Tale of the Underdog

TL MARSTON

This is a work of fiction. Unless otherwise indicated, all the names, characters, businesses, places, events, and incidents in this book are either the product of the author's imagination or used in a fictitious manner. Any resemblance to actual persons, living or dead, or actual events is purely coincidental.

ISBN: 978-1-7398565-0-2

DEDICATION

Endless thanks and appreciation go out to my mother and father for their lifelong love, support, and encouragement in everything that I do.

Also, I would like to thank Mel for being there with me, night after night when I write. It really does mean the world to me. I love you.

For my daughter Rachel. I am so proud of you. Dream Big!

For Ness, everyone needs a friend who believes in their hopes and dreams. Thank you, for your endless enthusiasm, wit, and boundless energy. Surely it must be time to go on another adventure.

CONTENTS

PROLOGUE

Was it ever a good time to leave?

The night was bitter cold and dark, as if a dense and blackened cloak had been laid over the entire planet, obscuring the moons natural light, and forbidding it any access to the planet's surface. Rainclouds, that were as black as a raven's wing in flight, held precariously onto what looked like an entire oceans weight of water, as infinite waves of icy, razor-sharp rain released to relentlessly assault the roof tops and the sodden ground beneath my feet.

The sting of each tiny droplet on my skin, left my face reddened, cold, and sore from the unrelenting bites of the tiny cold-water beads. The worst of it though, was the numbing chill. It cut deep and all the way through to the raw marrow in my bones, causing my bones to ache wherever my skin was bare. I was, at least thankful that I had chosen to wear such warm clothing for the short journey ahead of me, though I was more than a little concerned, where the clothing did not entirely cover my skin.

I hurriedly checked the left pocket of the heavy quilted jacket that I was wearing, first noticing the texture of the lining, it felt light and flimsy to the touch. I searched around the small void with my fingertips, making sure that the important item that I was carrying was still there. I worried for just the briefest of moments that I might lose it. I loathed the very fact that my life had come to this juncture, and I was determined that today of all days I would succeed, as failure was not an option, there would be no second attempt.

The item itself was valuable, and I would need it if I were to convince her to take the package. I just hoped that I would be able to find my way around on this unfamiliar, and previously unexplored rocky water planet.

I had never been here before… and yet, so far, my brief visit to this world was in fact the most important journey that I would ever make. I mused at the thought of this, it sounded ridiculous, even to me. Ridiculous… yes, but essential, I thought.

The ground was tough, gritty, and waterlogged. It crunched, surrendered, and broke under the weight of the heavy duty synth-leather boots that I wore. It was so damn wet here, that no sooner did I lift each foot off the ground, did murky, ice cold water quickly flow into the deepened tracks of my footprints. I was just thankful that my trail was almost immediately washed away, consumed by the continuous onslaught of this planets water.

There was just so much water here, I thought, as I hurriedly strode forwards into the darkness of this, a most wretched night. For just a few seconds, memories of Riesla 3 entered my mind, for it was the exact opposite of my experience here. I contemplated how contrasting a world it was to this planet, Earth. I was sure that it would soak up this entire planets water supply into its porous heat seared crust, without leaving a single drop on the surface.

I shivered momentarily, the cool night air of the evening gathering in my hood, lifting it just a little from my head and raising it slightly with every step I took. I found myself pulling the package even closer to my chest, in an effort to keep warm. I had made the decision to arrive just outside, of what was a large industrial town that sat on the outskirts of an even larger human metropolis. I did so, in the hopes that I could avoid being seen when I tele-phased onto the planet's surface. I just couldn't risk it… I couldn't risk them.

I knew that I needed to be swift, but I also acknowledged the necessity to be safe and to ensure that I remain completely hidden at all costs, as I had to close this loop. I had made every imaginable effort to blend in, and to be completely unseen and unnoticed by the planet's inhabitants of this world. I had to ensure that there were no loose ends. I had therefore chosen suitable human attire and accessories, to ensure that I did so. All, of course was an elaborate illusion, but one that I needed to fulfil in order to make the delivery.

As I walked a little further, I noticed that the dull orange coloured streetlights were straining to light up the crumbling roads below them, casting long and ominous shadows in some places. This combined with the darkness, and the watery heaviness of the blackened clouds and the lack of any natural light, made the view ahead look like that of a waking dream.

It looked to me to be a sinister place, it was strange, and unforgiving.

As I approached the more urban run-down outskirts of the town, I began to see a few modest homes and several decrepit retail units that were dotted around the bleak ruinous landscape. They were not in the best of repair, but I comforted myself knowing that I had seen much worse during my travels across the cosmos. This place, it was not a wealthy place, but it was the place that I had chosen. It felt right, it felt like the kind of place that made fighters, and the type of place where streetwise and toughened children grew up fast.

I laughed quietly to myself at the irony of it all, it wasn't the first time that I had made this journey, but I hoped it would be my last. My time in the universe had given me a unique perspective, one unlike any other. There had been so many lessons that I had learnt, and I hoped that today my judgement, and wisdom of the presenting situation would be the better for it.

I came to an abrupt halt on an empty street corner. Standing perfectly still, I stood for what seemed like an eternity, looking about my surroundings cautiously. It was eerily quiet, apart from the steady and persistent pounding of the pattering rain on the hood of my cloaked coat, and the tops of my shoulders. I was getting much closer to my destination now, and a tang of fear mixed with utter urgency began clawing and gnawing, like a caged wild cat in my now empty stomach.

Picking up the pace I began walking quicker, striding forwards and with renewed purpose towards the drop point. The streetlights were now becoming much more frequent in number. Standing tall, these tired and aged beacons of light were struggling in an endless endeavour to illuminate the now widening urban roads. It was as if their very presence were encouraging the worn path beneath my feet to light up, as the night pushed back against the light, creating an uncomfortable stalemate.

I continued onwards, hugging the stark buildings for any cover or relief that they might provide me with. I was optimistic at their presence, but their cold vertical facades shielded me only slightly against the worst of the misery and bitter cold of this foreboding night. Turning yet another corner, I immediately identified the drop point in the distance. It was around two hundred metres straight ahead of me.

I could just see an outline, it was a small block of apartments, which I knew to be just four stories in height. I looked at the buildings design and frontage, it looked tired. I was sure that in its day it may well have been regarded as the place to live. But in its current state of repair, it occurred to me that it probably housed people of very modest means.

I reflected on the journey so far, and I felt sick with worry… I was exhausted by it. This most modest of dwellings was where I would leave the most precious of cargos, something so valuable that it had no price, and yet it needed to be left here, here on this wet planet with this human. I smiled to myself shaking my head, whilst wondering how it would fare in all this water.

I stepped forwards, the length of my steps widening and becoming longer as I briskly approached the front of the building, only accompanied by the sound of my quickening footsteps. I was met by six steep and well-worn concrete steps that rose up from the street to the aged buildings ground floor level. An old and thin white metal sign was bolted to the wall, the black writing on it, identifying that flats one to ten were on the ground floor of the building. I was looking for flat seventeen, and so I made my way along the front of each apartment, whilst checking the numbers on each of the doors, just to be sure that the aged sign wasn't wrong.

I spotted a set of solid metal steps to the left hand side of the structure. They were fixed to the outer wall by large rusting bolts that were made of some kind of primitive metal. A sign read 'Emergency Exit.' I thought on the signs meaning for a brief moment. It amused me slightly, and I felt a wry smile cross my lips as the quiet building appeared to me, to be the last place that there would be any kind of emergency. I contemplated using the building's interior lift, but I decided against it, instead taking the exposed metal stairs. Mainly, because I thought that there would be much less chance of me being seen by any of the building's occupants, who I very much wanted to avoid.

The stairs creaked and groaned, they sounded strained and old, and I noticed that they were incredibly worn. As I climbed each one of the steps extremely carefully, I wondered if I would be the last being to ever use them. I was relieved when I drew close to the top, but there in front of me stood a tall iron gate. It had a thick, heavy metal chain that was covered in some type of red plastic sleeve. It had a strange and archaic locking mechanism that very much looked like it was attempting to secure it.

I lifted my right hand out of my pocket, tilting my wrist and hand slightly backwards. A fine laser beam of vivid yellow light, emerged from the small node that was embedded into the skin on the inside of my wrist, the fierce heat searing through the rusting mechanisms chain and sleeve almost instantaneously. The cut chain relinquished to the high temperature of the laser, dropping away from its hold on the gate and towards the floor.

A small amount of smoke arose from it for just a few seconds, as the heat of the chain cooled quickly, a consequence of the nights rain. I reached out and somehow managed to catch it before it hit the floor, placing it carefully on a small wall that was situated at the top of the steps. I was thankful that the heavy chain wasn't too hot.

I took a deep breath, gathering my composure for a second and checking for any movement or sound from my immediate surroundings. I then began to make my way along the front of the building.

'Eleven, twelve, fourteen, where was thirteen? Fifteen, sixteen… seventeen.' I counted the numbers out quietly and under my breath.

I came to a complete halt in front of a plain dark blue door and noticed that I was breathing quite deeply, this was most unlike me. I looked down towards my feet and tried to control my breath for a moment, whilst attempting in vain to wipe some of the rainwater away with the back of my hand, from my now saturated face. I studied the door for a moment and for all intents and purposes, it felt to me as if it might as well have been an interdimensional portal.

Then, bringing my cold hand up I pushed my index finger on the doorbell, just once. It rang loudly, and I could feel the vibrations of the bell resonate against the wooden frame of the doorway. A few moments later a dim yellow-white light appeared. It was just visible through the opaque glass panel in the centre of the door.

I stood perfectly still and waited, once again feeling my heart rate increase, as did my concentration. I could hear the jangle of metallic keys as the occupant inserted them into the lock. This door must be very old, I thought, for it to have a metal key. The door began to open slowly, there was just a crack of light at first, and then a small gap as a human face appeared between the old door and its frame.

'Hello, who is it?' She said questioningly, her voice sounded almost timid. I estimated that this was indeed the voice of a young woman, no more than twenty-five years of age.

'I have a delivery for you ma'am, may I come in? I need to speak with you about its care, it's… very delicate.'

'A delivery… for me?' She sounded a little anxious, her pale blue eyes were darting about, studying me, and trying to read my face. 'But I haven't ordered anything, are you sure it's for me?'

There was a little uncertainty in the woman's voice, and I knew that I must reassure her at once. I didn't want her to feel afraid of me, or the priceless gift that I was about to present her with.

'Yes, it's for Elana Mitchell. Is that you?' I paused waiting for any kind of answer from behind the old door.

'Well… yes. That's me, hang on a moment. She spoke a little more confidently now. 'I suppose that you had better come in.'

I let out a silent sigh of relief, and felt my shoulders relax as the door opened slowly. In front of me stood a woman with long wavy dark brown hair. She had high cheek bones and piercingly pretty eyes. She smiled at me warmly, and I smiled back at her. I was incredibly aware that I was an unknown stranger to her, one that was now entering her home, which was probably her only safe space.

The flat was clean, and modestly decorated. The furniture looked comfortable and well worn. I could tell that Elana had done her best to make the place look homely and welcoming. Candles were lit on the mantle and there was a scent, it was one that I had never encountered before, and I instantly decided that I liked it.

'Your home smells lovely Elana.' I commented as my nostrils took in more of the scent. 'May I ask you, what fragrance it is?'

'It's orange blossom, it's one I like a lot.' She smiled coyly at me. 'Just a small indulgence that I allow myself each month when I receive my salary.'

She stood up abruptly, looking a little uncomfortable at my noticing something so very personal to her, then suddenly she turned to me with a serious expression across her face.

'Now where are my manners, would you like a drink? It's cold outside and you must be frozen solid.' I smiled warmly. I was reassured by her consideration for my predicament.

I liked this woman, Elana. She was warm, friendly, and considerate. I had made a good choice.

'Do you have any tea?' I said in a hopeful tone.

I had read about this unique infusion whilst researching Earth's culture onboard my ship, and I desperately wanted to try it, to take it with milk or without though? I would need to decide, and quickly.

'Yes,' she said politely. 'How do you take it? She

asked.

'With just a splash of milk and let the tea brew for a moment.' I hoped that I had requested it in the right way.

'Ok, I'll just be a minute.' She uttered cheerfully. 'Please make yourself comfortable, it's cold enough outside. It need not be cold in here.'

Elana walked purposely through a doorway into what I assumed was her kitchen area. Leaning back into the comfortable winged chair, I unzipped the large black padded jacket and gently lifted the package out of my coat. It was soft, warm and… still sleeping thankfully.

I held her gently in my arms, looking at her rounded chubby face. Were all babies this chubby? I thought. She was an endearing child, and for just the briefest of moments I considered her future, as I did my own.

It wasn't long before Elana returned from the kitchen. She immediately noticed me holding the child in my now warming arms. The look on her face was a mix of both surprise and utter shock. She seemed to me to appear a little saddened by my apparent predicament, and then looking me straight in the eye, she said in a soft and soothing voice.

'I'm sorry, forgive me. I didn't know you had a child with you on this cold night. Do you need anything for her, him?' She spoke compassionately.

I looked up in earnest, as she was carefully placing the mugs of tea on the table, she then wiped her palms nervously down the lower front of her blouse.

'About her. The child.' I said apprehensively.

I was trying to hold onto her eye contact. A look of both recognition and surprise flashed quickly across her face as I began to speak again.

'The child… well…' I paused. 'I would like it very much if you were to consider raising her for me.'

Elana sat down immediately in the chair directly opposite me, first looking at the child and then at me in complete astonishment.

'Do you need money?' She sounded concerned. 'I do not have much, but I could at least help you for a few days. Maybe it would be enough to help get you on your feet.'

Her heart was true, for this reason alone I knew now, more than ever that she was the right choice. My heart was full of joy, the child would do just fine.

'I don't need money Elana.' I studied the expression on Elana's face. 'I need safety and a good upbringing for her. I know...' I hesitated once again before continuing. 'I know that you cannot have any children of your own, and well, I need someone to care for her. I have been searching for a home for her for some time now. I just need you to care for her and give her a safe home. I cannot take her where I am going. It's going to be dangerous, and it's no life for a child. Can you do that for me, care for her, raise her?'

Elana looked at the child, her bright blue eyes warmed, beginning to soften. She looked at my face, and then back towards the child.

'Elana, I have brought some money with me to give you for her upkeep. More than both you and her will ever need. My only request is that you live modestly. I need her to grow up in the same way that you were raised.'

I lifted my arms out and offered the child to Elana. She looked at me for the briefest of moments, just the once whilst holding my eyes in her gaze and then taking the child fully into her arms. She gently rocked her as she did so, never once letting go of my eye contact. She searched my face for deceit, but only found sincerity in my amber eyes. She looked once more at me, and I could see a thousand questions written upon her face. Then all at once, she pulled the child closely to her chest.

'I don't know what to say.' She said, looking about herself cautiously and then back to the child. 'I should report you to the authorities for this, but I just can't. I don't know why, but I can't.'

I studied Elana whilst I drank a few large mouthfuls of the now cooling tea, that I decided I liked very much indeed. I sat for a short while and watched the pair tentatively begin to bond. It was a wonderful sight, and my heart was filled with happiness. Seeing this, and acknowledging the bond, I reached into my pocket and brought out a small metallic cylindrical device, the one device that I had been keen not to lose.

'Do you have a chip fitted Elana?' I asked, she was still gently rocking the child who now had hold of her index finger in its tiny little hand.

'Yes.' She spoke in a quiet tone to me, so as not to startle the child.

'Here, hold your arm out.' Elana did so immediately.

I held the cylindrical device over the scanner that resided in her chip, that was located and embedded into her lower left arm.

'I've transferred you some credits to your account Elana. You can choose whether or not you continue to work. There's enough credit in there now that you do not need to, not anymore.' I gathered my composure. 'There is just one more thing that I need to say to you, and then I will be on my way.' Elana looked at me curiously.

'Where are you going?' she said looking troubled. I could see that she was trying to understand the words that had just escaped my mouth.

'I have a journey to make Elana before the morning sun rises. I cannot tell you any more of it, for the child's own good. But can I ask of you one last thing?'

Elana nodded sincerely at my bold request, she listened attentively.

'When she is grown, she will ask you many questions, including where she is from. She will likely be a very curious and intelligent child. You must not tell her about our meeting tonight, not until she is a grown adult. You will know when that time is right because she will ask you the right question. Until then, if she asks you anything about her parents, or her ancestry, tell her that she is adopted and loved, for that is the truth. Elana, there is an exceptionally important reason for this request, and it is vital for her safety that you keep it. Can I trust you, Elana?' I said imploringly.

'Yes. I know that I do not know you, but to me you seem familiar. I don't know why I feel this way, but I do know that I am safe with you, and that she was also safe with you. I believe your request is an honest one, and one that I will fulfil for you, as asked.' A gentle smile crossed her lips and she looked down at the child who was now awake but perfectly settled in her arms.

'Elana. That means more to me than I can ever express to you.' I paused and collected my thoughts as a slight twinge of sadness tugged at my chest. Finally, it was done.

'Thank you so much Elana, but I really must be going now. The journey ahead will be a difficult one. Thanks for the tea and thank you once again for…

everything.' I stood up and Elana walked with me to the door still cradling the child in her arms. I took one last look at the child, stroking her forehead with my now warmed hand, and bidding them both farewell.

I stood perfectly still, as the door to Elana's home began to close slowly behind me. I stood with my back to it, waiting for the meeting with Elana to finally end. Once again, I felt a momentary tinge of sadness, and then thankfully my focus and the reason that I had made this journey returned to me once more.

I began to retrace my steps past the decrepit buildings that had offered me little solace on the way in, quickly taking me back out of town. I would not miss the amount of water, nor the cold in this area of planet Earth, not for a single moment. Though I imagined that these humans, incredibly valued it, and the life that it sustained for them on their home world.

I continued to walk briskly back to my departure point. The taste of tea still lingering in my mouth, and the scent of orange blossom hanging precariously in my nostrils. I made a final turn to the back of an abandoned building. It was dark here and I was certain that I was hidden from the gaze of any passers-by. I did a final check about me, and once I was happy that there weren't any prying eyes, I touched a second silver-coloured node. This node was embedded into the back of my left wrist.

White wispy lights began to swirl, running up and down the length and breadth of my entire body consuming my entire form within them, after a few seconds I was tele-phased back up to my ship.

∞

When I arrived back on the bridge, I appeared in the exact spot that I had left only a few hours earlier. It was good to be back on board this ship, it was my ship. The interiors pure white strip lighting was in clear contrast to the far dimmer and inadequate lighting that I had experienced on the Earth. The first part of the plan had gone well, now I just needed to put the second part in place, and I could then call the mission a success.

I was content that no other innocent life forms would be at risk from this point forward, and I hurriedly prepared one of the ships small scout craft for a short, and urgent journey. A journey that I had thought about for the longest time. It was going to be significant to me, and I thought about what I wanted to take with me.

I thought of the simple things, those things that were not permanent. Things that I would enjoy, that would fill my senses. I would need music, some good food and drink. I peered out of the viewing window, my eyes taking in the clarity and the colours of this magnificent blue planet, as if for the very first time. It was breathtakingly beautiful.

She was now safe, hidden in a quiet corner on the outskirts of an average struggling city on planet Earth. She would have an ordinary childhood. She would learn to survive and thrive down there. She would develop her instincts, intuition, and resolve, and maybe, just maybe, she would be the one to get the opportunity that had been denied to myself and the many others like me.

I hoped that she would achieve her destiny… our destiny. It was a small and precious gift that I had given her, but I knew that it could be the greatest gift that I had ever given any living being during my forty years or so of life. My work here was almost done, and I knew that it was finally time to leave.

I set the coordinates on my ship, aptly named the Pulsar. Coordinates that would take her far out of this solar system, to a pre-planned destination where I would give Yahga, the ships onboard artificial intelligence, my final orders. I would then board the scout craft and send the command remotely once I had safely departed the ship. I felt a mixture of both sadness and joy.

I knew that today they would find me, as I had deliberately left them a trail of crumbs to follow. I had to make sure that everything was taken care of. I couldn't leave even a single trace of myself here, in this system, which is why I needed to send my beloved ship away first. I took one last look at her. She had served me well.

I loaded the scout craft with all of my favourite things, checking that everything was working and in order as I did so. I did not want any unnecessary complications at this stage. Today had been a perfect day, so far at least, and I didn't want that to change. I walked back onto the bridge of my ship and took one last look around its gleaming consoles and floors.

I will miss standing here, I thought, as I looked around trying to give myself a final memory of this ship, a ship that had been my home and base for the last twenty two years. I became aware of a single tear leave my left eye, it began to slowly roll down my cheek, leaving a narrow trail of moisture on my skin as it did so. I wasn't known for being overly sentimental and so I wiped it away quickly, almost not giving it a second thought, as emotion wasn't a luxury that I could afford right now.

I made my way to the docking bay and boarded the small craft, the hatch closed behind me with a short rush of air, I strode towards the small cockpit. On entering the small and compact cabin area I sat down, turning the power on, and as I did so, the crafts pilot seat neatly moulded around my body's shape, hugging my form as the engines fired up, the blue-white heat powering through the rear thrusters.

I released the craft from the ships docking bay clamps and slowly reversed out of the Pulsars hangar doors. Once the craft was clear, the docking bay door closed silently, leaving me with a perfect view of my beautiful ship. Her elongated and streamlined silver form reminding me of the diving birds of Nemeranth, their speed, grace and precision were to me, comparable traits.

I had been so very fortunate, my life's journey was so exceedingly difficult, but only ever intended for me. I sat in absolute silence for a moment looking at her, gleaming in the distance. The Pulsars sleek polished hull, powerful engines, and almost unstoppable fire power made her a highly admired and sought after vessel.

I reached down to the left of my seat and positioned in the centre between the two seats was a small rectangular black gloss console unit. This was where most of the crafts controls were. I placed my hand gently upon the scout ships control stick, whilst also checking the ships sensors. I noticed the Pulsar slowly began to move away from me, and into the distance. She grew smaller and smaller, and her engines grew brighter. Culminating in a mass of pure searing blue-white light, and then all at once, and in total silence the ship, my ship, disappeared from view. She was gone.

The space around me felt much emptier now, but I felt somewhat contented that my ship was now in a much safer place, away from this system, away from the coming danger. I just hoped that my elaborate plan would come to fruition, and soon.

Reaching for the controls once more, I piloted the shuttle to just outside the small white star's corona, eventually bringing the shuttle to a complete standstill. It felt a little more than ironic that my final stand would take place here by the heat of this small, but perfect star. I got up and immediately opened a large, brushed silver metallic case, inside was a bottle of Thrusken wine, a crystal glass from the planet Gnarth and assorted snacks from some of the planets of the Haruvean Belt.

'What a magnificent view.' I said quietly and out aloud to myself, as I opened, poured, and began to savour and enjoy the wine. Each sip was a marvel, and in all my travels I had never once found anything quite like it, though I had made extensive efforts to try, due to my absolute love of fine wine.

Looking out of the window, I thought back to some of the many faces that I had known during my life, a few of those faces I had loved deeply and passionately. Never had I imagined that my story would end like this, in both a feast, and a reckoning. Though in all honesty, I was thankful and acknowledged that I had probably lived the equivalent lives of many beings.

In just over the forty years or so of my existence. I had to admit that life had been one hell of a ride, and I had been grateful and incredibly humbled by the wonder of it all, even though I felt a little saddened that I was not the one. I had accepted that it was not my destiny, not by my choosing. I comforted myself knowing that my part in it had been significant, just as it had been for all those others who went before me. I paused one last time taking it all in and savouring it, in all its magnificent splendour.

The first ship that appeared to my port side was a scout craft, it circled about me, its darting movements reminding me of the stinging insects of the planet Platos Five. A few seconds after it had picked me up on its scanner, a second and much larger ship appeared in my view.

'Yahga, tell me. How many are on board the two ships?' I said in an urgent tone.

My on-board AI was one of the more advanced in the Cosmos, and was capable of many things, including advanced warfare and strategic capabilities. A male voice answered my request.

'There are currently ten lifeforms on board, lifeforms are split across the two ships. Two are on board the scout ship, and eight are on board the fighter. Your orders?'

I looked at the small crafts viewing screen once again as both ships grew closer, their blackened hulls with their sharp and bold features told me that I had indeed been right to plan this day, and that the drop on Earth was absolutely the right move.

'Scan their weapons and defences Yahga, this ends here, today, we take no chances.' I said assertively. Yahga scanned the approaching ships and responded almost immediately.

'You have several viable options. I can hack into their ship's controls. However, I must advise you that you have very little time, and because their defences are off the grid, I am unable to hack them. You could defend yourself, however I estimate your chances of success are currently between sixty-five point three and sixty-five point four percent that you will fail in the craft that you are currently onboard.'

I looked to the crafts console and then back out of the window. I could now see their insignia as clearly as I could see the inside of my own ship. A red elongated skull with jagged features surrounded by a golden circle which was outlined with stars, this represented the current number of their conquests.

'OK Yahga. We knew this day would come. It is time to end this pursuit, it's the right time for my own journey to end. Tell me, your consciousness Yahga, did you manage to ensure that it mostly remains on the Pulsar, as we planned?'

'Yes, my friend. I can withdraw myself from this craft at any time.'

'Good. I will need you to do that, on my order–'

Just as my final and determined words left my lips, two of the fighter's vicious assailants tele-phased directly onto the craft. I recognised them to be warrior class, and I knew that I would have a fight on my hands. Their armour was matt black, highlighted in places with metallic blood red markings.

Their faces, which could only be seen through their visors were truly hideous and dark red in colour. Small two inch long tentacles hung from their chins and where their eyebrows would have been if they had any. Their eyes were flaming orange in colour and filled the entire socket in their bony sharp skulls, a tiny dark pupil sat in the centre of each eye socket.

I reached for my plasma pistol, shooting the first one, the shot hit them clean in the head, thick brown blood oozing from the wound, as it fell heavily to the floor. The second fighter lunged at me, knocking the pistol out of my hand. It dropped to the floor and spun out of my sight. The next thing I became aware of was his bony fist hitting me in the face. I felt the sharp crack of my nose breaking, and then noticed the smell of iron in my warm red blood. I lifted my arm and a razor-sharp six inch micro-blade evolved out of my knuckles.

I quickly plunged my weapon straight into my assailant's chest. The look of pure shock and rage on its face would be the last expression that it would ever make. I held my nose, it ached and throbbed almost causing me to pass out. A wave of nausea swept up my throat, but I knew that being sick was not a luxury that I could afford right now.

'Yahga, take control of their ships immediately, wipe their communication abilities and direct both their craft into this star...' I shouted towards my AI whilst trying to gather my thoughts. 'And Yahga, do the same for this craft. We must secure this site at all, and any cost. We must protect all knowledge of the existence of the child on Earth. I need to make sure that there are no loose ends, no more breadcrumbs, and Yahga, that's an order.' There was a silent pause.

'Confirming your request. You may cancel this order at any time.' The shuttle heaved sharply and began to move towards the small white star, as did my adversaries scout and fighter vessels. I sat and listened to them, they were desperately trying to communicate with me, shouting obscenities and threats in their angry and frustrated voices. I ignored them and put them on mute, my job was done, my plan had worked, and I felt satisfied.

Wiping some of the now drying blood from underneath my nose with the back of my hand, the ship warning systems began to sound.

'Warning, imminent hull breach in sixty seconds. The lights in the cockpit turned to red and I knew that

I had just one thing left to do.

'Yahga, please remove yourself from this ship in thirty seconds.' I swallowed hard. '… and Yahga. Thank you.'

'Working with you, and knowing you, has been a pleasure. Relocation of ships AI in progress.' I smiled at the simple blurring of consciousness and logic in the AI's tone.

'This was it. This was really it.' I thought, as I watched the two predatory ships that we had just immobilised being pulled at pace now, into the small white star. Both ships finally surrendering to its immense gravitational pull. Complete peace soon came over me, and I felt a calmness, the like of which I hadn't experienced before. Of all the many things I had done in my life, this was the most significant. It was the only gift that I could give to the universe, and it involved me ending my own life to do so.

A few silent tears began to roll down my cheeks, though this time I chose not to resist them, I would allow myself this moment, I had earned it. I hoped that I had done enough for her, only then would it be worth the cost.

Taking one last look at the vivid colours of my beautiful and yet fatal surroundings, I accepted my destiny. It was all so magnificent, wasn't it? Then, slumping wearily and exhausted into my seat, I closed my eyes.

1 THE LONG WALK HOME

How to outfox the fox. This was the story of my life, a struggle, an endeavour… Since the day of my birth. I had but two choices, I either prove myself, or give in and accept my place in our crumbling society. I refused to accept the latter, and those expectations and circumstances that were laid out before me.

It would have been so easy to accept my lot in life, but I refused. Because of this, it meant that absolutely everything had been hard work. But at least I could say I'd earned it, every bit of it.

I had my struggles as a child. There were the many verbal and physical fights that I had gotten into, mostly because I wouldn't back down if I felt that something was wrong, or unfair. You could say that I was a stubborn child, and you would be right. But as I grew into adulthood, I came to realise that these fights were always and only with bullies, those who wished only for their own voices and perspectives to be heard, whilst pushing down and preying on those who were the complete opposite or were unable to defend themselves.

I soon recognised that they only cared about their own needs, that they were weak, and that they longed for power and control. They would always only ever pick on the quiet, the polite, or those who were different, and then they would push them until they broke, or fought back. I was in the latter category.

I fought, but only when I had to. I think that they hoped that me, and others like me, would stay silently and subserviently in our places. But I knew that if it were left unchallenged, they would ultimately benefit from their victims acquiescence, withdrawal, or submission. Their unchallenged power growing most of all, from every silent surrender.

I would spend much of my spare time during my mid-teen years paying back the bullies that I had encountered during my childhood. As I grew, I became fitter and stronger and more capable of taking care of myself. Some of the kids in the neighbourhood would let me know if there was a problem. I would then go out of my way to stick up for the small kid, the kid with a stammer, the kid whose parents had no money.

Mom would spend many an evening wiping the dried blood from my face whilst tending to the many bruises, small cuts, and scratches.

'Why do you do this to yourself?' She would say as she comforted me, whilst dressing my wounds.

'Mom, if I don't stand up to them, who will?' I said softly, tears filling in my young eyes.

'You could always turn the other cheek, walk away?' She said, her voice sounded full of sadness.

'No mom, I can't. What they do is wrong.' I said determinedly.

I had many battles in those rundown streets, with

so many bullies, the fights equally matching the number of bruises I acquired during my childhood years. But ask me if it was worth it? Hell yes, it was, even if just one of those kids learnt that it was possible to fight back.

As I matured into adulthood the career that I had chosen as an Earth Marine would, I thought, enable me to legitimately protect those that were more vulnerable to the galaxy's bullies. It was a hard yet rewarding career. It had been a constant struggle, and I had worked hard to progress through the ranks. It was an enduring and lifelong commitment that I had made to the planet, and its people.

I knew of course that I was still trying to prove myself an equal, twenty five years after my first bloody fist fight on those streets. But now at forty years of age, I was a matured and experienced officer in the United Nations Earth Marines.

Deep down though, and if you scratched the surface of my highly polished boots, you would discover that I knew what I was. I was still that street kid, who longed for justice, fairness, and equity. I wanted to do my best to ensure that all on our planet had their rights. Of course, I was serving with those from more affluent backgrounds, but I for one wasn't going to let my social class stop me from doing what I felt I was born to do.

During my early service, my day to day life, was at times a hard slog. It was often dirty, raw, and quite brutal. I was seen as a role model for every soldier from a poorer background who came after me. I knew that whatever it was that I was searching for, it was something worth striving for, something worth the effort.

I said I was stubborn, and I must be the most

stubborn person I know because something in me wouldn't quit, or let it slide no matter how hard our adversaries hit us, or regardless of how utterly exhausted I was at times. So, I continued onwards, and I pushed for that next promotion, and I worked hard to be given command of even more people whose lives were quite literally at times, in my hands.

I did have one advantage, I had my squads respect, and of course a genetically strong and agile body, decent gut instincts and a modicum of intuition, that would help keep me and others alive… well, it had until now. Many would call my success pure luck, others would say it was determination, or was it motivation? As I grew older, I was concluding that it might be something else entirely.

But today, I found myself brushing the loose strands of dampened dark hair from my sweat covered brow. I looked ahead and into the distance, everywhere looked bleak and parched, the wealth of the city's water supply not reaching out as far, to these the most desolate urban reaches.

The sun was beating down on the dusty arid terrain, and any moisture that had existed in this land, had long since gone having surrendered to the sun's blistering onslaught. I had no doubt that it had been redeposited elsewhere on the planet's surface, and that someone, somewhere, was enjoying a summer storm or a torrential downpour. But right here, it was sweltering hot, and I'd been walking for over three hours, attempting to get back to the city.

I felt parched, my mouth full of sand and dust. I had just one quarter of a canteen of water left, which was gently sloshing, protected from the days heat in the sealed container that was attached by a sturdy metal clip to my waist-belt. I was wearing a navy-blue vest, which had seen better days, some old blue-black combat pants, along with a pair of robust and well-worn black military grade lightweight boots, that made the scorched dirt crunch unwillingly beneath my feet.

I looked a mess. The dust and filth had gotten into every crease in my skin and clothing, it clung to my sweat, covering my body like iron filings that had been drawn towards a magnet. I calculated that it must have been at least ninety degrees in the shade, as I made my way steadily towards the sprawling metropolis. I needed to drink more water, and soon. I longed for the relief that a little shade would give me, some well-earned respite, and a little nourishment.

I looked upwards and noticed that even the sky looked bruised and broken, reminding me of the last four centuries on Earth. Or was it the last four broken bones in my body, I couldn't make my mind up which was more painful, but one thing was for sure, the route in front of me looked shadowed, and ominously far darker in some places than others. The decimated buildings that once rose up into the sky, were slowly crumbling and tumbling back into the Earth. In front of me was a stark, fractured, and ruined skyline.

The hairs on the back of my neck stood up, this was a warning to me that my current route was full of danger, and that there could be many unseen hazards and perils ahead. I stopped for a brief moment and considered my options. I could take an easier route, or I could head directly into the place that looked the most dangerous, and therefore more likely to cause me physical pain.

It would have been an easy choice for most, but over the years I had adapted myself to different situations, and to a myriad of conditions. I had learned to survive this place of many contrasts, I had to. I felt driven by it, and I had absolutely no idea why, though I felt it was probably out of necessity and instinct, my mind wondered for a second, and I began to think on it.

Earth, the blue planet, and my home. A planet of historic conflicts, a planet of politicians willing to sell their own souls, for just a small taste of power, wealth, or both. It was a planet full of hope, and yet so filled with fear that sometimes, it could feel hard to breathe. But at least I knew that I was not alone in how I felt. Many called this blue planet paradise, whilst others called it hell on Earth, though to be honest, at times even hell looked like a better option for some.

Historically speaking, everything had begun to change on Earth around three-hundred years ago, when we first started to invest in the interstellar jump drive concept. The only drawback being that it was incredibly expensive. Little by little, we began trading across a small corner of the Milky Way galaxy. We had been doing this for the last two hundred and fifty years.

During this time came the second most significant advance of our kind, when we befriended three other intergalactic species, the Okai, the Nadaal and the Crucians. Of course, this was of great benefit to the corporations, as the money and the scientific discoveries just kept rolling in.

But for many, these opportunities were not golden, and far greater numbers of people could not afford the advances in tech, and so there became a divide between the elites and the underclasses.

I was one, amongst many others that knew something had felt off for a long time, and at least as long as my own forty years or so on this planet. Many felt unsettled by the Crucian species, something felt deeply wrong about their alliance with us. But the bulk of people that felt the political change were, of course in no position to do anything about it. They feared the establishment run by the elites, far more than they feared the hunger in their bellies, or their desire for equality in a world built on hypocrisy.

The sad truth of the matter was, that no one could say exactly when, or why they felt as they did. But, for the longest time now, many of us including myself, thought that something was very much off, in relation to the intentions of the Crucian species. Our interactions with them, felt like a creeping shadow. It felt more often than not, like their promises were an insipid lie told by a loved one, or a so called trusted and close friend.

To me, it appeared that every word that left their tight lipped mouths would always be the exact right words, appearing velvety to the naïve, and slipping off their slick and narrow tongues, like poison, corrupting all but the most honourable among us. They would always make perfect promises to us. But those promises, well they always seemed to come at a great cost to humanities heart, and soul.

We seemed to lose a little bit more of ourselves with every decade that passed, and with every promise and deal that was made behind the elites closed doors. It just didn't add up.

For the majority of people on Earth, there were not many opportunities that could lift you from the dirt to the luxury apartment of your dreams in one of the cities wealthier districts. The military offered me a road out of the sub-city, into a reasonable standard of living, and hopefully, I could do a bit of good along the way.

I felt incredibly conflicted at times, I was a loyal servant of the people. But some nights, after a few large whiskies and when looking into the bottom of the glass, I would often silently question the very infrastructure and integrity of the military establishment that had paid my salary for the last twenty-two years.

I was most conflicted in that I couldn't decide if this, my questioning everything, was a good thing or not. All it gave me was some degree of anxiety, and I for one didn't think I had anything else to contribute. Even if I did, who would listen to a career soldier that came from the poorest part of town?

But for today at least, I found myself in yet another shitty situation, walking down an uneven and broken path. I strode in and out of the darkest of shadows trying to keep my edge. But it was hot, it was sticky, and I just knew. I felt them coming for me, though I did not know when, where or how.

I placed my audio device onto my head, it hovered just over my ears. It allowed me to listen to music, whilst also being able to hear my immediate surroundings, a marvel of technology that we humans had the Nadaal to thank for. The compact device enabled me to listen to my passion, vintage music. The music that I loved the most was rock music, from the late twentieth and early 21st century. I saw it as a distraction, or escapism, depending on how you wanted to look at it. It gave me a temporary escape from all that was familiar and known to us in 2425. To me, the humanity within the music was all still so relevant, no more so than today.

Listening to it, it almost felt like a memory of who

we were… before we lost ourselves to greed for the tech, beauty, power, and perfection. Was it simply materialism, or egotism that led humanity to this place? I could never work out which.

The music helped me concentrate and push on, in spite of my feeling drained and utterly exhausted. It added to the already atmospheric environment of my immediate surroundings. I began to sense some tension in my muscles as my bodily chemicals started to respond to the situation that was beginning to unfold in front of my eyes. I quickly re-tied my hair back in a loose ponytail, wiping my burning hot palms on my hips, man… that guitar riff was excellent and the intro just…–'

Before I could blink, they were upon me, there were maybe five or six of them, two of which had started to run towards me at speed. Oh, fucking hell… I thought. What the–.

In the distance about sixty meters in front of me I could make out a rusting, large metal shipping container, with a single metal chair bolted to its bottom. The chair had straps across the arms, and I could make out something similar on the floor, near the chairs legs. The container looked very old, like it had been purpose made for fuck knows what. Its light blue paint was peeling from it in large flaking pieces, and where there wasn't paint, there was rust.

The very thought of its possible use sent shivers and adrenalin coursing through my veins, stimulating my over tired body.

Right, I thought. The fuckers won't take me down. Time to go to work. The first two were big, and the male was incredibly muscular, the female was well built, but she looked more lean, like she might be fast.

I knew that the males size, also made him slower, but the female was going to be problematic. They wouldn't take me down, not today.

I knew that it was important not to let them make any physical contact with me, as I knew this would hurt a lot, and it could be a game changer. The large musclebound man charged at me, his arms grabbing for me, but he was only successful in catching the air.

I deftly moved out of the way to the left side of him. Momentum carried his bulky frame forwards, and on his way past me, I quickly brought up my right leg and slammed it down on the back of his right ankle. I heard a loud crack confirming that I had disabled the first man. I knew that he would struggle to continue walking, let alone get close enough to be able to hurt me.

I quickly picked up the gun he had been carrying, throwing it out of his range. I then took it upon myself to charge the second assailant, the muscular woman. She quickly dipped her body, trying to absorb the shock, but just before I connected with her, I leapt up, tensed my fingers, and jabbed her hard in the throat, my foot connecting with her leg as I landed. She immediately grabbed her neck with both hands, struggling to inhale. She stumbled clumsily forwards, eventually hitting the floor as she desperately continued to gasp for breath, the look of shock, clearly written upon her contorted face.

There were four remaining aggressors, of these, three looked incredibly agile, there were two females and two males. One of the women looked as fit as I was, and her body appeared to be much more toned, which for obvious reasons gave me the most concern. I glanced around at my surroundings and caught site of a three-foot-long metal pipe.

Rushing to the crumbling wall, the first of the four which was a blond haired female grabbed at me as I tried frantically to wrestle the pipe from its resting place in the rust-stained concrete. Two hands were now upon me, one hand was on my neck and the other on my left arm.

I brought my right arm up and slammed it back, hoping it would send her hurtling backwards, but it only had the effect of dislodging her from me for a few seconds. She was quickly back upon me, punching me hard in the back near my lower left ribs, I felt something give, and between the deep thudding and bruising pain, my instincts for survival kicked in.

With one final pull, the pipe came loose from the wall, and I gripped it in my hands tightly, jabbing backwards in an effortless motion, connecting with the assailant's leg. She yelped out aloud in pain and tried to grab me again, this time I finished her off with a crack to the head. She sank slowly on her haunches to the ground and lurched forward, her bottom lip and chin hitting the dirt.

The fourth attacker saw his chance, and reached for his stun gun, having realised that the others had not succeeded with brute strength alone. He raised the gun in line with my head, just as I raised the pipe. I then charged quickly forwards, and as his finger pulled the trigger, I rammed the pipe into the end of the gun, causing an electrical discharge that stunned him. He fell backwards and didn't move again.

I sensed the fifth behind me now, and without looking I brought the pipe to the side of my hip and threw it in a single seemingly fluid motion, connecting with the fifth woman's chest and sending her hurtling backwards. I charged up to her and dealt an explosive and quick jab to her jaw, knocking her out in the process.

This left one man who stood perfectly still, he didn't move, not even his eyes moved, but I could just make out a faint flicker, was that a hologram? Shit, I thought, they've brought the Crucian, how the hell? I walked slowly towards the Crucian who had taken the appearance of a human male. Standing proud and full of bravado, and in a forceful tone of voice, I said.

'Whatever it is that you think your gonna do to me, I will tell you right now, you can go to hell. You may be Crucian, but you have underestimated my understanding of your physiology. So, tell me… do Crucians also like the taste of Earths dirt?'

The Crucian bristled, its holo-projection losing its form, if only for a milli-second. That's right, I thought. The Crucians have no sense of humour, and they are so full of shit that it makes them almost brittle with pride. It was too good a chance to pass on. I thought, Piss the Crucian off and then the real dance could start. The Crucian moved towards me, and I towards him, never breaking eye contact, not even for a moment.

'Might have noticed, I've taken your five buddies out. I would say the odds are well in my favour that you will struggle to eat your food tonight. I would choose something soft, maybe liquify it first, as whatever it is you are able to eat, you will definitely be sucking it up through a straw later.'

The Crucian leapt at me roaring, his orange-red eyes full of rage. My plan had worked perfectly. I side stepped him and spun around instantly, grabbing his long arm, and holding it firmly up his bony back. He cried out in pain, trying aggressively, but fruitlessly to kick out at me. I leant in closer, placing my dry lips next to his ear.

'Tut, tut, don't you Crucians know when you are beaten. No? That's the fucking problem with your species isn't it, so fucking arrogant and such absolute and utter fucking assholes. You think your species is better than ours, or any other, don't you? Cos of what? Cos of the tech that you leech onto us, through our greedy corporations and the politicians that don't give a shit about us. Thing is, I see you for what you are, and I see your lies and deceit. Sooner or later buddy, this whole planet will, and when that happens you will have us all to deal with, and we don't play nice when someone pisses us off.'

I pushed the Crucian forward, his head hitting the ground and knocking him out cold, his holo-projection ceasing to work completely, and his angular facial features and deep red skin could just be made out under the fitted black visor that he wore. I then tried to think of a fitting end to this conflict, so I tied his arms behind his back, dragging him towards the chair, his boots leaving two perfect tracks in the scorched dirt.

I looked closely at the straps that were originally intended for me. Taking a long breath, I heaved him up onto the chair, in one clean motion and bound him to it, locking the restraints in place and then throwing the electronic locking key a good twenty meters away. Get out of that, you bastard. I thought.

Stepping back, I brushed the dust and dirt off my shoulders, patting myself down and checking that I had no open wounds of any real concern. I walked past the now silent, but fully utilised metal box. I rapped it hard with my knuckles, causing them to smart a little, but still I found myself smiling contentedly, in spite of the deep and throbbing pain that I was in.

I walked onwards and towards the end of the narrowing alley that would hopefully bring me closer to the end of what had been a gruelling day. As I turned the corner, I instantly saw six military field officers dressed in medical camo, which was white and grey in colour. They were carrying cases full of medical equipment, ignoring my presence completely, they ran past me and down the alleyway towards where the six neutralised assailants now lay. They were all either unconscious, debilitated or both.

Directly, set in front of me now, I could see three large military vehicles, a couple of fold up field tables with computing equipment and holo-screens on them. There were several military officers, who appeared to be standing more or less in silence. A medical officer approached me and began to scan my body as I continued to walk towards the tables. He looked me in my eyes and held a scanner to them.

'Superficial wounds and two cracked ribs, some dehydration. Drink plenty of fluids, apply some bio-fluid to your side and you will be fine.' He said confidently.

Turning quickly away from me he then headed off towards the alley to join his colleagues at pace.

'Captain Mitchell.' Said a brawny man who was stood behind the row of holo-vid screens.

'Yes Sir.' I said respectfully, whilst attempting to straighten my now throbbing side and aching back. I placed the palm of my left hand onto my ribs and felt the newest of the bruises, my touch was soon accompanied by a deep and cutting ache... Damn, that hurt.

'Congratulations Captain Mitchell, you've passed stage three of your assessment. See General Eastwick for a debrief.' His tone was assertive in manner.

He looked pleased with the outcome, but he did not smile. However, his demeanour told me that he thought I had done alright, and that was good enough for me. I hurriedly jumped into one of the vehicles that were parked to the side of the temporary site, and on a dirt track.

It was one of the few vehicles left in the military that still worked on an electronic battery. Most vehicles, including military vehicles were now powered by cold fusion. An invention of the 21st century, that was covered up by the fossil fuel corporations who wanted to dredge the last bit of money, and biofuel from the Earth's crust.

Two hundred and fifty years ago, this had resulted in humanity having to mop up a tainted legacy of heavy pollution, deforestation and a heart-breaking reduction in the planet's wildlife and ocean life.

I sat in the vehicle, getting as comfortable as I could, considering the pain that I was in. I reached for a pouch of bio-fluid, tearing it open and soaking my side and back with it. My vest was now soddened in part with the fluid, but it didn't matter as it was indistinguishable from my sweat.

The vehicle moved around two hundred and fifty metres, to the opposite side of the alley. It shifted almost completely silently, and after a few minutes I was joined by the group that had recently assaulted me, as part of their assignment.

There were now fourteen of us in the vehicle, including the medics and the military men and women from my squad, who had been tasked with taking me out. One looked over towards me, he was still tending to a bruise on his head, he looked affectionately towards a woman who was nursing her leg, whilst rubbing some bio-fluid into her arm.

'How is your leg Cat?' I said concerned.

I studied her swollen leg and noticed that she had a large cylindrical pad stuck to it, which she was pressing firmly against her skin.

'I've had worse injuries Cap.' She spoke proudly. 'Once the bio-fluid and these med-nanites do their job, I will be just fine.' Cat replied, her tone now relaxed, whilst she looked across to the large muscular man, giving him a friendly wink.

'It will take her just a few hours to heal properly, she's doing her best to encourage the nanites into her skin. She should be alright by the time you hit the bars tonight.' The medic accompanying Cat commented drily, and eleven of the twelve in the vehicle laughed. Those who could reach her, patted Cat on the back, all except that is, Jevargh, the Crucian, whose sharpened facial expression never moved at all, and this unnerved me.

It really was starting to bother me, I would bust his ass off my squad if I could, what the fuck were those Crucians on? I wasn't going to let him ruin my squads connection, and I certainly wasn't going to let it stop the faint smile, that now drew across my cracked dry lips.

'I'm sorry Cat, ya know… about your leg, I was running on adrenaline and had I not acted, you would have downed me, for sure. You are one tough cookie, couldn't risk it. Come on, you know how important it was to me that you all make a real effort today. You know I deeply appreciate what you did for me, I really do. You all tried so damn hard. You know you left me with no choice but to resort to my combat survival training, and that was the point of your assignment, I think. Had I failed it, well that would have meant that I didn't pass the final part of the suitability assessment, and that would also have meant that I didn't get a shot at my next rank.

I will make it up to you Cat, I promise.' Cat looked at me sincerely and held her hand up, slapping the palm of my hand in acknowledgement.

'Respect. Would love to have some of what you got Cap. I mean… how do you do that?' Cat retorted.

'I dunno, I was just in the zone, I guess. Hey, listen, tonight we need to celebrate the fantastic conclusion of today's assignment, and of course, because I love you all, the beers and the whisky are on me, as a way of thanking you for your enthusiastic and energetic contributions today. I mean it when I say that I couldn't have done it without you.'

All of the men and women of my squad were now in good spirits, all apart from Jevargh who still sat silently in the vehicle, not joining in with the rest of the squad and although I had no proof, I just felt that he despised me, despised us. I'd struggled to keep a lid on my true thoughts and emotions today. Since he had joined my squad six months ago, I had picked up some dark vibes from him, and from what I had observed, he definitely wasn't a team player.

I was frustrated with having to have a Crucian in my squad as I didn't trust them, or their species agenda. This combined with me being utterly exhausted, and wounded had resulted in my true feelings spilling out of me like a burst dam. I needed to get a grip, if Earth really was intent on cultural exchanges with the

Crucians, then who was I to get in the way of progress. I had better find a way to deal with how I felt, and fast.

The rest of the squad were also feeling tired and were very much ready for some rest and relaxation. We were finally on our way back to base, and before the squads assignment took place, we had pre-planned a night out in the city. Although Jevargh had declined the invite, saying that he had an important assignment for Crucian Command, and that he needed to write it up.

I needed to talk to someone about what I was sensing about him, but it was difficult, and as with all things in 2425, politics, agenda and ego's often overruled logic and common sense. The squad appreciated that I always thanked them for a job well done. They also respected that I would challenge them, when they were out of line, which thankfully they rarely were.

The military had helped me refine my talent for survival, finding my place amongst the loyal and the battle worn suited me. I had originally seen it as a way out from the under-city ghettos where I had grown up. I was typical military material. I had no large family to speak of, other than my adoptive mother Elana, who raised me, and I might add, did a damn fine job too, in my opinion. I was incredibly lucky, but the one thing that I always found that I yearned for, was to know more about my family and what my heritage was.

One day, when I was about fourteen years old, I asked Elana about my family. She told me that she could not speak of my mother, and that I was not to ask any further questions, she looked upset and worried, and so I didn't ask her again. In time, I eventually accepted this, holding off the DNA test that would tell me much more about my origins, but out of respect and love for her, I dropped it.

I felt like a mystery to myself, and I don't think I ever truly grasped the concept that I was unique. I did not understand or know anything about who I was at all. I think this helped me relate to all those people who felt the disconnect of our now fragmenting society. I could feel it, deep within me. I knew a great deal had changed in our society over the last ten years, much more so than the last two-hundred.

Then, there were the weird experiences that I was having. I didn't know what they were, at first putting them down to some undiagnosed ancestral medical condition. But deep down… I knew that something unusual had started to happen to me. I could feel a strong energy within me that appeared to get stronger the older I got.

At first it had felt like a hot flush or that I had some kind of fever, but as I aged, it began to feel like a deep searing heat, that sat firmly in the centre of my chest, wave upon wave of gently pulsating warmth would then softly run down my entire body, disappearing as quickly as it would start.

I didn't think of it as that different at first, I had no frame of reference for it, and it happened seldomly, and as naive as I was back then, in some way I tried to convince myself that everyone had it. One day a few years ago, I happened to mention it on a night out with my squad, whilst I was very drunk indeed. I did not live it down, and my squad teased me about it relentlessly for months. Earning me the nick name of 'Furnace.' I put the experience to one side, swearing that I would never speak of it again.

My mind quickly flipped back to the present moment, and the journey we were taking in the military transportation vehicle. My squad were chatting about this and that, as well as the day's events, but it was becoming more and more noticeable that Jevargh was not happy.

He bit his bottom lip, ever so briefly toying with it between his sharp teeth. Was I the only one who was noticing this? I swear that for just the most infinitesimal of moments, I thought I saw pure and unfiltered rage and revulsion for us all, within those burning orange eyes.

I did not mention the leakage that I had just witnessed to him or anyone else...it could wait, for now at least. It had been a long day, and from what I could tell, no one else had seen it. He was probably still reeling from what I had said to him during the assessment.

Maybe, I thought, just maybe I was incredibly tired. I was glad for now that today's exercise was complete. I was very relieved that I had passed the assessment, and for that matter, so was my body.

∞

The four o'clock air was relatively fresh and crisp, following a torrential downpour late afternoon that had released much of the heat from the air. I quickly showered, changing into my number two uniform, and headed out of the accommodation block to my debrief with General Eastwick. I felt heavier for some reason, and I could not define or describe why.

The heat in my chest had been more noticeable today, and that usually meant that something significant was going to happen. I couldn't fathom it, as the day had been a success. Of course, it was totally unexpected and a bit weird with Jevargh. I just tried to put that down to him wanting to throw me a curve ball… all the same, those Crucians more often than not, really gave me the creeps.

The base was relatively quiet, I parked my fusion-bike in the vehicle park, checked, and straightened the pressed creases of my uniform, right I thought. Time to get the official view on my performance today. I was a little anxious, but I knew not to show it, as this could be perceived as weakness. Right now, I had to be the persona that I had created for myself, and everyone else.

Sometimes, I just wished that I could put it all aside, but not this afternoon. This afternoon, I had to find out how I had performed.

I walked up the steps and swiped my chip, which was situated on my inner lower right arm and just above my wrist. The security panel was to the right of the entrance and as my security clearance was authorized, the door slid smoothy open. I saw in front of me the familiar sight of the reception foyer with its dark grey polished floor and the long corridors leading off it, were also like glass. I walked to the end of the corridor and made a sharp right. The General's office was in front of me, the name plate on the door read, General Eastwick. I paused, took a deep breath, and knocked on the door.

'Enter,' he said firmly. I pushed the smooth silver panel on the door, and it instantly slid open. I walked in, aligned my feet in front of his desk and saluted him.

'Captain Mitchell reporting for debrief Sir.' My shoulders ached… oh how they ached, and my side still throbbed, but nevertheless my stature remained solid, upright, and awaiting his next words.

'Captain Mitchell, never in all my service have I witnessed such a shit show of aggression, unruly conduct and a damn right fucking fiasco!' Oh fuck… I thought. 'However… that being said, in all my years I have never seen such an entertaining sight of absolute bodily control, technique, and damn right fucking excellence, and that move to the head, damn girl. I have waited twenty-five years to see such a beautiful thing, although you could have gone a bit easier on our Crucian guest… but hell those shackles sure looked good on him.' He paused, taking a large gulp from a heavy bottomed glass of water that was on his desk.

'I'm putting you forward for promotion, but if you ever do anything like that again, I may be forced to charge you, do you understand Captain?'

'Yes Sir, can I apolo–'

'No, you fucking can't, and furthermore against my better judgement, I'm assigning you to the Amaranthine, part of Earths Elite Intergalactic Division. You ship out in forty-eight hours, pick your own damn team, God dammit and try to make a fucking difference out there. Heaven knows we need it, whole damn world's gone to shit.'

'The Amaranthine, Sir… isn't that–?'

'Damn straight it is, it's where all the important shit gets done. Now get your ass measured for your new uniform and armor, and please don't make a fucking ass of me. Oh... and well done. Major Mitchell, your new cruiser, the Amaranthine awaits you, and your squad.' For a moment I was completely lost for words as to what to say…

'Thank you, Sir. I won't let you down.'

'Oh, I know that. Now get the hell out of my office and stand down Major Mitchell.'

'Yes Sir.' I saluted, turned on my heel and left his office, I couldn't quite believe what had happened, not only had he promoted me, but he had just assigned me to one of the most prestigious jobs that I could think of, and he had given me permission to choose my own team. It was time to celebrate.

I jumped back onto my fusion-bike and rode back across the base on the smooth plascrete roads, parking at the east vehicle park. I sprinted across the outer edge of the vehicle park to my quarters as I had to change out of my uniform, and quick. Celebratory drinks and food were in order.

I had a promise to keep, and some news to share with the squad. But how would I tell them I was leaving? How would I ask them to come with me? And how would it feel if some didn't want to join me, or couldn't commit to it?

This was going to be a brand-new adventure, a one of a kind, once in a lifetime opportunity… and my own ship… my own big ass space cruiser… How the hell did I manage that? I couldn't quite believe it, and I most definitely needed that drink now.

The squad had a leisure uniform code of sorts, nothing formal, more of a colour code really. We had decided one night, many moons ago that we would all try to wear something in black. We had all agreed that we could accentuate our outfits with either silver or gold.

Everyone had their outfits, and mine was a black synth-leather biker jacket with silver-coloured studs, black jeans, black synth- leather rocker boots, and a black crop top which had a silver metallic print on the front of an eagle with outstretched wings.

Once I had applied the finishing touches to my look, which was to add a little makeup, and make sure that I enhanced my best trait, my eyes. I managed to create a damn fine smoky look, and my outfit was complete. The rest of the squad were free to do their own thing, so long as they wore a mix of black, silver or gold.

Leaving my quarters hurriedly, I headed out of the accommodation block and towards where I would pick up my ride into the city. Whilst walking to the car park I noticed that the transport I had booked had thankfully arrived. The vehicle was identical to the last vehicle that I had rode in, and I contemplated for a moment that a different colour might have been nice, a bit of a change, or both. Why were all the autonomous vehicles (AV's) in the city the same colour?

The journey to the night life in LA was predictable and perfect. The vehicle was as smooth and streamlined on the inside, as it was on the outside. Cream synth-leather sculpted seating, for up to six people in the interior, this vehicle had everything you would require for your journey. It was simple, comfortable, and fully recyclable.

These vehicles had evolved over the last few centuries, as the vehicles original creator had intended. Though sadly, he had died three centuries ago, following a failed experiment to have his consciousness implanted into a synthetic. It had never been attempted since. But his legacy in motor vehicles did at least live on, and his companies' trademark could be seen in all the places that human beings explored in the galaxy, many centuries later.

The vehicle ride was incredibly fast, taking only ten minutes to travel the thirty miles or so to the center of the city, and that included navigating the other traffic and pedestrians. I tried not to look out of the window as it would often result in me feeling nauseous. But inside the car, and if I looked only within the car, I couldn't feel any motion at all.

I had discovered some time ago that if I looked out of the windows my eyes would not lie to me, not only seeing the speed, but every twist and turn. That along with the stops, starts and the close proximity of all the other vehicles and bystanders was something that I didn't enjoy at all. On a positive note, there had not been an automated vehicle accident for over two centuries, but it felt odd, to be driven by an AI. It was so extremely fast, everything measured to the last micro-millimeter, routes plotted and controlled by satellites with their own AIs on board.

I much preferred my fusion-bike, but as I wanted to have a few drinks tonight, that wasn't an option. I wasn't overly fond of the automated transport vehicles, especially as I had no control over the things. I still wanted some influence over the way I travelled, that was just how I preferred it.

The vehicle eventually made one last turn, stopping smoothly, it had been yet another efficient and uneventful ride. In front of me now, I could see multitudes of bright neon and LED lighting of every imaginable colour, it was enhancing the pedestrianised areas, in swathes of illumination.

The various premises in the area beckoned the multitudes of revelers to the many bars and restaurants doors, some with deep thudding music, and others with exotic dancers and brightly coloured holo-vid advertising that was everywhere, promoting the various diverse bars, restaurants, and stalls.

It had been too long, I thought. I really needed tonight. I had worked so hard over the last six months with little respite. The squad and I had only recently returned from Mars two months ago, after a four-month tour, Mars was great, but it wasn't Earth.

Mars had developed its own culture, which was vastly different to that of Earth. Mars was a planet full of elites, and tycoons that were ravaging the planet for its minerals, mainly metals. It was a hardened culture, and the population had evolved into this over the two hundred and fifty years or so, following its colonization and terraforming which initially began in 2150.

I treasured the atmosphere of the city at night, I loved the smell of freshly cooked street food, the colours of a thousand different types of alcohol, in the hands of so many people. People from all walks of life, all mingling together, enjoying the atmosphere, making conversation, laughing, loving, and having fun.

I walked into the tightly packed bar, looking around for familiar faces. I didn't see my squad at first, they were tucked into a dimly lit back corner, and it wasn't until Reece 'Deno' Martin caught my attention as I attempted to order my first beer, she was waving frantically to me, indicating that I should get a round in as promised. I signaled across to her using my hands and asking how many beers I needed to get, and she showed me both her hands, so I took that to mean that I needed to get ten beers.

The bartender was a middle-aged man of about seventy-five years of age, with hardened facial features, olive skin and deep creases on his forehead and cheeks. He had a full head of wavy and thick black hair that was cut just below his t-shirt neckline, heavy dark eyebrows, and a neatly trimmed black beard which was obviously dyed.

'What do you need honey?' he said in a deep and

gruff voice that didn't quite match his use of such endearing and friendly language. I leant forwards across the black and gold flecked marble topped bar, whilst speaking directly into the barman's ear.

'I'd be really grateful if you could keep the two tables at the back-left corner over there, topped up with ice cold pitchers of beer, and whisky chasers for those who want them, and a range of snacks would be good, to soak up the beer. Can you put it on my tab for the evening?'

'Yes ma'am, who shall I charge it to?' He held a scanner out and I passed my wrist over it smoothly.

'Thank you… Captain Mitchell, I'll see to it right away, you have a great evening.' He said cheerfully, whilst pulling out several empty glass pitchers from a cupboard at the rear of the bar.

In the near distance I could see Deno approaching me, she was nudging her way speedily through the many revelers in the overcrowded bar. She had that familiar smirk on her face. Deno, whose real name was Reece, was the first member of my team. When I say this, I mean she was the first one I got to pick for myself. Before I made Captain, everyone I worked with was assigned to me.

It was one of the few privileges of rank. It was a great relief when I was finally able to choose who had my back and hand pick the suitably skilled to be part of my squad, even if that meant they came with a few quirks. Deno was most definitely quirky, she had earned the nickname 'Deno' because of her love of all things western, and a distant namesake that she idolized from way back in the eighteenth century. She also owned the most cowboy hats and pistols of anyone that I knew.

Deno was an ace quick shot, she was a little eccentric, and drank her beer like the bad ass that she was. She was good in a fight, albeit she was a dirty fighter when the chips were down, and she would often use whatever she could lay her hands on to gain an advantage. I liked this about her, she was definitely a survivor, one that had a hell of a right fist.

She did have a softer side, but it would only tend to leak out every now and then, and she would always look a little embarrassed about it. I thought this was an endearing quality though. She was real, well as real as any of us were in 2425.

Deno was also fearlessly loyal and if any of her tribe, as she called it were threatened… well, very few ever saw this side of her and lived to tell the tale. She had hidden layers, much like an onion. I didn't blame her at all for wanting to protect her inner most thoughts. To me, her most endearing quality though was that she could tell when I was having an off day, and she always seemed to know the right thing to say to me, which was a skill because most people couldn't read me at all.

'You get the drinks Cap?' She said, her face was lit up with that endearing grin.

'I did, I just asked the nice man to keep the drinks coming all night and, on my tab. I must be feeling generous, and I have news, good news.'

'News… you got the promotion, didn't you? Damn, that's great news.' Her face lit up.

'I sure did, but there's more, much more and believe me I'm really gonna need that drink tonight, or maybe ten.' Deno looked excited, curious, and was clearly puzzling over what I had just said.

'Well, I think we need to get you a centre seat so you can tell us everything about what happened at the debrief. Cat's leg is fine now by the way, but we still gave her the best seat, for obvious reasons… I don't think she's ever gonna get over that move you pulled on her.' Deno laughed, which meant that Cat was definitely milking the sympathy vote from her squad mates.

The first squad member I spotted at the table was Tommy 'Guns' Kawolski. Tommy had the biggest arms I'd ever seen on a Marine, hence his nickname. Tommy was six feet, six inches of pure natural brute strength and toned muscle. He was the kind of guy you wanted by your side at close quarters in a fight. He was also the first of my heavy arms specialists. If it needed two people to fire it, Tommy could usually do it on his own. He was a gentle giant of a man, a really good soldier, and from what his wife alluded to, an even better husband.

We eased our way through the crowds of people to the tables that were designated as ours for the evening, even if the rest of the bar didn't know it. As soon as I approached, I noticed my squad stiffen and straighten, it was a natural thing for them to do, but we weren't on duty, and so I immediately gave them permission to ease up.

'At ease, we are here tonight as off duty squad mates, and I'm here mostly to buy the beer… and the whisky chasers of course.' I smiled at them all, it was good to see them.

'Whisky chasers… they are paying you way too much Captain.' Fetch said, the words escaping her mouth, aided by the vodka that she had been drinking for the last hour or so.

'Well yes, to be frank, they will be paying me a lot more from tonight, Fetch. I just made Major.' I said proudly.

At that point, my entire squad stood up and saluted me, all but Deno putting their hands upon my shoulders and sharing their congratulations. Deno paused for just a moment and then just leapt forward and hugged me.

'Why thank you all and thank you Deno. I think protocol aside, I needed that hug!'

Joe 'Hawk' Tanaka gave me the biggest smile, it drew across his face, causing his cheeks to crease deeply.

'Let the Major get herself a drink, there will be plenty of time to celebrate, and later you can tell us your other good news.' His tone was enthusiastic.

'Second Lieutenant Tanaka, always on target, pass me a beer… I think your aim is off tonight though.' Joe looked a little confused, but before he could say anything, I gave him some good news.

'Joe, how does Captain Tanaka sound?' I spoke openly, inviting Joe to take the promotion. Joe looked at me speechless, for a moment, trying to take in my words whilst looking around at the others who were all smiling.

'Are you shitting me?' His mouth was agape with surprise.

'Nope, it's all yours if you want it?' Joe bowed his head humbly for a moment.

'I would be honored to accept it.' He lifted his eyes up to mine and looked at me sincerely, this was one of the reasons I valued Joe, he had both integrity and sincerity in equal measure, and I knew that if he said something, he meant it. I smiled once again.

'Of course Joe, I wouldn't want it any other way, and the good news for me is that you get to remain my second, I need a good eye and a safe pair of hands Joe, now more than ever.'

Joe nodded, I could see that he knew I was going to announce something big, but I would bet all the money on the chip in my arm that had just paid for the drinks, that he wouldn't have guessed what, in a million years.

Frankie 'Fetch' Martinez beamed as she swallowed down a chaser in one long and meaningful gulp, my how that woman loved to party. Fetch was the shortest of my squad, badass, head strong, stubborn and the kind of woman that acts first and thinks later.

This quality was a bit of a mixed bag in my eyes, it was excellent in situations where bravery and immediate action were needed, but it could be problematic when strategy and planning were the best way forward.

We had pulled Fetch out of many a hole she had dug for herself, but then Fetch had pulled us out of many holes too. Fetch redeemed herself often, and I needed her guts, guile, and her aptitude for bravery in my squad. She was an ace pilot, could land a shuttle on a pin head if that were what was required, and was expert at weapons systems of any vehicle or craft.

The nickname Fetch, came from her unique secondary ability to acquire whatever it was the team needed, hence the nickname 'Fetch.' We didn't know how she did it, and we didn't really want to know. Whatever we needed, she could get it cheaper and faster than any of our military vetted suppliers.

Catherine 'Cat' Shaw was the second of my heavies. Cat was a five-foot ten-inch African American who was as lean as she was strong. Cat was not only strong, but she was fast and also incredibly intelligent, though she mostly tried to hide her intellect, often with humour. Cat would often take the lead and come up with efficient and deadly strategies that were not all too common for heavy gunners in my experience.

I liked Cat very much, she had a lot to offer the squad. She was also a science and engineering specialist, and if anything needed fixing or adapting, Cat was your woman.

Cat got her nickname 'Buzz' for two reasons, the first reason was her love of science and engineering tech. If you ever went to her quarters, she would be taking something apart, and working out how to put it back together, much better than it was originally, with her tools… and, well some of them buzzed. But the first time when she got called the nickname had nothing to do with her scientific or engineering expertise. It was more to do with her prowess with a seventy-five-pound buzz saw, that she clean lifted off its bench, managing to take out two assailants in one movement by literally swinging it around her head like a lasso.

Well, after that Buzz and her last name Shaw seemed to fit really well, and the rest, as they say is history.

The last member of my six was Summer Neilson, she looked like the girl next door… only Summer was everything but. Summer was our infiltrator. She was adept at getting in and out of places unseen, due to her gymnastic ability and her incredible bodily control, which is where she got her nickname 'Shade.' Summer had the looks of the girl you might take to the prom. Your only mistake would be believing what you saw.

Summer was also adept at hacking and using whatever she could get her hands on to gain information and intelligence for the squad. I needed

Summer, she was prepared to do the work some would find all too dark, all her weapons were silent, as was she, unless of course we were talking food.

Where food was concerned Summer would get very animated. Summer was an adept cook, and on missions would often take charge of the squad's nutritional needs.

The night and the beers were going down well, it had been a long time since beer had tasted this good. I paused for a moment looking at my squad, all relaxing, talking and laughing. Was this a good time to tell them, to ask them? I didn't get the option to mull it over, as I noticed that Deno indicated to Cat that she needed her place. Cat instantly shuffled over to sit with Tommy, and they immediately started talking shop, and big guns.

'So… Cap, I mean Major. What's the big story?' Deno looked like a reporter wanting a news scoop, her face full of inquisitiveness.

'Well… as much as I'd like to tell just you, I really need to share this with everyone.' I swallowed hard, as I thought about the reality of what I was about to say and then ask of them, and it really hit me. This was it, after tonight I may never see any of them again, and the thought of starting over wasn't something that I even wanted to consider.

'Listen up everyone, I have some news and it's really good… I'm extremely proud of you all. I just want you all to know that I am, grateful and thankful that you are... Sorry. I'm finding it difficult to know where to start with this, and the whisky is making me feel a little tipsy, and you know how sometimes...' I looked down at my whisky and took a large mouthful of the golden liquid into my mouth.

They all looked at me and I could feel myself feeling a little anxious and I most definitely felt in the spotlight, and that really wasn't like me. I think it was the realisation that things were going to change, one way or the other from the instant that I shared my news.

'Well… the promotions weren't the only good news I have for you all. There's news and it's good, if you want it and not so good for me if you don't.' They all looked concerned. I don't think I'd ever seen my squad sober up so quickly. I drew a deep breath…

'There is no other way to say this… I've been given command of my own space cruiser, the Amaranthine, they have apparently been looking for someone to command her for some time, and they felt that I would be right for the job. I'd like to ask you all if you would like to join me in my new command. There is absolutely no pressure, it has to be your decision. We will likely be away for months at a time and that won't be easy… the food will likely suck, as will the quarters, and we won't be drinking anything like real beer for a while… and–' Before I could even finish my sentence, Deno shouted up.

'I'm in.' She was followed by Cat who said.

'So, when do we leave? Then Tommy spoke, his deep voice booming.

'Consider me signed on Major.' Then Fetch blurted out.

'Your gonna need things that only I can acquire.' She laughed, and we all laughed with her. This left only Joe and Summer. Joe looked at me proudly.

'I can't let you go into space without your most excellent second in command, now, can I? I'm with you all the way Major, as always.' Followed by Summer who said.

'Your gonna need some good food, and… also you might need someone to get into all those dark shady places, and from what I see there is a hell of lot of darkness in space.' Deno just looked at me.

'This is big… really big. I wouldn't miss this adventure for the world.' She smiled and passed me another whisky, which I drank down in one large gulp, slamming the glass on the table. If I'd felt proud before I shared my news, I was experiencing it at a higher level now, if that were even possible.

I was humbled by them and recognized the gift of their loyalty and camaraderie. I acknowledged to myself what had just been shared with me. I was happy that I had several beers and whiskies to take the edge off this moment.

'Pass me another whisky.' Fetch passed me the whisky instantly, like she had it all stored safely in her back pocket. We continued talking about the new assignment for a while, what would the ship be like inside, what would our quarters look like, how many people did the ship hold? Then, standing up, whisky in hand I immediately gained their attention.

'I would like to propose a toast, in two parts. Firstly, I would like to toast the best squad a newly promoted Major could ever hope for. Secondly, I would like to propose a toast for the adventure ahead of us, may it lead us to places that we could never imagine or hope for, to the Amaranthine, and to our success!' All six stood up, glasses in their hands.

'Hoozaah!' they shouted and then they knocked back their chasers.

'Who's with the Major?' Joe said, loudly.

'We are, until the stars fall from the skies!' Everyone

looked at me and each other cheering jubilantly.

'To you all, the best of the best, and to those we have lost, and to the stars that rise before us in the clear night sky. Squad, report to platform three, Los Angeles Military Space Port in forty-eight hours' time, for your assignments to the Amaranthine.'

2 THE LATE NIGHT VISITOR

It was around 01:45 hours when we eventually stumbled out of the bar. The squad had their arms around each other's shoulders in both an act of solidarity and to help them remain on their feet. Most of my squad lived off base, all except Deno, who had her quarters within the barracks. I was considering options for transport, when I remembered that I needed to complete and sign Joe's digital promotion papers, and email them back to the military records office, and their internal mailbox at the Pentagon.

It seemed more urgent that I do it now for some reason. I also think though, that at the time the whisky was definitely affecting my better judgement, as there was no reason that it couldn't wait another day.

I looked across at Deno who was holding on to the mounting of a streetlight as if her very life depended on it. She swayed backwards and forwards like an amateur pole dancer, but thankfully and in support of her dignity, the streetlight remained upright.

'Hey Deno. Are you getting a lift back to base?' I shouted across to her, waving at her, trying to get her attention. Deno lifted her head and looked towards me for a moment, whilst still holding tightly on to the mounting.

'Yep Cap. I mean Marj, Majoor. I'm sorry, I can't seem to sleak lelly well at the mooooment. Is this lamp post moving?' Deno tripped over her words and was somehow far drunker than I. I walked carefully, whilst trying not to stumble, making my way gingerly over to where Deno was still loosely attached to the streetlight, I offered her my shoulder to lean on.

'Right soldier, let's get you home before you do yourself a mischief.' I said firmly. I just hoped that I would be sturdy enough for the two of us, as I tried to get my bearings.

'Yes ma'am.' Deno made her best attempt, to straighten up in vain. She was gently swaying all over the place. I tapped the chip in my arm and spoke into it.

'I'd like transport to take two people back to Los Angeles Air Force Base.' Within thirty seconds a vehicle identical to the one that I had travelled in earlier, arrived. It pulled up silently around fifteen metres away from where we stood. I put Deno's arm over my shoulder, and we walked, and stumbled more or less in a straight line to where the transport awaited us. I nudged Deno generally in the direction of the now open vehicle, as she was having some trouble locating the door.

Incredibly, we managed somehow to both sit ourselves securely in the vehicle, without acquiring any injury, as it moved off swiftly and silently. I passed Deno a large pouch of water that I had obtained from the bartender before we left the bar. I knew that if I drank plenty, the hangover might be slightly less encumbering the next day. The odds of this had now reduced by fifty percent, as Deno gulped down the water, like she hadn't drunk for days. Some of the clear liquid escaped her water filled mouth and began running down her chin, she wiped the flowing droplets off quickly with the back of her hand.

I was beginning to feel heavy with the alcohol, and I decided to make sure that I drank plenty before turning in for the night, once back at my quarters. I requested the vehicle not show us the outside windows. I didn't think my gut could stand it. Deno was now singing old country and western songs badly, I didn't realise that she liked the old stuff. I tried to join in but didn't know the words, so I tried to hum along to support Deno's valiant attempts. It made me smile, but all too soon the journey was over, and we exited the vehicle, though not nearly as elegantly as we had entered it.

It looked far gloomier on base than it usually did at night for some reason, and I soon noticed that there were just the bases essential night lights on. These were far dimmer than when the base was lit up as it normally would be. Usually, this lighting would only be on when the base was completing a military exercise. I thought that this was odd, as I hadn't been made aware of any that were taking place tonight.

I also noticed that in some locations visibility was far better than in others. Deno and I made our way carefully towards the accommodation blocks. Along the way, Deno was shushing me and herself in an attempt not to make any noise, but she was making far more noise than she would do normally. The two of us neared the corner of the block where Deno's accommodation was located, and where I would see Deno safely on her way. I was going to head over to HQ to sign the digital proforma for Joe's promotion from the console that was located in my office. I paused for a brief moment, readying myself to let go of Deno's arm.

'Are you gonna be OK Deno?' I said, a concerned look on my face, as Deno swayed ever so slightly in the breeze.

'Yes ma'am, I will be fine, thanks for seeing me home. I–.' From the corner of my eye, I saw something move in the distance. I looked immediately towards the movement, as it struck me as a bit out of place. I thought that it was only myself and Deno that were out as it was now around two in the morning.

'Deno! Shush...' I whispered. 'Over there, what's that?'

Deno spun around quickly on the ball of her foot, I thought she would fall over but she didn't, planting the heel of her boot firmly on the floor, steadying herself.

'Cap? I mean Major?' She whispered questioningly.

'Over there, I think there is someone going into HQ. Now why would anyone be so stupid to go into HQ at this time in the morning?' I took a brief moment, contemplating that I was going to do the very same thing.

'Unless of course, it is to sign on to the net in order to access the files for Joe's promotion. I mean obviously… that's a really good reason to go into work at 2 am.' I tried to re-focus my vision in on who it was that I could see. I didn't know who I was trying to convince, myself or Deno.

'Shit Deno, I think it may be Jevargh the Crucian,

what the hell is he doing? Come on, we need to follow him and see what he is up to.'

'I will try, I think I need to pee first.' I looked at Deno in astonishment.

'Really. Now, you need to pee now, right now?' Deno shrugged her shoulders, showing me a single digit, indicating to me that she would be one minute. She quickly disappeared behind a stack of heavy metal containers. I glanced over my shoulder, making sure that I still had eyes on Jevargh. I watched him climb the stairs of HQ, he didn't check if anyone were observing him, why would he, he probably thought we were all asleep.

Deno returned swiftly, looking a little less drunk now. We moved quietly across the side of the parade square that was directly in front of the HQ building, whilst attempting to keep as much as we could to any bit of shadow or area of darkness, where the lights glare couldn't reach us. We could see a single lit office to the right of the main entrance. The rest of the building though, other than some limited outdoor lighting was in total darkness.

'Hey Major, what we gonna do?' Deno whispered, as she shadowed me step-by-step in my footsteps, as we both carefully and quietly snook up towards the buildings entrance.

'Firstly Deno, we need to establish what, if anything he is up to. Something feels very off here. I mean, I've had my suspicions about him for a while now. I knew there was more going on, you remember my assessment. He was the last one standing, and it was just the two of us. We were on our own, Deno there was a look. I dunno… I almost lost my shit with him. I think it was just the way that he looked at me during the assessment, and afterwards, in the vehicle on the way back to base. It caused me some concern. I haven't been able to get it out of my mind since it happened. I felt that he definitely wanted to hurt me, or that I was going to have some kind of accident.'

'It sure did hurt his pride when you left him trussed up in that metal box though Major. You are sure it's not just that, ya know… wounded pride, or a big ego?' Deno smirked.

'Yeah, some of it could be. But quite honestly, I don't know what would have happened, had he succeeded. I'd probably be nursing some significant injuries in hospital right now.'

We reached the main door, which was dimly lit, just enough to see its outline and make out what was wall and what was door. To the right of it was a smooth metallic panel with two circular and flat lenses embedded within it. I recognised it to be a commonly used security device, a retina and iris recognition scanner. I placed my right eye directly over the larger circular lens, and pale light blue rays swept up and down across my eye.

The door began to slide open smoothly and I heard the familiar sound of a very brief air rush, as the door opened fully and within a few seconds. I signalled to Deno with my right hand in a forwards motion and crouching down together we both entered the lobby silently.

The floor was covered in dark grey rectangular tiles that were highly polished and took on the appearance of glass. Each tile measured thirty by fifteen centimetres and was edged in a silver, smooth polished metal edging. Each strip of edging had embedded within it, rows of two-millimetre holes which were around five centimetres apart. The edging did not simply look luxurious, but it had a practical use also, in that the tiles were part of the base's security measures. The idea being that if an intruder entered the building, the metal beading around the tiles was pressure sensitive and would flag that there was an intruder on site. No immediate, or audible alarm would be raised, but the offenders would be detained within minutes, by the bases military police.

Luckily for us, and because of my rank, I had access to the majority of the Headquarters site. I knew that once we entered the building, the security would thankfully be turned off, at least until we left and decided if we needed to raise the alarm. I wondered just exactly how Jevargh had managed to gain entry, he wouldn't have the appropriate clearances. This would need to be investigated later, in order to rule out espionage.

The two of us hunkered silently behind the foyer wall, to the left of a second door that led to a long corridor that had six offices adjoined to it. The corridors floor was also glass like, but unlike the foyer, it was light grey in colour. It had smooth white walls only broken intermittently by six smooth dark grey doors, each fitted with its own retina and iris recognition scanners.

I was running the viable options through my mind, whilst also trying to think of how we could possibly find out what Jevargh was doing. I wondered if there were any way that we could listen in to any conversation that he might be having or at the very least, see something of what he was doing. But whatever approach we took, I knew that it was vital to do it without being seen or heard. This would mean he could be intercepted more easily should the need arise to have him detained later.

I looked to my right and just happened to see one of the bases maintenance bots leave one of the vents that they travelled around the base in, in order to carry out their duties. I considered it an option and thought that crawling through the vent would be perfect for Deno, she would love it. However, she was still a little too intoxicated. But I… I would just about fit inside the vent, and in my current state I felt that I had a slightly better chance of remaining undetected by Jevargh.

'Deno, over here, quickly take a look at this, what do you think? Is it doable?' I pointed to the possible access point.

'We need to somehow get this vent cover open so I can try and crawl through it. I think, I mean if I recall rightly, each one leads to air access vents above each of the offices. So, if I can find the right room, I should be able to see something and if we are lucky, maybe hear something. Even if it's just a little, that will be much better than having nothing to go on. I know it's a big ask but–' Before I could finish my sentence, Deno had begun to examine the vents fixings and its accessibility. She nimbly felt around the outer side of the cover, and amazingly it just popped right off.

The vents access measured around seventy-five cm by seventy-five cm. It would be tight and somewhat claustrophobic, especially when navigating corners, but I felt that I was probably agile enough to get through it. I worried for a moment about how much alcohol Deno had to drink, and because of this and any risk of our proximity being revealed to Jevargh, I needed to make sure that she was well out of site. That aside though, I believed that using the vent was worth the risk.

'Okay, listen up.' I said assertively. 'Once I am in, can you replace the cover on the vent, just in case Jevargh leaves the building before I am out of there. I need you to stay put in the first office on the left-hand side of the corridor until it's safe. I will record anything that I can using my chip just in case I need to take this issue to command.' I stopped for a moment, drawing in a breath. 'Deno, no one, and I mean no one will listen to us without at least some credible evidence. I will open up and let you into one of the offices. I just want you to sit this one out Deno unless I need you. Do you have a sidearm?' Deno nodded and smirked.

'Of course, I do, but you will be happy to know that tonight it's on safety for a change.' She was never without a sidearm, though you wouldn't know that she had a pistol, let alone where she had it secreted on her body. This was another quirk, or was it a talent that she had, it certainly was one that I had yet to achieve any competence in.

'Here, take my stuff and keep it with you.' I quickly removed and handed Deno my boots and jacket. 'Once I have further information, and when Jevargh has left the building. I will make contact with you on my chip. We will meet back up here, by the vents access. I will be coming out feet first, so you may need to pull me out. Oh, and Deno, be careful, be quiet and don't get us caught.'

I dropped to my knees and slowly lent forward whilst crawling. Dropping again, lowering myself until finally I was flat on my stomach. I pulled myself forwards, slowly entering the metal framed access point. It looked dark inside, and this became even more apparent when Deno began to reseal the opening of the vents access panel, which she appeared to be doing efficiently and at great speed.

The vent was surprisingly warm, but it was incredibly dark on the inside, and other than multiple rows of tiny dark red LED lights, that were only just visible to my eyes. I noted that I could not see very much at all. The lights sole purpose was to help guide the maintenance bots around the vents, this time though, they would be the only light source that would assist me, as I made my way even deeper into the vents shaft.

I hesitated only for a brief moment, when I noticed the last bit of light from the foyer disappear behind me, as Deno closed the vents access cover fully. I was now on my own, crawling on my belly in almost complete darkness through a bots maintenance vent, and there I was only a few hours ago drinking to our success, thinking that the evening had gone so well. The irony of the moment was not lost on me, as I momentarily shook my head in disbelief.

I moved now, more rapidly and silently than before, making my way along the narrow tunnel. I was thankful that I had clothing on that wouldn't catch, drag or be noisy against the vents metal casing. The only thing that tugged in any way, was my bare skin. The warm metal of the vents casing causing the skin on my stomach and arms to stick to it slightly. As a result, these parts of my body were causing some additional friction when they came into direct contact with the vents smooth surfaces. The effect on my movement was that it took considerable physical effort and concentration to heave myself forwards, let alone do this silently.

I neared the first bend, fitting my now warming body into its unkind angles. I could feel a slight rise in the temperature in the vent. I felt the walls of the vent in front of me, I noticed a change in the gradient, which I mapped out quickly with my hands. The gradient was situated just in front of me, and I expected that once I had climbed the incline, that this would then take me up to ceiling height, or at least so I hoped.

The vent began to split, but directly ahead of me at least, I could just make out what looked like a single long ventilation shaft, with six other shafts that branched off it at regular intervals. I knew at this point that I was almost at ceiling level and in line with the offices upper ventilation panels. I was heading in the right direction, and more importantly I was nearing Jevargh's location.

I made my way down to the first intersection point, where the vent branched off to the right. I eased slowly and smoothly, making my way in absolute silence to where I could now see a single, and slightly illuminated vent. I studied the angle of the air gaps in the vent, noticing that they tilted downwards. Excellent, I thought. This meant that I would be able to see at least some of the inside of the occupied room, and if I were careful, I could do so, without being detected.

I took a final deep breath, lifting my head, shoulders, and upper bodyweight up and onto my elbows, at least now I had a little more stability. Looking down, and into the room I could see Jevargh below me, he was moving about the room. Was he pacing? He looked extremely agitated. Why was he pacing up and down the room in that way?

Crucians, I thought were well known for their mostly cold, emotionless stances and demeanours…

Jevargh though, well he was clearly very much on edge, he looked anxious, but why? I couldn't see anything odd about his situation, other than his apparent restlessness, and the small matter of him being in a room that he didn't have access to, as highly unusual.

I continued to observe him closely, noticing the increasing heat in the upper vent, some perspiration had begun to escape the pores on my body in an attempt to cool me down. It was beginning to pool now, in tiny droplets on my chest, back and forehead, I felt a single drop make its way to the tip of my nose. It began to tickle slightly, and so I blew it off silently using my bottom lip. I hoped that this was the worst of the heat, as I would struggle to cool myself down if it got much hotter.

Suddenly, and apparently from nowhere. I noticed a second person in the room, but that was impossible. Deno and I had only seen one person enter HQ and that was Jevargh. I instantly realised whilst studying the second figure that something didn't look quite right about it. Jevargh's seemingly invited guest was, in fact a holographic three dimensional projection. That would explain the pacing, I thought. Jevargh had seemingly been impatiently waiting for them, whoever they were to appear. This confirmed to me that his actions were pre-planned, this didn't add up.

The second figure in the room appeared to be a Crucian female. A few moments later and not long after her appearance in the room, a third figure could then be seen. But the third figure, from what I could just make out, was definitely not a Crucian. What the hell, and who the hell was that? I'd never seen anything like it.

I set my chip to record, as the solitary female figure

looked to the unidentified being, as if she were seeking permission from it to speak. The unknown being moved slightly, revealing a single long, white digit shaped proboscis from around the centre of its heavy and elongated bony shape. Its cranium was large and looked to be incredibly long from its forehead to the base of the skull. A ridge of raised sharpened bone ran down the centre of it, from the beings ivory white forehead all the way over the top of its head to the base of its skull. The being had tiny eyes, which struck me as odd. Its eyes looked almost jet black in colour, and it had a large and powerfully shaped jaw which made the being look vicious. I observed that it reminded me somewhat of a dinosaurs jaw, its jagged teeth were clearly meant for ripping meat, or prey apart.

I studied the beings proboscis further, at first, I wandered if it was something like a finger, but it definitely was not a finger, not in the human sense at least. It appeared to be frantically gesturing towards the Crucian female, seemingly communicating with her that it gave her its permission for her to continue. The Crucian female appeared to revere the being, but she too definitely appeared to be acting cautiously around it. This was something new I was witnessing, and something that I, and to my knowledge no one else had ever seen before, in all my years of service this was most definitely a troubling alliance that I was witnessing.

The female was dressed formally, in typical Crucian elite regalia which was black, red, and gold attire, that was reserved for the most powerful upper echelons of Crucian society. This female had some power, though from what I could make out, not nearly as much as the unidentified being that was next to her. She appeared to be wealthy, and her grooming and pedigree was clearly visible. Not a hair out of place, and every bit of her deeply angular face and complexion, like that of fine porcelain.

She held herself with some degree of authority and was making every attempt to play her part in this situation. She was clearly quite adept at upholding her position in society and maintaining her dignity and decorum, but it appeared to me to be an elaborate façade, put on to please the beings desire for dominance.

Like her facial features, her physique was angular and sharp also, her hip bones evident and protruding slightly from beneath her gown and robes. These features could be seen in all Crucian females, I observed that the deep red skin on her arms too, was likewise perfectly smooth, and almost radiant to look at. She was not attractive to me, but I recognised that in Crucian society, she would be considered as incredibly beautiful. She paused, gathering her composure once more, and then lifting her head slightly to meet Jevargh's eye level, she began to speak.

'Jevargh, it is good to see you.' She said contemptuously, as if Jevargh were merely a pawn. 'How are you finding the dirt and the putrid squalor of Earth?' Her tone was deliberate and condescending, as if she were inviting a river of insults to pour from Jevargh's blackened lips.

'I do so admire your resolve, many of us would feel sickened to our stomachs at the very thought of even walking upon its surface, let alone spending any time with these filthy humans. You must long to scrub the stench of this sickened planet from the soles of your boots.' Jevargh nodded respectfully, acknowledging her statement, and waiting for her to pause before he finally spoke.

'Chancellor, it is good to see you.' He uttered respectfully and subserviently. 'To hear and see one of my own again. It brings me some comfort. I can at least remind myself of who I truly am. It is a toil to have to endure placating this unworthy and primal species, but one that I do willingly for our combined interests. I long to end them Chancellor, and I long to see the day when they fall to their knees in recognition of how unworthy they are. That they even exist in the same galaxy alongside us is an insult to us, and our allies.'

Oh shit… I knew Jevargh had behaved like an ass hole in my squad, but this. This was the talk of war. This was the talk of a toxic agenda, of conspiracy, and of repulsion for our species. It was deeply disturbing to me, to have it confirmed.

I knew then in an instant that all along, and since he had joined my squad, he had been plotting and scheming, watching us, studying us, and reporting back. I recalled the look he gave me during my assessment. It was full of venom… I was right about him.

All at once, I could feel my human emotions begin to kick in. I was angry, I hadn't noticed at first, but I had begun to bite down hard on my bottom lip causing it to bleed slightly, whilst still trying to concentrate on the task at hand. I was battling every urge and instinct in my now tightened body to confront him, the bastard. I felt a second wave of anger, if only I wasn't in this vent. I could apprehend him. We could interrogate him and find out what he had been doing. Abruptly, Jevargh began to speak once again.

'I have all the information that you seek about

Earth. It didn't take me long. These humans do not protect what is dearest to them, they have little intellect, and they do not recognise their assets, in the same way that we do. The information was easy to obtain, a simple task, now completed and one that will see the demise of an even simpler species. Chancellor, I long to see it put to use.'

A cold shiver passed over my body, despite the heat in the vent, and the back of my neck now tingled. Adrenalin was now pumping around my physique, and a deep and consuming urgency gripped my core. I couldn't afford to lose my concentration, not now. I closed my eyes for a moment but kept recording, that fucking bastard, I thought. How dare he speak of our species in that way!

Then came the unusual heat once more. It was unrelenting, intense, searing, and lodged in my chest again. What the hell was this? It only seemed to happen when I was under extreme stress and duress, or when something was wrong, and from what I had just witnessed, this was much more than wrong, this was a cataclysm.

I glanced down at my chest, and for just a brief moment, and no longer than a split second I thought that I could see a soft shimmering glow, which appeared to be resonating and gently pulsating, just under the surface of my skin. I rubbed the sweat away from my eyes quickly, I was tired, I'd had a lot to drink, and I promptly persuaded myself that it must have been the glow of the red vent lights, playing tricks with my eyes. This combined with the emotion I felt, hearing the vile shit that was pouring out of Jevargh's poisonous, and condescending mouth had me feeling incensed.

It had been a long day. I looked down at my chest once more, and the faint shimmering and pulsating glow that I thought I had seen under my skin, had now gone completely. I inhaled deeply, letting out an almost silent sigh of relief. I was determined to continue to listen and record as much of this incident as I could, no matter how hot it got.

There was a brief pause in the conversation, as the Crucian chancellor appeared to be relaying some information, and Jevargh's words to the unidentified alien. She then walked to where she had originally been stood and began to speak once again to Jevargh, though this time her words seemed more deliberate and she appeared to be rushing what she was saying to him, it appeared scripted to me. Why was she doing that?

'Your efforts will be rewarded in the coming onslaught, and in our valiant future conquests. Are you ready to transmit the information to us Jevargh? Once we receive it, the cruiser will then forward the information to the fleet, from there it will make its way to the High Chancellor and the Council of Eight. They requested that I convey to you, that they salute your efforts Jevargh, son of Meghast.'

Jevargh bowed slightly, holding out in his left hand a small cylindrical red crystal shaped device. On Earth, we had similar devices that had revolutionised our computing ability, each crystal able to store more information on it than all the, now primitive storage drives of Earth, just one hundred years ago.

I considered what I had just heard. Whatever it was they were planning, they were being clearly devious, aggressive, and malignant towards us. This was an incredibly serious matter, and a politically volatile one at that. I felt validated though, in some small way that I was right, but at what cost did being right come? I really hated being right sometimes. This, what I was hearing… well, it was really fucked up. What the hell had I just witnessed?

I thought about it even more, how much more fucked up could this situation get? How the hell could I stop it? I still didn't have a clue, as to what it was that they were planning against us, but I knew it wasn't good. I knew I had to share this information… but who with, who could I trust?

The chancellor nodded to Jevargh and looked towards the grotesque and previously unknown alien creature. It seemed to be moving somewhat fluidly and it was ever so slightly shimmering, if you weren't absolutely still, you might not even have noticed this. Its movements creeped me out, and I had come to the conclusion that it definitely wasn't friendly, not to us at least.

The creature moved again, the two figures appearing motionless for what seemed like an eternity, but in fact was probably only a few seconds, my heightened state and the adrenaline that was coursing around my body, appearing to slow time itself.

All of a sudden, something changed. I had no idea what initially, but what happened next caused my eyes to be temporarily blinded, as multiple and intensely bright, fine lines of red laser like lights filled the room below me. One of the first things that I noticed was the smell, it was putrid, it was truly horrific.

By the time my eyes had adapted, I could only just see two figures. The Crucian female and the unidentified alien. They were looking out across the office as if searching for something. But where was

Jevargh? There was a vapour, rising in the room, like steam. I tilted my head slightly and looked down towards the floor where he had been stood. What I saw, I couldn't quite believe, but it was truly shocking.

Jevargh was part decapitated, part disintegrated. His smouldering corpse lay in heavy pieces upon the floor, and still the two malevolent figures stood looking into the room, as if checking to see if Jevargh was truly dead. At this point the Crucian chancellor looked to the other creature, before speaking.

'It is done. No loose ends.' She said ruthlessly. 'The humans will never know what hit them. We have all the information that we need now, including the information on the Okai and the Nadaal.'

Finally, the large white bony creature spoke, but I couldn't even make out what it was, let alone understand the language it was speaking, but at least I had it recorded and from what I could make out, it definitely sounded pleased with the outcome. Then, just as they had arrived in the room, they were gone. A feeling of urgency felt really appropriate in the circumstances, and I cursed under my breath. Shit, shit, SHIT!

I was in a building with Deno and there was a half melted, perfectly sliced, smouldering dead Crucian ten feet below me. I signalled Deno on my chip and made my way as quickly as I could, and in reverse towards the vents access. I bumped and knocked against the inside of the vents shaft walls, my warm skin fought against me with every forced movement, as I scrambled backwards and quickly towards the exit.

Deno was waiting and was looking into the shaft. Seeing my feet first, she reached in and pulled me out in one fluid motion, my sweat covered skin once again squeaking against the vents smooth metallic surfaces as she did so. I attempted to stand up, I was shaken, and noticing this Deno rushed to steady me. Trying to catch my breath and pushing each of the words out of my mouth, I was only able to utter one sentence.

'We need to leave. NOW!'

Deno quickly replaced the vent and rubbed the sleeve of her jacket along the smooth edges of the cover. I pulled my rocker boots onto my feet, then taking my jacket from Deno, I put it on, zipping it up tightly. We hurriedly made our way out of the building and across the open parking spaces we had both crossed just about an hour ago. I felt shocked by what I had seen and was trying desperately to make sense of it all. Deno looked concerned and I could tell that she was impatiently waiting for me to say something, anything.

'Major, what the hell happened in there, you look like you have just seen a ghost.' Her hand, rested on my shoulder, in an attempt to steady me.

'Deno, they just killed Jevargh.' I was still trying to take a breath, I felt sickened.

Deno looked shocked, her forehead creased up tightly in a frown, I could see her starting to gather her racing thoughts.

'They? Wait, what… are you sure?' Her usual smirk had gone, and she looked alarmed at me, her eyes were wide with shock as she began to process the gravity of the situation.

'Oh, I'm dead sure. Deno, I need to be straight up with you… he's in bits on the office floor. The security system is only meant to be pressure sensitive, its only supposed to send an alarm to the military police on base. I'm pretty sure it's not meant to decapitate and leave someone looking like butchered meat on the floor.'

We continued walking a short distance, and I turned to get a final look at the building, still trembling slightly and not quite believing what I had just witnessed.

'Wait a moment. Deno look over there, by the entrance.'

Deno turned and we saw a vehicle, it was silver in colour, but other than that it had no significant standout features that we could make out in the darkness. I touched the chip on my arm and a small plate slid back, out of which, on two wires that moved like liquid, emerged my recon camera. I urged Deno to be silent by placing my finger over my lips, she disappeared into the shadows, and I did too.

Just my forearm was in sight, as it protruded from the shade. I hope that it couldn't be seen by these unknown malignant visitors. We were around three-hundred meters away and it was dark, I hoped for the best. I held my breath once more, the camera moved about smoothly on its translucent wires, whilst I tried my best to aim it towards the mysterious vehicle that had just pulled up. The camera began taking pictures moving autonomously and quickly in order to get a better angle each time.

I glanced towards the vehicle and could see two figures emerging from it, their attire was non-descript and grey in colour. They were humanoid in their form, but I couldn't make out whether they were human or another species entirely. The only thing I could make out was that each figure held a large dark case. This evening was just getting weirder and weirder. Deno then whispered from the shadows.

'Can you see anything Major?'

'Yeah, well I can, sort of. There are two of them and they have silver cases, they have just gone into the building. Look Deno, I need to tell someone about this. Other than me, who do you trust?' Deno paused for a moment and then whispered loudly.

'I trust the man that just promoted you and gave you your ship, that's who I would trust right now.' I nodded; she was right. He was an honest man, and he must have seen something in me. Maybe he would listen, and if not. Well, I could probably kiss my promotion and the Amaranthine goodbye, but I just felt that I had to see this through. I had to do the right thing, regardless of the risk and the possible loss of my recent promotion.

Deno and I walked for a while until we were well clear of Headquarters, it was now three in the morning. Infinite stars lit up the darkness of the night sky and gave me some comfort as they blazed brightly, lighting the way across the cosmos. We needed to tell the General what had happened. All I kept thinking was, he's not going to believe this, he won't want to believe this. But in spite of the doubt I was feeling, I still felt it was the right thing to do.

I looked at Deno, just hours ago we were both drunk and celebrating my promotion and a new intergalactic adventure. Now, I began to wonder if my promotion would stand, let alone my new ship. I was tired and I rubbed my face for a moment, trying to make myself more alert.

'Deno, can you call a vehicle and try to locate General Eastwick, it's time to throw my career in the latrine.' Deno nodded in acknowledgement. She brought her chip up to her mouth and requested a vehicle, in less than a minute another identical vehicle, just like the one we had seen, just like the one I went partying in, arrived. Why did all the fucking vehicles look the god damn same? I thought, shaking my head.

∞

Deno sat opposite me in the vehicle, we were both heavily soaked in the surrealness of the evening's events. Deno was sat one leg crossed over the other, she looked like she was ready to burst at any time.

'Got something you wanna say Deno?' I spoke, questioningly. I almost couldn't bare seeing her throw the thoughts around in her head.

'Yeah Major. What exactly happened in that room, apart from Jevargh being turned into chunky paste?' I took a long deep gasp for air. I was struggling to find the right words to say.

'Deno, I think we have a really big fucking problem, that's what I think… but I don't know what it is. It feels really fucking big though, I've never seen the other species before. It was skulking in the room with the Crucian Chancellor and that concerns me.' Deno frowned again looking at her boots and then back at me.

'Another species, a Crucian Chancellor… what the hell did you see Major?'

'Deno, I'm not sure what I saw. I just keep thinking, why was it there? What's it's part in this? She, the Crucian Chancellor… she seemed to revere it, and yet we have never seen this species before. Why don't we know of this species… plus, it's really bothering me, what they said just before they killed him.' I sighed.

Deno looked out of the window, the vehicle was heading towards General Eastwicks home. We would be there soon, and Deno would then hear it all.

'Well Major, I've never seen you spooked in the way

that this thing has spooked you. Whatever it is, it has got a soft spot, a place we can hurt it, we just need to know where.'

The vehicle drew quickly to a stop, outside its windows I could make out some large gates. Were those iron gates? Hardly anyone had iron gates anymore. These were ornate, painted black, incredibly old, and quite magnificent. I got out of the vehicle and Deno exited behind me. We both stood looking at the gates for a moment, we rarely saw gates that were made by hand anymore. Most gates were regimented, uniform in design and one of ten standardised colours, as were most things on this planet.

Deno walked up to the gates and butted her feet and head against them, the gates moved slightly, and Deno looked perplexed. I let out a quiet laugh, whilst putting my hand over my mouth to stem the rest of it.

'These gates are not automatic Deno, you have to open them yourself.' Deno looked at me and then started to look at the gates as if they were some kind of elaborate puzzle.

'Look, here.' I showed Deno the metal latch that rested on an L shaped piece of metal on the opposite gate. I lifted the latch and pushed the left gate. The gate began to move slowly, and there was the sound of metal moving on the hinges.

Deno looked at me and I could see the quizzical look on her face, which I think meant that she was trying to work out why the General had such heavy and old gates, when he could have had automatic gates. I let her have her thoughts without interjecting further.

We walked up the gravel path, this whole estate felt very old, and I wondered what drove his desire for the antiquated, it was clear that the General clearly loved it. We turned a corner and were greeted by pleasant shrubbery that was dimly lit by the garden paths lighting. I could see a navy-blue front door to the house, again it was old, and I thought it was probably made of wood.

We strode forward, something felt more urgent now, and we climbed three stone steps before the door was right in front of us. Just as we were about to knock on the door, flood lights lit up the front of the house and I could make out at least four military drones circling above us. Bright lights glared in our eyes, and I had to partially cover them with my arm.

'You have got thirty seconds to tell me why you are trespassing on my property.' The voice I could hear was the Generals, it was loud, and he sounded pissed off.

'General Eastwick, it's Captain, I mean Major Mitchell. I, I mean we, need to speak to you Sir. We need to speak to you about something really important Sir. It's urgent Sir, it really can't wait.'

There wasn't a sound and the drones kept circling for what seemed like a lifetime, then all of a sudden, the drones lights went out and I was then able to make out a slit of warm light. It was emanating from the buildings front door which had just opened.

I signalled Deno towards me and we entered the house, closing the door behind us. Inside the house was a mix of the modern and the antique, it felt welcoming and efficient. I pondered that the General must have some highly technical equipment installed, considering our welcome.

The General stood in his nightwear, he had long soft pants and a soft top, both in mid blue and over the top he had a soft burgundy robe that tied at the front and on his feet were what looked like soft shoes with rubber soles. I mused at them for a second wondering what their purpose was.

'They're called slippers.' The General said. Obviously, he had seen me looking at his feet. I stood straight upright.

'Sir, with respect. I need someone to share some information with. Deno, I mean Chief Martin and I witnessed something disturbing, just about an hour ago. I need to talk with someone I trust, and well, Chief Martin suggested you.'

'Did she now? Well then Chief Martin, let's see if you were right. Follow me please, we need to talk somewhere safe and where we can't be overheard.'

We made our way through the Generals hallway which was painted duck-egg blue and had four light oak wooden doors. At the end of the hallway there was an almost identical door, however this one looked slightly different to the others in that it appeared to be decorative. General Eastwick pushed the light switch, the front of the plastic switch lifted up and away from its original position, revealing a small panel with a retina and iris scanner. The General positioned his face up to the device and the front of the oak door clicked and moved forward revealing a second metal door behind it, that to my trained eye looked to be blast proof. The General pulled the heavy door open, and turning to Deno and me, he said in a relaxed tone.

'Come on in. No one will be able to hear us speak in here.' Deno and I walked through the door and into what looked like a military intelligence operations centre. I could literally feel my jaw drop open as I took in my new high-tech surroundings. There were holo-screens on every wall, and sleek white consoles were positioned directly underneath each one of them.

But the main feature of the room that caught my attention was a central circular, three hundred and sixty degree holo-console, which had around ten personnel working at it. I began to do a quick head count and had gotten up to twenty-two personnel in the room, when General Eastwick finally interjected.

'There are thirty-five staff assigned here at any one time just in case you're wondering Major.' He looked at me and smiled as if he were reading my mind.

'You are also probably speculating on why this facility is here, hidden within my home, and not located on the base? I nodded again, acknowledging his comment.

'Well, I think it might have something to do with what you are about to tell me, but I would like to hear from you first, any questions you have, we can answer them later.'

We walked through a door into a large office that had blue glass windows and looked out directly across to where the military personnel were working. Deno was last in and shut the door behind her, she was looking tired now, I deeply empathised with her, I was exhausted. I secretly hoped that we could get some sleep soon.

'I really don't know where to start Sir. I had been struggling with the Crucian that was assigned to my squad. I always felt that there was something off with Jevargh but…. Sorry, Sir. This is very difficult for me. I always put my trust in people until they prove to be untrustworthy. But with Jevargh, well–'

'You were right about him, weren't you?' He looked me straight in the eyes.

'Well, yes but unfortunately for us, being right feels

much worse and far darker than I could ever have imagined Sir. What I am about to tell you, well it's pretty bad and I'm sure it's going to sound ridiculous. Thankfully, Chief Martin can back me up on the details if needs be.'

'OK. Major Mitchell, take it from the start, I want every detail.'

I shared the details of the nights events with General Eastwick. I explained in the best way that I could, just what had transpired, and he listened intently. I drew a deep breath and told him about what had happened at Headquarters. He raised an eyebrow as if it surprised him, but that it wasn't totally unexpected.

'Then we got straight in a vehicle and came right here.' He walked around his desk, slowly allowing himself time to think.

'That's a lot to take in Major, but thank you for bringing this to me, can you download the recording to my chip please.' I held my wrist out and he took a copy of the recording from my chip. He watched it through and when it had finished, he turned slowly towards me.

'Major, Chief Martin. What I am about to say next must not be shared with anyone else at this time. You can brief your squad once they have been scanned to make sure you're not shielding any further Crucians. Chief Martin, you need to be scanned before you leave this building.'

'Sir, I can–'

'Listen, Mitchell, Martin. We have known for some time that those damn Crucians have boots on Earth, Odomas and Nemeranth. We have been working with the Nadaal and the Okai, trying to root out their spies for over five decades now, whilst also trying to figure out what it is they are up to. But the damn politicians always want more proof. They fear losing the new tech they just sold their souls for, or the future rights to develop it. Truth be told, all most of them care about is their wealth, their ego's, and their damn prestige.

'It sickens me, it really does, and they don't seem to want to know or care that there are lives at risk. I've got my goddamn fucking balls in a vice here. We need to screen your entire crew and everyone on the Amaranthine. I want you to get yourself up there and await further orders from me.'

'Yes Sir.'

'Major, there's one other thing.' I turned on my heel towards the General.

'Yes Sir?'

'Good work. That video you brought in, well it's unique. We've long had suspicions that they were working with something or someone else, and that's the first time anyone has managed to get anything on video, let alone see one for real. I will get our experts on it straight away and get some of our people over to Headquarters to see if our two visitors are still on site. Sergeant Wilson will take you from here to the scanner.'

We walked out of the door and back into the main room, following closely behind Sergeant Wilson as he took us through the room and towards the scanner. Deno was then led over to where the scanner stood against the wall. It was a tall egg-shaped device, which was flat on the bottom, it had fifty-centimetre slits that rose vertically at intervals of two meters. The device was glossy white and there was a circular black foot plate in the bottom that measured around four meters in diameter.

At the top of the device was a ring of small cylindrical black objects that appeared to look like they rotated somehow on the ring at the top. They were fixed seamlessly to the inside of the egg-shaped scanner. On the outside casing of the scanner and embedded into one of the curved panels, was an interface, this was clearly how the device was operated.

Deno stood and looked up at the ring at the top of the device, studying it intensely. I walked over to where Deno was stood, she was fidgeting with the synth leather bracelet on her wrist.

'You OK. It's been a long night, hasn't it?'

'Yeah, I'm just so tired, tired out.' She looked down at the floor, somewhat despondently.

'It's been an experience, that's for sure. We'll soon be on our way back to our quarters and we can get some well-deserved sleep.' I smiled trying to reassure her, tonight had been surreal for us, and the rest of the crew had probably been asleep now for at least two to three hours. They were completely oblivious to what we had encountered. I would need to brief them on all of it, and soon.

A smart woman in a white smock walked over to the console, she looked across and beckoned Deno over to where she was stood.

'Boots off please, Chief Martin.' She didn't look or give eye contact to either of us. Deno slid off her boots and stood waiting to be advised of the next step.

'Walk into the scanner and stand in the centre. You will see some blue lights, then some red lights and finally there will be a warm orange light as the scanning operation draws to a close. You may also notice a low toned, heavy buzz. Some people can't hear it, whilst others can. Once the orange light goes off, you are done. OK?'

'Yup, lights, buzz, done. Got it.'

Deno stepped into the device and the bright lights within the operations complex were turned off. Then, and almost instantaneously the rooms emergency red lighting came on, which was enough for us to still see each other, just. The ring at the top of the scanner spun and I wouldn't have liked to have guessed how fast it was going.

In a way I was pleased to be seeing it now, as my entire crew of one hundred and fifty would have to endure this once I took command of the ship, at least this way I could provide some reassurance. The lights changed every thirty seconds and ran in exactly the order that the technician had said. At the end, the complex lights came back on and Deno was asked to walk forward until she was clear.

'Your clean, Chief Martin. You are now cleared for active duty onboard the Amaranthine.' Deno picked her boots up and put them on as we were walking towards the exit. I sensed that she couldn't get out of there quick enough.

We left the complex and the Generals home quickly, retracing our path back to the roadside, where we stood waiting for the transport to take us back to base.

'Well, that was certainly not what I expected the night to turn out like, when I left my quarters earlier this evening.' I mused. 'How about you Deno?'

'Not in a million years. I think I need a good night's sleep now, just to begin to process it all. What time do you want me to be at the armorers tomorrow?'

'I think we have earned a sleep in, don't you? How about we meet at 14:30 hours?' Deno smiled. But it was a tired smile, and she responded whilst trying to hold back a yawn.

'Sounds good, I'll meet you there.' The transport arrived and we both got in hurriedly, it was raining now, and it had definitely gotten colder. The journey back passed uneventfully, and Deno dozed on and off throughout. Within fifteen minutes the vehicle had dropped us both off. We said our good-nights and I walked into my quarters.

The accommodation block had its night lighting on, and I walked carefully down the corridor so as to not wake up any of my fellow officers. I reached the door, and I quickly scanned my right eye. The door slid open, and I walked slowly inside. My room smelt good, and the scent of orange blossom filled my nostrils. My bed beckoned me, enticing me into it, like the warm skin of a lover, who had been missed.

I quickly threw off my clothes, allowing them to drop to the floor in a heap. I climbed into my bed, pulling the soft duvet over my body, and fell swiftly and silently into a deep sleep.

3 FINAL PREPARATIONS

I awoke to the gentle sound of the ocean, sounds of the water and the morning tide drawing in and drawing out. It would have been bliss were it not the familiar sound of my alarm waking me for the day. I sat up in bed, and for just a brief moment, had forgotten about last night. I turned and put my feet on the floor and noticed my clothes in a heap.

Then it all came back to me in a rush, and for just a second my mind felt overwhelmed with the magnitude of what had taken place. I stood, pushing the palms of my hands into the crook of my back, stretching it out.

I looked at my clothes again and flash-backed to the figures in the office, Jevargh, the Chancellor, and the mysterious and unknown species that was full of ill intent. Poor Deno, I thought. It must have felt unreal when she pulled me out of that vent, and I told her what had transpired. I wondered to myself how Deno was doing this morning. I ambled sleepily over towards the kitchen area and began to make myself a coffee.

I sat wearily at my white gloss, curved, and streamlined breakfast bar, turning on the holographic entertainment viewing screen, which was positioned on the rear wall of my quarters. I flicked channels until I gave up looking for something entertaining, and then decided that I would watch the news. I wasn't surprised to find that there was nothing about last night's events, why would there be. I was sure it would be classified information.

Then something caught my eye, the French leader of Earths combined religious groups, John Bisset of the 'Light Seekers' was being interviewed live about some ancient ruins that had been found on Pluto. He said that they were going to be examined closely, due to their religious and spiritual significance. He then told the reporter that any finds, particularly those of religious importance were going to be brought back to Earth for further study.

I wondered for a moment why everything had to come back to Earth, and why some believed they had the right to take ancient history and relics from any planet that they landed on in the first place. It seemed bizarre to me that anyone would even contemplate connecting artifacts found on Pluto with Earth. It just didn't make any sense to me, but one thing that I was curious about, was what was it that they had found.

I didn't spend any more time thinking about it. I drank the last dregs of my coffee and placed the mug into the integrated cleaner which was fixed into the wall. Within a few seconds the door of the appliance opened, and the cup was clean and ready to stand next to my coffee machine once more. I walked back over towards my bed and scooped up the clothing on the floor, placing it in the same appliance. They would be clean within a minute or two.

I made my way to the bathroom. I went to the toilet first as the coffee had made its way through my body, along with the remainder of last night's alcohol. Then I walked across the small room to where the shower was, four sprays in total. There was one above me and three at the side. I pushed the chrome button on the wall and jets of warm water covered my body, soaking my body clean.

If only they could wash away yesterday's memories, I thought. If only we hadn't seen Jevargh go into Headquarters. Would that have made the evening easier. Was it better to know, even though we knew extraordinarily little at this time, which felt way worse for me at this point.

I lathered my body and hair with cypress scented soap, letting the warm water run over and off my smooth firm curves. I put my hands flat against the showers walls and pushed the button once more. The water stopped, and within seconds warm air blew over me, drying most of my body within a minute. I picked up a towel and dried the remainder of my body, I brushed my teeth quickly, and finished off my routine by brushing my thick, long hair, tying it back into a tight, neat ponytail.

I looked in the mirror at my fresh, clean appearance. Who would have guessed that this was the woman that had witnessed such savagery only hours ago? Certainly not me, that's for sure.

I decided to walk to the armoury, it was around five minutes or so from my quarters, and I hoped the fresh air would help clear my head. Above me, in the clear blue sky, the bases combat drones were circling in formations. I could tell that the base was on high alert following last night's security breach. Shuttles were also landing and departing, and there was definitely more activity than usual. I wondered what General Eastwick had ordered, following our departure from his home in the early hours of the morning.

I looked at the armoury as I neared it. It was an austere building that was built to withstand a significant attack. It rose into the sky and was at least two hundred feet high with large air force blue armoured panels that were interspersed with narrow, brilliant white and deep red decorative fascia's. At the front of the building by the entrance was a statue of Captain Ian Brown, a brilliant pilot who was officially the first human to interact with an alien species from a different solar system. The footplate on the statue read.

'There was a trio of bright lights. I felt an immense joy, as once and for all we knew that we were not alone in the vastness of this Universe.' He was, of course referring to the first contact event, when the human race first met the Okai back in 2160.

I gazed up at the statue for a moment, taking in his words. Everything had changed for humanity from that point forward, and I tried to imagine what Captain Brown must have thought and felt. In what was a single moment of realization. Everything dramatically changed for Earth, and a new age of spirituality and scientific advancements swept across the continents as humanity began to evolve quickly into the interstellar age.

For a long while after, things were really good on Earth, we traded in rare materials, exchanged technology, culture, food and history with our new friends, the Okai. The negative focus that some humans had on other humans differences dissolved, and we finally came together with the collective realization that we were just one species, of incredible diversity. In time many of the wounds that had existed between different groups of people began to heal. It was then, that we were finally worthy of calling ourselves, the human race.

I noticed two heavily armed guards in full white and blue moulded plate body armour stood at the entrance to the armoury. They were packing the latest E220 rifles which were the most powerful plasma bolt rifles that had ever been created on Earth. The rifles fired up to two hundred bolts per minute, they were both deadly and efficient.

Each rifle could be set to either stun or kill, depending on the situation. Each rifle held a small magazine which held ten micro cartridges which would discharge two-hundred plasma rounds. Ten small magazines could also be encased within a larger field magazine. This meant that at any one time each soldier had up to two thousand plasma rounds available to them, before they would need to change the field magazine on each rifle.

Each magazine was released with a single click and had a simple release mechanism, which was to the left side of the barrel, just in front of the stock on each rifle. Inserting a new magazine was as easy as holding it in your hand, pushing it up, and listening for it to click into place. I approached the entrance to the armoury, studying the two guards closely.

'Halt. ID please.' The guard on the left requested my ID and held out a portable scanner. I held the device up to my eye and the machines light changed from red to green.

'Major Mitchell, please enter and make your way to

the Tactical Supplies Department for armour fitting.' Both guards saluted me in unison as I walked past them. I smiled and said thank you to them both, they were doing their job well, doing what I expected them to do.

What I'd learned over the past forty-eight hours or so, was that I ought to follow my intuition more. I was right about Jevargh. But being right about this, it didn't feel good. I didn't want him to die, I just didn't want him to be a Crucian infiltrator either. I sure as hell didn't want him to betray the alliance between Earth and Kanarth, the home world of the Crucians. But then again, that Crucian Chancellor and that creature that was with her were the real culprits here, and if they represented Kanarth… then this changed everything that we thought we knew about them.

Jevargh may have been a willing pawn, but I bet that even he didn't think they would end him in the way they did. That told me all I needed to know about the depths that these two species would go to. They would kill their own to prosper, or to keep a secret. I knew one thing… that nothing good could ever come from that.

I entered the room where my armour was to be fitted and was greeted by my six. Five of them were busily showing off the parts of their armour that had already been made, whilst Deno sat on a metal bench playing with the rim of her cowgirl hat. She was fidgeting loudly, and I could see that she was still toying with last night's events that appeared very much to be at the forefront of her mind.

Joe caught sight of me and immediately stiffened his posture. He stood to attention and saluted me, following his lead, the rest of the six stood up and saluted me within a few seconds. 'At ease soldiers, how goes the armour fitting?' I smiled as they all looked at me like five-year olds with the latest craze toy. Joe answered, finally relaxing his posture.

'This armour is amazing ma'am. It fits like a glove. See that scanner over there?' I looked to the corner of the room where a device similar to the one Deno had been in last night stood. It was turned off, but perhaps that was why Deno was a bit quieter than her usual self. She had been like this before, and I knew she would work the kinks out in her mind. She probably just needed some bourbon, some good company, and a few laughs.

'Yeah, I see it.' I looked around at my six who were all eyes on me, their excitement was palpable and infectious, and the room definitely had an energy this morning.

'Well ma'am, it scans your whole-body shape and then sends it to that 3D armour printer over there.' I looked across the room where a large rectangular device stood, it took up the whole side of the wall and stood around ten feet in height, it had a panel on the front and was white in colour, it didn't look like an armour printer to me, but if Joe said that was what it was, I was inclined to believe him.

I looked across and saw Tommy was flexing his biceps, the look of amazement on his face was endearing, as he closely eyed the armours fit and durability.

'You approve Tommy?' I spoke. He took his eyes off his arms for just a moment.

'Do I approve?' He laughed, showing off the fit and flexing his biceps to the squad.

'The missus would love this. I'm feeling romantic

already.' He laughed heartily again, and everyone else laughed with him.

'Well, maybe you can show her it later, just so she can see what your ass will look like in space, you understand. Don't go getting any ideas. I wouldn't want you to have to explain to me why it has dents in it.' I raised my eyebrows and winked at Tommy.

He let out a roaring laugh and Fetch and Summer, both nudged him, Fetch then ruffled his short, cropped hair. They were all in good spirits. Suddenly a different and unknown voice came from behind me.

'Major Mitchell… I'm Chief Engineer Watts.' The woman looking at me was around twenty-five and had a bookish appearance, with dark hair that was tied up in a loose bun.

'Hello, I'm–'

'Major Mitchell, I've been briefed.' She smiled and looked briefly over the electronic eye piece she was wearing, before tapping something into her holo-pad.

'I will be fitting you for your armour today, the order came from General Eastwick himself. I fully understand that the crew will need to be scanned before they depart.' At that moment all but Deno looked towards me, but it was Fetch who spoke first.

'Scanned? What the hell are you on about? Major do you know anything about this?'

I inhaled and took a deep breath, looking around at my six. I wasn't going to say anything to them until I briefed them later, but the Chief had let the information slip, she wasn't to know, and I felt she was genuinely trying to be helpful.

'Yes, well. Fetch's outburst aside, I suppose now seems as good a time as any. I will give you the shortened version and Deno can fill you in on the detail later, that is if you feel you want to know more. I'm sorry that you all had to find out this way. I have no way to soften what I am about to say, so I might as well just say it. Jevargh is dead.' They looked at me, their mouths slightly open and their eyes wide, all except for Summer who didn't seem surprised at all.

'Long story short, Deno and I got back to base last night and saw Jevargh enter HQ. We both thought it was odd, so we followed him. I crawled up and into the maintenance bot's transportation shaft and recorded him meeting with a Crucian Chancellor, who is yet to be identified. There was also an unknown species present at the meeting, and when I say unknown, I mean, as in unknown to us, the Okai and the Nadaal, but most definitely known to the Crucians.' I paused and then continued, trying to find the right words.

'Jevargh transferred some currently unknown information about Earth to them, and shortly afterwards they killed him. We made an immediate withdrawal from the site and as we were leaving, we saw two unknown beings enter the building with large cases, no doubt a clean-up crew. Luckily, for us I recorded most of this and the entire conversation with Jevargh, and his two guests on my chip.

We then travelled to General Eastwicks home, which is an intelligence operation centre by the way. We needed someone we could trust, and Deno suggested we shared the information with him. It was a good call. He told us that he had been looking into the activities of the Crucians on Earth for a decade or so, but that Earth had begun looking into the agenda of our so called allies for at least the last five decades. Our evidence was the first time he, or anyone had actually seen the other species accompanying them, so it is incredibly significant.

We still don't know what it is, or what it wants, and we have absolutely no idea what the Crucians intentions are at this time, though we know it can't be good, for any of us or our allies. General Eastwick later insisted Deno was scanned to ensure she wasn't a Crucian spy, or anything else, and to check that she is human. That's what Chief Watts was referring to in relation to you all being scanned.

Obviously, we can't have Crucian boots on the Amaranthine, which is why you all need to be scanned to make sure you're not Crucians, or anything else for that matter. A scanner will be available at the Space Port before we leave. I'm sorry you had to find out this way, I had intended to brief you later today, as I wanted to tell you all myself before we finished.' I smiled, and then glanced at Chief Watts who was looking a little embarrassed.

'However, it is what it is.' I looked down for a moment, gathering my thoughts. Deno stood up and looked at me and the rest of the squad, she looked determined, like she was going to say what came next, no matter what.

'Something big! I mean really big is going down guys. These beings, they don't care about Earth, and they are definitely up to something, and it isn't good, any of it. I need to know what that is, Major. Just point me in the right direction, I'm taking these fuckers down.' Fetch, Summer, Tommy, Joe, and Cat just looked at Deno, their eyes wide. I could tell they wanted to know more, talking it through later would help Deno process it all.

I was glad that she had said how she felt because I felt exactly the same. I felt worried and angry. I felt it was my job to get everyone through it, but how?

We needed to know much more about what they were planning, and to figure out how to stop them. I had so many questions in my head, but not one of them would be answered until we had left Earth. I refocused my mind and turned towards Chief Watts.

'Well Chief, I guess now you know why the General wanted his best armorer with us.'

Chief Watts looked at me surprised and a little shocked.

'Oh, you didn't know. We take off tomorrow morning at ten, see you at the Space Port.'

Chief Watts walked off slowly, obviously taking in what I had just told her. She then came to a complete standstill, turned on her heel and headed towards a large cubicle that was elevated up six metal steps and had a large window in the middle that overlooked the entire room. I could see her giving instructions to two engineers, then slowly walking out of the cubicle, and looking straight at me, she said.

'Right, Major Mitchell, we had better get your armour made. Please ensure you wear only a vest or t-shirt and shorts or pants whilst in the scanner, all other clothing must be removed. There are changing rooms to the left, meet me by the scanner once you are ready.' Her tone was efficient, she was professional, and the top of her field. She struck me as someone, that aside from the qualifications that she needed to do her job, was competent and definitely knew what she was doing.

I walked to the changing area and took off my clothes, all except my pants and a vest. I walked over to the scanner and waited to be told what to do next.

'Step in, it's quite alright. There will be some bright

blue lights that will cross hatch over your body as they measure you. The whole process should only take a minute, then we will assemble your armour for you. We can customise it in several ways. For example, you can choose the colour of your visor. Your default setting is an exceptionally light smoked grey, but you can have any colour you like, it's mainly for when you are out in bright light. The light in space is quite brilliant when it's there, but you don't want too much of it. Is there a colour you would prefer?' I paused for a moment, thinking on my options.

'Hmm, I think I would like a blue, do you know any good blue shades?'

'Oh yes, cerulean blue is just wonderful and looks amazing with the pearl white armour. Of course, it would look even smarter if all your six had the same colour, what do you think?'

I looked across to my six, who were still enthralled with, and still testing the manoeuvrability and various options in their new armour.

'Blue visors guys, what do you think?' I shouted across to them, all six turned to me and gave me the thumbs up. Good, that was one less thing to have to think about.

'Now, there's just a few new features I need to explain, you requested the pearl white armour and the cerulean blue visors, this colour scheme will be uploaded to all crew on the Amaranthine.'

'Won't that cost a lot of money, if it's any cheaper we can just go with what the crew already has.' Chief Watts smiled warmly as she turned towards me.

'These suits are fully customizable and can be set to any colour you want or need. Each piece can be coloured individually, or as a complete outfit to suit any environment you are working in. When I'm on board I will ensure that whatever happens, your armour suit will always be ready for each situation and any environment that you or your squad find yourselves in.' She paused and then carried on. This woman clearly loved her job.

'Your suit is completely airtight, flexible and manoeuvrable, you won't even know you have it on once you are in it. It comes with an emergency supply of oxygen that lasts twelve hours, in normal circumstances, just in case you find yourself detached from your ship, or on a planet that has an unbreathable atmosphere. It also has gravity plates in the boots, which should ensure that you are able to walk around safely in any zero-gravity environment.'

I stepped into the scanner, and it began to read my measurements, fine blue needle thin lights cut right across the surface of my entire body. The lights were circling and intermittently pausing, the machine repeated this action for around a minute and a half. I found it hard to concentrate, my mind drifting. But in between the bursts of bright blue light, I could see my six, who were showing off the various different modifications that they had embedded or attached to their armour, they appeared to be paying particular attention to those that were specific to their chosen specialisms.

Summer transformed her armour to a dark grey that was almost black, her visor turned the same colour and I have to admit she looked every bit the infiltrator that I knew her to be. Fetch was admiring her visor which had a full instrument panel installed, which was clearly visible from the inside of her helmet. She moved her head about and tapped the sensor pad to the right of her jaw, tabbing through the different modes available to her. I just knew that this would come in handy, and as our best pilot, I was certain that we were going to need those ace piloting skills in the months ahead.

Tommy and Cat were admiring the additional lightweight exoskeleton that was embedded into their armour, though to look at it, you would never know that the silver-coloured strips woven in at the front and back of their arm and leg plates gave them an additional twenty-five percent upper body strength and fifteen percent lower body strength, respectively. They were lifting the benches and each other up off the floor, testing their newfound strength out, much to their delight.

Joe was stood upright and was stretching his arms and legs, and generally checking out the manoeuvrability of every joint. Deno, meanwhile was paying close attention to her right thigh, where she had some sort of attachment that was either wrapped around it, or embedded into her thigh armour, it was a holster… for a weapon of some kind.

'You are all done Major.' I felt myself drift quickly back into the present. Chief Watts beckoned me out of the scanner, and I followed her at speed to the changing area.

'Once you are changed, meet me in my office, it's up the stairs and through the observation cubicle. We can discuss personalizing your armour suit and making the appropriate upgrades to your chip.

'My chip is getting an upgrade. Will it wake me up and make me coffee?'

Chief Watts laughed. 'Not quite, I'm afraid. But it will enable you to command your ship to land within a meter of your location anywhere in the known galaxy, or would you prefer coffee?' I laughed at the Chief's humour, despite the initial embarrassment, I could see that we were going to get along just fine.

I changed and made my way up the metal stairs, walking through the cubicle that was lined with computer banks and into the office that was entered via a single gloss white automatic door at the far end of the room. The door slid open, and I walked through into a square room, it was different to the rest of the department in that it was personalised. Pictures of different parts of Earth adorned the walls, some I didn't recognise, but I could make out some were definitely European. They were beautiful, and the thought crossed my mind that I should travel more and see more of the planet I was now helping to defend.

'Italy, if you're wondering?' Chief Watts said calmly.

'It's my mother's country of origin. It's quite beautiful, and the people are deeply passionate about, well just about everything. Have you ever been?' She smiled. It was clear that she loved talking about the place.

'No, I plan to travel someday. It seems I'm bound to travel the stars first, which when I think about it seems a little bizarre. But maybe one day I will make the time, though it might have to wait a while.'

'Well, when you are ready, let me know and I will show you around. I'll find any reason I can to go there, it just feels right, like it fits me.' I nodded and smiled, and then something caught my eye, on the desk was a commendation and a medal which was framed in antique oak, it was the purple heart. Chief Watts immediately saw me focus in on it.

'Oh that, well. I ended up in a scrape two years ago. I was once like you, a warrior, but I decided to train in a different specialism, after the incident. Lost my lower left leg, and arm.' She rolled up her sleeve showing me her arm up to her elbow, which to the untrained eye was almost indistinguishable from the real thing. There was just an exceedingly thin pale line that was two millimetres wide. It was clearly a surgical scar. It circled around her lower arm just below the elbow.

'I'm sorry, I didn't know.'

'Please don't apologise, I was incredibly lucky and fortunate that I could have the surgery. I lost three of my command that day… and well, it never really felt the same after that. I decided that I would use my other talents and take a back seat until I figured out what I wanted to do, and here I am. The Amaranthine's newest addition to her crew and hopefully a damn fine armorer. Please, sit in the chair and we will take a look at your chip.'

I did as she requested, and the Chief pulled her chair up to the sterile white medical chair, that I was sat upon. The chair began to rise up a little, then it moved slowly and began to ease me backwards until I was almost laid entirely flat. Chief Watts took my arm and placed it onto a moulded arm rest that was attached to the chair. She adeptly strapped my arm to the chair, at the wrist, and the elbow. I knew that this was to stop my arm from moving as she needed to open the skin up on my lower arm, to access my chip.

'Major, I'm going to numb your arm now, the incision will be slightly larger than the last one as your chip needs replacing with a newer model, so I'm going to remove it and attach the new one. It should only take a few minutes to complete the procedure.'

She moved her eye piece over her right eye, I could see its digital interface in red and a light purple, though it was too small for me to read from where I was sat. I heard the sound of the local anaesthetic enter my arm, within seconds my arm was completely numb, I couldn't feel a thing.

'OK, now just a little incision.' I watched as the Chief deftly opened my skin up, the cut was three inches in length, an inch longer than the last procedure I'd had. She eased the chip's casing out using a fine instrument and disconnected the plug that sat under the case.

The connections to the chips port had fine hair like strands attached to it that went further into my body. These electro-organic strands eventually connected to my central nervous system, and I was thankful that I wouldn't need to have this procedure again, as it was much more invasive than having my chip upgraded. It would have meant I needed to have a general anaesthetic.

'Would you like to see your new chip before I connect it?' She looked over her eyepiece at me, raising her eyebrows, though I couldn't see her nose or her mouth as she was wearing a blue surgical mask.

'Yeah, it might be nice seeing it, as it's going into my body.' She reached to her left side and within a few seconds in front of my eyes I could see the casing which looked very similar to the one she had removed, but it was definitely larger in size. The casing did have a few minor differences, such as the fine grooves that were etched into the sides with a small hole at each end. The top had several more round and flat nodules, which I assumed were how I accessed the new upgrades. The Chief began to attach the device into my arm, her gloves were now moist on the outside with my blood.

'Let me talk you through the upgrades to your chip. Your camera and recording equipment are vastly improved, the device also has several single dose medications, such as an acute pain relief drug, an adrenalin drug, and a new knock out drug that is very ingenious. When used, to all intents and purposes you will appear deceased. Not sure why they thought that would be handy but, in this galaxy, who knows what could happen. I'm sure you would agree, yes?' She paused.

'Yes, up until twenty-four hours ago I thought things were much simpler than I do right now, so thanks for the info. Anything else?' The Chief paused, before responding to me.

'Yes, just a couple of things. The new device comes with a tracker, so your ship can find you to within a meter, anywhere in the known galaxy. I really wasn't joking Major. Also, this button here.' She pointed to a small red button.

'This will bring the Amaranthine to you, wherever you are. It allows you full control of your ship and will reroute her to you and remove navigational control from the crew. It's quite remarkable really. It is also fully voice activated, so if you can't control the device manually for whatever reason, it will respond to your voice commands and no one else's.

Finally, and I've saved the best for last, it comes with a quantum communications device, basically you can talk to anyone, anywhere in the galaxy, and as long as they have an equivalent device. The Nadaal and the Okai both use quantum communications and they kindly gifted their tech to humanity a decade ago. We have just finished working the kinks out of it, and adapted our technology to accommodate the advancement, and you Major Mitchell, are the first enigma class ship commander to have this particular upgrade of the device installed and fitted. This, by the way, was the express instruction of General Eastwick. There is one thing you might find a little unusual though.' She paused.

'The communication isn't audible at your end. What I mean is, you hear the conversation in your mind and not out aloud, so you might want to let your crew know, just so they don't think you are talking to yourself.' She smiled, clicking the plug into place whilst continuing to embed the device into my arm.

'It wouldn't be the first time I've found talking to myself helpful, but yeah… I will let them know.' A few minutes passed in silence as the Chief neatly closed up my skin and applied rapid bio-fluid to the area. It felt cool and soothing, and I knew that by morning that I too would have a fine white scar, though mine would not be where my lower arm or leg used to be.

I would be sure to make sure that Chief Watts was made welcome on the Amaranthine. She had given enough during her service. The mere fact that she wanted to continue serving, told me everything I needed to know about her, and her continuing commitment to Earth.

There was a slight swooshing noise from behind as the door slid open. A young technician walked in holding a computerised pad in his hand.

'Major, your armour is ready for you to try on, and your squad is awaiting a final inspection before we pack away their armour and send it up to the Amaranthine.' The Chief looked at me and quickly unclipped the restraints on my arm.

'Your good to go Major, I will see you on board the

Amaranthine tomorrow for your first ship's briefing, let me know if there is anything else you need in the meantime.' I slowly got up and out of the surgical chair as it was still moving, not wanting to waste a moment longer on it.

'Will do Chief Watts and thank you for today. I'm sure we are all a lot safer thanks to your expertise.'

I quickly left the office and walked out of the long medical cubicle and down the stairs, I could see my six stood together. They were still admiring their armour which was all manner of different colours. However, it had all now been fully assembled. Each suit was stood upright and was completely open at the front. The wearer merely needed to step back into the armour, and it would then wrap and seal around the wearer at the front, becoming completely airtight on closure.

There was a seventh empty suit at the end of the row, which was still in default mode, it looked like soft brushed steel. That armour, I knew to be my suit, though I hadn't tried it on. I was still excited to see how well it fit, as I knew I would be using it a lot in the coming months.

Joe automatically called the squad to attention as I grew closer towards them.

'At ease.' I paused and then spoke again. 'I don't know if this is a good thing, but I've chosen our ships uniform colours. These colours are to be worn by everyone on the ship or under my command. New uniforms will be issued to those that need them. These will complement the armour suits, and the entire crew will be briefed about this tomorrow at 14:00 hours. Earth insignia and rank will of course remain the same.

I can see you have all had a play with the colour changing mode…, loving the pink Fetch. Chief Watts will work with us to make sure that any adaptations we need can be made as seamlessly as possible, you need your armour fixing, see Chief Watts, you need camouflage or a tweak to you breathing apparatus, see Chief Watts. Now let's try this armour on. Chief Watts would you do the honours and sync the colours of my six and myself to the colours that I chose with you earlier?'

Everyone walked over to their armour and turned to face away from it. Each one of the six and myself stepped back in perfect unison, aligning our feet on to the moulded foot plates in the armour suits. Once we were all ready, I nodded towards the Chief and our armour instantly closed around us. My visor in the helmet shifted colour to the richest shade of cerulean blue. As I glanced across the room, I could see the colour on the armour change on all my squad's suits until they were all pearlescent white. The suits webbing, which was a body suit that lined the armour was dark blue, and the rank and insignia was dark blue also.

Each squad member checked out the rest of the crew, they all looked fantastic, and I was exceptionally proud of them all. I still couldn't quite believe that I had the appropriate rank and permission to decide the colours we would wear, but it was a nice feeling to be able to have some commonality, and I hoped that my new crew, and the established crew of the Amaranthine would welcome the changes I had made.

'Joe, what do you think?' I beckoned Joe towards me.

'I like it Major, its smart and yet it looks modern, like a future soldier. It's a million times better than Khaki, and I really like the white pearlescent finish, and the blue vizor's are great. I really like the last names over the right breast plate too, Mitchell, Tanaka, Martin, Kawolski, Martinez, Neilson and Williams, and the rank on the front of the lower neck just below the helmet. It looks really good Major.' I smiled at Joe and patted him on the shoulder, the rest of my crew continued to pose in their armour, they looked great, and they knew It.

∞

The day had been practical, entertaining, and fun, and I was feeling quite tired as I walked back to my quarters. Everything I had, was kept in the modest military issued accommodation that I currently occupied. I needed to pack it all up, so that it could be shipped and transported to my new quarters on board the Amaranthine. As I neared the door, I could see a large stack of boxes and foot lockers, apparently left for me to use in the corridor.

They stood empty, waiting for me to fill them with all my worldly possessions. Over the past two years I had grown quite fond of my neat open plan room, it had served me well, and I felt a little sad to be leaving it. I comforted myself knowing that a new and different path awaited me.

My new quarters would be on board the Amaranthine. I still had many unanswered questions circulating in my head. I needed to find the answers for these and do what I could to ensure Earth's safety. But before I could get remotely close to achieving this, I would need to take care of the practical tasks, such as packing up all of my stuff.

I spent around three hours putting everything into boxes until only one set of uniform and what I could carry on me remained. I walked towards the fridge freezer, opening it, and placing several large ice cubes into a heavy bottomed glass. I really wanted to enjoy a last night cap in my room before I retired to bed. I filled the glass half full of my favourite Speyside malt whisky.

I had ordered half a case, and with what I had already drank, this left me with four and a half bottles of pure night-time bliss. It was, of course coming with me, as I doubted it would be easy to get hold of, once on board the ship. I lay back on my bed and waited for the ice to cut into the bronze liquid, cool it and dilute it slightly which was my preferred way to drink it.

Suddenly, I began to feel strange, a little lightheaded and almost dreamlike. This had happened before, but it felt much stronger this time. No, please not now. I could feel the heat in my body grow exponentially, and I then began to sweat. But this time it was different, because unlike on previous occasions, the heat didn't subside.

I felt my head, it was red hot, and I was burning up now, it was almost as if I had a high fever, though a few moments ago I was completely fine. I got up off the bed and began to remove my clothes. Pacing about frantically now, I took everything off aside from my bra and pants. No, no, no, what is happening to me?

I began to feel overwhelmed as the heat began to consume me from the inside out. The skin on my forearms slowly began to glow. What the hell was that shimmering underneath my skin? I began to panic, my breath catching in my throat. I can't breathe… What was happening to me? I knew I couldn't ask for help, if anyone saw me like this, they would probably either shoot me or take me to the nearest lab and I knew that from that point onwards, both my career and my life as I knew it would be over.

I ran to the bathroom sink to soak my face in some water, in an attempt to cool myself and I looked at my face in the mirror. What the hell was wrong with my face? Fine orange, yellow and red tracks were snaking their way down my skin. I looked like I was burning up, like I was combusting. Why was this happening to me now? The tracks flowed downwards, resembling fine molten rivers.

Something was very wrong with me. I touched my skin once more and it felt too hot, my skin wasn't meant to be this hot, I thought. My chest began to pound, heavy, deep thumps that appeared to me to be slower than my usual heartbeat. I placed my hand onto my burning chest, and I could feel my heart push against my hand. It felt like it was trying to beat its way out of my chest.

Something is very wrong… Then, it came again. Heat, so damn hot within my core, I felt like a volcano this time, I felt ready to release. I looked down at my arms and the molten rivers and shimmering were now there too.

My whole body was now consumed in these rivers of fire, or some kind of shimmering fusion that I could not explain, and yet in all of this chaos I could still think. I was still me. Several thoughts began to hurtle through my head, which felt as if it were now being crushed by the weight of a thousand suns. What was this? Had I been somehow infected by the Crucians with some kind of new and deadly virus? Was I becoming unwell? Was any of this real? It felt like a living nightmare.

I instinctively reached for the shower, setting it to the coldest setting and standing under it at first, but to my surprise my legs had no strength in them and eventually they just gave way. I sank down slowly, my back against the wet wall, and eventually stopping at the shower floor. Steam poured off my skin and filled the room in a heavy and hot fog, but despite this I did not cool, not one bit. At that moment, for some reason I thought about my mother, and the one thing that I had never fully pursued came into the front of my mind. Why did she tell me never to ask or speak about my family? There must have been a reason, but those answers would have to wait, as either I was going to die, or I was shipping out to my new command in the morning. I was in denial, I was probably going to die, I thought.

It was an immense effort, but I managed to reach up to the dial to turn the shower off, slumping against its walls in a heap. I was soaking wet, but the water appeared to have made little difference to me, and steam continued to rise from my skin. Within seconds my skin was dry again. I didn't understand this, how could I understand something so different, my only comfort was that I had survived. I needed to find out what this was, but how could I even begin to explain it... to anyone.

I eased myself onto my knees and made my way on all fours, slowly towards my bed. I felt ill, all my life essence felt like it had been drawn out from my body, leaving me with barely enough energy to breathe. I needed to gather my thoughts, and so I climbed sluggishly onto my bed, I needed to lay down and think things through. If I were going to die tonight, I needed to make a will or at least get a few things down, I could record something on my chip.

I brought my arm up to my chest, the very effort

sent driving searing heat and pain up and down my entire body. I groaned in pain, but daring not to scream out aloud, I drew a slow and deep inhalation into my empty lungs. I slowly began to speak into my chip.

'Chip, record on. This is Major Stephanie Mitchell. The date is the second of July 2425, and this is my last will and testament. Video on. The chips camera lifted up and out of my arm and I wondered in all honesty how it was still working, but this train of thought only lasted for a very brief moment, as I knew I needed to gather my thoughts and act quickly.

'I'm recording this as I really don't think I will make it through the night. All of my worldly possessions go to my adoptive mother, this includes my death in service provision and any savings I have. However, my personal sidearm and my collection of antique weapons, currently held in a safety deposit locker at the Bank of America, code 983761, oh and my collection of antique music from the twentieth century, I leave to my friend Deno, I mean Chief Reece Martin.

When they tell you what has happened, you are going to have questions about it all. The truth of the matter is that I don't know what is happening to me tonight, and it's not something that I can explain. I'm sorry… I'm just so sorry. I don't know what this is, and I'm sorry that I didn't visit more mom, you always told me that I was special, but I think I was the lucky one, to have you. Maybe… maybe they will work out what is wrong with me, maybe you will get some answers and then find some peace.'

I was exhausted and didn't have any energy left in my body to continue speaking. I was struggling to breathe now, and I felt so damn tired and sleepy. Everything just felt so final, and I began to let go, relaxing my body. I was pleased that my life's earnings were going somewhere that they would be valued, mom could certainly make use of the money and Deno would certainly cherish my weapons and antique music collection. I felt myself struggle to keep my eyes open and finally, I closed my eyes, letting go. What a way to end it all, I thought, as my eyes betrayed me, and everything went dark.

4 LEAVING SOLID GROUND

I slowly opened my eyes, somehow half expecting that I had finally arrived in the afterlife, or in the final moments of my consciousness leaving my unconscious body. I could see shards of sunlight coming in through the window which had been only slightly filtered by the tinted glass, its brightness causing me to sit for a moment until my eyes adapted to the light's intensity. After a few moments, I opened my eyes fully and immediately reached for my skin, it felt warm, normal, and the shimmering, fusion and intense heat had gone.

I sat up, expecting to feel exhausted, but I felt great, energised and like I had just had the best night's sleep ever. I stood up and looked at the pile of clothes on the floor. Walking to them, I bent down and picked them up. They were still damp and heavy with last night's sweat, and the condensation they had absorbed. I then looked around the room looking and checking for any trace of intense heat damage, but other than a lot of condensation, a few tracks of water running down the walls and some droplets that had pooled on the smooth surfaces in my quarters, everything appeared just as it had done before I was consumed by that damned heat. What was wrong with me?

I looked over my shoulder at the clock on the holo-screen and it said five minutes past eight. I had slept around ten hours straight by my reckoning. Both my sense of duty and my conscience started to rise to the surface, and I told myself that I would get a full medical examination once I was on board the ship.

I showered quickly, and dressed in my number one uniform, as it was customary for a commanding officer to greet their new crew in their best uniform. I had to admit it, I looked smart, the lightweight zip shirt, the dark blue trousers, and smart zip up jacket which had gold accents for decoration, the trousers had fine gold piping down each side of the outer leg, I looked every bit the part and I was honoured to wear this uniform, it meant everything to me.

The insignia that identified my rank had been changed for me by the bases supplies personnel, and my insignia was now a single golden leaf, which indicated the rank of Major. The leaf was on both of my lapels that ran over the top of my shoulders. I pulled my best boots on, they gleamed, and I could almost see my face in the highly polish sheen of the black synth-leather. I adjusted my jacket, it fit flush against my trousers. I combed my hair until it was neat and tight against my scalp. I clipped it into place and twisted my pony tail up and into a tidy bun, which I fastened to the back of my head with several clips.

Today, I looked my rank. This was a special day for me, and one that I couldn't have imagined making, even just twelve hours ago. That feeling last night, when I felt my own body take all of the control away from me, well it was terrifying, and one that I never wanted to experience ever again. I thought I could deal with anything, but this, this was a whole other level of fucked up. Looking at my composed reflection in the mirror, I moved my head around looking at my face, looking for cracks in my composure and playing with the skin under my fingers, checking that it was still my skin that I could feel.

From what I could tell, I appeared, at least on the surface to be myself. But I had a nagging, twisting and sickening feeling in my gut that last night's events were far from over. There was definitely something wrong with my body. This, this fusion and the shimmering, other people's bodies don't do that, I thought. Inside my mind, I was becoming more and more concerned about what was happening to me. I felt like a freak, I felt ashamed and weak that I dare not tell anyone for fear that it would end my career, or my life as I knew it. Why was it getting worse?

I took one last look in the mirror and looked deeply into my own eyes expecting to see something… But I didn't see the burning, melding, and shimmering humanoid shape that I had become last night. I only saw myself. What did I expect to see?

I took one last and long look into my room, turned, and then touched the outer door control panel on my now vacant living quarters door. I walked down the corridor where a young sergeant was waiting for me in the foyer. He stood to attention and asked for my electronic room key, which I handed over to him without giving it a second thought.

He respectfully and succinctly explained to me that my gear would be taken to my new quarters and safely stored there, for me to unpack once I arrived onboard the ship. I acknowledged the information he gave me, and I thanked him. He then waved half a dozen men and women into the building whom, I assumed were quickly making their way down towards my quarters to collect my packed up belongings. I saluted him, turning on my heel and leaving the buildings foyer for the last time, stepping out of the shade and coolness of the air-cooled building and into the unescapable light and warmth of the sun.

Outside, and adjacent to the accommodation blocks main entrance was a large military supplies vehicle, which was parked up. Once loaded, it would make its way from the base directly to the spaceport. The entire contents of my quarters would then be efficiently transported on a cargo shuttle up to the Amaranthine for me to unpack once I arrived onboard the ship.

I continued on my way towards the parade square, where only two nights ago Deno and I had uncovered Jevargh's dark betrayal of Earth, before he himself had been betrayed by his own species, and whatever the other unknown being was. The irony of his situation was not wasted on me. I stood mulling it all over, and I began to contemplate what else he had told them of our world, as I continued waiting patiently at the designated pickup point.

This was where I would begin the next phase of my career, but I found that for some reason I was still thinking about Jevargh and that terrible nights events. After a few minutes, a single military vehicle began its approach towards me. It was to take me to the spaceport, its presence relieving me only temporarily from this particular train of thought.

Seeing it slow silently as it approached me felt very much like a significant part of my life was drawing to a close. But truth be told, as the vehicle drew closer to me, I was still struggling to push the darkened undertones of the last few days from my mind.

The vehicle was navy blue in colour and quite large, seating up to fifty troops. It's smooth and curved surfaces made it more aerodynamic than most military transportation. Vehicles like this were known to travel at speeds of up to two-hundred miles per hour. Most were now fully automated, but still able to be driven manually. This feature hadn't been available in newly manufactured civilian vehicles, all private vehicles had all been installed with autopilot systems since the year 2050.

The vehicle gradually slowed to a complete stop, its large, heavy door sliding open without a sound. I stepped inside and was immediately greeted by Fetch, Summer, Cat and Deno who were looking down the vehicle and towards its entrance. The group instantly beckoned me towards them, and I walked carefully up the vehicle's central aisle using the headrests of the empty seats for balance.

'Good morning, how you all feeling? Todays the day huh? Where are the guys by the way?' Fetch spoke first as she quite often did. The thing with Fetch was that you never knew what would come out of her mouth. But this time, and before she could get a single word out, my mind flipped me back to the events of last night, and for just a millisecond I was back in my room consumed by intense heat, thinking that I was going to die. I really needed to talk to someone about this, and soon.

'The guys got an earlier transport, so we had coffee and spent a little time catching up ma'am. All of our stuff was picked up earlier this morning. We can't wait to see what she's like.' Fetch beamed with enthusiasm. Her energy was evident today, like a wild rushing force of water pushing speedily into a vast ravine, it felt powerful, magnetic, and highly contagious.

'Well, let's hope there is coffee on the ship, I hear she's a beauty, and one not to be messed with. From what I've been told, she has a ton of firepower.' Whilst our journey continued, we talked and speculated for a while about what we thought the ship might be like, all except for Deno that is, who was a little quieter than her usual self.

The journey to the space port took around twenty minutes, and as we approached, we could see the massive, developed site which had a twenty square mile footprint. It had everything from its own cargo port to shopping, hotels, and nightlife.

The actual space port itself, which was colossal, was a site to be seen. There were two titan class cruisers in dock, each one was enormous, and could support crews of five hundred and four hundred and fifty souls, respectively. There were hundreds of different coloured cargo and transport shuttles that were ferrying passengers and supplies to and from their ships to those that were docked on Earth and those docked in space at other ports.

Our transport pulled up to departure point twenty-four. Stepping out of the vehicle felt very like the final act of a play. I knew this would be the last time for a while that my feet would touch solid ground. We hurriedly walked together up towards the departure aisles, where two marines were standing resolutely in full combat armour. They saluted me, and we continued onwards, walking through a large archway, which I recognised as the initial chip scanner. Once cleared and through the archway we continued through a security checkpoint and into a large shuttle hanger.

I could see a scanning device which was identical to the one Deno had been in, except this one was black in colour. I sat on one of the many metal benches whilst my crew were scanned. I breathed a small sigh of relief when Fetch who was the last one, came through all clear. I stood up and walked over to the device, stepping into it felt strange but it had to be done. I had to show the crew that I would not expect them to do anything that I wasn't prepared to do myself.

The lights were much brighter than I had imagined, and I closed my eyes as the scan continued, flexing my fingers, and rocking on the balls of my feet. I couldn't wait for it to be over, I felt like an imposter, surely it would pick up that I was different to the rest of my squad. But it didn't, it just whirred and completed the scanning process, leaving me feeling confused about myself and what I thought I knew.

I stepped out of the scanner and was given the all clear by an engineer who was operating the machine. Walking over to the middle of the room I called my six over to me. They stood in front of me, eagerly waiting for me to speak.

'Final check everyone. Has everyone got everything they need? It might be a while before we get any shore leave.' Everyone nodded and said yes, they looked excited. It was somewhat comforting to me that the six people I trusted the most in the entire world, other than my mother, were with me.

'Right, we are on shuttle B-twenty-four which is over there towards the front of the hanger. Let's get on board, today is going to be a long day.' I nodded to them all, acknowledging that it was time to move. We walked in unison across the smooth grey causeway towards our waiting shuttle.

There were two shuttles readying to leave which were docked at the front of the hanger, they were an impressive sight. The craft were white with blue accents on the side, nose, and wing tips. The wings of the craft were small, and had they belonged to a bird they would have proved to be dysfunctional much like those of a Dodo, or Penguin, there for effect but not for purpose.

The shuttles only flew because they were powered by six immensely powerful cold fusion engines and their associated thrusters that ran along the entire length of the underside of the ship. The shuttles sleek and aerodynamic shape was a signature mark of its modern design and advancements in human engineering. There were two boosters to the rear of the shuttle and four small boosters that were situated underneath each corner of the craft, these were for added stability when landing. The windows of the shuttle gleamed against the suns light and were dark blue in colour.

We reached the boarding ramp, climbing the slight incline quickly as we were all keen to board. I made sure that I entered the craft last, engaging in some banter and pleasantries with a few members of my new crew who had been ordered to pick us up. It wasn't every day that a crew welcomed a new commanding officer to their ship. I was keen to ensure that the crew knew that I had arrived on board the ship. It certainly wouldn't go amiss if word got around that I was easy to talk to, and not a military stuffed shirt, with little personality.

The seating on the shuttle was simple and ran half the length of the vehicle, we sat with our backs to the shuttle walls, and the lightly padded and neatly moulded seats would hold us snuggly in place for the entire journey. I pulled the harness over my shoulders, across my chest and downwards towards the top of my hip bone, pushing it into a secure fixing that was situated to the left of my hip.

To the front of the arm rest there was a small black control panel with illuminated blue symbols on it that displayed the seats several different comfort and safety functions. Each seat had its own panel, one of the symbols had a blue diagonal line across the shape of a torso, this symbol had to be pushed to secure the shuttle seats harness into place. The harness pulled snuggly against my chest as I touched it, soon afterwards the flights on-board narrative began, and we were all told that expected journey time to the Amaranthine was around twenty minutes.

The crew were now unusually quiet for them, and I could see that they were all trying to gather their thoughts. I wondered if they were thinking about the loved ones that they were leaving behind on Earth, or perhaps they were having thoughts about what the journey ahead would hold.

I was thinking intensely now, about how I was going to command my ship. My ship, our ship. It certainly was both a daunting and exciting prospect. It was an adventure that I was very much looking forwards to. I knew deep down that I wouldn't be truly tested in leadership until I had led a large crew.

Majors usually led thousands of people, at least this was the case back in the old days, but I had a very specific set of skills. I had led just fifty specialists as

Captain, all of whom, had they not been serving with me, could have led at least fifty people on their own.

The on-board flight narrative ended, and I glanced around at my six. Fetch was pulling at the harness and trying to make it loosen off, the harness was clearly winning, but the look on her face had me trying to hold a smile back from my lips. Why was she always so incredibly stubborn?

Deno was fiddling with the rings on her fingers, this meant that she was a little anxious. She kept looking out through the windows as if she were trying to catch the last glimpse of solid ground. Tommy had pulled his cap over his eyes, and from what I could tell he was either sleeping or was about to. I wondered if he and his wife had been up talking all night?

Cat was sat reading an article on the culture of the Nadaal, Cat always liked to be well read, and I guess for her, she probably saw this as research for the mission. She sat silently with a studious look upon her face, deep in concentration.

Summer was also reading, but her reading material was much lighter. Japanese cuisine in the twentieth century, and, as her always incredibly willing guinea pigs, I hoped that we might all get to taste some of that food at some point in the near future. Joe sat silently with his eyes closed, his posture was relaxed, but aligned, and I knew this to mean that he was probably meditating. I didn't wish to disturb him, and I wondered just how clear his mind was right now. I envied him that, as my mind was anything but clear.

The shuttle gently lifted off the launch pad and glided slowly and smoothly out of the hanger. It was completely silent, and it felt like we were floating on air, there was no noise but our own and no turbulence whatsoever. We glided out and along the shuttle runway for about a half mile, and then without any change in motion the vehicle began to ascend in complete silence. Buildings became smaller, the rivers began to look like arteries, and the sky turned to the most glorious pure blue. The stratosphere was so bright even through the dark blue of the windows that it lit the inside of the craft. I could see the gentle curvature of the Earths horizon become more and more apparent, and then there was a change, and for the first time in several months I felt myself leave the Earth's atmosphere.

Leaving Earth always felt such a wrench, like having to move out of a beloved apartment, because it isn't big enough anymore. I always felt a little saddened to leave home, it wasn't perfect, far from it, but it was all we had, and it needed protecting.

From the window opposite I could see two space ports in the distance. Each had their own assembly docks, where most of Earths Titan, and Enigma class space cruisers were serviced and stationed when in dock. The most noteworthy ports were Atlanta 2, and Britannia 3. They were gigantic in size, and each one held the equivalent personnel of a large city, being home to more than one million residents from Earth, Kanarth, and Odomas which were the home worlds of the Okai, and the Nadaal. The Crucians had a small diplomatic contingency on both stations but had shown no real interest in developing a residential area to speak of. I now understood why.

The edge of the Milky Way cut through the darkness of space, and I marvelled at the sheer size and scope of it. Most of it still calling out to us, waiting for us to explore it. All that life and all those souls, still unknown to us for now. I longed for the day that we might traverse those distant stars and discover new systems of habitable, or inhabited worlds. It had always been awe-inspiring to me, and I thought once again, about what it must have been like for the people of Earth, the day that they were told that they were not alone.

The shuttle continued onwards in silence, and I noticed a slight change in its trajectory. We had changed our original course away from Earth's atmosphere and were now bound for the Amaranthine. I tried to look out of the window without drawing too much attention to the fact that I felt really excited, like I felt on Christmas Eve as a child, before I got to open my presents. I could see numerous space vehicles moving to and from in the windows that were directly in front of me, but I could not yet see my ship. The anticipation was almost unbearable, and I stretched my torso in an attempt to try and see a little more.

Then, all at once, there she was… I was overcome by the sheer size of her. Her sleek hull was colossal in size, her strong and powerful design, was only matched by her aerodynamic and toughened hull. Row upon row of decks with large windows and viewing areas could be seen. At the front of the ship was the bridge, which could be identified by a seamless window that ran around the front of the ship in a semi-circular curve, this reminded me somewhat, of a smooth and curved arrowhead. Each of the windows were coloured an iridescent reddish purple, they were quite striking to look at. This was a special coating on the windows, that could only be seen from the outside of the ship, it's function was to minimise the light that entered the ship from the sun, or any other star for that matter.

The ship had a 'V' wing fighter craft attached to its underside that was a massive craft, in itself. It was almost one sixth the size of the cruiser. At the rear of the Amaranthine, were four decks of fighter craft. I realised that this ship, for all her aesthetic beauty, was in fact an incredible feat of human engineering. She really was a bad ass assault and defence craft. I couldn't quite believe that she was now under my sole command.

'You gonna close your mouth ma'am before we dock?' Deno smirked at me. I closed my mouth and looked out of the window once more.

'Well, Deno. She is a sight to behold. I can't quite believe it, this is like, well this is like something that only ever happens to other people.' Deno glanced at the ship and was studying the 'V' wing underneath the main hull.

'Tell you what, I would really like to take a look inside that 'V' wing. I don't think I've ever seen one quite as big as that one. I bet she looks awesome when she's in flight.'

'Agreed.' I said, looking across at Fetch, trying to gauge if she had seen it too.

'How bout we take a good look at her in a few days, and take her out for a spin? Though, we will need to bring Fetch along too, you know she will never forgive us if we don't.' Deno's face lit up and she nodded towards me, I could see that she approved.

Over the next few minutes, the ship grew larger and larger as we made our approach. On closer inspection, the vessel was covered in smooth hexagonal white plating, each plate was approximately five meters in diameter and was exquisitely edged with a silver chrome like fine strip which made me think that no expense had been spared on this vessel. There was no denying that she was magnificent, and I wanted to be worthy of the trust that had been put in my command. I hoped that General Eastwick would be proven right over time, in that he had put his trust in me. I would not let him down.

The shuttle made a sharp but seamless turn, and we were now moving much slower, ultimately heading into the rear of the ship and towards one of the four flight decks. We passed through the atmospheric shield that separated the vacuum of space from the oxygenated area at the rear of the ship, and I could just make out some crew members that were busy doing their jobs. Some were loading vehicles whilst others were carrying out maintenance. I could see a larger group of people waiting by one of the docking areas and I wondered if they were our welcoming party.

The shuttle slowed even further and then set down, light filled the crafts seated area and our seat harnesses released. Some of my six stood up stretching, whilst Joe and Fetch sat in their seats waiting for the shuttle door to open. I moved the harness off and over my shoulders and lent forward.

'Well, here we are guys, shall we get the formalities out of the way?' I stood up and stretched out my back walking towards the door as I did so. I felt a sharp pinch of apprehension and then pushed through it. Taking a deep breath, I opened the door and stepped out of the craft. I reckoned there must have been fifty people waiting to meet us, and everyone on the platform that I could see, paused from their work for a moment to see if they could catch a glimpse of their new commanding officer. A tall, well-dressed man stepped forward, and I could see that he held the rank of Captain.

'Major Mitchell. I'm Captain Dawson and I'm your new Chief of Tactical Warfare on this ship. I wanted to welcome you personally, to what is Earths best all-round battle cruiser, the Amaranthine. I nodded to Captain Dawson and tried to gauge him. He had an air about him, and I wondered if his family history had generation upon generation of military expertise.

'Thank you, Captain Dawson. She certainly is a sight to behold, tell me, how long have you served on-board her?'

'The Amaranthine has been in commission for just three years ma'am, and I have had the pleasure of her company since she cast away from Britannia 3 back in July 2422.' He smiled, I could tell he had a genuine fondness for this vessel, and I could understand why. I was overcome by the sheer size of her, I hadn't dared imagine how magnificent this vessel would be. I wanted to see every part, and I would make sure to give my six time to explore later. I knew it would be on their minds, as it was definitely on mine. Captain Dawson walked with me through the docking area and onto deck eighteen of the ship.

'How many decks does she have Captain Dawson?'

'The Amaranthine has twenty decks, not including the command deck, so I guess in total twenty-one decks. At the rear of the ship there are four flight decks that accommodate two hundred fighter craft, as well as auxiliary craft and the ships shuttles.' I was extremely impressed with what he had just told me.

'Twenty-one decks… two hundred fighters and the 'V' wing, that's one hell of a ship Dawson, how are the decks split. So how many crew decks etc.?' I couldn't wait to hear his reply.

'So, deck one is command, it includes the tactical bridge, all comms and warfare control. Decks two to ten are quarters, our accommodation is the absolute best that Earths fleet has to offer. Decks eleven to fourteen are our leisure decks, everything from cinematic entertainment, to pools, gyms, saunas, and bars.

I promise you Major, when you want to kick back this ship has everything you and your crew needs to relax. Decks fifteen to twenty are combat research, science and agriculture, engineering, and maintenance decks. Deck twenty one also has the 'V' wing controls, docking mechanisms and is where all training exercises take place, so all in all the Amaranthine excels, at just about everything. I know I must sound like a kid with his favourite toy, but this ship, well I'm very fond of her Major.' I acknowledged that I had heard him, with a reassuring nod.

'Thank you for sharing your thoughts with me, I would value your counsel, once I have had a good look around. I'm the new one here and I appreciate your openness Captain. I look forward to us working together over the coming months, to do whatever we need to, to protect our planet.'

Captain Dawson looked towards me, he had genuine concern written all over his face.

'Is there something I should know Major?' He furrowed his brow.

'Yes. I will be briefing you and the entire crew at 14:00 hours today. We do have a mission Captain, but I promise you, it is an endeavour entirely worthy of this ship and her crew.'

Captain Dawson thanked me for my honesty, and we continued down the corridor towards the ships lift.

'Allow me to show you your quarters, Major.' We stepped into the lift and within seconds we were on deck two. Captain Dawson escorted me down the long immaculate corridors. We must have walked at least three hundred meters when finally, we stood in front of a dark blue double door which had a gold door plate on the wall to the left of it. In black writing, it stated my full name and rank.

'Your quarters Major. You might want some time to settle in and have a look around your room. You probably wish to familiarise yourself with some of the ship. I will see you on the bridge at 14:00 hours sharp.' He turned and walked away, back towards the lift.

I spun around on the ball of my foot and faced the door to my new quarters. I studied it a little before walking in, even the door was impressive. On entering, I was immediately taken aback by the sheer size of my new quarters. To the right of me was a shower room, I peered around the corner of the doorway and was astounded to see that my quarters also had a jacuzzi bath. I don't think I'd seen a jacuzzi bath in around five years, and this wasn't just any bath, this one could host at least four people. Who would I even want in my bath?

Baths were considered an absolute luxury, and very few households on Earth had them due to excessive water use and the high taxes on them across the planet. I walked further into my quarters, I touched the luxury seating, enough for a dozen people, my feet sank into the thick carpeting, and I noticed the latest digital entertainment system was also installed.

I walked through a second doorway to the bottom right of my quarters and into the bedroom. I stood and looked at the bed, it was three times the size of the one

I had back on Earth. It was surrounded by fitted wardrobe units and sleek cabinets. I sat down on the large and comfortable bed and rubbed my face with my hands, hoping that it would all sink in. But when I opened my eyes, I still had just one short word running through my mind. Wow!

I spent the next few hours exploring just five of the decks, Captain Dawson was right, she certainly was a special ship, everything had been considered to make the Amaranthine a home away from home, she was equipped with the latest technology, that would help protect her and her crew.

I looked out of one of the massive viewing windows on deck eleven and could see Earth. Her blue oceans and green lush lands, jagged snow-capped mountains that cut across continents, the arid sands that edged the great seas, carpeting patchwork like across much of the great continent of Africa. All those colours, so bright and vivid to my simple human eyes.

I felt unworthy, humbled, and grateful that this planet was my home. A rare jewel in the Galaxy, and a place of many contrasts, a place of wealth, love, human culture, art, poverty, and cruelty. A place of openness, truth, and compassion, misinformation, lies and deceit. Earth was perfect. We were not.

I pondered on these contrasts for a moment, thinking about it. It had been written many times throughout our history, and in the blood and tears of our ancestors, that we humans would always fight, if the cause were just, whatever the odds, for the underdog.

My eyes caught sight of the stars of the cosmos and my reflection, together in the glass. I glanced down at my chip as it lit up. The blue holographic displayed inches above it showed me that it was 13:45 hours, and that I was expected on the bridge.

∞

I entered through some double opaque automatic doors and into a large area of glossy consoles and command chairs that were all fixed seamlessly to the floor. There in front of me was the largest curved viewing window on the ship. It was positioned to the front of the bridge, making the space feel cavernous, and like it was open to all of the space of the galaxy outside it.

The bridge had a complement of thirty people, navigators, communication experts, technical experts, and weapons experts. At the front of the bridge, was an open area with high gloss flooring, and I knew that this was a good place to brief the crew. I walked about three paces before Captain Dawson called the bridge crew to attention.

'Major on the Bridge.' He bellowed. Everyone stood, turned, and saluted me as I made my way to the front of the bridge.

I was feeling extremely focused and ready to give my briefing to the crew. I could see the bridge crew studying me as I walked past them, but I tried not to let my thoughts wander across towards them too much. I noticed a different sound as I heard my feet begin to stride across the high gloss floors. I took one last glance at Earth which could be seen clearly behind me, through the window. As I turned, I noticed that the holo-screens were showing different parts of the ship, each screen was filled with crew, and I was absolutely sure that everyone on board the ship was watching me on the holo-screens. Great. No pressure then, I thought. I smiled and looked at the screens, whilst also acknowledging those crew that were with me on the bridge.

'Good afternoon. I wanted to start by saying that you might find this briefing a little different from anything you have experienced previously. Firstly, I want to introduce myself to you, and I've thought a lot about how I would do this. Well, to start with my name is Stephanie Mitchell, though I prefer Steph. Because of the rank I hold, I will probably be known to most of you as Major Mitchell.

Before I speak with you about our mission, I wanted to share with you what my hopes are for you all, and this magnificent ship, the Amaranthine. Secondly, I want you to know, that I am quite aware that I'm the new one here, and because of this I wanted to tell you a little bit about who I am, rather than you just seeing me as my rank.

But if you are interested, and if you want to know anything about me after this briefing, feel free to ask my six.' I looked towards them, they smiled and stood looking proud.

'My six know my skills, and they know how I like to treat my crew. They know what I believe in, what I like to drink and eat, and what lengths I would go to in order to get the job done and protect my home world.' I paused and pointed towards Earth whilst still looking at the faces of the people on the bridge and on the screens.

'We have a task, and it's one like no other. I'm going to brief you all about our assigned mission. Then I'm going to tell you why every life form on this ship will be scanned following this briefing. No one will be allowed to remain serving on the Amaranthine, until they have been checked and cleared for duty.' I looked at the holo-screens and across the bridge, it appeared that I had their attention, and also their surprise.

'Just over forty-eight hours ago Chief Martin and I encountered an alien species that has yet to be identified. The unidentified alien was in the company of a high ranking Crucian Chancellor. On the night in question a second Crucian, who shall not be named, was murdered in cold blood by his own species, in what we think was a bid to cover up a covert mission.

We now believe that their objective was to infiltrate and obtain sensitive and critical data from Earth. The content of the information taken is yet to be ascertained, as is the sensitivity and importance of it in relation to our planet. However, it is acknowledged that the data must have been significant enough for them to plan and make a concerted effort to retrieve it. Someone high up in Crucian Command gave the order to then kill their own agent, and call in a clean-up crew, thus closing the evidential loop, leaving no loose ends.

The reason you must all be scanned is to ensure that all crew on this ship are human and loyal to Earth. I take no pleasure in telling you this and certainly no pleasure in you having to be scanned. I know that this is a highly unusual situation. I'm sure you will understand that I need to know that in the coming months, everyone on board this ship is with me, standing up for Earth.

We do not know yet what we will discover, we do not know who the unidentified species are, or what their true intentions are. What we do know is that they have taken something from us, and that it is of great importance to Earth. We do not know how, or for what purposes they intend to use this data, but from what we observed they are definitely up to no good.

We must assume therefore, that their intentions are hostile because their actions were aggressive towards one of their own, they also went to great lengths to conceal all the evidence. They stole sensitive and yet to be identified information from Earth. This was a deep cover operation by the Crucian species and the unknown species, known from this point forward as species X. Their mission was most probably authorised at the highest level of their combined governments.'

I heard some gasps from some of the crew and this appeared to be echoing around the holo-screens. I felt myself strengthen and straighten my stance.

'Our mission is to find out what information was taken from Earth, and for what purposes. But I need to be honest and transparent with you all. Right now, a mere thirty thousand miles away, and in Earth space is a well-armed Crucian warship, which is docked as part of its mission to improve diplomatic relations. I ask you all. Who sends their most advanced warship on a diplomatic mission?

I'll tell you who, a species that must not be trusted, a species that kills its own, and a species that lies whilst stealing critical information about your planet, our home.' I pointed out of the window.

Look at her, she's beautiful isn't she. We are so fortunate to call her our home world. Your families, loved ones and your friends are down there right now, they are oblivious to this threat, they are relying on all of you to keep them safe.' I turned and walked towards my six.

'Today, when I left Earth, I had a close squad of six. As I stand before you on your bridge today, as your new Commanding Officer, I look to those screens, and I see a crew of thousands. The Amaranthine and her crew will get the job done, we will succeed in our mission. We will do, whatever it takes to protect our home. I ask you, as your leader, join me in this mission. Use your skills and knowledge to help me protect our home.

However, if any of you aren't sure you can do this, and if any of you want to leave this ship, you can do so right now, with no impact on your career or your rank. I want you to know, that I only want you on this ship if you are with me, with Earth. Whatever your rank and specialism, I want you to know that you are all vital to the success of this mission.

Over the coming days, I will be getting to know the ship better and I hope that I can meet you all. I will be eating with you, and I will be drinking with you, and I expect the same from all senior officers on this ship. From this point forward, the officers mess will close and re-open as a new ship's mess. I hear that a large number of you wanted a Caribbean restaurant. On this ship, we work as a team, we are one unit, each with a job to do and I do not want pomp to get in the way of that.' I looked towards Captain Dawson. He smiled, and I knew this decision had been met with his approval.

'I'm going to hand you over to Captain Dawson, who will now provide you with details about how to report in for your scans. Thank you, and I look forward to getting to know you all much better over the coming months.'

I stepped to the side, turned, and walked towards my six. Captain Dawson stood on the bridge and began issuing the itinerary and timescales to the rest of the crew.

The ship returned to its usual activities quickly, and

I stood discussing the ships capabilities with my six. Fetch was extremely animated about the navigation features and the weapons systems, she asked if she could take the 'V' wing out, as expected. I said she could be on board the next time it flew. You would have thought I'd doubled her pay, but I definitely was not going to let her fly the 'V' wing, without the proper training, then Deno suddenly chirped up, midway through Fetch's excited outburst.

'Got a new gun!' She smirked and looked to see who was listening. We all stood and turned our heads in unison towards Deno who looked to be chewing on a small stick.

'Firstly. Where did you get a stick from on this ship?' I paused.

'And why the hell are you chewing it… and what's this about a new gun?' Deno stood up and pulled up the holo-screen on her chip.

'Looksies, this is the Zeta Carbine KV-1N 500 Magma Infusion Cannon.' Her eyes were transfixed on the image, the look she had reminded me of how a young child looks when it gets its first puppy or kitten. Yep, Deno sure loved her guns.

'It fires six rounds of six bursts, a bit like the old wild west Colt forty-five. Only thing is, this packs more of a wallop, downside is, I need to transport the cartridges around with me. But the mega upside is, this little beauty will put a hole in just about anything.' I suddenly found myself smiling, wanting to laugh and remark on its size.

'It's a little small Deno. Are you sure that gun is what you want, we have the latest automatic plasma rifles and long-range laser cannons, perhaps you would like one of those?'

'Oh, you know what I think Major? Size isn't everything, and besides this little beauty will sit just fine in my new hip holster. It's arriving today and I'm gonna be taking him for a spin down at the range, if you wanna join me later?'

'Him?' I looked at her puzzled.

'Yes, him. Meet Kevin.'

'Kevin? You named your new gun, Kevin.' I tried to close my mouth, but it wouldn't shut.

'Yup.' Deno beamed.

'OK…' I turned to face Joe, who just raised his eyebrows at me. Fetch actually stopped talking, whilst Summer glanced out of the window looking very awkward indeed. Cat and Tommy just glanced at each other, but other than that they were all completely speechless.

'I don't think I've ever seen you so enthusiastic about a new gun. I look forward to seeing it… him in action. That didn't sound right at all.' I coughed, shook my head, and looked down at my boots whilst trying to suppress a smile, before raising my eyes to Deno once more.

'Run it through safety checks and store him, it in your locker. I will catch up with you later about testing him… it out at the range.'

An interruption came, thankfully in time to stop me considering sending Deno to the ships doctor for a check-up. It was the senior comms officer Lieutenant Thirkhill.

'Major, we have two incoming Omega class ships. The Jadaal 1, and the Setune 3, they are currently docking to port. Both the Nadaal's Ambassador to Earth and the Okai's Ambassador to Earth are accompanied, each by a small crew. Your orders

Major?' I turned to Lieutenant Thirkhill.

'Let's welcome them on board. But tell me Lieutenant, is it usual for this to happen?'

'Not at all Major, it's the first time since the ship took on its duties that we have welcomed dignitaries from other worlds, your orders?'

'I want a full complement of security staff lining the corridors to welcome them. Ask hospitality to put on some refreshments that are appropriate to their cultural and dietary needs. If this is a first, let's enjoy it and do it right.' Lieutenant Thirkhill nodded.

'Yes ma'am.' I beckoned my six to accompany me, and we made our way quickly to the docking bay to greet the incoming dignitaries.

'Thoughts?' I said, asking my six for their views. Joe spoke up.

'Well Major, they must be here for a reason, but what that reason is?'

'Agreed.' I said, then Summer spoke.

'I think we should welcome them openly but keep an eye on them all the same, at least until we know why they are here.'

'I agree. Summer, can you check any incoming or outgoing communications from both ships.'

'Of course, Major.' Summer left my six and headed off towards security.

'I want you ready in case this goes south. The Nadaal and the Okai are our allies, but with the strange things that have been happening lately we just need to be cautious. OK?'

'Yes Major.' I noticed a slight change in how my crew were now walking. They were now striding forwards at pace, like they were preparing for action. The long corridor opened up to a space that was square in shape and around forty meters in diameter. Four corridors branched off the open room, two led directly to the ships docking airlocks, and two led back towards the ships central corridors. It was obvious that this particular area was an arrivals and departure lounge. There were two console desks and a number of comfortable seats. We stood in silence, patiently awaiting our first guests.

The first door to open was the one immediately to our left. Six Nadaal walked through the door and into the room. Their skin colour was the first thing that struck me. They were golden in colour, ranging from a dark mustard to an almost bright and sunny yellow.

They struck me as regal in the way they carried themselves. I remembered that they could all receive communications at the same time, directly from their queen. They also had the ability to turn this off to allow privacy if they so wished, though their queen could bypass this ability in times of great need. Their hair colour was dark brown to black, they had an eye shape that was similar in shape to ours, though theirs were slightly larger. Their eye itself, was solid in colour and brown to black, with no visible pupil. Each eye was made up of small facets, again like that of bees. Their other facial features were very much like ours, although each one had an identical shaped nose. On their forehead they had two small black antennae that were in line with, and at the same angle of their eyebrows.

The clothing they wore struck me as bold, and the rich colours and fabrics flowed from their cloaks, as did the tunics they wore. The group approached me and smiled, acknowledging my presence.

'Major Mitchell, we are grateful to meet you. My name is Ambassador Bereatia. Queen Calaria sends her warmest wishes to you. We understand that you and your crew have played a significant role in identifying a new threat to our combined species. We all thank you and would like to offer the services of one of our most expert communications officers, Soldier Adari.

Soldier Adari will ensure that the Amaranthine is in full communication with our Queen at all times. We hope that Soldier Adari will prove himself as an essential member of your crew, helping us all to stand together in solidarity against this new threat. His head twitched and moved, as if he were listening to something that we could not hear. Queen Calaria wishes you to know that the Nadaal stand with you on your endeavour. She also says to let you know, that if you need additional resources that the Nadaal will ensure that the Amaranthine and its new commander has everything that she needs.' His head stopped moving and he engaged his eyes once again with mine.

'Major, the Nadaal are a peaceful species, but know that we will join with the humans in an attempt to protect our hives, and the cities and communities of the Earth and Nemeranth.'

'Ambassador Bereatia, we welcome the Nadaal's kind offer, can you convey our deepest and most humble thanks to Queen Calaria. We too hope that we can stand united together and face this new threat. With our combined forces and our combined numbers, we stand a much better chance should anything serious develop in the future.' With that and a simple nod, the party turned and left the room. Only Soldier Adari remained.

'Your orders Major?' Soldier Adari stood, a single Nadaal on-board a human ship.

'Soldier Adari, welcome to the Amaranthine, the

first thing I would like you to do is choose a living quarter for yourself. Cat, can you show Soldier Adari around the ship and ensure that he has everything he needs. Once you are settled in, please return to the bridge for briefing. Oh, and one more thing, what should we call you, Soldier Adari is a little formal.' Soldier Adari nodded.

'Major, I am most content to be called Adari, I trust this will be acceptable?'

'Yes, Adari that's fine, welcome to our ship.' In the briefest of fleeting moments, I thought I could see a faint glimmer of a smile as he and Cat left the docking area.

The next group through the docking bay door were a group of three Okai. The first thing that struck me was the different coloured skin, pink, light violet, and pale tangerine, an interesting mix. Their hair was in dreadlocks of different lengths which contrasted in colour to their skin. On their faces were tattoos, in designs that were significantly relevant to their culture. Their clothing was relaxed, and much more casual than the Nadaal's. It was loose to allow freedom of movement. The party was made up of three females, an older female to the front and two younger females to the rear. They approached me, stopped, and bowed their heads to us.

'Welcome to the Amaranthine.' I said, bowing my head slightly to the party.

'Thank you. Major Mitchell I am Counsellor Jardanae Vaen, and this is Blanave and Raena. We ask humbly and offer one of our finest strategists and combatants, Raena of house Willaen, as an Ambassador to this fine ship.'

I glanced across at Raena and noticed how

incredibly attractive she was. I almost caught myself having to nudge my jaw back up, but fortunately for me, Joe saw my pause and quickly intervened.

'Major Mitchell would like to accept your generous offer.' Joe nudged me gently.

'Yes.' I cleared my throat quickly.

'I do indeed accept and welcome your support. Welcome to our ship, Deno would you escort Raena around the ship and help her to choose a quarter please.' I turned and acknowledged Joe, thanking him with the quick glance of approval that I gave him.

Jardanae smiled, she had obviously noticed my body language and my slightly awkward moment and blush. The Okai were telepaths with their own people, but I was just really thankful that they couldn't read human minds.

'Major Mitchell, the Okai thank you for your generosity.' She smiled and there was a sincerity and warmth to it.

'Would you care to stay for refreshments before you depart?'

'We would like that very much. May we tour the ship before we leave?'

'Yes. Captain Tanaka will escort you to hospitality and then around the ship.' Joe nodded and guided the Okai out of the room and towards the hospitality suite.

I made my way back towards the bridge, walking the ships long corridors, the glossy black floors and blue lighting that was inbuilt and embedded flush to the floor, identified where to walk at all times. My mind drifted to the ships two newest crew members. I had never worked directly with the Nadaal or the Okai, another learning curve for me for sure, but one that I hoped would cement our worlds relations even further.

I was looking forward to getting to know them both better and learning more about their cultures. They fascinated me, so different and yet so similar. Each species sharing commonalities, even though each one was at least six and ten light years from the Earth.

5 GUNS, WHISKY AND FRIENDSHIP

The Amaranthine certainly was a magnificent ship and over the last thirty-six hours or so, I had managed to walk many of her corridors, meeting with many of the crew. Deno had messaged me a couple of times on my chip, inviting me to meet with her at the firing range. She said that she wanted to have what she called a fun night watching movies, which usually meant drinking lots of whisky and bourbon, and generally putting the world to rights.

I had arranged to meet Deno at 18:00 hours and found myself for the first time since landing on the ship, in my synth jeans, a t-shirt, and a pair of trainers as I hurriedly left my quarters. I felt quite excited to be off duty, if only for the night. Deno and I always had the best times and although I didn't have a lot of people that I could call true friends, I did have a Deno, and I felt blessed that she liked me enough to want to spend some of her off duty time in my company.

I walked towards the lift noticing that some crew members were evidently taking a second glance at me.

Some were checking me out generally, whilst others were clearly trying to work out if it was their commanding officer who had just walked past them giving them a friendly wave or a smile. I always wondered what difference it should make. I was a human being first and a Major second. Deep down though, I felt that I was just an average woman doing a less than average job. I arrived at the firing range and was quickly checked in by a crew member.

'Major. Chief Martin is waiting for you in aisle two. Which weapon would you like to check out?'

'Hmm. Do you have the Provost T12?' This was a side arm, it was uncommon, but I'd always wanted to try one out.

'Yes ma'am. You can retrieve it from locker forty three, over there on the left.'

'Thank you.' I approached locker forty-three and held my chip against the scanner. The locker opened and inside was the weapon I had requested with six cartridges, each holding fifty rounds. I made my way to aisle two, where Deno was cleaning Kevin.

'Hey. How's things?' I spoke, trying to get Deno's attention, waving my hand in her peripheral vision.

'Hi. I'm nearly done, I'm looking forwards to showing Kevin off to you, he's proper mint.'

'I've been looking forward to this, you say he packs a punch?'

'Yep. Small gun, big punch. He's very powerful. I like him a lot.'

'That's great Deno, will you be bringing him on missions with us?'

'Oh yes. Wait until you see what he can do.' I smiled. I couldn't wait.

I loaded my weapon, as did Deno, she stepped up

to the counter first, pushing a red button, holo-targets appeared. Deno drew her weapon and–

The weapon discharged and Deno was flung backwards, just missing me by an inch or two. I rushed to her aid, whilst trying to gauge if she was okay. Turning to face her I found that she was on the floor in a crumpled heap, cursing to herself about planting her feet, or words to that effect. None of the words that left her mouth were polite, and some of them I had never heard before.

'Deno. Are you alright, you literally just flew past me there.'

'Yep. I'm fine. Told ya Kevin was a powerful gun. Sorry about that Major, I forgot to plant my feet, caught me slightly off balance there he did.'

'Right… well just make sure you plant your feet next time. I don't wanna have to get the medics out to you. Deno, is this going to be practical when we are on missions if you have to plant your feet every time you use him?'

'Oh yes. Once I get into the habit, I won't even think about it. I will just do it.' I knew Deno, and I knew that she was probably right. She stepped back up to the counter and I pushed the button again. Targets dropped and Deno planted her feet. She reeled off thirty-six shots, all on target. She stood looking at the targets with a wide and endearing smile on her face.

'Well, that certainly was impressive. You have improved your aim even further since we last did this.' I said sincerely, as I carefully checked the accuracy of her shots on the ranges viewing screen.

'Practice makes perfect Steph, now it's your turn.' She stepped aside, beckoning me to the counter. I stepped forwards, gun in hand, turned to her and nodded. She pushed the button and the targets appeared. I fired off the rounds in quick succession.

'Hey, how did I do?' I looked across to Deno who was looking at the score panel.

'Not bad, is how you did. You know you aced it Steph. Why'd you even ask?' I laughed with Deno, the expression on her face was priceless.

'Well, I'd wanna know if my aim was off. You going again?'

'Yup. Kevin is reloaded and ready to go.' She stepped forwards again, but this time she closed her left eye, and this meant only one thing. That she was taking this very seriously indeed.

I pushed the button once again and the targets appeared, this time they were moving about more, appearing, and then disappearing and then reappearing elsewhere in the range. Deno fired her shots off, again in quick succession.

She had gone into a different place in her head, the endearing smile had gone, and she looked incredibly absorbed by the experience. This was the Deno that was usually reserved for combat, but the best bit about it, was that she could turn this on and off, like a faucet. I envied this about her, and I wished that I could do the same. She turned to me, the look of concentration gone and a wide smile on her face once more.

'How'd I do, how'd I do?'

'You did great, oh wait… actually you did better than great. How the hell… You just got a perfect score!' Deno jumped up and down fist punching the air, waving Kevin about jubilantly.

'Told you he was epic. He's like the perfect weapon for me.' She brought the spent gun up to her lips and gave it a quick kiss.

'It's your turn to go again. Want the moving targets or static?

'Think I'll stick with static. I can't compete with you tonight, Deno you are on fire my friend.' She held her hand up and I grabbed it, patting her on the shoulder and congratulating her.

After a few moments I stepped forwards again, nodding to Deno to push the button. The targets appeared and I began to fire off my weapon. Then, my mind disengaged from the task at hand, and I was back in my room on Earth for a few moments, I saw my face in the mirror again and--

'Steph are you alright, Steph, Steph. Is everything ok?' It was Deno, she had hold of both of my shoulders and was gently shaking me. I snapped back into the present.

'Sorry… I think I zoned out there for a moment.' I gathered my wits, shit… not again.

'You just stopped firing, well your arms lowered first, and then you let off a single shot, that missed all the targets by the way. But then, well you were just staring into space, so I took the weapon out of your hands, I was worried. It was only for a few seconds, but I've never seen you do that. Are you sure you are alright?' Deno looked at me the weight of her concern written across her face.

I didn't feel alright. I felt uneasy. I'd never had an issue like this, and I thought that it must be linked to how traumatic that experience of… whatever it was, that I had a few nights ago. It was obviously playing on my mind. Maybe I just needed to talk it through, well as much as I could. I didn't feel able to share it, not fully. I mean, who would believe me?

'You know Deno. I think I would really like to

watch that movie now.' I took the half spent cartridge out of my weapon and handed it back to the armourer, so that he could check and book it back into the ships armoury. Deno packed Kevin back up in his case and we headed out and back to my quarters.

I realised when we arrived, and shortly after Deno walked through the door, that she hadn't seen my new digs. She looked about, taking it all in.

'Take a good look around if you want, I was the same when I walked through the door for the first time.'

'It's big. It's very sleek isn't it, our quarters are very nice but this. This is luxurious, is that… Oh shit, it is. Wowzers, you have a jacuzzi bath, a real jacuzzi bath.'

'That was my reaction too, maybe later we can take it for a spin. I've not used it yet, it looked too big for just one person, and a bit of a waste of water. But for two people, maybe I could be convinced. Let's choose a movie, is there any that you have wanted to watch?'

'Yes, I found this movie whilst browsing the net. It's a bit of a western, but not in the traditional sense. I read somewhere, that it was critically acclaimed when it came out. Maybe we could give it a watch?' Deno told me the name of the movie and I searched for it on the system.

'There, I found it. Oh, it does look good. Let's get some drinks and nibbles sorted and put it on.' I went to the kitchen area grabbing some chips and dips. Deno, was searching about for the alcohol and she soon found the half bottle of Speyside Malt that was next to the other four bottles in the cabinet. She held it up to the light, reading the label, and then she began to put it back.

'It's ok, I think we deserve to drink the good stuff

tonight. It's been a strange week for us, all in all. Mostly good, but strange.'

'Mostly good… I would have thought from your perspective it had been fantastic. So, what's bugging you?' We sat down and Deno passed me a glass, then poured whisky into it until it was a third full. I held the tumbler in my hand, noticing the weight of the glass, whilst circling the golden liquid around the inside of it for just a moment before taking a sip.

'There's something that I've been struggling with for a while now, it's really getting me down and I feel I can't talk to anyone about it.'

'Steph. We know, it's really not an issue.' They couldn't know, could they?

'What do you mean you know. What do you know?' I looked at her apprehensively.

'Well… that you like the ladies, and maybe that you put your career above your personal happiness. That sort of thing.'

'Deno. I know it's not an issue about who I'm romantically or sexually attracted to, that really isn't what has been bothering me. Why on earth are we even talking about this. It's the whisky, isn't it?'

'Could be I've got the wrong end of the stick there.' She moved her fingers across her lips demonstrating that she ought to zip it.

'Seeing as we are talking about the subject, though I'm not getting into the specifics… I made a choice to put my career before my own personal needs. You know what this life can be like, hell Tommy is the exception, I think. Still, it must be hard for his wife, having to say goodbye to him so often. I would struggle with that a lot. So, my way is simpler… no complications.'

‘Complications, who doesn’t like a few of those. Tell you what. If my cowboy walked through those doors right now, wouldn’t even think about it. You can’t pass up your soul mate Steph, that’s just not how it works.’

‘Managed to do a pretty good job of it so far. Soul mate, ha. Now we are talking deep. Not sure it’s meant for me anyhow. I’m forty and single, I wouldn’t even know where to start anymore.’

‘You sure about that Steph, cos the way I see it. Well, let’s just say, if it comes… it’s not likely that you can ignore it, just saying.’ I smiled at Deno’s optimism.

‘I’ll keep that in mind. Now pass me some dip and I will tell you what’s really bothering me.’

Deno passed the dips and I sunk a tortilla chip into the guacamole, consuming it in one mouthful. I chewed it around in my mouth, thinking of how I could share any of what the real issue was, with my friend.

‘I think I might be ill or something…’ I looked at Deno, and she at me, her face full of worry, the smile had gone once again.

‘Ill? What do you mean ill, in what way?’

‘I dunno, maybe it’s some family condition, or something wrong with my bodily chemicals. I keep having these episodes. I get very hot.’ That’s an understatement, I thought.

‘I feel very tired. Actually no, I feel utterly exhausted. Then just as I’m about to get myself checked out by the medics. I feel absolutely fine once again.’ Deno took a large mouthful of whisky before finally speaking.

‘Well, you don’t know anything about your blood relatives do you, so no family medical history. So, that kinda makes it a bit more difficult. Sounds to me like it could be a chemical imbalance of some kind though. Maybe your thyroid or something else. A lot of women have these hormonal imbalances sometimes, you've seen Fetch… I have to literally hide my chocolate and snacks from her for two days every month.' I laughed, mainly because it was true.

'But seriously… aside from Fetch taking my chocolate, some women have it really bad… affects them physically and emotionally too sometimes, I hear. Listen… I'm no expert on these things. But if I, were you though. I'd get yourself checked out by a doc.'

'Yeah. Maybe your right. Maybe it is some kind of chemical issue I have going on. Thank you, I will think about it a bit more Deno. Could be you are onto something there.' I didn't know why, but I felt a little better. Deno had helped me semi-rationalise the unfathomable. Perhaps as frightening and concerning as these experiences were, maybe there was a valid reason for them.

The whisky was going down well, and we watched the movie, discussing everything from the period of history that the film was meant to represent, to a scene where several cows that were penned up appeared to be rollerblading across the screen. They were of course getting frisky, but we liked the idea that they were rollerblading much better.

'You know what. I think we need to take a closer look at that Jacuzzi. I have several swimming costumes, I'm sure there will be one that you will be happy about putting on. We walked into my bedroom, and I touched the front of a drawer, it slid out and Deno began rummaging through it, trying to pick something out. She picked up a shocking pink two piece. It was one that I hadn't worn. I had always been waiting for the right moment, a bold moment, as it was extremely bright and very bold.

She disappeared off into the bathroom to change. I picked out for myself a dark blue bikini. I turned on the Jacuzzi and it began to fill. Deno came out of the bathroom and as I went in, I realised that I had made an error of judgement.

'Deno, woah… I'd forgotten just how bright that thing was, if you like it, you can keep it, it suits you better than it would suit me. Tell you what, whilst I get changed why don't you ask the mess to send us up a selection of cocktails from the era that the film was made, circa early 2000's to 2020's.' Deno quickly brought up the holo-screen.

'Search cocktails from the early 21st century.' The screen began to reel off numerous cocktails, as I went into the bathroom to change. When I reappeared Deno was sat finishing off her whisky.

'They are bringing a selection up. Six of each should do it. Jacuzzi is ready to go too.'

'That's great, you get in and I will get the door.' Deno headed for the jacuzzi, and I wandered towards the door, still feeling the effects of the last whisky. I waited for a moment or two, and then the intercom went. I threw on my robe and answered it quickly, I was very much looking forwards to trying these ancient cocktails.

A stewardess was stood in front of a large metallic trolley that was hovering slightly above the ground, she introduced herself and asked if she could bring the drinks in. I nodded, feeling slightly more visible than I had done when Deno had suggested the idea of cocktails. I thought to myself that she must surely be thinking who is going to drink all of this.

She pushed the floating trolley efficiently into the room, turned on her heel, smiled and quickly left. I felt somewhat relieved that she had gone. I nudged the drinks trolley over to where Deno was now luxuriating in the bubbling and frothy water.

'Which one would you like to try first, they have labelled the jugs for us, and given us some ice in a bucket. I guess that's so we know what we are drinking. Oh, that one has a good name. Sex on the beach. Ha, that's a really good name. Let's try this one first.' Deno held her hand out, and I smiled. I was happy that she felt that when we were off duty, she could be herself, be my friend.

A few hours had passed, we had finished the last of the cocktails and Deno and I were now very drunk indeed, and no longer in the jacuzzi. Deno was lounging about on the largest of my two sofa's, talking about her interest and fascination of her namesake, and why it was such a cool nickname to have. I could barely keep my eyes open and had had far too much to drink. Ultimately, this was my favourite time of the night. I'd never seen a dishonest drunk, and Deno was the most honest drunk I knew.

'Sooo, Majooor… I mean Steph, are you ok with meeee callen you Steph. Noo that you are a Majooor? Cos, I can probably try and stop that… ya knows… if it was an issue for you Steph, I mean Majooor.' I struggled to contain my laughter whilst trying to sit upright on the sofa and respond coherently, my brain appeared to be having trouble keeping up with Deno.

'Ya know what I think Deno, I think that so long as you adreeess me by my rank, when we are working… it really won't be an issue. It never haas been for meeee.

Even Majooors need freends.' I raised my glass, realising that I was having some trouble seeing what it was that I was drinking. Oh hell, I thought. I really was very drunk.

'Good to knoow Steph. I am mighty happy… that yooou are my friend.' That was the last thing I remembered of the night as we both collapsed into sleep.

The next morning, I awoke early, as was always the case after I had been drinking the night before. I sat up and rubbed my eyes. I feel rough as… I need to get a glass of water, I thought.

Deno was still asleep on the other couch, and I could only see the back of her head as I walked slowly to the kitchen. I got myself a pouch of water, promising vehemently to myself whilst I opened it, that I would never ever do this again. I sipped the water that I had poured, just moments ago, it tasted odd. Though I knew full well, that it was my mouth that was off, and not the water.

I walked back over to the couch and sat down, taking a few more mouthfuls of the clear fluid into my body. Then across the lounge area, there was movement. Deno was stirring, she slowly turned over, her hair was pressed in thick strands across her face.

'Morning, how'd you sleep?' Deno sat perfectly still for a moment and then began to push the hair off of her face. I sat and just stared for a few moments trying to take in what I thought I saw on her face. But no, it couldn't be, could it? I gestured to Deno, pointing at her face, I definitely didn't remember that.

'Deno. You have something on your face… what is that? Is that pen?'

'What? I have something on my face, what do you

mean?' I got up and walked across to where Deno was now sat. I sat down next to her.

'It looks like you have some marks…' I tried to concentrate on what I was seeing.

'You have pen on your face, how did that happen… Oh wait, you have… 1, 2, 3, 4, 5… 9 shapes on your face, if I didn't know any better, I would say they look a bit like guns… or… no, no I prefer guns. Let's stick with guns.' I began to smile, and my smile turned into a laugh, as Deno leapt up and ran to the bathroom.

'Aww shit. How the fuck did that happen? Shit, shit, shit. I can't get it off, it won't come off.' She ran back into the room and sat down.

'Well shit… I'm gonna have to get some advice, I can't get it off. Who might know how to get permanent marker pen off my skin?' She pointed to a slim item that was on a small table.

'Hang on a minute, what is that?' I picked the slim item up and examined it closely.

'It's a pen, everyone used to use these a couple of hundred years ago. I found it under the floorboards of an old and ruined house that we searched for explosives about a year ago. It didn't work until I poured a drop of solvent into the top, then it worked just fine.'

'It reads 'permanent marker' Deno. Do you think it is truly permanent? I'm gonna have to give you some time off until you can get it off your skin if it is. I mean I can't have you on duty with those… guns on your face. Get showered and dressed, I will call a medic out and we can get it sorted, hopefully.' I smiled, I couldn't remember drawing on Deno's face, maybe she had done it herself whilst she was drunk, my friend did love her guns and spending down time with me, and for that, other than the fact that I was really hung over. I felt truly blessed.

6 THE RUINS OF CTHULHU MACULA

Three days had passed since I took command of the Amaranthine and everyone in the squad had begun to settle in. It was much to my relief when I was informed that the entire crew had passed their scans, and thankfully there wasn't a single Crucian among us. I felt incredibly relieved by the scans results, knowing that we had done our very best to ensure that there were no enemy spies onboard.

Adari and Raena had started to socialise and work with the crew, and the crew had been getting to know both of them much better. Everyone had lots of questions and they were all genuinely interested in their history and culture, this included how similar and different each of their cultures were to those back on Earth.

I had spent many hours of the last two days exploring the ship and introducing myself to as many crew members as I could. I knew it would be hard to have a relationship with them all, that aside I wanted them to know me a little, even if I wasn't splitting a bottle of McHawles malt whisky with them all.

I was walking slowly back to my quarters, when I received a new message on my chip from the bridge, it was Captain Dawson.

'Major, it's General Eastwick. He's asking to speak with you and only you, something about an urgent mission.' I looked at my chip and replied whilst trying to work out the fastest way to the bridge.

'Tell him I will be right there.' I ran to the lift, entered, and stood impatiently waiting for it to ascend.

What could he want, and what was the mission? I was both excited and a little anxious, as this would be my first assignment since I took command. The doors opened and I stepped out of the lift. Cat and Fetch were the only two of my six that were in attendance on the bridge, and I nodded to them both as I walked hurriedly past them towards the privacy of the briefing room and its holo-screen.

Stepping onto the briefing rooms high gloss floor, the door closed silently and smoothly behind me, the holo-screen lighting up as I did so. General Eastwick immediately appeared on the screen, larger than life.

'Major Mitchell, I have a request to make of you and your crew. A group from the Light Seekers has asked for our support on Pluto. Apparently, we have discovered an ancient ruin there, the Light Seekers are saying it holds significant religious implications for faith groups on Earth. I want you to support them in their efforts, but I also need you to report whatever is there, directly back to me and no one else.

I need to know more about their activities, is this relevant to Earth and if so, is it really a new site of faith, or is it something that was left there by someone or something far more advanced than us, but not linked to faith groups on Earth at all. Don't get me wrong Major, if it has religious significance then they can have it, but if it is something the whole of humanity can benefit from, well I say we let the science lead on it. The thing is, I need an objective view. Can I trust you to do that Major?' I paused and paced slowly around the briefing floor trying to gather my thoughts.

'General, do you have any idea why the Light Seekers believe this site is linked to their faith?'

'Not a one, but you know how these things are, though there aren't many would say it, the Light Seekers are indirectly sponsored by the elite, all of whom are trying to soothe their consciences on what and how they spend their money, and among the elite are also the deeply desperate, those who desire something to cling on to, to remind them that this hot mess of shit we are in isn't all there is.' I looked down at my boots for a moment, trying to conceal my own emotions and thoughts on this matter.

'General, do we have an ETA, when are they expecting boots at the site on Pluto?'

'Three days from now, so enjoy yourself tonight Major, you leave for Pluto in the morning.'

The briefing ended as quickly as it had begun, and General Eastwick faded from the holo-screens view. I left the briefing room, returning to the bridge and made my way to the very front, turning to face my crew.

'Open a ship wide channel.' I looked to the communications operator who was sat at a console to my left, she lifted her head and nodded towards me, her eyes told me that she had actioned my request.

'You're live Major.' Her glance returned to her

console.

'Attention all hands. This is Major Mitchell. This is a ship wide briefing, attention all hands.' Everyone across the ship paused, or immediately stopped what they were doing.

'The Amaranthine has its first trip out in a while. Tomorrow at 08:00 hours we leave Earth space for Pluto. We will be taking it easy, reaching Pluto in two Earth cycles. If there is anything you need, I suggest you order it now, we may be out there for some time. All day shift Officers report to your designated stations at 07:30 hours on the day of departure. I don't think I need to tell you how much I am looking forward to this trip. Pluto, although small, has always fascinated me. I look forward to seeing it up close and personal. Mitchell out.' I smiled at Cat and Fetch, acknowledging them as they approached me.

'Well, this is really happening, we have our first mission. Pluto.'

'We do, can we expect to suit up Major?' Fetch said excitedly. Cat glanced towards the bridge, watching the crews movements for a moment, and then looked back at me.

'What kind of mission is it Major? Are we playing politician?'

'To the Light Seekers, yes, maybe in part. Though, I have been ordered to provide an objective report on an excavation site on Pluto. Can I count on your counsel?'

'Yes, of course Major, always.'

'Good, have everything ready, this is a peaceful mission to support Earth and maybe even support the Light Seekers, ironically though, we will be the ones out there looking for the truth.'

I turned and walked towards the door, I wanted to call on our new crew and let them know, I knew Fetch and Cat would tell my six, six, then I thought… maybe it's time to up the numbers to eight. I made my way to my quarters, the emptiness and limitlessness of space at every window reminding me of how special we were, how special all of this was. There was so much space, and yet within its emptiness there was light, and there was so much life. I entered my quarters and sat at my desk, opening a communications link to the Bridge.

'Can you request that Adari and Raena meet me in my quarters, I would like to brief them personally.' The communications link went silent, and I sat looking out at the window, yet again I felt pulled towards the vastness of space and the cosmos. I felt very small, and for just an infinitesimal moment the whole ship felt small, Earth felt small, and I suddenly had the strangest sense of Deja-vu, like I had thought this very thought before. I tried to think how that could be, and then, in an instant the door intercom buzzed loudly, someone was at my door. I got up and pushed the button to open it. Stood there in uniform were Adari and Raena. Both stood looking at me expectantly.

'Please, come in. I would like to speak with you both, I realise that we haven't had much time to talk since you came onboard.'

They entered my quarters in unison, Adari walked to a chair and waited patiently, whilst Raena was inquisitively looking around, studying the decor and some of the features of my room intently. She glanced over towards me and caught me observing her, she paused for a moment, looking a little embarrassed.

'I'm sorry Major, I am unfamiliar with human culture and my inquisitiveness must appear… well, very relaxed in nature.' I stood and slowly rocked on the balls of my feet.

'Take all the time you need, but if I may ask, can you do this after our conversation, else I won't be able to concentrate on what I need to say.' I smiled warmly and noticed that Adari hadn't moved from where he was stood since he had come in.

'Please, won't you both sit down and relax, can I get you some refreshments?' Adari sat down and a gentle smile rose to his lips, his eyes looked slightly larger than they had been when he initially joined us.

'Major, do you have Nadaalian tea?' I smiled and acknowledged his request.

'Yes, of course and Raena, would you care for a drink, I can get you anything. Perhaps you would like to try something new?'

Raena looked across at me, she had chosen to sit in my reading chair, its over-sized cushions of turquoise and teal crushed velvet had drawn Raena to it, she sat enveloped and surrounded by the soft cushions and I could tell that she approved of the comfort.

'Major, I would very much like to try orange juice, I hear it is wonderful and similar to our Sanori fruit.' I nodded and ordered the drinks on my chip, then walking to the centre of the room I turned to face them both.

'I guess there is no other way to say this, and I am unfamiliar with your customs, but I wanted to take some time to welcome you in a more informal way.'

'Major?' said Raena, Adari looked across to her and then back at me.

'Let me explain, yes I am the highest-ranking officer on this ship, but up until quite recently I was a Captain with a specialist squad of six operatives back on Earth.

This is my first tour of duty in space, with my own ship. That's one of the main things I wanted to speak with you both about.' I paused gathering my thoughts for a moment.

'I know that the best outcomes need the best people, or to put it another way, the best of our combined species. My people tell me that on your home worlds you are both highly commended and highly respected. Therefore, it makes good sense for you both to join my six and be an active part of my closest circle of command onboard the Amaranthine. I realise that this is something new and it's never been done before, but I'm sure you will both agree, our aims are the same. We want to protect our species from any malignant threat, I think we will do that better if we work together.'

At that moment, my door buzzed again, the refreshments had arrived.

'Enter.' I said as one of the ships stewards appeared with three drinks, orange juice, a coffee and a Nadaalian tea. The steward put the tray of drinks onto the coffee table and left the room as quickly as they had arrived. I gestured towards the tray.

'Please, let us enjoy our drinks, I trust you will find them to your liking?' Raena picked up the orange juice and returned to the comfy reading chair, she sat and studied the colour and consistency, peering into the glass, smelling its contents. She tipped the glass up, slowly. Her lips touching the glass, as she tilted it, and easing some of the cold and newly experienced orange fluid down her throat. I found myself utterly mesmerised by it, and then for just the shortest of moments, she raised her eyes to mine and then looked back down towards the juice. I waited expectantly for her verdict.

'This 'orange' juice is delicious. Surely one of Earths hidden treasures.' Once again, her eyes met mine. 'I bet you all take this delight for granted. It is wonderful and much more than I expected it to be.' Her smile was warm, I found myself completely and utterly drawn to her explanation of orange juice. It's orange juice! I gathered my composure and continued. I turned to Adari, studying his face.

'How is the Nadaalian tea?' Adari was halfway through a sip of his tea.

'Oh, it is wonderful, though a touch more honey would make it absolutely perfect. I will speak with the steward and let them know this.' I nodded my approval to him and continued.

'Joining my six would, of course, be voluntary. It would have to be your choice alone, but I trust that you can see the benefits of our species working closely together.' Again… those eyes. At this rate I was going to need to run ten miles around the decks and take a cold shower. I was just thankful that the Okai's telepathic abilities were only functional between their own species. I looked down at my feet, and then out of the window, again towards the stars.

'I don't need a decision from you right now, please think about it and let me know in your own time.' Raena gulped the last mouthful of her juice, putting the glass down on the table.

'This receptacle, it is glass? No doubt another thing taken for granted by your people. How wonderful it is, so fragile, yet completely transparent, a rare commodity indeed. Major Mitchell, I will join with you and your six. I look forward to working closely with your team.'

She raised those eyes up to mine once more, stood up, bowed ever so slightly towards me, and then left my quarters. Adari soon followed her words with his own.

'Major, let me discuss this with my queen, and I will advise you of our mutual decision in the morning.' He put his cup down and left the room. Suddenly I was stood on my own. Well, that was a bit weird, and I didn't even mention Pluto. I had definitely felt some kind of connection with Raena, but the soldier in me told me to ignore it, to be practical. The mission must come first. I sat on the couch but found that the more I thought about it, the more it intrigued me, and I became acutely aware that I couldn't take my eyes away from that damned empty glass.

I cleared the drinking vessels, placing them onto the tray. I still couldn't get used to the ship's stewards clearing up for me. It felt a little uncomfortable, if I was being completely honest with myself, and even now I had to keep reminding myself that it was the accepted norm. I sat down in my reading chair and pulled up the mission briefing on my chip. I liked to be thorough, and so I ordered a second cup of coffee and settled down to brief myself fully on the coming mission.

The chip in my arm requested security clearance, and its screen turned red. I knew that it would stay in this state until the code had been entered correctly. I spoke my authorization code, holding my eye directly in front of the chip's scanner. The automated voice was indistinguishable from any living human, speaking in a calm tone it said.

'Security clearance accepted, welcome Major Mitchell to your briefing on events at the ruins of Cthulhu Macula, Pluto.'

∞

It must have been only a couple of hours, I had read the brief on Pluto, and was making some notes on my chip when my door intercom buzzed again. I wasn't expecting anyone that I knew of. I got up out of the chair and walked to the door. On opening the door there stood soldier Adari and Raena. I must have looked a bit surprised because Raena smiled and then looked briefly away, though she appeared to be smiling. Was she trying to conceal good news, if she were, then she was failing miserably?

'Hello again.' I said, gesturing them both once again into my quarters and following into the room behind them.

'I have news Major.' Soldier Adari announced proudly.

'News?' I said, expectantly. 'Please, do continue.'

'May I?' Soldier Adari gestured towards my couch, clearly, he approved.

'Please, and yes of course, please make yourselves comfortable, and for future reference you don't need to request permission to sit on my couch.' I spoke warmly, remembering that it must be strange and perhaps somewhat difficult for them to be the only two non-humans onboard the ship.

'Our Queen… Major, she can be persistent. I sent word to her aides, and she immediately asked for an audience with me. I didn't expect her to reply so quickly. She has taken a determined and genuine interest in your mission Major. It is rare, and a considerable acknowledgment of your leadership that she has done so. Our Queen has many decisions each day to make, and she must communicate with thousands of Nadaal simultaneously, it must be exhausting for her.' Adari glanced out of the window, his reverence to her clear, and I could tell his thoughts took him to his home world.

'Queen Calaria has asked me to respond and accept your request. She asked me to convey her thanks for putting your trust in the Nadaal, and to wish us a successful and safe mission.' I looked into Adari's eyes. I had my eight.

'Please relay my thanks to Queen Calaria, and welcome to the team Adari. There is something else I need to discuss with you both, Raena did you want to say something before I begin?'

'It will wait Major. I feel that what you are going to tell us is important.' She once again plopped herself down onto my reading chair. She really does like that chair. I thought.

I turned to face them both and I began by telling them what had happened on Earth, they both listened intently and from time to time I could see both intrigue and surprise flash across their faces. I was about to move on to the mission briefing, when Adari interjected.

'Major, I am fascinated by this, what do we currently know about species X?'

'We don't know much at all currently, only that we believe they are working with the Crucians. We don't know what their agenda is, but we intend to find out. We do know that they are aggressive in their nature, as are the Crucians in their intent. They seem to want to cause us harm, but again we do not know how they intend to do this.' Adari began pacing up and down, it was clear he was thinking it all through. Raena spoke next.

'Major, the Okai are a peaceful species, can we be

sure that their intent is hostile?' I found myself questioning and reflecting on my own beliefs for a moment.

'Raena, when you know me better you will know that I stand by my principles. What Deno and I witnessed in HQ was horrific, only an aggressor would behave in such a way, tell me Raena, what would it take for an Okai to kill one of their own loyal subjects?' Raena looked at me puzzled.

'I cannot imagine that any of my people would ever do such a thing.'

'Exactly, Raena this wasn't normal behaviour, it was the behaviour of an enemy trying to cover its tracks. Our aim is to try and work that out. To work out the what, and the why, and hope that it will be enough to protect our combined species. That's all I ask from you both. Help me to find out the truth.' I turned and looked at the holo-screen.

'Now, let me tell you about our first mission. What we know is that most species have some kind of spiritual or religious belief or beliefs, Earth is no different. We now believe that some elements of Earth society are acting in their own best interests, gas lighting and misleading the general populous, it would appear that they have an agenda.

The thing is we don't know who is pulling those strings. So, we have been tasked with finding out if one of Earth's religious groups the Light Seekers, who are currently trying to excavate a recently discovered ancient ruin on Pluto, are doing so for their own gain. Our intelligence tells us that whatever is on Pluto may have been left by something far more advanced than us, and something incredibly ancient.

Of course, what the Light Seekers are saying and

saying very publicly, is that the find is of extremely important religious significance. Our mission on Pluto is to establish if the ruin contains anything of historic or of scientific relevance, or if the ruin really is a spiritual site that can be linked to Earths religions.

We depart tomorrow at 08:00 hours sharp, so if there is anything you need for your quarters, or any supplies you need on board the ship, you had best order them soon, as we could be away for some time.'

Raena and Adari talked the situation through with me for some time, staying for a short while afterwards. It struck me, that although we were from different worlds, we still shared many of the same values, we were all resolute in our determination to protect our species.

The evening came and went uneventfully, the crew prepared the ship for its journey to Pluto, stock was ordered, and delivered. The crew relaxed, dined, and entertained themselves and my, now eight, continued to get to know each other better at the bar over a couple of drinks. I ordered another half case of whisky, and enough coffee to get me to Alfa Centuri and back, plus a few other indulgences for the trip, as we didn't know when we would return to Earth. I knew that the average surface temperature on Pluto was around 44 Kelvin or -229 Celsius or -380 Fahrenheit. I really hoped that Chief Engineer Watts expertise would mean that our suits would keep out the cold, and anything else for that matter.

∞

I awoke abruptly to the sound of my alarm at 06:30 hours. I opened my eyes wide and looked towards the window, but only the darkness of space greeted me once more. I felt excitement, and the gentle touch of anxiety tug within my chest. Today, I thought, we leave Earth's orbit for Pluto a dwarf planet that resides within the Kuiper belt, majestically different to anything else in our solar system, and sitting peacefully amongst a ring of much smaller objects that lay far beyond the orbit of Neptune. Pluto was the largest Kuiper belt object and was to me by far the most interesting.

It felt like an incredibly long way to travel for what was an archaeological dig, and then I remembered that the Amaranthine was capable of travelling much further and could hop to other star systems using its interstellar jump drive, which didn't really make the ship jump at all. The drive enabled the folding of space around the ship in order to move it from one point in the galaxy, to another, almost instantaneously.

For reasons of cost, and risk, this capability was used rarely, and only when absolutely necessary. The element used to enable this technology was expensive to produce in the quantities needed for the jumps. Moscovium, originally known as Element 115 had taken Earths best scientists nearly two hundred years to master and was the key to unlocking and progressing Earths great technological halt, which occurred between the years of 2210 to 2250.

I got up, showered, and put my uniform on, whilst drinking my first cup of coffee of the day. This was a tradition of mine and it was a rare day that I left my quarters without first enjoying a good cup of coffee. I tied my hair back tightly, fastening it in a tight knot at the back of my head. Today at least, I would look every part my rank.

This was my first voyage as commanding officer on the Amaranthine and I wanted to set a good example to the crew. I checked myself in the mirror, my skin looked fresh and almost dewy, my hair was glossy, and my eyes were bright. I straightened my posture, taking one last and long look in the mirror, then headed for the door.

As I walked the long corridor to the lift I was joined firstly by Cat, she looked full of anticipation. Her uniform appeared to be fitting her more snugly than usual, and from the definition of her physique, she appeared to have been working out in the gym more of late. I would need to send her to the supplies department for some new uniform before it burst open.

Then Joe appeared, he looked calm, composed, and ready for the day, as he always did. A few moments later Fetch and Deno both spilled out of Fetch's quarters, they were laughing, and Fetch was pointing at Kevin, I mean Deno's new gun.

Deno had her palm on Kevin who was strapped tightly to her thigh in what looked to be the new holster that she had mentioned. Then Tommy appeared, he was still tying his tie, but at least he had a shave, and Summer wasn't too far behind him, she was gathering her hair up into a loose ponytail which she twisted up and clipped neatly to the top of her head.

We turned the corner and stood by the lift were Raena and Adari were stood together patiently waiting for us. Everyone appeared to part to the side as I approached the lift door. I gently touched the control pad to call the lift to us, once it arrived, I turned to them all gesturing them with my hand into the lift.

'Shall we?' I smiled, whilst encouraging them to get inside.

Everyone swiftly entered, we stood in silence for

only a few moments until the lift reached the bridge. We exited together and I walked to the briefing floor, making sure that I approached each of the occupied consoles saying good morning to all of the crew that were on duty with us.

I looked momentarily out of the viewing window at Earth, this would be the last time for a short while that we would see her this close up. I felt a deep twinge of personal sadness at having to leave her, but I resolved this by telling myself that what we were doing, was for Earth, and every living creature that lived upon her.

I looked at and checked my chip, it was exactly 07:28 hours. I stood and faced the crew, once again all eyes were upon me, and I knew that this would be happening throughout the entire ship. I would have to try and get used to this, it felt strange to me to be so observed. I straightened my back, trying to stretch the tension out of it whilst keep a good posture. I made eye contact with some of the crew on the bridge, seeking their attention by clearing my throat.

'All comm channels are open Major, you are clear to speak.' A crew man spoke in a serious tone, from behind his console. I acknowledged him and turned to view the numerous holo-screens, where I could see many crew members across the ship.

'Good morning. We will be departing for Pluto shortly, but before we engage the engines, I wanted to wish you all a safe journey. We are due to arrive at Pluto in just over forty-six hours' time. At which point, I will be taking a small squad down, and onto the surface for our mission to assist and support in the excavation of the newly discovered ruins at Cthulhu Macula.' I paused and turned towards the navigation console, where two crew members sat at their stations, one male and one female.

'Major, we are ready to depart, on your order.' Said Lieutenant Barnes, who looked keen to get the journey underfoot. I smiled and looked once again out of the window.

'On my order… take us out of Earth's orbit Lieutenant Barnes.'

'Yes Major.' I stood for what felt like the longest time, and although surrounded by crew, I was completely alone with my thoughts, thoughts of home, and of my mother. I felt her with me in this moment, and I knew that she was proud of what I had achieved. Hell, she was probably watching this on the news right now, I thought. I needed to call her, I needed to check in with her, I wondered how she was. I also needed to ask her what she knew about my blood relatives. I had so many questions, but for now these would all have to wait.

The ship began to move, slowly at first, but I could sense no motion from the ship, only what my eyes told me, and this was from what I could see through the windows. I couldn't hear the engines at all, and the ship began to glide slowly out of orbit, as the Earth disappeared from our view. The ship quickly flew past several large space stations, and then all at once they were behind us. Now it was just us, our thoughts, and the vast expanse of space that lay before us.

The journey proceeded as planned with no issues, and at 06:00 hours, forty-six hours later we arrived just outside Pluto's orbit. I made a determined effort to rise earlier than usual as I wanted to see Pluto's surface and colour with my own eyes, and preferably as soon as I could.

Looking out of my quarters viewing window, I

could just make out the many icy mountains and valleys, though to me, its surface looked to be extremely cold and utterly lifeless.

There were no blue, life rich oceans soaking this dwarf planet's surface, or glass like lakes to reflect the beauty of the suns light. There were no green lands of lush tall forests, or carpets of fertile grass. I looked and squinted towards the sun, noticing the bright spheres reach touching the planet's surface, though as powerful as her light was, even she could not carry her warmth this far out in the system.

I reflected for a time on the situation we were in, and I wondered why anyone would build anything down there, it was just so far out from Sols goldilocks zone. I could feel the bitter cold and consuming darkness of all the space around Pluto and around my ship. I felt empathy for Pluto, out here surrounded by its many rocky companions, like a million acquaintances you could pass in a bustling city, but none of whom you would ever call a friend.

I walked slowly to the mess, pondering more on what might be down on Pluto's surface. I struggled to imagine anything down there, and yet we already knew that the Light Seekers had found a site. It didn't make any sense to me, but what did I know. Clearly, there must have been some reason to put something down on that planet, but I just couldn't fathom it out.

I remembered that Chief Watts had requested that my eight report to her for a final fitting, and reprogramming of our armour suits, before we departed the Amaranthine in the shuttle that would take us down to the surface, to the ruins.

I entered the main dining hall and saw that there were only a handful of crew who were enthusiastically eating their breakfasts, their plates were piled high with food. These were quite obviously the hungrier staff of last night's shift. Making sure that they grabbed something to eat, before returning to their quarters to sleep whilst the rest of us worked. I walked up to the counter and could see a vast selection of hot and cold foods for the many different tastes and cultures that were onboard the ship.

I ordered myself some toast and a couple of poached eggs, along with a large spoonful of baked beans. I filled a standard mug with coffee and carried my food to a now empty table. I sat down on the metal bench and began eating the hot food, it tasted so damn good, and the coffee was strong and hot.

Suddenly, and from nowhere, I thought I could hear a low and persistent noise that reminded me of an Indigenous American Indian chant, only there were no words, just some very interesting, and what sounded like incredibly spiritual sounds. I quickly looked about me, but I couldn't make out where the noises were coming from, I turned and looked around the dining hall once again, trying to gauge, and to see if anyone else around me could hear it.

No one moved, so I decided in that moment to try and ignore it, but as I picked up my fork once again, I could see that my right hand was shimmering warmly and the veins on the back of my wrist were once again like molten magna. I quickly moved my right hand from on top of the table and placed it on my thigh. I slowly sat back in my chair and looked at my hand again… it looked completely normal. What the hell was going on? I felt sickened by what was happening to me, and I felt anxious.

I didn't know why the hell I would think this, but

part of me had hoped that I would leave this issue back on Earth. It was now very clear that this wouldn't be the case. This latest experience was different. For one, I didn't feel like I was literally burning up and two, it came and went very quickly. Was it linked to the low chanting sounds that I thought I had heard, and what the hell were those sounds anyway? Perhaps it was just the rhythmic sounds of some machinery in the mess? Yes, that was it.

I finished my coffee and stood upright, hoping that no one had seen what had occurred. All at once it began to dawn on me that at some point someone was going to see it. I couldn't control it, and I didn't know what it was, what the hell was happening to me, or how to stop it, and I was damn sure others wouldn't either. I tried to compose myself, taking a few moments to gather my poise, and then I set off towards the armoury.

The armoury on board the Amaranthine was well stocked and equipped, it had all the features of any military armoury on Earth, the only difference being that it was scaled back in line with the ship's crew size. As I headed into the armoury's reception area I was once again greeted by two armed guards who checked my identification and welcomed me.

I walked through the double security doors and into the main hall. Stood there were my eight whose eyes were all fixed on Chief Watts who was carefully checking their gear. Each squad member was fully suited up in every piece of their personalised armour, all apart from their helmets which they held in their hands. They looked good in those suits, and I for one couldn't wait to try mine, as I strolled across the room towards them.

'Good morning, Chief, is everything going as planned?' Chief watts looked up and finished adjusting Joe's webbing around his left thigh.

'Major, good morning. Yes, all is going fine, in fact everything is just perfect, which is just how I like it. I need you to get into your suit so that I can check the fittings for you.' She then pointed towards my open suit, before continuing to finish the adjustments on Joe's webbing.

I walked across towards my armour and slipped my boots, uniform jacket, and trousers off in quick succession. I was now stood in my navy-blue under-armour garments. I turned to face away from the suit and took a single step backwards manoeuvring my feet until they were flush with the soles of the armours moulded foot plates.

Once again, the suit began to move towards my form, enclosing me slowly within it. It sealed tightly shut at the front and I could feel the vacuum begin to pull my body snugly to fit the melding of the armour, as compressed air was pushed rapidly out from the numerous seals on the suit. I studied all the armour pieces on my suit, each one shaped and contoured perfectly to fit my body alone, protecting me but also allowing for incredible comfort and freedom of movement.

The suit felt light and comfortable, and I was incredibly impressed with it. I jumped up and down a little to get an idea of the weight and movement again. I could feel that the suit was enabling me to jump a little higher than I would usually be able to do, which was a really good feeling. Each movement in the suit required less effort than what would normally be required.

Chief Watts called out to us all as she approached, instructing us to form a line. She walked up and down, her face was serious as she checked both the front and the backs of our suits. She held, in her hand a device that was testing for air loss from the suits. Thankfully, for us, all our suits were completely airtight. She then studiously asked us to put our helmets on. Each Helmet had a full ultra-clear vision visor, and these were shaped around the contours of the head.

The helmets were slightly larger at the front, the front of the helmet was approximately three inches out from the tip of the nose to the chin to allow for easy breathing and facial movements. At the top of each helmet and towards the back was a semi-circular curved halo that was a solid, and smooth loop that went from just behind the left ear to just behind the right ear, hugging the back of the head. This was a new type of fitting that allowed us to communicate with each other, and the ship.

Cat and Tommy had additional fittings on their forearms where their heavy weapon mods could be attached. Summer had a series of fixture points for all of her equipment. Adari had fixture points on top of his shoulders, these were for his Nadaalian micro stinger turrets and Raena had two smaller fixtures on the inside of her forearms. I didn't know what these were for but would make sure to ask her later. The rest of us, other than Deno who had managed to acquire a bonded and fitted holster for Kevin that was secured on her right thigh, had the standard military armour set up.

At Chief Watts command, we all pulled our helmets on and over our heads and pushed the small buttons, located near our left ears which activated the helmets sealing mechanism, at which point all the helmets sealed shut. The helmets could now only be opened by the wearer, a medic, or commanding officer.

'Major, have you got a moment, can I have a quick word?' Chief Watts called me over to the console that she studying closely, her eyes were fixed upon the data on the holo-screen.

'We need to talk about temperature control.' I thought back to the last night in my quarters on Earth and the intense heat that I had felt, and then my mind switched back to the present. I was going to have to try and put this thing, this, whatever it was out of my head, why couldn't I just let it go?

'Yes Chief, about that.' I said calmly.

'I would advise a constant suit temperature of twenty-one degrees Celsius. That should keep you all very comfortable. The suit will compensate accordingly to either heat or cool the squad whatever the conditions.' I nodded in approval and turned to face the squad.

'How about we get some of these fine boots on Pluto?' Everyone stood up other than Deno who was still fidgeting with Kevin.

'Let's make our way to the shuttle and see what all the fuss is about, but before we go can we just take a moment. I need to remind you all that this is a culturally sensitive mission. Deno, you good?' Deno stood up, Kevin was holstered snuggly against her thigh, Deno beamed with delight. She nodded and gave her thigh a gentle pat.

'Alright then, let's go.'

We left the armoury and took the lift to the sixteenth deck, which took us straight to flight deck one where the shuttle was waiting. We swiftly boarded the shuttle, sitting in our designated seats. The shuttle lifted off from the platform. We slowly moved out of the flight deck and through the atmospheric shield and into space.

Pluto, though small at first grew larger and larger, and after around fifteen minutes or so we began to make our initial descent. As we entered its thin nitrogen atmosphere, I almost felt lucky that we were visiting it at its warmest cycle. I knew that if it were much colder, Pluto's nitrogen atmosphere would solidify and fall to the dwarf planet's surface, awaiting warmer temperatures that would reawaken it from its deeply frozen state.

∞

The shuttle began making its final descent. The nitrogen rich atmosphere causing the windows to freeze around the edges where the cold of the thin atmosphere met with the warmth of the inner glass panes of the craft. The shuttle descended vertically for the final two hundred feet before landing with a gentle jolt. We all sat patiently awaiting instructions to disembark the craft, whilst wondering just what was out there, and just how effective our new suits would be.

We must have waited for at least five minutes whilst the shuttles pilot completed their final safety checks, it felt like an eternity to me. It must have been to the rest of the squad too, as they had begun to fidget in their seats. They all looked agitated and restless, like wolves awaiting permission to take their share of a fresh kill. After several more long minutes, we were finally given the all clear by the shuttles pilot. We were told by the shuttles pilot, who must have fancied himself as some sort of comedian, that we could depart the shuttle and put our armoured boots onto the surface of Pluto.

I noticed, that once out of the craft my armour felt incredibly light, and I was happy with the fit and the level of comfort that it provided me with. Chief Watts certainly knew her stuff, and I would make sure to thank her on our return.

Fetch was the first one off the shuttle, she pounced energetically onto the rock solid and blackened nitrogen ice. Once she had gotten her bearings, she spent the next few minutes jumping about and prodding the ice, and just about anything else she could find with the toe of her right boot. I wasn't entirely sure what she was hoping to discover with her boot, but at least we knew that the surface was solid enough to bare our weight.

I looked about me stepping out of the craft. The first thing that I noticed was the amount of light that reached Pluto's surface. It reminded me very much of night-time moon light, only there was no moon here and the space around us felt very empty indeed. The light, though very dim was in fact from the sun, our sun.

The tiny planets ice looked far brighter at close quarters than I thought it would. It seemed to magnify the sun's light rays in some way that was very different to the water ice of the Earth. I examined my surroundings and saw that we were in fact standing on a flat plateau, for the most part it looked quite smooth, at least for the short walk to where the Light Seekers had set up camp.

In the distance, about three hundred meters away I could see some bright blue field lighting which was marking the perimeter of their site. There were several white domed field housing structures and hardware that to me, at this distance looked most likely to be power generators. I could also see what I thought were a couple of cold fusion terrain vehicles.

I gave the signal to advance, and we began to walk carefully towards the camp. Every one of my squad was on duty now, so for the most part the jokes and banter had stopped, at least for the time being. This was unknown territory for us, and although we didn't anticipate any trouble at the site, we had never been to this dwarf planet before, and so we were all naturally, a little on edge.

Our feet crunched as we strode on the heavy ice, we wouldn't have heard it at all, if not for our suits carrying the sounds upwards, through the various materials and to our ears. I could see an infinite number of Tholins, which were a kind of tar made up of hydrocarbons that had interacted with the suns light. The mixture of blackened rock ice combined with the glow of the white nitrogen ice was in stark contrast to the planets mountain ranges, which we could see in the distance. They cut into space like razors, the jagged two mile high ice mountains a stark and contrasting reminder of this planets beauty, and it's enduring hostility towards life.

I looked upwards, planting my feet firmly on the diamond hard surface, before placing my right hand on Fetch's shoulder to ensure that I did not lose my balance. I could see millions of stars all around us, in a inky black and deep purple haze, that was as much of the cosmos as my human eyes could take in. The stars lit up the outer rim of the milky way and illuminated the space all about us, it felt like being inside a cosmic snow globe, looking outwards and into infinity. The stars celestial light calling out and beckoning us all to explore their beauty, and their limitlessness.

As we grew closer to the site, the pale blue glow of the camp lights got steadily brighter. We could make out much more detail now, including the fact that it was apparent that no one was home. We would need to journey beyond to the archaeological site, if we were to establish contact with the only other sentient life, other than our own on this rocky, hard, and icy sphere.

We were met by tall lights with powerful pale blue beams that lit up the camp. If not for them, it would have been almost impossible to see anything at all without the aid of our helmets lights. Fetch pointed towards some smaller white lights in the distance, they illuminated what looked to be an enormous, flat, and blackened vertical stone surface that appeared to be at least thirty feet in height and diameter. At first glance it appeared to be seamlessly fused into one of the nearby mountain rises.

This perfectly flat surface stood out against the natural rock and ice formations of its surroundings. From what I could see, this definitely did not appear to be a natural surface, it was way too smooth. I found myself being drawn towards it. I felt a strange sense of déjà vu as we drew closer to it, though I didn't know why. What on earth could it be?

We slowly made our approach towards the blackened structure, noting once again that there was no one around in the camp that we could ask for guidance. We assumed that the camps inhabitants must be working at the site. On reaching what now appeared, at closer inspection to be a perfectly flattened, symmetrical, and massive doorway, I called the squad quickly to a halt.

I stepped closer to the smooth, vertical surface,

examining it slowly with the fingertips of my suits gloves. I was certain that this was an entrance of some kind. There were some very faint, and what looked to be incredibly ancient markings on the outer frame of the gigantic panel. Perfectly smooth and angular edges joined flawlessly to the mountains natural form and were almost undetectable to my eyes, so perfect was the join. I concluded that this was indeed a doorway of some kind, and whatever had built it here, many eons before had decided to embed this structure deep into the mountainside. The only logic that I could come up with for this rationale, was that it was to protect something from the elements of space... but what?

I raised my left arm and activated my suits mobile camera. It flew upwards and closer to the ancient etchings, its bright light illuminating small sections of it. As it began to record and magnify the markings, I could make out much more detail. At first appearance, the fine scrawls looked to me like astral markings of some kind, though I had never seen anything like these before, nor could I interpret or understand their meaning.

They reminded me very much of galaxies and the cosmic web of the universe. The one thing that this told me for certain though, was in fact the most important thing. Something had definitely been here before us, something incredibly ancient, and incredibly advanced.

Deno stood for a moment gazing at the flat surface, curiously examining the markings upon it, looking at her feet and then at me, she raised her eyebrows inquisitively as if she had an idea. She took a single small and deliberate step forward, touching a small circular nodule that resided in the centre part of the door.

She waited a few seconds and then turned to me, shrugging her shoulder quickly as she did so. Suddenly, the flat surface began to move upwards and into the mountainside. Deno, stepped backwards quickly as the movement had caught her momentarily off guard, she looked towards me in disbelief. The door rose slowly at first, and then all at once there was a thirty foot, perfectly symmetrical doorway revealing our way forward. Its unnatural shape now beckoning us to enter, into the side of the mountains rise.

I entered first, trying to get an idea of where to go. In the distance I could see a row of dimly lit blue lights that stretched out even further into the structure. This was most definitely the entrance to the ancient ruins that we had been briefed about, and we now retraced the Light Seekers tracks deeper into the site. I touched the side of my head, and my helmets temple light came on, lighting up the immediate area around me.

We cautiously moved further and into the site together, checking it was safe as we moved far beyond the ancient doorway. We could see a long smooth, and black glossy corridor in front of us, its sides, roof, and floor were all perfectly smooth and had the appearance of polished glass. The corridors walls were engraved with fine symmetrical channels of what held some kind of blue lighting.

On closer inspection I noticed that it looked like the walls fine indentations were actually glowing blue, but I couldn't see any obvious power for the light source anywhere. There was no wiring to speak of and no hidden chamber or panel that I could find. It was as if the power source and the rock had been perfectly fused together. I couldn't think of anywhere that I'd seen this kind of technology, I felt a light shiver run down my spine as I had no rational explanation for what we were seeing here.

We carefully continued making our way down the long black corridor, its walls felt endless. I noted amongst other things, that the corridor was approximately two meters squared. Joe who had been leading initially, hung back and made his way towards me, gently tapping me on the shoulder to gain my attention. I turned to him immediately wondering if there was a problem.

'Major, we should be careful, I've never seen anything quite like this.'

'Noted, me neither. Let's pause for a moment and check out everyone's thoughts on this.' I stopped and turned to face everyone.

'Listen up.' I said seriously. I felt very aware that wherever we were it must be incredibly ancient, it could contain anything, or have been for any use, including uses that we didn't want to consider at this point. I had a myriad of questions in my head about this place and I was sure the others would have their thoughts too.

'We need to take extra care from here on in, we don't know what this site is, what it's purpose is, or even who put it here. It's obviously incredibly old. Cat, can you get any readings from this place at all?'

'Yes Major, but you won't like it. You won't like it at all, it makes no sense.'

'What's the issue Cat, what makes no sense?' Cat held her scanner against the walls, and I could see her eyebrows raise, though she didn't say a word. She took the reading again, and again, and then she turned to me.

'I'm not sure you wanna know Major. I mean I

know you wanna know it's just–' she tapped the scanner, and then tapped it once again.

'Cat, please… tell me. What's going on.' She turned to me, and then looked at the rest of the crew apologetically. Her voice was quieter than usual when she finally spoke.

'You're not going to believe what I say next Major, no matter how I say it, so. My scanner indicates that this corridor is a very spritely four point two billion years old…' She shrugged her shoulders at us, as if she didn't quite know what to do with the information she had just shared.

'Wait, what? That's highly improbable. Four point two billion years…' I looked at Cat, and then at the rest of my squad. Everyone looked at each other and then they all looked back at me.

'Four point two billion years, well that would put the creation of this corridor just after the formation of the Earth and most of our entire solar system. How can that be? We need to be very careful here. Whoever, or whatever was here, probably watched the Earth's mantle cool, and that means we are dealing with something far more advanced and ancient than anything we have ever known or dealt with.' I felt a cold shiver run up and down my spine as I looked once more upon the perfectly smooth walls of the corridor.

We continued walking silently for a further five minutes, processing what Cat had just shared with us. As we got further into the site the corridor began to open up and widen, there was an immense sense of space here now. I looked up and could see a high square archway which was marking the entrance to an even more massive and much more open space.

Lights were planted at five-meter intervals now, and

I thought it must have taken the Light Seekers some considerable time to do this. On the archway were even more markings, this time they were much clearer than the ones we had seen at the entrance.

'Stars.' I thought, as I gazed at what looked to be a massive star chart that ran all the way around the archways form. Small and large crystals of all the colours of the universes suns adorned the archway, these were embedded deeply into the arches surface. They glistened and glittered, in colours from white, white-blue, yellow orange and red in their millions, as each one caught the bright light of our helmets. It was both impressive and beautiful. There were fine white lines that linked each of the crystal stars and I wondered for a time at this marvel. The archway was magnificent, and if nothing else, I was certain that the beings that built the archway definitely revered the cosmos.

We finally stepped through the crystal archway, entering a large and cavernous room, I could see five humanoid figures examining some of the engravings on the walls. We walked towards the figures, and they turned to face us. They were clothed in white suits, they wore no armour and had on the most simplistic headwear. The simplicity struck me, and I could tell that these people were not soldiers, nor were they armed as far as I could see. I stood and waited for the leader of the five to step forward, and after a few moments a man aged around seventy years of age approached me.

'Major Mitchell?' he said, questioningly. His voice was warm, and he was incredibly well spoken. I could imagine him teaching or delivering sermons as his voice was rich, deep, and worldly.

'Yes, I'm Major Mitchell and you are?' I paused, waiting for him to answer.

'I'm Archdeacon Rhodes. You could say that I'm the head of archaeological studies for our organization. It's good to meet you Major. We have done our research on you, and you come highly recommended. It is surreal, don't you think that this little rock solid sphere could hold such knowledge, and such religious significance. We are thrilled with what we have managed to decipher, so far.' He looked at me as if he knew what my mission was, there was definitely an air of coercion about his manner and tone. Almost as if he were attempting to convince me that this sites origin was a forgone conclusion.

'Well Archdeacon Rhodes, I'm sure once I understand more about what has been discovered here, we can establish the true nature of this site. Either way, I'm sure our scientists on Earth will be extremely interested to have a look around too.' He looked at me and almost dismissed my words immediately with his eyes, I could see that his mind was already made up on the matter.

I had brought my open mind with me, and I intended to hold on to it, even if I was not that impressed by his demeanour, and the ever so slight manipulation that I had just experienced and witnessed for myself. But I wasn't going to rock the boat with the Light Seekers at this point, just because of this mans entitled attitude.

We moved to the rear of the room, the other Light Seekers were busily studying and taking notes on their findings. One man of small and wiry stature turned and watched us walk around. I noted that his eyes were upon us for the majority of our tour with the

Archdeacon, he seemed to be making a point of it. We stood for a brief moment and the Archdeacon paused.

'Major, there is something I want you to see.' He pointed to a smooth rectangular table that was on a slight incline, it reminded me somewhat of our consoles on the bridge, and yet there were no visible markings on it. But as the Archdeacon grew closer the table appeared to activate and there were many small lights and symbols that lit up, albeit dimly upon its darkened surface.

'That's incredible, we scanned the corridor and the archway on the way in and it–'

'Four point two billion years, give or take a few million. Yes Major, we know. It is astounding isn't it, that this site was here before the Earth's crust solidified. I am a man of faith and science, and I still can't quite get my head around it. We have interpreted some of the glyphs as best we can, look here, we believe this says.

'One that will come in a great time of need.' Look right here just to the left of the first markings, we are not sure, but we think this one says. 'Of the light, an end to darkness.' Finally, here, 'The ancient one, born again.' We are of course not entirely sure that this is what it says, but nevertheless wouldn't you say Major, that this has some religious significance?' His eyes looked proudly at me, they darted about my face, gauging my reaction. He clearly felt like he had scored a victory of some kind. For the moment at least, I couldn't deny that these writings appeared to be incredibly 'spiritual' in their nature.

'Archdeacon, these glyphs are certainly mystical in both their nature and in the way that they are written, but I don't believe we can say they are religious in their origins just yet.' His eyes narrowed. His apparent disapproval of my words evident. As quickly as his eyes had narrowed, they quickly reverted back to their usual size and shape, as he tried to conceal his emotions whilst plotting his next move.

'Quite so, though we do believe that in time this site will become a pilgrimage for Light Seekers across the Earth. It is truly wonderous.' I could tell that he believed every word that came out of his mouth. I chose not to engage with him further at this point. Cat then waved towards me, beckoning me over towards where she was stood, as I left the Archdeacon unattended for a few moments.

'What is it Cat, what's going on?' Cat turned her head, looking across the room towards the wiry man who had been observing us earlier.

'Major, if my gut is right, that man pacing around over there wants to speak with you. I also wanted to mention, these glyphs are noted down somewhat like a memoir. This site has a story to it, and I'm betting it's an interesting one. Whoever, or whatever put them here, left them for someone to find. But I gotta tell you, this place gives me the shivers and I can't decide if I should be excited or... I think that there is much more to this room Major, but I haven't got a clue where to start with all of this... I've seen a lot in my time Major, but I've never seen anything like this.'

I acknowledged and thanked Cat for her insight. Noting that the wiry man was still subtly trying to make eye contact with me, I started to walk quickly over towards where he stood. He looked at me somewhat hesitantly at first, his shoulders dropping in what I thought looked very much like relief.

'Hi, I'm Major–'

'Mitchell, your Mitchell. Major, I need to speak with you urgently but not here, please follow me. Try to look casual, they have eyes everywhere.'

We walked together out of the main chamber and into a smaller room. If I didn't know better, I would say that this room looked like some kind of medical facility.

'Major, my name is Professor Michael Adams. I hoped that we might speak in private about this room, this site. I haven't told the others because… well, I just don't know where to begin….'

'Easy Professor, it's ok. Just gather your thoughts and get your head together. I'm here to help us all try and understand this site, this discovery.'

'Well, as you might have gathered this room is a medical facility, which is why I have brought you here. The thing is, and I don't want the others to know because heavens knows what they would read into it.' He paused again, taking a long gasp for air, whilst trying to steady himself.

'Well, the thing is, I'm a geneticist and I specialise in gene coding, splicing, and genetic engineering. I could go on, but that's not really the point. Well, I. Well… the thing is… this facility has been used recently. There I said it, please don't share this discovery outside of this room.'

He looked genuinely worried, and I tried to reassure him by placing my hand on his left shoulder and looking sincerely into his eyes.

'When you say this room has been used recently, just how recently do you mean?' He gathered his thoughts.

'Well, whoever or whatever was here tried to destroy or wipe away any traces, so we can't be exact on this, but my best guess would be, as in the last fifty years or so. This entire facility self-repairs itself, I believe. I don't think we have ever found anything quite like it, certainly not in our history. Major, I do not wish to share my findings with my colleagues, which pains me a great deal. You must understand, I am a man of faith, but every bone in my body is telling me that this isn't a religious site at all. It is the site of a creation of some kind I believe, but I do not believe that it is of religious significance. I believe this site is an ancient birthplace. But it is also so much more than that. I believe it is also a starting point, like the first pin on a map.' He looked at me relieved, like an immense weight had been lifted from him.

'And your colleagues, they are all unaware of this, you are certain?'

'Yes, they think this room is a research room or something similar. They have no clue and that's the way it should stay.' I looked towards Cat who was examining a large flat table in the centre of the room.

'Thoughts, Cat?' She paused for a moment, before turning to me.

'Major… I have never seen anything quite like this, I feel like I should just press repeat, every time I speak. If this is what Prof Adams believes it to be, then my first question would be, why?' She looked around the room.

'Why go to all this trouble, putting a site out here on Pluto? It's one of the coldest places in our solar system, so, my thoughts are that there has to be a reason that they chose this place?'

She picked up a smooth round grey-blue item from the table. It looked a little like a large smooth sea washed pebble. It was around ten centimetres in diameter and perfectly smooth. She passed it to me, and I held it in my hand for a moment. I gently rubbed my thumb over its smooth surface and could see what looked to be faint, orange-coloured tiny lights beneath the objects exterior. I turned the object over in my hand trying to establish which way was up, studying it for a time. I felt drawn to it, it was an immensely tactile object, and it sat perfectly in my hand.

Suddenly, the stone like object appeared to flicker and move slightly. But before I could put it down, it puffed out a fine mist like substance into my face that looked like a million tiny diamonds. They hung still in the air perfectly motionless for a moment, and then without any warning they rushed towards my face, all at once, disappearing as they made contact with my suits helmet. I staggered backwards momentarily in shock, as my squad rushed towards me, the shock of the stones awakening action, catching me momentarily off guard.

'What the hell was that?' I shouted to my squad and Professor Adams. He rushed immediately to my aide, checking my helmet for any trace of the contagion.

'Major, I have no idea, but I would suggest that you return to your ships quarantine for examination, just to be safe.' At that point one of the Light Seekers from the chamber entered the room at speed.

'Professor, you need to see this, the entire central chamber has just lit up.'

We all ran out of the room, and back towards the central chamber. The chamber was fully illuminated now, it was much brighter and well-lit than it had been just minutes ago. At its centre was a large holographic star chart. The chart contained six maps of star systems, a couple of them I recognised immediately to be Sirius A and B which are 8.58 light years from Earth. I also recognised the system of Wolf 359, a red dwarf star located in the constellation of Leo which is approximately 7.9 lights years from Earth. The other four systems, I didn't immediately recognise. I looked at the Archdeacon, and he to me.

'Would it be too simple an idea to state that this looks like a series of maps to me. I'm calling General Eastwick and requesting a military presence here. If only to protect this site, regardless of whether it is of religious significance, or scientific significance. Archdeacon, I'm afraid this is too important a find to not protect it, for all of humanity. Cat, can you write up an initial findings report and send it to General Eastwick to provide an interim briefing for him.' She paused briefly and then looking like a woman with a sense of urgency, she walked towards the edge of the room.

The Archdeacon appeared to look visibly displeased at my decision, he skulked off silently and began searching in his backpack that rested on the floor. He closed the bag, stood up, and turned around. He was holding an object, an object that he was now pointing at me.

'That's quite enough Major Mitchell, I'm afraid I can't allow you to contact General Eastwick. You see this site is ours, it belongs to us, and we will not allow you to take it from us.'

He paused and looked towards the other Light Seekers, all except Professor Adams who had disappeared from view. They all pulled out their weapons and although we outnumbered them, they had us at a disadvantage. I slowly raised my hands and nodded to the squad to do the same.

'Archdeacon, this site belongs to all of humanity, and maybe all beings in the galaxy. We don't understand it fully yet. If you harm us, you will have the full might of the Amaranthine and Earth Force to contend with. Is that really a fight you want, because I can guarantee it's one that you won't win, so please put the weapon down.' He waved the phase pistol in the region of my head.

'You, you are so very ignorant. Do you not think that we have our own allies Major Mitchell? Do you not understand that we are everywhere, in every organization and in the upper echelons of power across all the inhabited worlds?' His toxic bravado was beginning to ring alarm bells, but I couldn't stop the words from coming, as they began to pour out of my mouth.

'Archdeacon, if I didn't know any better, I'd say that you sound like a Crucian with his knickers in a twist. There is one thing that I know about Crucians, it's that they don't like to lose, anything. Tell me, do your colleagues know that you have infiltrated their faith? Are your colleagues willing to die for you here today, let's ask them, shall we?'

The Archdeacon had a look of concern on his face, it was the first time I had seen anything like a flicker of vulnerability in him. He looked across to his colleagues whilst still keeping his weapon pointed at me.

'Are you going to let this soldier, who has no faith, dictate to you? Ask your heart what you feel God would want you to do.' The three Light Seekers began to look uncomfortable, looking across at me, and then back to the Archdeacon. I saw this as an opportunity to reach out to them.

'Listen, if we protect this site, I promise you that it

will be a collaboration between our best scientists and your own. I want everyone to benefit from whatever knowledge there is here, for the greater good of humanity, surely you can understand this.'

At that moment, the Archdeacon's hollo-projection deactivated, now instead of a human there, right in front of us all stood a very angry Crucian. He took a step forward and lifted his chin up so that his eye level was in line with mine.

'Mitchell. What a weak and pathetic human name, you do not know what forces you are toying with. Your ignorance of the facts blinds you to what will be, your destruction, it is inevitable. We were once like you, proud and stupid. We fought until our planet's surface ran black with generations of our blood. It's already too late for you and–'

Unexpectedly, there was a loud noise, which echoed throughout the chamber at which point the Crucian fell to the floor motionless. Professor Adams emerged from the shadows and was walking towards me with a phase rifle in his hands. He looked to the other Light Seekers and told them to put their weapons away.

'Major, we have suspected for some time that our organization had been infiltrated, but sadly we had little or no evidence. Do we have your word that this site can be of joint benefit and exploration for the good of our planet and our allies?'

'You do.' I said, and I meant it. It was good to know that the Light Seekers were also aware of this threat, though worrying that they too had been subject to espionage.

'But, if you don't mind me saying so Professor Adams, I wouldn't have had you down for the gun handling type.' He smiled and looked at me his eyebrows raised.

'Major, I've lived an interesting life. But to answer your thoughts, before I found my faith, I was a marine. I learned many things as a soldier, which is why I knew that the moment I met you, I could trust you.' I immediately reached forward and shook his hand.

'Professor Adams, would you consider joining our ships mission. We are looking for an ambassador of faith, a chaplain, and an acting science officer. the post is vacant, but I can't think of anyone more suitable for the position. It looks like we might have a few other sites to visit, and I would very much appreciate your knowledge on these discoveries as we progress.' He continued to shake my hand.

'Major Mitchell, I would be honoured to accept the commission on board your ship.' He stepped away from me, just for a moment whilst bending down to reach the dead Crucian. He removed the weapon from its now cooling hands, covering its face with a simple synthetic cloth.

He turned slowly towards me, whilst studying the reaction written across my face and evidently visible in my eyes, to this, his simple act of unrequited compassion to a nameless malignant assailant. I could see that he was carefully considering this act, his act, and his next words.

In a low and calm voice, just as if he had witnessed the very same words upon my lips, or in the single burning question that was now in the forefront of my mind, he looked down towards the Crucian, and then directly back towards me.

'We are all creatures of the light, Major. Even those who have lost their way.' There was no comment that I could make, for his words were spoken true.

Deno ran towards me, she had news. 'Major, we need to get you back to the ship, we need to get you checked out. I've contacted medical and they have an isolation unit waiting, ready for you, now.' I acknowledge Deno and looked at Fetch and Summer.

'Will you two accompany me please? Joe, can you clean this mess up and have the Archdeacon transported to the Amaranthine for a post-mortem examination. Also, confiscate any property that he has here, and in the camp. Bring it up to the ship for examination by our investigative team. Also, ask General Eastwick if he can contact central command on Earth to search any of his known residences. I want them to look into all of his friends, acquaintances and any other links that might tell us how he did this. I think we need to presume at this point that sadly, the real Archdeacon is dead.'

'Yes ma'am.' And with that Joe got straight to work.

7 SILENTLY IN DARK PLACES

Fetch ran quickly towards the Light Seekers shuttle. Taking a sharp left as she entered the door, hurtling powerfully down the centre of the shuttle's middle aisle. She jumped into the vacant pilot's seat, taking a long glance over her left shoulder towards where Summer and I were sat, as we were hurriedly securing ourselves into our seats.

Summer was sitting directly opposite me, she looked tense and on edge, as though she was preparing, readying herself for anything. The one thing I knew about summer, was that she could switch between the two sides of herself instantly and effortlessly. She was both beautiful and deadly, and her professional mask was always on regardless of the situation. Even when you saw her out of work, I was convinced that it was all a facade and that no one knew who the real Summer was, except Summer.

The crafts white hot engines were lit up and ready for take-off. I looked towards Fetch and gave her a single nod, indicating that we were ready for transportation back to the ship. The lights of the camp and the site soon disappeared below us in an instant, as Fetch took us away from Pluto's surface. We sat in complete silence for a minute, and then Summer spoke. It was unexpected and I would never forget her next words.

'That mist, it was like some kind of weird glittery substance that came out of that pebble shaped object. Did you see that it hovered and held perfectly still, just moments before it went towards your face. Why, I wonder?' I shrugged my shoulders.

I didn't have any answers, but I certainly had many questions that were as yet unanswered. Such as, what was that mist? Had it done something to me? Was I now infected with some incurable virus or malignant nano-bots? But my racing thoughts didn't stop there, my mind coming up against wall after wall. I was trying to problem solve the unfathomable.

What had been at the site under fifty years ago? How could the site be billions of years old? How was that even possible? Who put it there? Summer looked out of one of the shuttle windows towards Pluto and then back to me.

'That place, it was so old. Professor Adams, he seemed to have resolved so much of it, in theory. The maps, we need to figure them out. It's like a very fucking old bread crumb trail, isn't it?' Summer paused and was massaging her temple, the stress visible on her face.

'It could be, yes. I think that it was always waiting to be found.' Trying to fill my lungs, I gasped for air. I felt warm and a little spaced out. It must have been the shock, I thought.

'Fetch, how long until we dock with the

Amaranthine?' She immediately turned to me, a steady look of concentration on her face.

'Three minutes Major, I'm just beginning our approach now.' I took a long deep breath and gazed out of the window with only the blackness of space to occupy my eyes. I touched my arm and the electronic pad that was built into my armour, opening a communications link to the Amaranthine.

'Hello, this is Major Mitchell. I want everyone checked out by the medics on their return from Pluto. I want to be sure no one is contaminated or injured.

'Yes Major, we will see to it right away.' A voice spoke through the device.

I sat for the next few minutes whilst Fetch took us through the Amaranthine's atmospheric shield and landed the shuttle perfectly. We got up out of our seats and opened the shuttle door. A digital red, isolation tunnel stretched out in front of us, and out of the hanger. I assumed that this ran all the way to the medical facilities.

The three of us began to walk towards our quarantine. The corridors along the way were empty and I realised that they must have been cleared to allow us safe passage. It felt strange, and we did not see a single soul on our walk. It felt surreal and like there was just the three of us onboard the ship.

We finally reached the medical facility. On entering we saw three medics and the ships Chief Medical Officer, who was running some tests across several holo-screens. He turned to us after a few moments.

'Please enter your designated quarantine space.' Each of the three medics called a name out, my name was said first, followed by Fetch, and then Summer. We entered our quarantine areas, these were remarkably similar to the quarantine tunnel, only instead of being red, they were blue. Each one was a perfect cube, within it was a bed, a chair and various monitors and medical equipment. I stood for a moment looking at Fetch and Summer who were both looking at me and then at the medics as if waiting to be told what to do next.

'Please step out of your armour.' The voice of the Chief Medical Officer was loud and commanding, we were on his turf now, and I knew his tone was one that was intended to get us to do what we needed to do, quickly and without question. We each removed our helmets and stepped forward, releasing the suits from our bodies.

'When called please enter the decontamination chamber. This will remove all contaminants. Your armour will be taken in sealed containers to be deep cleaned. Major Mitchell, please enter the chamber.'

I walked towards the chamber, but instead of stepping out of the field, it surrounded me and continued as I did, all the way across the room. Finally, I reached the doors of the chamber. I stood, and after what seemed like forever, the doors opened.

I stepped in and looked at the white smooth, sterile walls which had row upon row of circular ringed holes that were four feet from the floors surface. I considered these and thought they must have been vents of some kind. Each one was circled in black and blood red, and to me they looked quite ominous. A voice came into the room.

'This won't take long Major. We will have you out of there in a few minutes.'

The voice went silent and as it did so, what looked to me like steam vapor began to come out of the vents.

It was red in colour, blood red. I sank to my knees and closed my eyes. In an instant, my mind took me back to Pluto and I recalled the strange vapor, or whatever it was that left the smooth pebble like object. Perfectly still, in my mind's eye I could see it, frozen in time. I remembered it pausing and oddly, I also remembered that I felt observed by it, watched, and studied by it, in that single moment. I thought, I must be imagining it. How could a vapor observe me? But what concerned me more than this, was the following thought. Why?

No sooner had this question entered my mind, that I started to feel odd, lightheaded and a little woozy. I looked down at my skin which was now covered in droplets of the vapor that had begun to condense, coming together, it ran like rivers of blood and tears down over my entire body. My hands felt warm, and I noticed heat within them once more. I turned my palms down-wards and saw the lava like tracks glowing and running like liquid where my veins and arteries ran. I immediately tucked them under my armpits, in a panic I tried to hide them. As if merely hiding them would make a difference. I looked down at the now reddened floor.

'Please… Not now.' I muttered under my breath. I tried to gather my thoughts and willed the changes to leave me. A single word. Stop. I rocked back and forth on my knees for another few seconds. It was getting harder every time this happened for me to deny that something was very wrong with me. I cussed in a panic under my breath.

'Shit, fucking shit. Stop now, please just stop.' I was angry at myself.

Hardly daring to bring my hands back in front of my eyes, I began to move them out from underneath my armpits, I then felt an emotion so uncommon to me. I felt fear. But logic told me that I needed to see my hands to gauge what was going on and what action I would need to consider next. As if I even had a term of reference for this weird fucking shit. I knew that I would have to buy myself some time if they were still glowing. Glowing, I thought… I felt sickened with the fear of what was happening to me. Suddenly, and immediately I brought my stomachs contents up and onto the floor in front of me.

'Oh great… just fucking great. What next?' My teeth were now clenched and gritted together, and I felt a rage begin to stir within me, whatever this thing was. It was really pissing me off.

Slowly, I raised my hands to my eye level, my body shivered from the shock, and I felt immensely weak. I examined my hands and once again, they were mine. I felt overjoyed, at the mere sight of my own flesh. I turned the backs of my hand to the palm, again and again. I had to be sure that the shimmering had stopped.

Wiping the remaining traces of the vomit from my mouth and chin with my arm, I looked to the floor, all traces of the vomit had now gone. As had the blood red fluid that had just moments ago covered my entire body. I looked at my skin, that too showed no traces of the red liquid that I was drenched in. The lighting in the room had changed also, and I knew that the decontamination procedure had concluded.

The doors on the room slid open and I walked back to the examination area that I had started in. My suit was gone, having been taken away for cleaning, and both Summer and Fetch had been moved to different rooms. I was alone with my thoughts once again. I sat on the bed, some of my energy was returning now, and I noticed that I felt very hungry. The Chief Medical Officer entered the room. He was carrying a small white hard case. He spoke to me calmly.

'I trust that the decontamination was relatively quick?'

'Yes, though the red liquid thing was a bit unnerving.' I looked to see if I could gauge any emotional response from him.

'Yes… I'm told it can be quite disturbing to anyone who has not experienced it before, perhaps I should have mentioned it. I will make sure that I do so in future Major.' I nodded to him and in that moment, I couldn't stop myself from glancing at my hands. Still me, I thought.

'The mist like substance, I have spoken with Summer and Reece, and they have both described the exact same thing, which leads me to believe that this was some kind of organic or synthetic intelligent compound. That is, when I say intelligent, the compound was clearly meant to seek something out. I believe it just happened to be you, though we do not know, and may never know what it did to you, what it gained, or what it learned from you.' I looked at the monitors on the doctors holo-screens.

'And what do my test results tell you doctor?' I sighed.

'Well, you're in perfect health. But I want you to contact me if you experience anything out of the ordinary.' I shook my head and smiled, restraining a small laugh from leaving my mouth.

'Something has amused you. I trust that everything is alright?' He looked concerned.

'Well, there is something doctor, but if I could

discuss it with you later? I'm tired, hungry, and I need to report my findings on Pluto directly to General Eastwick.' I eased myself off the bed.

'There are clean clothes in the locker. Make sure that you have some food and drink brought to the briefing room, or your quarters as soon as you are able to Major, and that's an order.' He smiled and then continued to examine my medical data on his chip, whilst he casually walked out of the room.

I touched the front of the locker and it slid open. Inside was a full set of uniform, my underwear, and boots. On the shelf below was a comb, a hair tie, and clips. I dressed quickly, making sure that I made myself look as neat as I could, given the circumstances. I left the medical centre and made my way to the briefing room. I walked straight in without speaking to any of the crew that were on duty, and I ensured that I had closed the door behind me. I stepped up to the communications console and entered my authorisation code, Delta Omega, Shiva, Phoenix 880120. The console lit up and a retina scanner rose up out of the console, I leant forward, and it efficiently scanned my eye.

'Welcome Major Mitchell, General Eastwick connecting.' I took a step back so I could take in the full screen. General Eastwick appeared in front of me. He looked concerned.

'Major, I heard what happened on Pluto. Well, done for identifying another one of their agents. Who would have thought it, an Archdeacon? I understand things got pretty intense down there?' I pushed my shoulders back and straightened my posture.

'You could say that Sir. The site is extremely ancient, as old as Earth and the technology is… well

Sir, I don't have the right words to describe it. Unusual, in the fullest sense of the word. The site Sir, it self-repairs. Chief Shaw has dated it to around four point two billion years old.' General Eastwick had a look of concentration and deep thought written upon his face.

'Tell me Mitchell, I understand you also had an encounter with some tech, or some kind of device?' I reflected for a brief moment before answering.

'Yes Sir, there was a small, smooth object that I examined. It released some kind of mist, this mist held in mid-air and then travelled directly towards my face. Immediately after this the central chamber at the site lit up and we saw galactic maps of six systems in the centre of the room. You know the rest, the Archdeacon, now known as a Crucian infiltrator, did not wish us to claim that tech, information, or knowledge. It was clearly important to them, though what they thought they would gain from it at this stage is beyond me.'

'And the age of the site, doesn't that intrigue you Major?'

'Yes Sir, it does. But… It confuses me also Sir.'

'Meaning?' he focused in on my face.

'What put that facility down on that rocky ice ball Sir? I mean think about it, what could build something so ancient? What could build something that is able to self-repair itself, and why leave us maps, maps, and directions to where? It's like whoever they were, they wanted someone to find those charts. Otherwise, why go to all that trouble. Why put all of that information in a highly advanced self-repair facility?'

'There are a total of six maps Mitchell, yes?' he said, his tone of voice full of intrigue and interest.

'Yes Sir. But for now, we have more immediate and

larger concerns, concerns that are much closer to home. I think we should focus on finding out what the Crucians are up to in our combined systems, I don't trust them. Let the investigators on Earth look into our findings about the disappearance of the real Archdeacon. This should buy us enough time to find out just what Jevargh transmitted to that ship. It strikes me as both odd and concerning that both the Nadaal and the Okai each have their own almost identical Crucian Cruiser docked just off their home worlds too, though for some reason the one docked off Earth is much larger in size.'

I still remembered the conversation that took place in the room on that night, and it still sent chills down my spine, whenever I thought about it. Although I confess, that I too was interested in these remarkable finds, I wanted nothing more than to make sure that the discovery and wonder of the Pluto site would not be a final distraction for humanity. I hoped that its significance would not take our eyes away from the true intentions and possible plans of the Crucians. Now, I thought, we just needed to find out what those plans were.

'Major, for what it's worth I think you are right. I also want to know why there was a Crucian operative on Pluto. Why are they interested in that site, so much so that their operative was prepared to die for it. He must have known before he pulled his weapon on you that it wasn't going to end well for him. No, something doesn't add up, I agree. I want your operatives on that Crucian ship. Who is your best for this type of mission. I'm talking get in, get out, unseen.'

'Without a doubt Sir, for this type of mission I would recommend First Lieutenant Neilson, and I would pair her up with Chief Martin, if nothing else but to watch her back, should the shit hit the fan Sir, but I'm hoping it won't come to that.'

I was confident that Deno would have Summers back all the way. I had observed them in action before and oh boy were they quite the pair. A silk glove around a clenched fist. The fist being just what was needed, should the glove tear.

'Major. Your mission is to get your best operatives onto that ship and retrieve the information sent by Jevargh from Earth. Any other intel that you can obtain in relation to their wider plans would of course be of extreme value. I cannot stress enough that this mission is classified as above Top Secret and if at all humanly possible, other than in certain death, your team is to infiltrate silently and get back without being detected, unseen, unknown and not fucking there. Do I make myself clear?'

'Crystal. Sir, I will brief my team immediately.'

I glanced towards my arm which had started tingling. It felt warm and for just a moment a brief jolt of anxiety ran once again up the length of my spine, the only thought that entered my head was, 'Not now.'

'Major, are you OK?

'Yes Sir, I'm fine… just running the mission through my head.'

'Good, I will await your report following the successful conclusion of this mission. Oh, and Major before you go…'

'Yes Sir?'

'It really was damn good work down on Pluto. I look forward to us exploring those maps together and seeing where they take us. Now Major, you need to get your ship back to Earth's orbit as soon as you can.

Permission to use the jump drive is granted. Eastwick out.'

Instantaneously, he was gone, and I was left to my gently tingling arm, and my own thoughts for the mission. I needed to call the squad in for their briefing. This would be one hell of a dangerous mission, but I was confident that Deno and Summer would be up for the challenge.

∞

I stood perfectly still, in front of the communications console for a few minutes whilst gathering my now racing thoughts. The present situation was an extremely dangerous and serious scenario, boarding a Crucian cruiser without the proper permissions would, if caught get my operatives killed, or far worse.

The Crucians weren't exactly known for their good treatment of those who were taken prisoner, and they certainly weren't known for fair treatment of anyone who went against their species, this included those who wittingly or unwittingly entered into their territory without their explicit permission. The troubling thing for me was that I was about to ask my squad to go against everything that the Crucians had demanded from our species for the past hundred and eighty-five years or so, including our silent subservience to their will.

We needed a plan, and it had to be a good one if we were to have any chance of succeeding. I moved my hand over the smooth control panel that was situated below the holo-screen in front of me, its blue hues reflected onto my bronzed skin as I did so.

'Operatives Martin, Tanaka, Martinez, Shaw, Kawolski, Nielson, Raena and Adari please report to the briefing room immediately. Code nine, I repeat code nine.' I drew in a long, deep breath. This was it, for all I knew the next conversation with my squad would put their lives at substantial risk. This would need to be done right as we would only get one shot at this, but all I needed was just one carefully placed shot. I needed their insight and their expertise like never before.

My hands gripped the edges of the console, and my knuckles began to whiten with unease as my eight entered the room. I felt tense, and they all looked at me as if they knew the very words that were to cross my lips and yet… How could they sense what I was feeling, how could they know that I would ask more from two of them today, than I had ever asked from anyone that I had ever served with.

It was a sobering thought and one that I didn't take lightly. I felt the heavy weight of responsibility and leadership on my mind and my conscience. I studied them all intently as they quickly found their places at the table.

So, who would it be? Summer, so capable and so very deadly and Deno, my quirky sharpshooter and the closest thing that I had to a real friend. I could feel the loyalty that I had to them both pull tightly at my chest, as I contemplated our next move. I knew that all eight had entered the room, knowing that what I would tell them next would be extremely significant to the mission. There was a crackle of energy in the air, like that of electricity about to make direct contact with a lightning rod. But truth be told, I was scared for them, no… deep down, I was terrified.

All eight looked ready for business and ready to do their jobs, they sat up straight with their shoulders back, they looked proud to be sat at this table, my table.

This table was where ultimately a crucial decision was about to me made. Adari and Raena seemed to me to be fully engaged in the mission, for the first time since they joined us. Their cultures were so vastly different to ours, but their aims and values were the same. They both looked at me, waiting for me to speak.

Both of their species were united in their support of the mission. I paced about in front of the table, running through my head all the different scenarios and what I would say next. Standing at the top of the table having now left the console to my rear. I looked down the room, studying all of their faces as they studied mine.

These were the most trusted, loyal, and most capable soldiers that I knew. There was so much riding on this mission, and so much risk attached to it. We needed to know what information they had taken from us, and we needed to know how they intended to use it, I just hoped that the cost to my squad wouldn't be too high.

'At ease, please. There is something that I need to discuss with you all. Something that is of a highly sensitive nature, and of critical importance to any future relationship between Earth, Nemeranth and Odomas and the Crucian Species.' Deno looked at me and I could sense that she was reading me. I was absolutely sure that she knew why I had the look of someone who was about to deliver bad news to a friend.

'We have our next mission. We are jumping back to Earth immediately after this briefing.' All eyes were now fixed on me, and I felt the pressure of it, the weight of it, though I could not share this burden with any of them, it was mine alone. I needed to be strong, appear confident and I needed them to trust me, and furthermore we all needed to trust one another, if we were to get the job done.

'Cat, can you bring the data up on the Crucian ship please.' Cat stood up and walked to the console, connecting her chip to it almost instantaneously. At once, there it was in holographic 3D. it was enormous and every detail of the ship that housed our enemy, every room, and every corridor was there in full view for all of us to see.

'Any thoughts about how we enter this thing, we know of course that it's both highly armed and defended?' I looked across the table hoping to start the discussion off.

'It's big.' Said Tommy, as he raised his thick eyebrows, and I could do nothing to stifle the smile, or the laugh that escaped my lips. I smiled at him warmly.

'That it is Tommy. It most certainly is, big.' Everyone laughed and I was glad that it broke the tension that had hung in the room.

'What is our objective Major?' asked Raena, it was the first time she had spoken since our meeting in my quarters.

'Our objective is to infiltrate that ship and retrieve sensitive information from it, without being caught. Deno, Summer, I've assigned you both to this mission.' The rest of the team looked at Deno and Summer, trying to gauge their response.

'Can I take Kevin?' Deno asked. Some laughed whilst others smiled. But I knew that she was trying in her way to make me feel better about what I had asked her to do.

'Deno, you can take Kevin on two conditions. 1. You only use Kevin if your own, or Summers life is at imminent risk, and 2. That you both get back here alive.

Those are my conditions, do you accept?' I looked at Deno's contemplative expression.

'Yes, we accept.'

'We…?'

'Yes, Kevin and I.' I coughed, stifling another laugh, trying to push it back down my throat with a deep swallow.

'And Summer, how do you feel?' Summer looked at the holographic 3D representation of the ship, and then back at me.

'Piece of cake, when do we go?' Summers expression was a casual acknowledgment, it looked like that of a close friend that I had just asked out to lunch, or to go to the movies.

'OK. Thanks Summer, I need all possible access routes into the ship. Does anyone know where those assholes store their data for example?' Raena raised her hand and spoke.

'I do Major, it's in the mid-section of the ship.' Raena's slender finger pointed to the location on the holo-screen.

'The Crucians store all of their data on devices that utilise organic crystals, the ships mainframe is located here.' She raised her hand up, pointed, and kept it perfectly still, so as to indicate a section of the ship that appeared to be central, but was in fact quite close to the ships outer hull. I hoped that perhaps it might just be close enough to not draw too much attention to Deno and Summer.

'So, the next question is how do we get in without being detected?' Summer then interjected.

'Easy, we take a small vehicle, something that they won't be looking for on their scanners. One of the ships repair vehicles should do it. We glide in slowly and silently and then we pop open one of their hull plates, and in we go. I reckon we can be in and out within an hour, two at tops. Adari spoke next.

'Major, I can set up one of our cloaking devices on the craft. To all intents and purposes, it would give Deno and Summer a much better chance of reaching the ship's hull undetected.' I nodded in acknowledgment and approval of Adari's support.

'That's a great suggestion Adari, I will take all the help and ideas I can get, if it gets my crew back here safely. Thank you.' Fetch spoke next.

'Let me go with them.' I turned to face Fetch who had a rare look of concern on her face.

'Go with them? Fetch, stealth really isn't your thing. Why do you want to go with them?'

'Yeah, I know but I wanna go as back up.' I looked around the table and everyone was looking at Fetch as though they were trying to understand her intentions.

'Give me some context Fetch, this mission is a two-person mission, and I really don't want to put any more of you than absolutely necessary at risk, so make your argument a good one.'

'Well Major, a great deal can go on in space whilst you're wandering around trying to succeed at a one of a kind espionage mission, on the inside of a very large and extremely hostile ship. Just let me cover their escape route. I can take the same type of craft. I too can be cloaked, I will mind their transport, entry and exit route, whilst they get on and retrieve the data.' I raised my eyebrows, that wasn't a half bad idea.

'Thoughts everyone?' Nods went around the table and then Joe spoke.

'Major, I think we have our approach and retrieval covered, but what about getting to the data itself?' I acknowledged him, looking first at Summer, then at Cat. Cat held her hand out, and in her palm was a small black circular device which was around four centimetres in diameter. It had a small purple liquid like crystal that was one centimetre in diameter in its centre. The device was smooth across its surface and if Cat hadn't been holding it in her hand, I would have thought it a broach or some kind of elaborate decorative item.

Cat then walked around the table and handed it to me. I felt its smooth surface, toying with it in my hand for a moment.

'What is this?' I said curiously. Cat looked across at Fetch who was now smirking and looking extremely proud of herself.

'This is one of the outcomes of Fetch's arrangements. I looked again at Fetch who was still smirking across the table.

'Fetch, care to enlighten us?' I said interestedly. I was genuinely curious, and I would bet all the money that I had that this would be good.

'Well, it's a data retrieval and storage device, compatible with our systems. To be completely transparent with you Major, its compatible with any system. I acquired it on Makon 5, in the Rigel system several years ago. The really impressive thing about this device is its speed and storage size. I'm told it can download all data from any drive or computing system in a matter of seconds. I'm sharing this item now because I think we need it, and because I want Summer and Deno to have the best chance of getting in and getting out of that ship quickly and safely. If this helps, then that's great.' Fetch had stopped smirking and had a satisfied and proud look across her face.

'Just one question, how did you acquire it?' Fetch rolled her eyes briefly, looked around the table and then spoke again.

'Truthfully… I won it in a card game.' She looked at me a little embarrassed.

'A card game…for real? Do you even know if the damn thing works?' I raised my eyebrows. This wasn't exactly what I hoped she would say.

'Well yes, of course I have tested it.' She said boldly.

'Cat, go with Fetch and test the device, when you have tested it, test it again and then both of you report back to me asap.' Cat nodded, as did Fetch.

'Get that done right now, we need to know the results as soon as it is tested and hopefully ready.'

They both hurriedly left the briefing room. I hesitated before I spoke again, thinking for a moment about how Fetch's ill-gotten gains could help us get Deno and Summer back to the ship safely. I turned and looked out of the viewing window once more, sighting Pluto in the distance.

'Summer, can you share with everyone what the plan is once you reach the Crucian ship.' Summer stepped up to the holographic display and highlighted a small section in the middle area of the ship.

'Just, here, this is our best way in. It's the safest too. It does mean however, that Deno and I will have to navigate our way down three decks to retrieve the data, but in terms of distance and in terms of the number of obstacles that we are likely to encounter, this is the best route by far.'

Summer enlarged the image on the screen and drew a path with her index finger. It looked simple enough, but I knew that what I was seeing on the screen would not be entirely accurate as to what they might encounter once they were on board the ship.

The briefing room door slid open, and Cat and Fetch strode back in. I could see that they both had a look of accomplishment on their faces, and I hurriedly invited them back to the table to report in.

'Major, we can confirm that the device works perfectly. We trialled it with the Amaranthine's data and then deleted it. It took us exactly forty-one point two seconds to complete the entire process, including deletion. I would however like to suggest that Summer takes a backup just in case there are any unforeseen problems with it, or the Crucians technology.'

'That sounds like a solid plan. Summer was just showing us all the route that she and Deno will take. Got any thoughts, Cat, Fetch?'

Fetch looked at the screen closely, I could see her trying to work out if there was a quicker route, whilst Cat ran several calculations on her chip. Then at the exact same time, they spoke.

'No Ma'am.' They looked at each other and Cat magnanimously allowed Fetch to continue first.

'Looks solid to me, when do we leave?' Cat nodded, acknowledging Fetch.

'I was going to say almost the same thing. When do they leave Major?' Cat commented, her tone serious.

I took a second to consider when they would leave to begin the mission, gnawing irritatingly at my gut was the feeling that holding off too long only meant that we would have less time to plan any actions from the outcome of the mission. But going in now, without food and some preparation time could mean they weren't going to be at their best. I needed them to be at the top of their game. I needed them to come through this.

'I want you to get some rest, eat, and be ready to go at 01:00 hours sharp. Report to deck seventeen at 00:45 hours. We need as fewer Crucians as possible walking around that ship when you breach their hull. This mission is above Top Secret and as such you are not permitted to discuss anything that has been shared in this room, with anyone. Am I clear?'

'Yes Major.' they all said in unison.

'Dismissed.'

They hurriedly left the room, all except for Raena. I stood gazing out of the window. My mind drifted and I once again began studying the terrain and the many mountain ranges that covered much of Pluto's surface. I thought I was on my own, stood in my own silence, until I turned around and saw her standing there. She was still looking at the holographic screen, studying it with a concerned look upon her face.

'Sorry Raena, I didn't mean to be rude. I didn't know you were still there.' I said quietly.

She looked down for a moment and then directly out of the window. 'It's an interesting Planet, isn't it?' she said, her voice soft and calm.

'Well, you know, that exceedingly small dwarf planet has been through a lot. Hundreds of years ago they said she was a planet, then they said she wasn't big enough to be one, I think they kind of got caught up in the whole, size matters thing. But to me when you look at her and see the geology, the mountain ranges, and the basins, how can she not be a planet. Small, but perfectly formed. Sometimes, I think even scientists miss what is right in front of them.' Raena laughed.

'Major, our people would say that Pluto is a planet. I think your people, do her a great disservice. But regardless of what they say she is, she is certainly incredibly special. She has held a mystery, and a secret for over four billion years. A secret that I believe is yet to fully unfold, and one that starts with a star map and an ancient pathway. Think about it Major, if this site is so old, then how old are the map makers?' She smiled at me, contemplatively and then looked back at Pluto.

'A pathway, don't you mean multiple pathways there were after all, six charts.

'No Major. I believe that all seven are part of one larger destination. I believe that all seven are also integral to the other seven.'

'Don't you mean six?' I said curiously.

'No. I mean seven, including Pluto. I believe that Pluto is the first, leaving another six.' I acknowledged her with a look of pleasant surprise, I could see her logic.

'Think of Pluto as the first light on the path to wherever this journey will take us.'

'I really do like how you think Raena, are all Okai so intuitive and such deep thinkers?'

'Many are, yes. Can I be open with you Major?' She looked a little pensive.

'Yes of course, please go on.'

'The smooth object you held in your hand on Pluto, have we retrieved it to the ship?'

'I imagine so, but I've not seen it since the incident.'

'Would you mind if I studied it Major?' A surprised look crossed my face.

'Not at all, but I must insist on safety measures. We still don't know what it did to me, and I must state that for the record, that I am still pretty concerned about it.' I touched my arm and opened a channel on my chip.

'Can you give full access, but with all appropriate safety protocols to Raena for full examination of the object that was retrieved from Pluto.' A voice replied acknowledging the order. Raena was still looking at Pluto, studying its surface and the empty space around it. Then she turned to me and spoke once again.

'I wonder what and who was there less than fifty Earth years ago.' I paused and thought back to the beautiful crystal archway, and all of those stars. I hadn't thought once about that, since Cats initial scans alerted us to the possibility. Too much had happened in the space in between, but the comment was not lost on Raena, and I was grateful for her recall of it. I took a moment to compose my thoughts once again, looking out towards Pluto, as if she alone could give me the answers that I sought.

'I think I'm curious as to what, as well as who. I must acknowledge to myself that it all seems utterly impossible… 4.2 billion years old, and yet if Cat's and the Light Seekers scans are accurate, it was utilised by something or someone just a mere thirty to fifty years ago… If that is true, I cannot even begin to speculate on its purpose, or its origins.

It blows my mind if I'm being honest with you Raena.' Raena approached me, standing only a couple of feet away. She looked genuinely intrigued by my emotions and she raised her hand, placing it momentarily on the top of my arm. I could feel the heat of her warm hand, as it gently rested on my uniform sleeve. She looked deeply into my eyes, with real and absolute honesty in her manner, which was written across her face. I was a worldly woman, but I confess that I had not experienced the Okai's pureness of thought and sincerity before, and for just a few seconds, it utterly pierced my resolve, as did her words.

'Major. We will find the answers you are looking

for. I promise you this.' She looked away briefly and then directly back at me, her tone was now much more serious and determined.

'We can begin exploring the pathway, once we have dealt with those Crucian brutes that are docked just off your home planet. I say we jump to Earth and get the mission underway as soon as possible.' I smiled at her determination, but not for a single moment did I doubt any of it.

'Thank you Raena, I think we are going to need that strong will of yours in the coming hours and–.'

I immediately stopped mid conversation as the door slid open almost silently, as Deno strode into the room, the soles of her boots squeaking against the high gloss floor. She must have felt really awkward, as she paused for a brief moment in mid-flight, she stood perfectly still and then made this little coughing noise. It was something I had never heard her do before, but it certainly got my attention.

I noticed the most inquisitive look on her face, her right eyebrow was raised, and I was certain she was intensely studying Raena for whatever reason. She was trying so hard to be subtle, but it was probably the most unsubtle thing I had ever seen her do, and that was saying a lot.

'Well… will you please excuse me Major, I had better get back to it and take a look at the object retrieved from Pluto. But please do let me know if I can be of any further assistance.' Before I could respond to her, she headed speedily towards the door and it closed quietly behind her, which left just myself and Deno who was momentarily speechless and in absolute silence, just looking at each other.

'What the hell was that?' I felt stunned, I needed a

moment to understand what had just happened. But why did I feel like a five-year-old whose mom had just caught her with her hand in the cookie jar, just before dinner? Deno smirked and then her smirk became a grin.

'What?' I said trying to work out why she was beaming.

'What? Why the hell are you grinning like that Deno?'

'Oh, we need to talk, but properly and off duty, after this mission, see now this mission just has to be a success because you and I, we deffo gotta talk about dat body language, right there and observed by yours truly… And Kevin of course.'

'What are you talking about? Body language? What body language?'

'Uh huh, it's OK ya know. It's kinda normal, even for Majors, I mean these things happen, certain number of people, all tightly packed together on a ship, no room to breathe.'

'What on earth are you talking about, Raena and I were just discussing the object that was retrieved from Pluto and the mission ahead of us, she actually makes a lot of sense you know.'

'Uh huh, but damn you got some kinda connection with her.'

'Connect… what? Oh… connection…Nah, Deno you are imagining it, it's just not there, we were just talking about that object we retrieved from Pluto, and besides.' I paused, trying to gather my composure, but for some reason I just couldn't get the words out of my mouth right, I could feel myself heating up, but this time, oddly it was just my face.

'Chief Martin, I will gladly drink your ass under the

table after the successful completion of this mission. Hell, I'll even buy the drinks, but this topic is now closed.' I smiled.

'Do I make myself clear, Chief Martin?' I was still smiling.

'Yes Ma'am, but can I say, purely and just for the record and only ever once in this room, that chemistry is like water, eventually it's gonna find a way through the cracks.' And with that she turned on her heels and bounced out of the room. I stood frozen to the spot momentarily, but I somehow managed to run my hands through my hair whilst trying extremely hard to take in what had just happened, paying full attention to the moment, whilst also trying to absorb what Deno said she had just noticed. It couldn't be true, no, put it out of your head… Deno had dreamed it all up, in that fertile little imagination of hers and besides… I couldn't spend any more time on it, I had a job to do.

∞

There was a buzz of electricity on deck seventeen, the kind of buzz that I had only ever experienced when about to start a critical mission. I made my way towards a group of personnel, there must have been at least fifty of them, all surrounding my squad. One of the first things that I noticed was the bright white lighting that illuminated the area around where the small spacecraft were being kitted out. Engineers were busily working on the two vehicles that would be utilised for the mission.

Fetch, Deno, and Summer were stood together talking, it looked to me like they were running through the missions plan. All three of them were fully engaged deeply within their conversation, so much so that they didn't look up as I approached them.

They looked mission ready and were wearing their fully equipped armour suits, minus their helmets. Chief Watts had changed the colour of their suits to adaptive carbon black which meant that the suits would change colour based on their surroundings. The three of them looked different somehow, and I couldn't make my mind up whether it was the stealth like colouring of their suits, or just the way that they were all stood. But one thing was for certain, everyone I could see on the flight deck looked to be taking their responsibility to the mission very seriously, this put my mind at rest, if only a little.

I knew that Deno was quirky, boy was that an understatement, but I also knew that she could switch in an instant to become someone you really wouldn't want to encounter as your adversary. Summer just looked as sleek as ever, even in the suit. How did she do that? I could almost see the cogs turning in her mind’s eye, she was weighing up the options and outcomes, and she hadn't even left the ship.

Fetch stood stretching her back out, she looked as tense as a coiled snake ready to strike and was clenching her jaw. This was one of her tells, and I knew she must be feeling just a little on edge. But when push came to shove, Fetch was one of the best pilots on Earth, and if anyone could pull Deno and Summer out of trouble, should the need arise, it was her.

As I approached them the ship’s crew members that were stood around them parted quickly. I acknowledged them all, walking past them as they immediately saluted me. I beckoned Deno, Fetch and Summer over towards me and I asked the staff around me, to clear some space so that I could talk with them in private.

They stood in a small semi-circle, and I had to admit they looked the part. I for one, was glad that I wasn't a Crucian. I had every word planned, what I wanted, no, needed to say to them. But when I looked at their faces, I just chose to go with my gut and not the rehearsed garble that I had toyed with in my head.

'You all ready? How are you feeling? I found myself caught in the moment, wondering what the next couple of hours would bring.

'I er… well. I wanted to tell you how proud I am of the three of you. Who would have thought that a couple of weeks ago we would be stood here?' I swallowed deeply.

'Anyhow… I just wanted to wish you luck and a safe mission. I know I don't need to tell you how to do your jobs, because I know you are all the best at what you do. But I just wanted to say that if there is anything you need or any questions you have before you leave, now is the time to ask.'

I rested my hands behind my back and noticed that damn tingling again in my arms… *not now*. I gripped my hands together tightly, almost to the point of pain.

Fetch spoke first, her jaw tight and her stance equally so, her purple hair catching the lighting of the flight deck, every strand taking on a slightly different hue. It looked quite incredible.

'We'll get the job done Major and thank you for listening to and considering my request. Ya know I just couldn't let my pals onto that ship without a plan b… just in case. But hopefully, it won't be needed.' She nodded, turned on her heel, and made her way swiftly towards her craft.

'Safe journey Fetch.' I shouted, as she turned slightly towards me raising a single arm in acknowledgment, before turning back to face the ships atmospheric shield, and her way off the ship.

I could see the Amaranthine's technicians running final tests on her craft, checking everything was in order. Fetch straddled the craft like she was preparing to ride a powerful motor bike, easing slowly into position, almost becoming one with its form. I looked at the tiny craft, hoping that they would remain undetected on their approach to the cruiser. Summer and Deno were stood waiting patiently for the go ahead to board their craft and get the mission started.

'You two ready? Listen, I know this is a big ask, like really big. I just wanted to say stay safe and look after each other out there. You are the only two people on the entire planet that I trust with this mission, so it goes without saying, get the job done and get out fast, and take no unnecessary risks, and definitely no sightseeing. That's an order.' Summer was the first to speak, her soft voice was filled with strength.

'Major, leave it to us. Deno has my six and I have hers.' She looked at Deno and then across towards where a handsome man stood by a stack of freight, he paused checking some of the contents off his holo-pad, occasionally glancing up from his task, he was most definitely fascinated by one of us.

'Lot's to come back for Major.' Summer winked mischievously as she took one last look at the man with the cargo who now appeared to be doing extraordinarily little with it. She smiled, turned, and headed towards Fetch. Deno stood there smirking like she was reading the entire deck of a pack of cards.

'Ha! Remember Major, it's just like I said, certain number of people, all tightly packed together on a ship, no room to breathe.' She smirked once more, winked at me, turned, and headed off towards Fetch and Summer.

Summer was now sat upright on the small craft and Deno quickly alighted, fastening herself into the rear seat. She turned to face me briefly and yelled at the top of her voice.

'Remember. When we get back Major the drinks are on you!'

'And… there it is…' I smiled to myself as I walked briskly to the front of their craft, the engine thrusters were on, and I knew that they were about to speed out of the hanger and into the vacuum of space. I didn't get the chance to say another word to them, as they began to move slowly at first, then gaining speed, they sped out of the hanger. As I watched them, and their craft begin to disappear from my field of view. I pleaded silently, looking out to the cosmos that it wouldn't be the last time that I would ever see them.

∞

Summer and Deno's craft led the way, whilst Fetch kept a respectful distance of around one hundred meters behind them. The vehicles moved swiftly at first, the plan was to gather speed, switch off the engines and then cruise in silently with just a brief and final blast of the thrusters to stop them all from hitting the Crucian ship.

I left the hanger as soon as they were out of my sight and made my way towards the bridge. I was thankful that I was alone. I recognised the need for just a few minutes to myself and my own thoughts, as I walked in solitude along the long corridors from the hanger on deck seventeen that would take me to the lift.

The entire ship's crew had an energy, this was what the Amaranthine was built for, and what her crew were trained for, and I was as sure as I could be that she, and they would be tested soon enough. On entering the lift, I was joined by Joe who entered a few seconds after me, he looked pensive as if his mind were ablaze with a myriad of thoughts.

'Major, did Cat happen to mention to you that we recovered several new artifacts. Some of which we managed to translate, well small segments of them at least… from the site on Pluto?'

'No Joe, but then I have been busy, and we haven't really had the chance to catch up since we got back, is everything alright Joe?' Joe shuffled on the balls of his feet.

'Yes Major, it's just…' This wasn't like Joe. He was holding back.

'Yes… what is it?'

'Well, Pluto….' He paused again.

'Yes, what about Pluto Joe?'

'Well….' Again, another pause. What the hell was going on?

'Joe, please just say what's on your mind.'

'We found something else, Cat and I wanted to tell you but…'

'What did you find, please Joe, it has been a long day and I'm tired'

'Well, it's a record of some kind, our science team are still trying to decipher it fully.'

'A record, a record of what?' I was intrigued, it wasn't like Joe to be as preoccupied as this.

'Well Major, this is where it gets… well, I don't even have the words for what I'm about to say.' He looked at me somewhat anxiously, again this was unlike Joe.

'Joe, you need to find the words. But make it quick, I'm heading to the bridge to see if we have an update on the current mission.'

'Major, part of the records we found contained a DNA profile, as you know DNA is like a universal thing, and well…'

'Joe, where on Earth is this going?'

'The profile, we looked at it, ran some tests on it, and ran it through the AI. As I said we are still trying to interpret the rest of it, but the DNA at least we understand some of what it is telling us.'

'So where did you find this DNA trace?'

'It was in the room, you remember the medical room, the one where the Professor and Cat picked up the initial DNA trace. The one that identified that something or someone was there as little as thirty to fifty years ago.' His face looked tired and strained, he was struggling with this conversation, and it was not like him. He was usually so calm, he was utterly reliable and a logical thinker, and yet this appeared to have him rocked to his very core. The lift opened and I stepped out onto the bridge.

'Major, can we talk in the briefing room, it will only take a moment?'

'Yes of course Joe.' I followed him into the room and the sounds from the bridge disappeared as the door closed silently behind us.

'What is it, what's going on? I don't think I've ever seen you like this.'

'Major, there is no other way to say this and before I start, I want you to know that we will get to the bottom of this, I promise you that. The DNA profile we found… well we ran it through Earths databases, really, we only did this as part of our standard protocol, and well with the situation being as it is. Well, we wanted to rule out further espionage. We really didn't expect... well, we really didn't expect what we found. Major, the DNA, it matches yours.'

All at once I felt myself become completely confused and lightheaded. None of what he had just said made any sense, nothing made any sense anymore, what the hell was happening to me? I felt panic run the length of my entire body, and then Joe's hand steadied me.

'Major. Is everything alright?' He said, concerned.

'I'm fine Joe, it's just… are you sure? Could it be a mistake?'

'Major, it is as it appears to be, a perfect match, of course it will need to be tested further but–'

'Who else knows about this?' I almost spat the words out of my mouth.

'No one, only myself and Cat. We wanted to let you know, but we also wanted to ask you, do you have any knowledge about this? Anything at all, any memory of Pluto, or any possible reason this could have occurred?'

'No Joe, I'm afraid I don't. Can we keep this between the three of us, just for now? I will allow full testing of myself and whatever else needs to happen, but let's get Deno, Summer and Fetch through this mission first. OK?'

'Yes Major, Cat and I would like to speak again with you, once it's dealt with. By then Cat may know more. I have to say, she is really intrigued by this.'

'As am I. To be honest with you, that's an understatement. I am also very concerned about this. Thanks Joe, I mean for telling me. I don't understand any of it, and the longer this goes on, the more questions I have. But this… well. How can anyone have a frame of reference for this? You are telling me that my DNA was found in that room, on the text of an Alien document of some kind, that we found on Pluto, in a building that's just over four billion years old, that self-repairs, and... Oh….' I stopped speaking, as it slowly began to dawn on me.

'Major?' Joe beckoned me to continue speaking.

'Joe, the device, the mist!' My mind flashed back to the device activating when I picked it up. The look of shock on Joe's face was evident, as he too realised the same as I.

'The mist. Major it went towards you. The device, it must have activated when you picked it up.' Joe spoke excitedly.

'Yes, yes it did, but why?' We stood and looked at each other trying to work it out.

'So, my DNA is connected to that base in some way?'

'We must acknowledge that it is a distinct possibility.' Joe said, as I began to pace back and forth, as a solitary piece appeared to fit the puzzle, but still I couldn't put it all together.

'OK. Joe, update Cat in private. No one else is to know at this stage. I want to speak with you both later and we can take it from there.'

I left the briefing room, as did Joe. A voice called out from the console. It was Summer.

'Making our final approach, going to radio silence. Wish us luck, complete radio silence in 3. 2. 1.' And with that the comm cut out.

∞

The blackened hull of the Crucian ship grew closer, its sheer size was immense and utterly overwhelming to the threesome who looked smaller than ants against its enormous hull. Deno leant forwards tapping Summer gently on the shoulder and pointing towards the section of hull that they were soon about to enter.

Summer steered the craft steadily, holding her breath and inching her way closer to it, until they were only a few feet away from its gigantic, blackened metallic surface. The sound of the thrusters were like that of loud whispers through their suits, but they were sufficiently silent in the vacuum of space and hoped that they would not be detected by sound alone.

Fetch arrived soon after, repeating their actions perfectly and placing her craft flush against the hull. Both craft now held their positions, they were merely feet away from the outer shell of the ship and their intended point of entry.

Deno unbuckled herself first, removing a long two pronged fork shaped tool from her pack, she glided effortlessly to the ship's hull, the tips of her antigravity boots acting like magnets on its outer surface, holding her steadily in place. With the specialist engineering tool gripped tightly in her hand, she began to hurriedly work to remove a small section of the outer plating of the cruisers hull. Meanwhile, Summer ran a series of diagnostic scans to check that they hadn't been detected. Fetch retrieved her weapons from the storage locker at the rear of her craft. Then moving carefully, she mounted the craft once more, sitting in total silence, flush against the Crucian cruisers hull.

After several minutes Deno waved to them both and gave the thumbs up to Summer as she made the final adjustments to the hexagonal section of the outer hull. Seconds later, it lifted clean off revealing a small access shaft that led deeper inside the ship to a maintenance airlock, this would be their single point of entry. Deno then attached several small magnets to the inner hull plate that she had just removed, resting it gently against the ships outer hull where it lodged firmly into place, the small magnets holding it perfectly secure.

The hole was one and a half meters in diameter which was more than enough space for Deno and Summer to squeeze through, Summer signalled to Deno that she was ready to begin her entry. With a final hand signal to each other they began to carefully enter the opening. They signalled to Fetch that they were ready to continue onward, as Fetch began to hunker down on her craft. She resembled a lioness, silently waiting for its prey.

Inside the entry shaft were markings and measurements, all in Crucian. Deno lead the way as the pair crawled slowly on their hands and knees for around twenty metres or so down the slender metal tunnel, before reaching the small maintenance shafts airlock. Deno placed her hand on the circular mechanism that would release the hatch. With a single twist, the mechanism turned, and the hatchway opened, releasing a sharp gust of residual gas that had been trapped in the airlock previously. Moving slightly backwards Deno gently pulled the hatch to the fully open position and then she carefully continued forwards.

Inside the airlock around four metres in, was a second hatch that led to the interior of the ship. Even so, they both were aware that there would be no gravity in the second, larger section that they were about to enter. Though if the intel was correct, the atmosphere would at least be breathable. Once summer was inside the airlock, Deno closed the hatch behind them, whilst checking it was secure. She then moved across to the inner airlock and repeated the process, this time there was an even greater rush from the airlock, it was breathable air.

'Take or leave the helmets?' Deno whispered, as Summer began to move carefully towards the hatch.

'Take them and wear them just in case. What if we need a new route out? We'll be pretty stuffed without our helmets Deno.'

'Good point. Helmets it is then.' She said, as she tapped the side of her head, to signify where her brain was located.

The pair swiftly left the hatch and soon encountered a cavernous, dark and eery space which was filled with miles of white electro-organic wiring. The entire inside of the cruisers vast space was dimly lit by masses of dark red safety lighting, intended only to guide Crucian engineers with their maintenance tasks and routine ship repairs.

Deno and Summer quickly realised that they could barely see anything at all, other than the outline of the ships inner hull and the framework of what looked like the cruisers many decks. The red safety lighting wasn't illuminating the dark spaces of the ships interior space nearly enough for their human eyes to compensate for or adapt.

They began to carefully follow the route of the many wires and panels that were situated right in front of their faces. Suddenly, Deno signalled to Summer, indicating for her to change the setting on her helmet, both switched their helmets to night vision which immediately revealed a much clearer pathway, whilst also exposing the bulk of the inner structure of the ship. The ships internal void was enormous, revealing just how vast a space they were navigating. They descended slowly down two of the outer decks in almost pitch blackness, carefully and gently they went, allowing their anti-gravitational boots to pull them even further down, until they eventually reached the outer walls and ceilings above where the two rooms they were seeking were located.

The rooms were situated off the main corridor of the deck, the outer shell of the inner hull looked identical to every other floor, both above, and below. Deno studied the outer structure of the deck that was immediately below them and sighted a larger area off to one side of the ships corridors, a room that she immediately recognised from the holo-plans at the briefing to be the mainframe server room for the ship.

This was exactly what they were looking for. They made their way cautiously and quietly towards it, trying not to make contact with any other part of the ship, as they proceeded slowly downwards one final deck, allowing gravity once again to do the work for them.

Deno's boots touched the outer ceiling of the mainframe and server room first, her feet slowly and softly connecting with the flat blackened surface, she bent her knees to cushion the impact, and this resulted in her landing almost completely silently. Summer landed soon after and directly opposite Deno, motioning her to locate and remove the ceiling panel so that they could enter the room.

Deno worked steadily and carefully, eventually removing the panel and placing it to the side of her. Summer then entered the room soundlessly, dropping to the floor whilst quickly gathering her wits, taking in her immediate surroundings.

Her poise though, told a much different story, Summer was ready to do whatever it took to retrieve the information. She would remove any apparent threat in the room, efficiently and without a second thought. She was an effective and deadly operative, and this was by far the most important mission of her life.

Once she knew it was safe to proceed, she looked up at the gaping hole above her head and beckoned Deno down towards her. Deno landed on the floor, Kevin in hand, ready to engage any hostiles, but fortunately for the Crucians, on this occasion non were to be found.

Summer identified and approached the Crucian ships main server. She could see countless tiny red lights that were blinking on and off, these indicated power flow, to and from the unit. Taking a small flat device from her pack, which was scarlet red in colour, she located an access slot and steadily pushed the device into the server, inserting a bio-wire from it directly into her facial visor port.

She stood observing the rows and rows of complex data that appeared in front of her eyes for a moment, trying to locate the information that Mitchell had asked her to retrieve. There was just so much of it, what were the Crucians collecting, why was there so much information on Earth culture, music, the arts, and social activities? Suddenly her facial expression changed from calm and determined concentration, to one of sheer horror and shock.

'Oh, no, no, no. This can't be… No! Deno, we need to tell them, they have no idea what's coming. We need to get back to the ship!'

Summer was hurriedly searching the Crucian Ships database, she looked panicked, and Summer never looked panicked. Deno took a couple of steps back to where Summer was still reading what had appeared on her visor during the data search.

'The storage device… take it.' Deno pushed the device into Summers palm, and she attached it to the server. The device lit up immediately and began downloading the ships data. Deno turned to Summer and touched her shoulder, trying to get her attention, but Summer wouldn't look away from the servers operating panel.

'Summer! What are you doing?' Deno said, her voice concerned.

'The data we must… pass me my pack now!' Summer pleaded with Deno, there was exasperation written across her face. Deno paused, just for a split second, and then reaching for Summers pack, she quickly handed it to her.

'What's wrong Summer, what the hell is going on?' Deno looked shaken, she had never seen her like this.

'Thanks, Deno, I'll explain later, but this should buy us some time... I hope.' She opened the pack revealing ten data sticks, pulling one of the sticks out of the pack and studying it, she held it for a moment in her hand, toying with it. The stick had a single black spider image on it, but other than that it was completely blood red in colour.

'Please work…' She said expectantly, as she pushed the stick into a socket on the server.

'Deno, is the download of the ships data complete?' There was a look of panic and utter urgency upon her face.

'Yes, it's just finishing, it will be complete in… twenty seconds.

'Deno, we must make it back, we need to do everything right and get back undetected, do you understand. I've done my best to try and buy us some time but….'

'What's going on? What do you mean buy us some time?' Deno's face changed from concern to one of high alert.

'It's bad Deno, really bad… but now is not the time, I can't distract you anymore than I already have. Quick, help me make this room look like we were never here.'

Deno and Summer straightened the room up, Fetch's device completing its download with no issues. Deno removed it quickly from the server, slipping it into her pack and double checking that the item and the pack was secure. She then gestured without a sound to Summer that the download was complete, letting her know that the storage device was secure. They hurriedly made their way back to the entry point in the ceiling of the room, checking the room to make sure that it looked as if they had never been there.

Deno stood under the open gap in the ceiling and clasped her hands tightly together. Summer then lifted her leg placing her boot snuggly into Deno's hands. Putting all her physicality into the boost by pushing every bit of her strength into that single movement, Summer was able to effortlessly pull herself up and through the open void to the entry points exterior.

'Shit that really hurt.' Deno mumbled to herself.

'What's wrong, are you ok?' Summer looked down and directly into Deno's pained eyes.

'Think I've pulled my shoulder somehow. It will be fine. We just need to get back.' She winced.

Then lying flat on her front, Summer reached down towards Deno, who raised her arms towards Summers hands. She pulled Deno upwards and through the same small gap with every bit of her body's power, grabbing Deno firmly under both of her armpits in the hope that

Deno would at least be able to lever herself upwards.

Deno winced once more, as she exerted herself again, her body weight fighting against her own bodies strength, as she finally managed to heave herself onto the roof of the now vacant room. Once Deno was safely through the void, Summer quickly looked into Deno's eyes, she was clearly concerned.

'You alright?' Summer said, there was a worried tone to her voice.

'Yep, that sure was a bit of a stretch though, but thanks… I'm fine. Think I might have pulled my left shoulder pretty bad though. I'll get the Medics to give me the once over when we get back.' Deno grimaced again, she was making light of it, as she always did, but was clearly in some considerable pain.

The two gently replaced the panel over the void in the ceiling, clicking it back into place. Simultaneously, they released the anti-gravity controls on their boots, utilising two small boosters that were fitted to the rear of their suits on their backs, and two boosters that were located on the outer edge their boots heels. This had the effect of slowly elevating and easing them upwards and back towards the outer hull hatch, which only thirty minutes earlier they had entered.

Fetch was sitting perfectly still, scanning for any activity around her, her posture had become set, like that of solid ice waiting to be carved and heated into the fluid movement of water. The only part of her body that had any movement whatsoever were those pale blue eyes, eyes that could convey whether or not you would live or die, if ever you were to cross her.

The vehicles clung to the outside of the enormous craft, like ticks on a dog, and were almost completely imperceptible to the human eye. Fetch silently hoped to herself that they would give the Crucians much more than an itch to scratch. From where she was positioned, she could see the Amaranthine clearly in the distance, its lights twinkling like beacons, calling them home.

She pushed her emotions back down into her chest as this was where she was most comfortable with them. She wasn't known for her sentimentality and usually came across as a bit of a hard ass to those that didn't know her better, but today, even she couldn't get away from the fact that other than Deno and Summer, everyone, and everything that she secretly cared about was either on board that ship, or on the distant blue planet directly in front of her.

The first one to appear at the access point was Deno, followed just mere moments later by Summer. Fetch drew in a deep, and unspoken breath of relief into her lungs. She indicated with a simple thumbs up that she was pleased to see them both back at the craft safely. But truth be told, inside herself and under thinning the shield of her emotions, she was elated.

Being the oldest of Mitchell's eight, she felt responsible for their safety, and this was one of the reasons that she had volunteered herself for the mission. The other being that underneath her tough exterior, was a deeply caring person, though she would rather shoot you between the eyes than acknowledge this to herself, or you for that matter. No, where Fetch was concerned matters of the heart were definitely subjects to steer clear away from.

The three began to make their way slowly, silently, and steadily away from the Crucian ship. All three held onto their breath, barely daring to inhale, no one uttered a single word, as every second felt like a great cavernous vacuum that was only filled by the perilous urgency of their situation.

Summer found herself repeatedly running through her mind time and time, again and again, everything that she had just observed, knowing that she couldn't afford to doubt herself now.

She felt the weight of it, it lay heavy on her conscience as she was tried to work out how she would relay the information that she had uncovered back to Mitchell. She felt it in the pit of her stomach, a sinking, and an uncomfortably strange feeling that arose in her throat, which she soon realised was a symptom of extreme emotional upset. She swallowed down hard, trying to force it to leave her, but it wouldn't go, it sat with her like an unwelcome guest, refusing to leave.

Meanwhile, back on the bridge, crew members were bustling about in a haze of activity, checking sensors again and again for any sign of their away squads movements. Then a call out came from one of the tactical operations crew.

'Major, all three are on their way back to the ship. They've just left Crucians ships inner sensor range, if all goes to plan, they should be back on the Amaranthine shortly.' His voice was clearly energised with the news.

'That is excellent news.' I said, my tone was one of relief. 'I'm going to go and meet them when they arrive. Joe, contact me on route if there are any further updates.'

I made my way quickly off the Bridge, beckoning Raena and Adari to come along with me. Running at pace, we soon we entered the flight deck. Two of the decks shuttle landing plates were lit up, the bright blue lighting was strobing towards the centre of the

Amaranthine, indicating that allied craft were incoming.

I looked out of the flight deck and into space, but I couldn't see them. Their craft were small, and we wouldn't know that they were back safe, until they were almost upon us. I turned towards Raena and Adari, Raena saw me looking towards them and spoke instantaneously, it was as if she had been waiting for the right moment to say something.

'You are deeply concerned Major, and yet they return unharmed.' She said warmly.

'Yes, Raena. I am very worried about all of this. Ever since Deno and I witnessed what took place on Earth with Jevargh, I just can't shake the feeling that there is going to be some kind of a reckoning, and soon. I put their lives at risk today in order to try and piece together what is happening, and I feel the responsibility of it, I really do. I know that it's their job, hell it's my job to deal with these things… but still.' I immediately drew a line on this train of thought, as I felt it begin to engulf my emotions with the sheer magnitude of it all.

Not surprisingly, the tingling sensation in my arms began to return once more, running from the tips of my fingertips all the way up my arms over my shoulders and into base of my skull. I wondered for a moment if it might be linked to the stress, anxiety and worry that I was feeling right now.

I squeezed my hands tightly once again, applying significant pressure at the palms, hoping that the sensation would cease, as it had done before. From what I could tell, it didn't appear to be subsiding. This phenomenon was making me feel really uncomfortable now, and I could only hope that I wouldn't be consumed by it on the deck of my ship.

'Raena, Adari. I need to fully debrief them on their return. Please can you contact and gather the rest of my eight? Ensure that the briefing room is prepped and cleared of all non-essential crew. This is a pivotal moment for us all.' I swiftly turned around, facing towards the decks entrance once more, my eyes solidly fixed upon it's opening.

Standing there, looking out to space felt like an eternity. Even after being reassured by many of the engineering and deck personnel that it would only be two minutes and thirty seconds before their crafts re-entered the flight deck. I felt sick to my stomach, I couldn't shake the stress that I was feeling, and I kept asking myself what, if anything they had found. My eyes were now aching in an effort to blink once more, as I continued to wait in earnest.

Thankfully, a few minutes later I acknowledged that the deck crew were right. Fetch sped in, touching down first. She hurriedly unbuckled herself from the craft and began walking over towards me. Summer and Deno followed suit soon after. Deno was hurriedly helping Summer off the craft, and I noticed that the left side of her body looked to be a little stiff. She appeared to be grimacing, her left side did not look as mobile as the rest of her body. I jogged quickly over towards them, and the three immediately gathered around me.

'Welcome back, let's make our way to the briefing room. Deno are you alright?' I asked curiously.

'Yep Major, I just pulled my left shoulder on the way out. It's giving me some pain, but I will be fine.'

'And you, Summer, are you ok?' Summer had a look of gravity written upon her face.

'Major, I need to brief you. Can we speak in private?' She spoke with urgency, and this was not like Summer.

'Yes, of course. I've asked Raena and Adari to gather everyone to the briefing room, let's go there right now.'

As we entered the briefing room, everyone sat down. The room was quieter than usual, everyone looked unsettled and somewhat serious. I made my way to my chair, sitting down and then looking across the table towards Summer, Deno and Fetch. Their faces looked severe, gone was the banter and the smiles. Everyone in the room seemed to have noticed Summer's demeanour in particular, and if they were picking up what I was, it would explain the look written upon their faces.

'I guess I don't need to explain why we are here, Summer, Deno and Fetch have just returned from their successful mission to infiltrate the Crucian ship currently docked off Earth. Summer will brief us on her findings, and then we can discuss these in further detail, OK?'

Everyone around the table nodded, recognising my request to allow Summer to speak. I glanced once again towards Summer who was doing something on her chip. She then stood and began pacing a little, as if she were trying to work out where she should start.

'Major, I'm going to try and take the emotions out of what I am feeling before I deliver this debrief. This is because what I have uncovered will evoke an emotional response in you all. I err… I just need to get it out there before I begin, I can't prepare you in any other way.' She sat back in her chair stiffening her back before she continued. 'As you may be aware, we successfully managed to board the Crucian battle cruiser V124. Once Chief Martin and I located the ships mainframe, I was then able to hack into the ships onboard computer in an attempt to source further information on main objective of the mission, which was to retrieve the data that Jevargh had recently transmitted from Earth up to their ship.' She looked up and down the table, ensuring that she had our attention before continuing.

'The data is that which Jevargh spoke of in his conversation with the unknown Crucian chancellor and a representative from Species X. Our mission was also, if we were able to, retrieve the entire Crucian ships database. With the assistance of Chief Martin, and Second Lieutenant Martinez's device, we were also successful in doing this'. She looked directly at me, both her demeanour and tone of voice becoming more serious.

'Major, I'm sorry… There is no other way to say this. Major, the Crucians are planning to attack Earth within the next twenty-four hours.' Summer's voice petered off, revealing her sadness.

I stood up, leaving my chair, looking out of the viewing window towards their ship.

'Summer. You say they plan to attack us, are you absolutely sure?'

I turned and placed the palms of my hands onto the briefing room table, realising that that damn tingling sensation was back in my hands once again. I clenched my fists tightly, moving my hands from the table and resting them upon my hips. The sensation ceased in my hands ceased as soon as I did so, providing some momentary relief.

'Major, it gets worse, much much worse. I need to

tell you what their plans are, and then I need to tell you what I have done. I hope that you will support my decision… there just wasn't any time.' She looked resolute, but I needed to know just what in hell she had done.

'Tell us Summer, and don't spare any of the detail.' I urged her to continue.

'The information that Jevargh transmitted to the ship. Well, it was in relation to the location and infrastructure of our entire education and childcare systems on Earth. There was also additional information in relation to childcare centres, creche's, youth recreation, schools, and universities etc. I found detailed information on every country, that currently has a child under the age of five years of age. Basically Major, all known locations of where all of Earths children and young adults reside and socialise, specifically those under the age of twenty-one. The data also suggests that they have acquired similar strategic information on the Nadaal and the Okai.' She finally took a breath.

I moved away from the table and my eight for a moment, trying to gather my thoughts, whilst noticing that my heart was racing.

'So… why did they take information linking to our children's whereabouts? Oh shit! They are going to attack and kill our children. Summer, do you have any further information that might validate this?'

'Yes, Major I do. Hidden deep within their systems was communication reports from the Crucian military command. These records suggest that they have wanted a war with our worlds since they first encountered us. However, they have had to hold off of this plan, due to our combined strength outmatching theirs.

The theory is, that they know that a war with the three worlds will be a long one, one lasting many decades. So… they figured that if they kill our children, it will weaken us and demoralise us. There won't be a next generation of Earth soldiers, and so the Crucians would then have a massive advantage, and one that would probably see them to victory. But it gets far darker than that Major–'

'Darker! Darker than them killing our kids, this is a whole different level of fucked up. The evil fucking bastards. I fucking knew they were up to something, all those years and all those lies, sickly insipid dark lies. Summer give me everything you know. I'm going to take this to General Eastwick. This is very serious.' I spoke, my voice was raised. I was unable to stop the words from escaping my lips. I was angry, angry at them. Summer then continued.

'Major, it appears that they wanted to see… and enjoy our suffering, they would appear to be… striving for it. I think you are right, they are extremely malevolent Major, in the purest sense of the word. They want to demoralise us, and they also want to create emotional pain for us, they seem to feed on it Major.' Summer looked around the table as the shock and horror of what she had just revealed washed over everyone, her words were like that of a devastating Tsunami.

'OK… OK. Let's think for a moment. What is their plan of attack?'

'Major, their ship is filled with millions of AI micro-fusion missiles. Each one is targeted at a specific site on Earth, thanks to Jevargh's intelligence. Every one of these missiles are targeted at our nursery's, schools, and universities, whilst others are targeted at housing.

For example, every household with children aged under five years old, basically ordinary family Earth homes, and in every country on Earth. These missiles can be released at any time, which is why I had to act Major. I had to do something to try and buy us some time, time to try and figure a way out of this.' I walked across the room to Summer, whose eyes were now beginning to fill with tears. I placed my hand upon her shoulder.

'It's OK Summer, tell us what you did, and we will take it from here.' I said sympathetically.

'Major, I didn't have a choice. I uploaded a virus spike into their mainframe.'

'A virus spike. And what does this particular virus spike do Summer?'

'It buys us time, from the moment that they realise that we know of their plans, or if they decide to launch those missiles before we have a plan of attack.'

'OK, so what you are telling me is, that when they are about to launch those missiles at Earth, the spike will activate and slow them down?'

'Yes, it should give us around six to seven hours maximum. That's how long I think it will take them to crack the encryption. It will effectively lock the ships weapons systems, including their ability to launch those missiles.

'Summer, you may have just given us an ace up our sleeve. However, time is now of the essence. Bring up the holo-screen, and let's take a look at their defences.'

In the centre of the table was a three-dimensional model of the Cruiser. The decks could be clearly seen, as could the bays that held the missiles, along with ten fully operational fighter decks.

'Anyone, what is the complement of Crucian personnel on board that ship? Fetch immediately responded.

'According to our latest recon, the ship has one hundred thousand Crucians currently serving onboard, with a compliment of thirty thousand fully trained fighter pilots, and upwards of sixty thousand available ground troops. All in all, the largest threat to our planet are their fighter pilots, and those missiles of course. They don't have sufficient ground troops on that ship to cause us a problem, unless of course they tried to board our ship.' I shook my head. I didn't like the sound of that.

'Weak points. Are there any weak points on that fucking ship?' I said assertively, Summer then spoke once again.

'Yes Major, but only the one, here.' She pointed to the stern area of the ship, and to the sixth deck of the ten decks. Moving her hands deftly, she manipulated the display of the holo-screen, zooming in on the rear view of the ship and its fighter decks. We could now clearly see the entry area of deck six that Summer thought was their most vulnerable to attack.

'Right there.' She pointed nimbly. 'Behind the back wall of that flight deck is their ships fusion core, it's just thirty metres in, hit them right there, in that sweet spot with a well-placed fusion missile and their ship goes boom! A blast like that is certainly gonna cause enough damage to destroy their entire ship, including everyone, and everything onboard. Getting to it though, well that's another matter.'

My mind was suddenly full of ideas, they came at me fast and all at once. Land a team on the stern of the ship, or try to infiltrate it, plant a bomb near the core…

no, no, too risky and not enough time. Then, finally 'a missile of our own' yes that was perfect.

'We could take a fighter in, load it up with several armour tipped cold fusion missiles… Providing that we can get level with that deck of course... we'll need support, and a lot of it. Hell Summer, we might well be able to destroy that ship and clear our planet out of those two faced nasty fuckers once and for all. I will take a squadron of our best fighters from Earth, and we will take this route.' I pointed to the top and bow of the ship.

'We don't want them to know what we are trying to do until the last minute, or preferably until it's too late for them to launch any counterattack. So, we will need all our other fighter squadrons from Earths ships, and any docked in the space ports. We need to work together to do this, it will be a multinational strike. This will be Earths first Major space battle, ever. I'm going to need to call on all of Earths nations to even stand a chance of pulling this off.' I walked up to Fetch who had a sombre look written across her face.

'The 'V' wing, we will need her too. Fetch, I want you to prepare immediately to board her and support her crew in any way you can.'

'Yes Major. I've been looking forward to it,' she said efficiently. She then smiled, nodded, and left the room punching the air.

'Cat, Joe and Tommy. Full armour and heavy weapons at the ready. I want you to take a squadron of fighters and clear out those stern decks. Clear out anything that moves or might get in the way. I need as few distractions as possible before I launch those missiles. Joe, I want you to take a squadron of fighters from the amaranthine and get them to this point here.'

I pointed to the rear of the ship.

'You will be acting as both a sweeper squad, and a distraction. I'm hoping that we will have some support from the other Earth nations, but we can't rely on that just yet.' Joe, Cat and Tommy then left the room to prepare, they looked focussed, their usual laidback demeanour had gone. They were going into battle.

'Deno, Summer. I want you to remain here on the Amaranthine and support the ships troops, but I also need you to help lead them, and should the worst happen, and if these bastards try to board us. I can't think of any two people better than the both of you to slow them down and keep them from taking this ship from us.

You are both now dismissed to prepare the ship, use whatever force you feel is necessary to get the job done, and Summer, Deno… you ought to know that you have probably given us the only chance we have. The Earth and all of us, well, great job and thank you. If we do manage to get through this, I will be speaking to General Eastwick personally about a promotion for you both, you've more than earned it.'

Summer and Deno saluted in unison and then left the briefing room to prepare. This left Adari and Raena in the briefing room with me.

'Raena, Adari, I think that you should contact your home worlds immediately and advise them of the risks to their offspring, but make sure that you tell them that if they are able to infiltrate the Crucian ships, now is the time to do it. We won't get another shot at this, and we are all going to run out of time, and soon. Earth will not act right now, as we wish to give your worlds the chance to prepare if you can, but you only have a matter of hours, so please tell your leaders what they need know, and what they need to do. Once you have done this, report directly to the bridge.' Adari and Raena bowed their heads, leaving the room quickly.

I felt a mix of both anger and urgency. What a fool I'd been to feel any compassion, or sadness for Jevargh, he didn't deserve it, not one bit of it. He didn't deserve anything from me, but my utter and absolute contempt for him. How dare he and these bastards try to take our children from us. How dare they plot and scheme our species ruin. How dare they lie, coming to us at first, as new allies, as friends. It was now quite obvious to me that they were selling us their tech for our subservience, our silence, taking advantage of our ego's, our vanity, and our greed, so that they could manipulate us into complete ignorance and silence.

All along, all they wanted, no, longed for was humanities pain and suffering. I looked up briefly seeing the reflection of my face in the briefing room viewing window. My entire forehead, chin and jaw line were ablaze with fine tributaries that ran the entire length of my face, onto my neck and down to my collarbones. The fusion was now shimmering softly underneath my skin, it was like that of the sun's surface.

At least now I knew that whatever was happening to me was linked in some way to my emotions. I took several deliberately deep and slow breaths trying to compose myself, ease my anger and fear for our world, our families, and friends. After a few seconds, I glanced back up at the viewing window and the skin on my face had once again completely returned to normal.

Whatever it was that was happening to me would now have to wait until after the battle. I very much wanted, no I needed, to send those Crucian bastards back to hell.

8 FOR THE LOVE OF THE CHILDREN

I sprinted onto the bridge, and I could feel my heart pounding in my chest as I knew what we had to do now. We only had but one choice, a single option, with no allowance for mistakes. If we managed that, we might succeed. I had to update the General and hoped that he would agree with my plan, it would come as a shock, even to him. I don't think I'd ever felt the need for urgency more in my entire life.

'Get me General Eastwick,' I commanded, 'and put him through to the briefing room. Tell him it is extremely urgent that I speak with him.' The comms operator acknowledged my order, instantaneously sending a communication request to the General. The bridge crew must have sensed something different about my tone and demeanour as they all turned their heads to look towards me, eventually returning their concentration to the bridges operational consoles.

I ran back into the briefing room that I had been stood in only moments ago. I didn't think for one moment, that on that night when Deno and I had followed Jevargh, that it would ultimately result in this, in war with the Crucians. I was now seething at his betrayal. I should have killed him on that exercise, it would have been worth the price. It would have been worth it, to stop this.

But I was no fool, had it not been Jevargh, it would have been someone else. Yes, it may have taken them a little longer, and I recognised that I wouldn't have been any use, if I'd been rotting away on the inside of a military prison cell. Those bastards would have found a way, no matter what, and I wouldn't have been here, now, in this moment trying to stop them. The holo-screen lit up and General Eastwick appeared.

'Major Mitchell, what's the situation?' He said, concerned.

'Sir. It's bad. Really bad.' He looked away for a moment towards something or someone in the distance, and then back towards the screen.

'Tell me everything Mitchell, and don't spare the detail.'

'The Crucians, Sir they aim to attack Earth within the next twenty-four hours, but specifically, all Earth's children and young adults. The want to kill them all. Everyone from birth to twenty-one years of age is a target. The plans Sir, that's what Jevargh transmitted to them. Our infrastructure, everything that tells them where our children and young adults will be… across the entire planet.'

'Jevargh. That son of a bitch!' His face became reddened and stern, and more serious than I had ever seen him before. He looked furious, tense and like a man about to burst.

'We have a plan Sir, purely as a result of one of my squad members quick thinking. She has managed to buy us some time. She put a spike into their mainframe when she realised what they were going to do... and how little time we had.

This will give us approximately six to seven hours to launch an attack, from the point of them becoming aware that we know of their plans, or if they try to fire those missiles. We have already advised both the Okai and the Nadaal to try something similar. We have done this in order to attempt to put us all on an equal footing, potentially buying them some time before the Crucians realise that we are well and truly on to them.'

'What else do we know Major?' He said seriously. I could see that he was running the options through his head.

'We know that they have a weak spot Sir, a weak spot that I fully intend to take full advantage of. Sir, we need to call on all of the nations of Earth to support us. We will only get one shot at this. If we lose, it's literally game over for humans on Earth. They will eventually crush our species, taking everything from us, including the things that we hold most dear… our children and our freedom.

They will apparently get some sort of sickening pleasure out of watching us lose our children and then… once we have lost what we fight for, we lose our planet. They have the exact same fate planned for both the Okai and the Nadaal Species too. We cannot allow them to continue to threaten our species. I won't let that happen Sir, you have my word.

My plan, if you accept it is to lead a handpicked squadron, twenty-four strong of Earth's best space fighters. I will be taking point and will fly inverted over the top of their cruiser. The fighters will shield, escort, and hopefully protect my fighter from the worst of what the Crucians have to offer us. For this reason, Sir, I would like to request the very best that we have for this part of the mission. The rest of Earth's fleet will act as a both decoy, and distraction. They will attack the bulk of the Crucian fleet, in an attempt to lessen their numbers and weaken their ship.

Sir, I will be targeting their ships fusion core, which is situated thirty metres or so to the rear of deck six on their ship. It won't be easy Sir, it's a gamble at best, but I don't see any other way.'

I could tell that General Eastwick was considering my plan. His steely blue eyes were searching for other options. I didn't want to appear overconfident, but I knew that there were none.

'Major I think it's a solid plan, and potentially the only one that could work, from where I stand. We don't have much of a choice, do we? No, this is our only option. I will call the United Nations and request international support. I can't see any of them refusing this, not with the weight of evidence.

Most of the leaders will have children of their own, or plan to have them, and those that don't have children, must have nieces, nephews or brothers and sisters. Surely they will see that if we lose our children… we lose everything.'

'Sir, may I make a suggestion. You might think this one is right out of the box though Sir.'

'Yes, of course Mitchell.' He said, curiously.

'Call the Russians.'

'Call the Russians? Major we haven't worked with the Russians for over three hundred years. Hell, we don't even trade with them anymore.'

'Sir, with respect. The Russians have a vested interest in this too. If the Crucians do succeed today, that means the Russians, as good as they are in battle, wouldn't stand a chance. Sir, please consider it, at least speak with them. This is a fight for the entire planet, for our entire species. They have a right to be asked.'

General Eastwick paused, taking back the words that were about to leave his mouth.

'OK Major. I will call them, but I don't expect a response. Await my further orders, I will keep Earths fighters on solid ground for now, so as to not give our game plan away. Let's just hope that it will give the Nadaal and the Okai enough time to prepare. Eastwick out.' The screen disappeared and I knew what I had to do. But first, I needed to see Raena and Adari, I needed to know what the response was from their home worlds.

Running all the way to the crews living area, I touched the intercom on the door panel that was situated at Adari's living quarters, his door immediately opening. I could see him pacing about inside.

'Adari, have you managed to contact your Queen?'

'Yes indeed,' he replied, 'she asked that I thanked you for the intelligence that you provided. She said that she would take care of the Crucians docked off our home world and then join Earth and the Okai in the defence of their planets. I don't think I have ever sensed such anger in my Queen before now. We are a peaceful species Major, but I do believe, how is it you that humans say it? That the Crucians have poked our Queens hive.

We will utilise our technology to rid our combined systems of this threat. She told me to pass on her regards, and she also mentioned something that I did not fully understand. She said that you are becoming 'more than you once were.' She said that you would be able to relate to this.'

'Well, Adari. Yes and no. I'm not sure exactly what she means, but I hope that whatever this, more that I am becoming is a good thing. Adari, all I really want right now is for us to all get through this next few hours and kick them back out of our systems.' I said candidly.

'As do I Major. My role on this ship is now complete as I have done as requested by my species, but I would like to contribute, in whatever way I can, to your efforts until my people join us in battle.'

'Your people will have their work cut out Adari, they may not get back to us in time to help.'

'Major. My people will be here. My Queen has directed our hive into action. It is merely a short matter of time before the ship docked off our home world, is… under our control. In fact, I imagine operations are progressing very smoothly, and as we speak. The Crucians have not felt the sharp point of our combined sting. Let me assure you Major, it will leave a mark, a mark that even the Crucians will struggle to recover from.' Adari smiled.

I hadn't seen the Nadaal in action, but I imagined that a poked hive would be something that the Crucians wouldn't forget in a hurry. Swiftly leaving Adari's quarters, I made my way towards Raena's quarters. On reaching her quarters, I pushed the touch panel on her door, the door instantly slid open. Raena was kneeling and appeared to be meditating in the centre of the room. I walked towards her silently, I really didn't want to disturb her, so I sat for a few moments, observing her silence. Then, all at once her eyes opened and she caught sight of me.

'Major?' she said, somewhat surprised.

'I'm sorry Raena, I didn't mean to disturb you. I just

wanted to see how you were and if you had a response from your home world?'

'Yes, though I believe my people are all in a state of shock.'

'We will help them, I promise. The Nadaal are going to send forces to help the Okai and the Humans once they have dealt with the Crucians. Adari, well, let's just say that he sounded confident. I think we should put our trust in the Nadaal and believe what he says.'

'Major, we have recently sent a team to infiltrate the ship in the exact same way that the humans did, we believe this is a solid plan.' It will take us a little time to infiltrate the ship. My understanding is that they have already set off.'

'I wish them luck. Is there anything you need Raena, is there anything that I can do?'

'No. Major, you have given us the chance to save everything and everyone. One day we may be able to repay you for this gift. I hope so, I do not believe you are fully aware of what your actions have done. They have given us a chance to live, to survive. Without you and your crew, well Major… I don't think.' She looked saddened.

'Raena, this was a team effort. We have all played our part, now comes the hard bit. We need to rid our combined systems of this threat, once and for all.'

'Major.' She touched my arm once again. 'Major, if we get through this, I would very much like to take you to see the trees of insight, on the western side of my planet. I believe you will find them to be… breathtakingly beautiful and inspiring.' She looked deeply into my eyes, but I couldn't hold her eye contact for long. It felt too intense, in a way that I couldn't describe.

'Thank you Raena. I had better do my best to make sure that we all get through the next few hours safely then. That sounds like something that I don't want to miss.'

∞

Soldier Barantha walked out of Queen Calaria's chamber. She felt stimulated and energised and was ready to instigate the Queens orders as requested. The Queen herself would be leading the assault on the Cruiser that was docked off the Nadaal's planet, Odomas.

But for now, Barantha had but one mission. She pushed the door open and entered the chamber of echo's, standing directly at its centre. Hexagonal brushed golden panels lined every wall, and at the centre of the room there was a solid gold hexagonal platform that was slightly raised off the floor.

The chamber was used rarely, as its only use was for the guardians of the Queen, to call other soldiers to action. Barantha, because she was a loyal and trusted protector of the Queen had been given the distinction of opening mass communications within the hives defences, whilst the Queen prepared herself to lead the assault.

Once at the centre of the chamber Barantha dropped silently to her knees, placing her hands carefully upon her thighs. Then, closing her eyes, she tilted her head backwards which allowed her throat to be fully clear. She would sing today, and all who were able would come. They would form a swarm massive in numbers that would joyfully pay their tribute, in courage and respect to their Queen. The act of singing would open sonic channels to all Nadaal, wherever they were in the Galaxy, calling them to assist their species in defeating the Crucians.

Barantha began to sing, quietly at first, incredible tones that sounded mythical in nature. There were no words as such, just a pulsating and rhythmic deep hum, which changed pitch and tone with every movement of her mouth and neck. Barantha's head moved about, joyfully, swaying like tall grass in the breeze. The incredible sounds undulated, from her very core and continued for a further three minutes, then all at once they ceased. She had performed well. Her Queen would be pleased. She stood up, straightening her garb and then quickly left the room, closing the large hexagonal door behind her.

Queen Calaria stood in her quarters whilst her attendants fussed about her. Every inch of her attire was immaculate, and the golden robes that adorned her looked exquisite, flowing like rivers of molten gold down the length of her body. She picked up a brush and combed her black hair, an attendant rushed to help her fasten it up in a simple twist knot on the back of her head.

'Dalaern, would you accompany me to my private chamber, there is work to be done to protect the hive.' Dalaern soon finished fastening her Queens hair and took a long and reverent look at her.

'Of course, my Queen, it would be as always my privilege to support you. If I can do anything to assist or to help make you more comfortable, please do let me know.' The Queen smiled, but she knew that she required no help or assistance for her next task, for it was hers alone. The Nadaal would respond to her commands, this time those commands would remove the scourge of the Crucians from the Nadaal's planetary systems space, once and for all.

She entered the chamber and, in the middle, and at the far end could be seen a plain chair. The Queen would command her forces from this chair with nothing more than her mind, her thoughts, and the purest of love that she felt for all her subjects. She turned and sat down in the chair, her gown spilling over it like molten lava, it flowed around, down and over the simple chairs frame, the chair struggling to contain the extravagance of the Nadaalian Queens lavish and liquid like garment.

'Dalaern.' She spoke softly. 'If for whatever reason I do not survive this. Please ensure that my daughter Arvina succeeds me. She is courageous, wise and kind and will make a good Queen.'

'Please, my Queen.' Dalaern replied. 'You are stronger now than ever before. There is no need to fear this battle. You alone command your armies, and they will crush every one of the Crucian forces in this sector. We will drive them from our skies, as one and as it has always been.'

'Thank you Dalaern. I hope that I am able to complete this task. I very much look forward to drinking a cup of your tea upon our victory, it is the sweetest I have tasted in all my years. Now, my loyal and trustworthy friend. I must prepare, alone. I will need all of my energy to link our species minds together. I need to see for myself just how many Crucians are on that ship, and I also need to view their exact locations onboard.'

She closed her eyes, and one by one at first, and then by the tens of thousands the minds of the Nadaal connected, only hearing one voice between them all. That of their Queen. In her mind's eye she could see the ship and the locations of every Crucian onboard.

'Listen my children. We, the Nadaal will teleport onto that ship, in unison and together as one mind. We will remove the Crucians one by one, and the threat to our planet will be gone within a single moment. We will continue until our skies are free from their poisonous and hostile intensions. We, the Nadaal are a peaceful species, but today we show no remorse, for they come to attack our hives and take our children from us, this is why they must be stopped.

Prepare to telephase onto their ship, three Nadaal to each Crucian onboard. Kill them, show them no mercy, my children. Prepare yourselves for war, we begin telephasing in three minutes.

Across Odomas they prepared. Swarms of Nadaal gathered their weapons, whilst the Planets fighter craft were boarded by tens of thousands of Nadaal, ready to take up the fight in space, if needed. They sat, silently. Their entire planet in silence, other than the sounds of their preparations as the hive mind became one.

'Telephasing in ten, nine, eight, seven, six, five, four, three, two, one.' In less than a second, thousands of Nadaalian troops disappeared from the surface of Nadaal, reappearing instantaneously onboard the Crucian Cruiser.

Wherever there was a Crucian there were at least three Nadaal. The normally peaceful Nadaal killed each and every Crucian on the ship, quickly, efficiently and without unnecessary cruelty. Every Crucian onboard the cruiser lay dead within ten short seconds, their ship had fallen silent and other than the hum of the ships engines, not a sound could be heard. Their anger, malignancy and cruelty had been silenced by the Nadaal.

'It is done.' Said the Queen calmly, her eyes were

still closed. She looked exhausted. 'Send that craft into our star. Let them have no burial rights, let their family's mourn them, never knowing how they died, for they were going to take everything we care about from us.'

Thank you, my children, we still have much work to do. I wish for one third of our fighters to remain here with our ground troops. One third are to travel immediately to Earth, to assist the Humans, and one third are to travel to Nemeranth to support the Okai. Know this, I am proud of you all, my children.' Queen Calaria finally opened her eyes, as Dalaern was knelt at her side, sobbing.

'My Queen, you still live.' She raised her head humbly to the Queen.

'My dearest Dalaern…' She said warmly. 'It will take more than a few Crucians to kill this Queen. Now, Dalaern, my dearest friend. Would you be so kind as to make me some of your fine, sweet tea. I find that I have developed quite the thirst.'

Meanwhile on Nemeranth, the Okai were still waiting to establish if their infiltration mission had been a success. Vast numbers of Okai were gathering by their trees. The trees represented strength and wisdom, as well as many other traits that the Okai truly revered. Counsellor Massarah stood, his stance was tense, as he waited for news, any news.

'Get me our commanders and get me them now.' He said, his tone full of strength and energy.

'Yes Counsellor.' A low voice uttered, from his communication device.

'Counsellor Massarah, we have good news. The mission was a success, and the team are on their way back to us… oh no, oh no, no, no.'

'What is happening? Report, what is happening?'

'The team was just attacked and destroyed as they were leaving the ship and –'

'Did they deploy the spike?' He said urgently.

'Yes Counsellor, we believe they did.'

'Then we will honour them fully, after the battle. Inform Earth, no, inform Major Mitchell that the Clock is ticking, and get our forces up there, we have much work to do.'

∞

General Eastwick opened a channel to the United Nations of Earth. On the screen in front of him he could see hundreds of representatives that were sat in neat rows waiting to hear his address.

'Welcome General Eastwick, you are cleared to speak openly.'

'Thank you. I'm really very sorry, there is no other way to say this. Earth is under serious threat. At this very moment we are on the verge of war with the Crucians. They plan to kill all of our children and young people on Earth. All of them, and without exception will be killed or seriously injured unless we act now.

The Crucians intention is to weaken us into submission. They do this for pleasure, to see our suffering and they long for our species demise. They want full control of our home planet and all of its resources. I urge you to consider my words and to join us in driving this threat away from our solar system.

The Nadaal and the Okai face similar threats and will join us if they are able to. I call for unilateral support from every nation on this planet, join us, please join us.' He paused for a moment, gathering his thoughts.

'We will be converging near the Amaranthine. Major Stephanie Mitchell is preparing the assault, as we speak. It would be good to be able to give her some good news from the leaders of Earths nations.'

'Thank you, General Eastwick, we need to break now to discuss this. We will be in touch very soon.' General Eastwick sat down at his desk, his usually strong legs felt weakened, and he held his head in his hands. He didn't know what else he could do, then he remembered Mitchell's plea to call the Russians. He immediately opened his screen.

'Get me the Russian President.'

'Sir, the Russian president?' A voice questioned at the other end of the comm.

'Yes, get them on screen, now.'

'Yes Sir...' A few moments passed, when suddenly his screen lit up. A middle-aged woman appeared on the screen, she was dressed elegantly, and her poise was one of calm and confidence.

'General Eastwick. I have to say that I was most intrigued by your call. We don't usually communicate in this way, ever.' She smiled.

'President, I have dire news, but news that I believe you need to know. Once I share the information with you. I am sure that you will agree that it is of great importance to the Russian people, and to all people on our planet.'

General Eastwick continued, briefing the Russian President as quickly and succinctly as he could. He told her everything that he believed that she needed to know. Information that would enable her to make the most important decision of her Presidency, to fight or to abstain. She listened intently, her demeanour changing and her once relaxed expression becoming more and more alarmed as the stark words continued to flow from his candid lips.

'General Eastwick, we anticipated that one day that we would need to join forces to protect our planet, but never did we anticipate it would be to thwart such an evil and callous plan. No, General Eastwick. No one threatens Russian children. You will have our fleets to assist you. Oh, and General, we the people. We wish you a swift victory.'

The comm fell silent once more, as General Eastwick lifted his fist in the air, punching it jubilantly. The Russians, who would have thought it. He dearly hoped that it would make a difference, as he sat back down at his desk. He needed to call Mitchell and tell her his news. But more than that, he hoped that they would all have enough time.

'Major Mitchell.' General Eastwick spoke at speed.

'Yes Sir, do you have an update for us?'

'I do. I'm still awaiting an update from the United Nations, as to which nations will join us. I should be notified any time now. You were right about the Russians. They are as angry as we are, and they have agreed to join us. Just one moment, I'm getting some messages coming through on my comm.' There was a long pause and silence, and then he spoke once again, his voice was energised.

'We have Europe, including the Brits. We have Australia, New Zealand, Canada. We have all of South America, Brazil and now China has joined us. We have India, we have Japan and Korea. There are too many coming through to keep up with. Major, I believe you just might have your fleet.' His eyes looked tired, and if my intuition was right, I would say that the overwhelmingly positive response from Earth had deeply moved him.

I felt optimistic for the first time in a while. But I knew it was just a matter of time before I would be asking that fleet to risk everything, for everyone. It weighed heavily on my mind. I sank heavily into my chair, thinking about my service history, the hard work I'd put in during my career. I kept thinking about the people. It was always about the people, that's why we did what we did. In the same way that I had protected those kids from the bullies during my childhood. Now, more than ever I wanted to protect my people, and my planet, and I was damn sure that I wasn't going to let some Crucian assholes get in the way of us trying to do that.

'Major.' A voice bellowed out over the comm.

'Yes, Mitchell here.' I replied.

'We have the Crucian ships commander on the comm, your orders Major.'

'Put them through, I will take this in the briefing room. Get me General Eastwick, now.' The comm went silent and then General Eastwick came back on the line.

'Major?' He said questioningly, his face full of intrigue.

'General, the Crucian commander has just requested he speak with me. I believe we may be about to start a war. Your orders Sir.'

'Keep that smug bastard talking as long as you can, whilst I organise the fleet, Eastwick out.'

I ran towards the briefing room, only stopping momentarily because I had yet another communication flag lit up on my chip.

'Mitchell here.' It was the Okai, with news.

'Major Mitchell, we need to inform you that

although the mission to implant the spike on the mainframe of the Crucian Cruiser that is docked off Nemeranth was a success, unfortunately, the away missions crew are now all presumed dead as their craft was attacked whilst they were on their way back to us. We believe that the Crucians may now be about to take some form of action. Major, are you ready to join with us and the Nadaal to save our offspring?'

'Hell am I ever! But yes, in answer to your question. The Earth is united, in well, the first time for a long, long time. We also have a plan. I'm sending our strategy over to you now. Perhaps it could work for your species too.' Mitchell tapped her chip. 'Do you, have it there?'

'Yes, Major and thank you. It looks solid. I will take it to our briefing. May you fight with the courage and ingenuity, that we Okai have witnessed as two of your species greatest traits.' And with that the comm went silent once again.

I stood at the communications console not knowing what would come next. I had prepared for this, had the training for this… But this one moment, the sheer gravity of it all. I would try and keep him talking as long as I could, but I knew the Crucians weren't the most talkative species. I would need to engage him in some other way. I opened the comm channel, looking to the holo-screen, waiting for him to appear.

'Major Mitchell. We wish to inform you that your allies the Okai have been thwarted in an attempt to board an infiltrate our cruiser, docked off Nemeranth.'

He doesn't know they were on their way back having completed their mission, interesting.

'And what exactly does this have to do with Earth?'

I cast my line out into his vicious river of hatred for us all. His face contorting, as he continued.

'You may have noticed that we have our best three Cruisers docked off Earth, Nemeranth and Odomas. They are our fleets mightiest battle ships.' He sneered.

'Yes, of course I am aware. We are in talks for trade with you, I believe. I am saddened to hear that the Okai suffered losses having taken such action against you. We humans only look forward to forging closer relations with all allied species.' Saying those words out aloud made me feel physically sick with rage, but I couldn't show it, not yet.

'Yes, those trade talks. About that Major.' Here it comes, I thought. That fucker is about to reveal his hand to us, and in so doing, their hostile intentions towards us.

'Yes, I hope the talks go well.' I replied skilfully. I had to play this as if I were completely ignorant of the facts. I knew he would be getting some kind of sick pleasure from my apparent ignorance and naivety of their plans for us.

'Major, there won't be any talks.' He hissed, his demeanour changing, his mask had finally slipped.

'Oh. But I thought the talks were going so well?' I could feel the anger and frustration barely held in, it sat in my throat, but I would not, and could not give him even one second less of my full attention, for now at least, I just had to keep him talking.

'No Major. It was never our intention to build peaceful relations with you. We just needed a plan, a plan to destroy you. A plan to wipe your pathetic species from the Galaxy. But more than this, we wanted you to know that we will enjoy it.' From what he had just said, and the look of satisfaction upon his face, he was definitely deriving some kind of warped pleasure from his own hate fuelled words towards me and my species.

At that very moment I realised that my intuition had been right all along, there definitely was something off about the Crucians. If I could just keep him talking a little longer, long enough to give General Eastwick the time he needed.

'I don't understand, are you saying that you want to destroy us?' I said innocently, the longer I could keep this act up, the better.

'No Major, we will do much more than destroy you. Your species could never understand, you are weak, a wretched blight on the galaxy but you will never stop our glory and us attaining our rightful place in this galaxy. I want you to know this Major before we end you today. We will rub your species away, like the old dirt that rests upon our polished boots.'

I almost couldn't bear to look at him, but I kept my eyes steady and focussed on his. I would not give him, or any other Crucian the satisfaction of anything that could be interpreted as a non-verbal submission. Now was definitely the time to reel him in, I was absolutely furious.

'Ya wanna know something? You Crucians are full of shit. You can try to rub us out, but we will fight you. We will fight you with everything we have, and everything we are. You have thought us to be the underdog, whilst you have plotted and schemed, when we sought peace between our species.

You may believe that we humans are weak, and you may see us as a blight to your glory. But at least we are not the rotting carcass of this Galaxy, that the Crucians are. No, we are much more than that, we are better than that, we are better than you.

We humans are at our very best in extreme circumstances, we humans will fight to the death for those we love. We will never surrender to you. We will always fight if the cause is just, whatever the odds, for the underdog. You will not take our liberty or our freedoms, you will not take our humanity, and you will certainly not take our planet, not today, not any day.

Let it be known that you have met your match. We will show you no remorse, there will be no surrender. We will light up the sky with our victories, and we will win. We will fight for a future for all our children and the right to raise them to adulthood, and once this battle is won, we will then return to peace.' That should keep him engaged for a bit, I thought. Though, I had meant and felt every single word of it.

He looked at me with bitter contempt once again, just as the final words left my lips. He didn't allow them to settle, he didn't appear to look moved in anyway by what had just been said to him. Was that coldness, or arrogance that I had just witnessed?

'Oh… but Major you will not. You see this battle is already won. We will kill all of your children first. You cannot do anything to stop us. Once we kill your children you will lose all hope. We will fight you and with no heirs, and with no one to replace your dying soldiers, it is only a matter of time, and your planet… it will be ours.

In our worst scenario estimates, this will happen in less than two decades. A short war, and I must say, a brilliant plan from the Crucian High Command.'

We were fast approaching a tipping point, and I just hoped that General Eastwick would be ready. I placed the palms of my hands on the console, leaning on it for support as I raised my head and eyes to meet his.

'Try it.' I said calmly.

'What? Didn't you understand my simple words human?' He continued, muttering some profanities under his breath, as if he didn't understand my logic.

'I said, try it! Go on. Launch your attack, try it! Would you like me to say it to you in another way, perhaps a way you could understand? How about, go for it, hit it, or bring it on. I can think of many ways to say it. So why don't you do just that?

While you are at it, maybe you might wanna add in that we are at war, because that's what you have just confirmed to me, and that is exactly what I was waiting for you to say, you Crucians… you really are just so full of shit!' His deep red face lit up, as he was furious. His anger was clearly visible to me, and his red eyes glowed with rage and hateful intent.

'This is my ultimatum to you and every other Crucian in our system, withdraw your forces from our combined systems and abandon your vessels. If you do this, we will let you return home, free. I do this because I am giving you a chance to live, a chance to leave the three systems in peace. I will not compromise my humanity, even though I despise you, and everything that you stand for. So, what's it going to be?'

'Major, you can have the death that we have had planned for you and your people.' He gazed at me smugly.

'Release the missiles.' There was a pause, a few seconds later he appeared to be in urgent conversation with his crew, was that panic I could see on his face. He returned to the screen, but I made sure that I spoke first.

'Now, on Earth asshole, that is what we humans call

a Check Mate. You might want look that up or try and do something about that problem you are having on your ship.' I cut the comm link and sprinted out of the briefing room and back onto the Bridge. Just as General Eastwick appeared on screen.

'Major, you should be seeing the fleet at any moment.'

I looked out of the viewing window and in the distance, I could see them amassing, numbering in their thousands. The different colours of the craft representing the different nations. Earths nations, united as one and fighting for the love of their children.

Then, in an instant, many golden craft with red insignia appeared too, by the thousands, the Russians had joined us. Then the Brits arrived, their red, white, and blue insignia, like the beacon of hope that they had been over five hundred years ago during the second world war. The space around Earth was now full of our planet's best fighters that were awaiting our orders.

I knew, now more than I ever had done before, that we needed to make the next few hours count. They were going to be the most important hours of my life, and the most important in our planet's history. I opened a ship wide channel.

'Attention all personnel, this is Major Mitchell. RED ALERT, BATTLE STATIONS. I repeat, RED ALERT, BATTLE STATIONS, report to your assigned war role posts immediately.' The ships lighting instantly changed to red. We were at war.

9 UNDERDOG

I gathered my fleeting thoughts together, running once again, from the bridge all the way to the flight deck, as this was where most of my eight were now waiting, all except Fetch who was onboard the 'V' wing awaiting further orders. They had been preparing themselves, whilst I had been finalising the plan.

Cat and Tommy were both suited up in their heavy armour. Tommy had a single heavy fusion cannon that was strapped around his back to give his arms a little more support, whilst Cat had two smaller fusion weapons that ran the length of her arms and were melded into her suit. Chief Engineer Watts was stood running last minute tests and checks on their equipment.

'Major, you need to choose a colour. Or at least you should consider it.' A colour, I thought.

'A colour for the suits?' I replied.

'Yes, for all the suits, for all of Earth forces.

'Right, well… I… Blue. The colour of the seas and the sky on a clear day. Yes blue, but the countries flags stay. OK?' Chief Watts smiled.

'Yes Major.' She touched the control panel on her chip and instantaneously all the armour changed across all forces changed colour.

'Now, we have our battle colours, let's get this job done. Joe. Cat. Tommy. Clear out that deck. Don't care how you do it, just make sure that I have a clear shot at the rear wall. Deno and Summer, support the defence of the Amaranthine in any way you can. Summer, have one of those spikes ready should it be needed to slow the Crucians down, should they board this ship.'

'Yes Major. Already in hand.' Summer replied, and Deno smirked once more, both of them withdrawing from the immediate deck area to make their final preparations. On their way off the deck, Deno's hand reached down her thigh, and she tapped Kevin for luck.

'Raena and Adari, I want you to support Deno and Summer in any way that you can. We need to do our best to hold on to this ship.'

'Yes Major.' They both paused for a moment and then Raena spoke, her pale green eyes full of warmth.

'Safe journey Major… and thank you.' Adari nodded in agreement and they both headed off in the direction of Deno and Summer.

'Fetch, you there?' There was a momentary pause on the comm and then Fetch responded.

'Major, I am onboard the 'V' wing. We await your orders.'

'Permission granted to engage the Cruiser, weaken it in any way possible. We have under six hours to get the job done. Give those smug bastards something to think about, Mitchell out.' Fetch spun around in her seat and faced the commanding officer of the 'V' wing.

'Time to engage, we have our green light.' The officer released the docking clamps, and the 'V' wing was released from the Amaranthine. It rose majestically at first and then swooped forwards towards the Cruiser like a hungry hawk diving for a mouse.

All at once Earths fleets charged forwards in their hundreds of thousands and at speed, the first sights of battle filled my eyes with a mixture of both concern, strength, and resolve.

'Is my squadron ready?' I asked the decks chief engineer.

'Yes, twenty-four fighters are readying just off to port. They await your craft Major Mitchell.'

'And it's loaded with the armour tipped fusion missiles, that I will need for this mission?'

'Yes Major, it's fully loaded. Your craft awaits you.' We walked to the port side of the hanger, where a single silver craft stood. Engineers and technicians were conducting their final checks, and I could clearly make out the fluorescent yellow tipped missiles that were two metres in length, as they were pulled into the underside of the craft by its hydraulic mechanisms. I stood looking at the craft and turned to Chief Watts who had followed closely behind us.

'Chief, remind me when I get back, that a promotion is long overdue. Take care of the Amaranthine for me.' She smiled and watched as I began to board the craft, the windows of the fighters cockpit retreating seamlessly into the crafts silver structure, allowing me to then enter it easily.

I jumped in and touched the seating adjustment panel, the five point harness quickly closed in around me pulling me snuggly into the seat. Transparent fluid arose from the fighters structure and quickly began to enclose the cockpit in a layer of toughened liquid memory glass. I was now completely sealed inside the airtight craft, almost one with its form. It was then that I noticed the silence, I couldn't hear a single sound from the flight deck.

I touched the system control panel for the fighter and its engines came online, it was still completely silent, but I could feel a little turbulence underneath the craft. Steadily, the craft rose up from the decks landing plate, I switched the comm channel on. Finally, I could hear the voices of the commanding officers from each of Earths nations. They were giving orders and discussing their combined strategies and tactics. I switched channels to that of my squadron, my eight, and General Eastwick.

'This is Major Mitchell reporting in for active duty.' I said, making the effort for my voice to be clearly heard by all. The squadron commander immediately responded to me.

'Major Mitchell, General Henderson reporting. We await your arrival and hope to provide you with a smooth and steady approach to your target. We have the best pilots, representing six countries. We have, of course six of the best from the USA, we have four of the best pilots sent from her majesty Queen Anne, and her British armed forces. We have six from the Russian empire, we have three from China, three from Europe and two from Australia.

We will be flying over the top of the ship, from bow to stern, taking out everything that gets in our way whilst doing our level best to provide shielding for your craft. My understanding is that you will fly inverted in order to pull a one-hundred-and-eighty-degree half loop. Is that correct Major?'

'Yes. Once we are clear of the cruisers port and starboard defences, at the rear of the Cruiser, I will instigate the half loop manoeuvre. I just need you to get me safely to the rear of that ship, I will do the rest.' I took one last look at the deck and gave Chief Watts the OK signal. Letting her know that I was ready to leave the deck.

I shot out of the hanger, immediately pulling up and away from the Amaranthine. I could see the awaiting squadron held perfectly still in an arrow formation. They were waiting for my craft to join them.

In the distance, the battle was in full swing, and the 'V' wing looked to be bombarding the port side of the cruiser and I figured that Fetch would be somewhat involved in this. Then, from nowhere the Nadaal arrived. Thousands of them moved together in a swarm, and as one, their unified movements reminded me of a swarm of angry bees, or was it a flock of birds heading south for the summer? I couldn't make my mind up.

It was then that the tingling sensation returned once again to my hands, it began moving slowly at first, up and over my body and towards my face. It felt like tiny pleasurable needles underneath my skin, stimulating my nerve endings but with intense heat. Why was this happening now, and why did it always seem to happen when I, or someone I cared about was at risk, or if I was under extreme stress or duress. I tried to ignore it once again, but I couldn't, the sensation was deepening, growing, and intensifying. I looked down at my hands and removed one of my gloves.

'Shit.' I shouted out aloud. My hand was once again showing signs of fusion. Its surface reminding me of that of magma, no, I thought, it wasn't magma, it was like that of the surface of the sun. But how could that be? This didn't happen to anyone else I knew. How could it be happening to me? Why hadn't I had it checked out, as if that would have made any difference, I thought.

I made a promise to myself right there and in that very moment that I would see the Chief Medical Officer on the ship on my return, and that I would ask them to run tests on me, that was, if I could complete this mission. I would give it all up, everything. If I could just rid our Solar System of these malignant Crucians. I was not about to let them take our children, or our freedom.

I quickly changed the cockpit windows from clear to carbon black, as I wasn't sure if my face had changed visually also. I didn't want the other pilots to panic or freak out if they saw me. I needed them to have their wits about them, and not be puzzling over my strange appearance.

I positioned my fighter right in the centre of the arrow formation. There were two rows of six, that formed the point of the arrow, my craft was the third fighter of the arrows tip. The rest were shielding the tip from the Crucian aggressors, whose numbers were growing.

We began to move forwards, slowly at first but gradually reaching full combat speed within thirty seconds. The battle raged on all around us, and I hoped that the Crucians would think that we were just another squadron that was attacking their ship, I hoped that they wouldn't identify our strategy before I could launch those missiles and achieve our mission.

Thousands of craft danced around us, each fighting

for its survival, every pilot trying to take another Crucian fighter out of commission. I could see the many losses that must have numbered in their thousands. I could see the remnants of the multitudes of craft that had been obliterated and torn apart. Their carcasses were all around me now, like fossils of metal, bone, and blood, they littered the void of space, so many were there that it made the void feel full. It was the worst carnage that I had ever seen.

In war there was always a cost. Even to the winning side, any war, no matter how righteous always left a deep wound on the victor's soul. This war would be no different, our relations with the Crucians would cease, and they would be considered our enemy. We would not trade with them. We would not welcome them. Our alliance would be reduced from four species to three. It was the only viable option, and it was the lesser of the two evils, the Crucians would have to be beaten and driven back to their home world. We just couldn't afford to trust them. They were in league with something so menacing that any peace we had once wanted with them had dissolved into oblivion.

I opened a comm channel to my eight, the tingling sensation continued sweeping up and over my upper body, but apart from the personal anxiety it was causing me, I felt completely fine and strangely, I was feeling completely energised.

'Joe. We are about to start our final fly over to the rear of the cruiser. Is your team in place?'

'Yes Major, but Cat and Tommy have… Well, they have jumped their transport to deck six of the cruiser.'

'They have what? Why? What on earth are they thinking, are they trying to get themselves fucking killed?' I had forgotten for the briefest of moments that they could hear every word I was saying, Tommy responded, his laughter full of vigour.

'Major, Cat and I are fine.' He continued to fire his weapon into the rear of the ship, it cut through the vehicles and pretty much everything else like a hot knife through butter.

'Tommy has one hell of a weapon.' Cat said, her humorous tones cutting through the sound of their intense weapon fire. I shook my head at their audacity, they were incredibly brave, I couldn't fault them for that. The risks to themselves though… I would need to think further on it.

'Joe, make sure that they get back on board asap. My ETA is one minute and thirty seconds. By my counting you have a maximum of one minute left before you need to high tail it out of there. Is that understood Joe?'

'Affirmative Major, dropping retrieval lines to them now.' His comm cut off and I was once again alone in my own head space. I could see the many turrets and weapons on the top of the Cruiser as we began our approach to the rear of the ship. In the distance, I could see Earth, her blue and green colours vivid and most visible to me.

I thought for a moment of all the children that would be ignorant of this war, for the moment at least. I thought of their futures and their hopes and dreams. They deserved the opportunity to grow and thrive. To live their lives without this threat hanging over them. I would do my best to give them that chance, to give them all the chance to reach adulthood.

'Major we are thirty seconds out from your final approach. What are your orders?'

'Do what you can to protect my flight path. I must

get these missiles into the back of that ship. Other than that, stay safe… and thank you General for a smooth escort.'

'It's been a pleasure Major. I don't think I'm underestimating this, by any means, that we all look forward to the coming celebrations.' His radio fell silent.

The rear of the ship slipped way beneath me, I moved my back and shoulders, stretching out the tension in them. I looked to my hand briefly, it was still pulsating, just underneath the surface, and my flesh looked mottled due to the shimmering fusion that was occurring beneath it. I had seen images and videos of the sun's surface, and this was what my skin looked like now, it was exactly the same. The cockpit glowed with the yellow, orange light that was being emitted from my hand and I hurriedly covered it back up with the glove.

'Mitchell here. We are golden. I am beginning my approach.'

∞

Deno tapped Summer on the shoulder as they looked out of the hanger and towards the Cruiser in the distance. They had both been listening intently to every word of the communications, whilst they prepared the ship, as they had been instructed to do. Summer raised her hand up, pointing towards the Cruiser.

'There, look can you see them? Boy, are they moving fast, wish I were there to assist.'

'Me too,' said Deno. 'I guess it's her prerogative to be the one that delivers the payload, it's not something I think I could do.'

'Of course, you could, I mean… if you had to. She has to, she feels responsible. I think she has felt that way since that night when you and she went to HQ. I think she wants to put an end to it. Sometimes when you see her and she is not aware, she looks troubled, it's like she has the weight of the world on her shoulders. But she never takes that stress out on anyone does she, nope. She carries it all, and us all through it.'

'Well, yeah… I guess you are right. She always puts us first. I guess we just must have gotten used to it, it's who she is. Her anger about this situation though, is normal, and it's understandable. I mean, after all, they want to murder our children.'

'You know Deno, she won't allow that to happen. I mean look up there, she is about to wipe that smug grin from the faces of every Crucian in the Galaxy. Hell, we should have ordered popcorn.' They both laughed and continued on with their preparations.

It was time. Every fibre of my body was on high alert as I began to pull the craft into its one-hundred-and-eighty-degree half loop. Disorientated. I felt disorientated and I knew this was not normal. My body began working against me and I struggled for control of it. My hands began to shake, and intense pain coursed through my entire being. No. Argh... no… NOT NOW, NOT NOW! I could make out the target deck in the distance and I knew that I didn't have much time. If I could just keep it together… for a moment longer.

'Major, are you alright. Is there a problem?'

'Just feeling the effects of that one-eighty. I will be fine.' I bit my bottom lip, trying to take my mind away from the pain that was wracking my body.

'Major you are clear to fire. The target is hot, weapons are online.' I reached for the missile touch panel and flipped up the protective cover. A single smaller panel was revealed that was gently flashing green.

'Releasing the pay load.' I touched the panel. Nothing happened. Panic gripped me.

'Major, is there a problem?' I touched the panel again, nothing.

'Major, what is your status?' A swell of cold fear ran up my entire body.

'The missiles, they won't release. Could they be damaged?'

'Major, return to base immediately, we believe the Crucians may have hacked into your crafts weapons systems.'

'I can't return… not now. What are my options? There must be another option.' The thought ran around my head. What options did I have? Was there any way to release the missiles from the craft, was there something that I hadn't thought about, was there something that I had missed?'

'Major, abandon your approach. Turn back now or you won't be able to pull away in time.

'I CAN'T DO THAT.' I yelled. 'WE DON'T HAVE TIME FOR A SECOND ATTEMPT!'

I tried to think, but my mind went almost blank with fear.

'The missiles, they will activate on direct contact with the ship?'

'Yes, but Major, please…' I cut the comm channel. I didn't have any other choice. I was out of options. I was just one woman. I could end this now and they would all be safe. Nobody else had to die.

The Crucian hanger entrance grew closer and closer, and I was still desperately trying not to scream out in pain. My hands trembled and I was unsure if it was fear, or if it was my body which seemed to be trying its best to tear itself apart. What a way for it all to end, but I was determined that I would not let those bastards take Earth.

I knew the end would be quick but trying to make sure that the last thoughts I had were good ones, was a challenge at this point, even for me. I looked to my right and could see the Earth. My reason for being on this craft, my reason for choosing this option.

I loved the Earth, my planet and home. It was a small price to pay to save the young. It was then that I felt a single teardrop leave both of my eyes, and as they began to roll slowly down my cheeks, I tried to regain my composure once again, soon realising that it was now too late to pull up.

Closing my eyes for one last time, my journey ending instantaneously as my fighter hurtled at incredible speed into the rear of deck six of the Crucians hanger, hitting it with tremendous force.

I thought that I was meant to be dead at this point. I watched in what seemed like slow motion as the wings ripped away from the main body of the fighter. They hurtled away at incredible speed, as the remainder of the craft plummeted through the hanger incinerating and taking everything inside of it.

Everything seemed to be moving much slower, slow enough for me to observe my own motion. I turned my head and could see the bulk of the craft and everything disintegrating and breaking up around me, as we approached the rear deck wall. I closed my eyes, this is it. I must be dead. This surely must be the last moments of my consciousness leaving my mortal body. But I don't feel any pain, I don't feel any pain.

I looked about me, and, in every direction. I appeared to be surrounded by the smooth and soft hot edges of the cruisers molten metals, which were still glowing brightly. I hovered still for a moment, and I noticed that I was directly above the ships fusion core. I appeared to be absorbing its energy, pulling the energised white-hot sphere in to my very core.

My body appeared ravenous, as the white hot threads of pure energy poured into me in thickened strands of pure and wispy light that was absorbed into my very being. After a few seconds it appeared that I had absorbed the ships core completely.

I sensed that I was once again moving. I looked down at my body. Where had my clothes gone. My skin. My skin was gone. I looked at my arms. I was covered from head to toe in some form of fusion, just as I had experienced before, many times, though this time it was sustaining me. I must be dead, I thought. That's right, I'm dead and this is the beginning of my journey to the afterlife.

I expected that it would end once my brain had shut down. I expected to just cease to be, but I continued, noticing that I could move my arms and legs, in line with my thoughts. Surely, I shouldn't be able to do this? I then looked in front of me and could make out what looked to be the innards of the ship's infrastructure. I moved forwards and noticed that I could see the split of the many decks, the occasional corridor, room, and other features as I moved past and through them all.

Everything in my path was quickly destroyed… by me, I appeared to be obliterating it, leaving an empty collapsed and ash like void in my wake. I still believed that I must be dead, and this, this was definitely some kind of weird afterlife experience, for sure, that's what it was. I had read about these things in magazines, but never for one moment did I think that I would be conscious, or aware for any of it.

∞

Deno looked up at the Cruiser, hearing Mitchells final moments clearly over the comm. She sank to her knees, bereft. Summer ran over to her an put her arms around her. Raena ran towards them both, whilst Adari tried to organise the medical shuttles for a rescue attempt.

Deno cried out, her heart full of pain. She had just lost her commanding officer and the best friend she ever had. Summer pulled Deno closer, she was inconsolable and sobbing quietly. She lifted her head then towards Raena seeking answers, that would not come.

The four of them all heard Fetch screaming and shouting obscenities at the Crucians over the comm. She was more angry than she had ever been. There was a brief pause and then a scream, the like of which they had never heard before, as the sound of the V wings rail guns began to tear into what was left of the Crucian ship.

Suddenly Raena froze, sinking to her knees, Summer looked across to her and was just about to intervene.

'It's alright Deno, don't worry, everything is going to be alright. Fetch everything is alright.' She stood perfectly still, looking out of the hanger towards the Cruiser and the V wing.

'What do you mean everything is fucking alright?' Fetch screamed. 'What the fuck just happened, where is Mitchell. Someone fucking answer me. Where is

Mitchell?' Summer responded, trying to speak calmly and clearly.

'She is gone Fetch. The missiles, they wouldn't release and…She's gone. I think Raena is in shock, I don't think she can accept it. I don't think any of us can.'

'What are you saying?' Fetch shouted through the comm, the sound of battle still raging in the background.

'Fetch, she is dead, Mitchells dead. She flew her craft into the hanger, the missiles they wouldn't release. She wanted to complete the mission.' There wasn't a sound for a moment, and then more of Fetch's screams could be heard over the comm, along with her pure anger and rage.

'You… you fucking bastards, every one of you. This is for her. Here. have it!' It was truly clear from her tone, that Fetch was pummelling the Crucian craft with everything the 'V' wing had. Fetch's comm cut off and then a different voice spoke.

'General Eastwick here. We have eyes on the cruiser and there is something… what the fuck is happening, what is that? Can anyone else see this? I repeat, can anyone else see this? Has anyone got eyes on this, other than me?' Everyone instantly looked to the skies, as he continued.

'No... That's impossible. Missiles just don't do that.' Radio chatter could be heard by all of Mitchells eight.

'Something… something is hollowing the inside of that Cruiser out. Tell me, you can see this? I… don't know what that is, but… it looks to have created a fifty-metre-wide hole from the rear of the ship. As I speak, there are now multiple decks blowing out along the port and starboard sides of the ship. It's running along the entire length of the ship.

Clear your craft from the front of that ship, now! I don't want anything destroyed when whatever that is blasts through and exits the forward bow. Take me to the rear of the ship, immediately.' Eastwick commanded. His voice full of urgency.

'My god… It can't be. How is that even possible?' He looked down the centre of the ship, desperately trying to take in what his eyes saw.

'It's gone, there is an entire cylindrical section gone. Something has borne a hole through the entire centre of the ship and… I can make out some kind of light or is that a fire at the far end. It should be out of the front of the ship soon. There is nothing left, no metal, no debris of any kind. It's like it just disintegrated or did it disappear? I want all, and any available eyes to observe the front of that ship now.'

∞

I had expected this vision to end. It didn't, it continued. I seemed to be becoming more aware of my surroundings. I was still me, but I was not. I was definitely self-aware though. I felt my own conscious and had begun to run ideas through my mind as to what had just transpired. What was I? Who was I? How could I have done this? The thoughts went around and around my mind in a spiral that wouldn't untwist. Where were my clothes? Why was I still alive?

I became aware that I had left the craft, as the ships debris cleared. I was in space. I should be dead, space is a vacuum, and if hurtling through the middle of a Cruiser didn't do it, then the vacuum of space surely would? But no… I was definitely still me.

I was definitely alive, though I felt utterly and completely exhausted. I looked to Earth and noticed that I was surrounded by thousands of intact fighter craft. I held my body still and hoped that they wouldn't engage me. I hovered in the void, I felt at peace. I had achieved my mission. We had won.

General Eastwicks voice echoed once again across the Comms. 'Tell me. Somebody, anybody tell me, what am I looking at? It's moving slowly, it appears to be coming to a complete stop.'

Deno lifted her head to listen to the Comm. She had stopped sobbing, but Summer was still consoling her. Raena, then turned slowly towards them.

'This shouldn't be happening. I don't understand. Not from a human, how can she do this?'

'What Raena? What do you mean, what are you talking about?'

'Your Mitchell. She says to tell you to, 'catch her on the other side.' I shouldn't be able to hear her, why can I hear her?'

Deno leapt up and ran at full speed to the waiting medical craft that Adari had commissioned, she turned and beckoned Summer to accompany her.

'Coming with?' Summer ran at full speed towards the shuttle, Deno pulling her onboard only moments before it took off.

'This is General Eastwick, do not fire on the… Well, the… I don't know what to call it. Please steer clear of the humanoid, form that is… lit up. The same life form that just obliterated that Cruiser. We need a medical shuttle immediately, is it on its way?'

Deno rummaged about in the lockers in the medical craft, desperately seeking every available medical supply stored onboard.

'Chief, we have all the supplies we need for any casualty, we don't need every piece of gauze and tape on the craft.' Deno looked at Summer and Summer looked at the medic, shrugging her shoulders.

'She means to help. We both would like to help.' The medic smiled across at them both.

'Well, over in that locker are some thermal blankets. Can you get a couple out for me?'

Deno responded by leaping up and charging to the locker. The blankets were in packs of two. Deno pulled a pack out of the locker, tossing it across the shuttle to Summer who deftly caught the pack.

'There she is circle around her. Let's get a closer look. The shuttle began to circle Mitchell's form. Deno rushed to the window and looked out, Summer wasn't far behind her.

'She's moving… but she definitely looks different, it's her shape though. What the hell has happened to her? And why is she glowing that way? Did the missiles do something to her ya think?'

'No, we don't know what this is, but it isn't the work of any missile that we are aware of. It looks to me like a mystery. But I'm sure that right now she is probably incredibly scared and wondering what is happening to her unless she has done this before?' Deno frowned at the medic.

'Before? No, we would have known. She would have told us, she's not the type to hide something like this.'

'Well, you know her better than most. But tell me, what would you do if you were changing and didn't understand why?

'Well, I'd… I'd probably shit myself to be honest.' Summer Laughed at Deno's response.

'She probably would literally shit herself, and then she would probably get really drunk and shit herself again.' They laughed for a brief moment.

'That's right, you see how well we know each other.' Deno looked out of the window again.

'We are going to need something to cover her up, she appears to be naked. Open the back of the craft. I'm going to bring her in. Oh... before I go, what are her temperature readings? She looks like she could melt steel and I just want to make sure that Kevin doesn't melt.' The medic looked confused and wondered who Kevin was.

'Her temperature, believe it or not is perfectly normal. She may look hot, but I don't think you, or Kevin... whoever that is, are at risk. That is so long as you're not a Crucian.' Deno frowned once more at the medic trying to work out if she was being serious or not.

'That was a joke, her temperature is fine. Go get your Commanding Officer, she needs you now.'

Deno checked her helmet was secure and opened the pack of blankets that she had taken out of the locker only minutes before. Removing one, she opened it out, tucking it quickly under the strap on her thigh. She removed Kevin from his holster and handed him to Summer who was standing suited up at the rear of the craft.

'Look after him for me, I won't be long.' She placed the overpowered pistol in Summers opened hands, turned, and leapt out of the rear of the shuttle, her boosters kicking in shortly after.

There was debris and devastation everywhere that she looked, the sharpened edges of space fighters and blown out glass, rolling, twisting, and turning in infinite motion. A reminder of the battle that had only just ceased.

In the distance, and around two hundred metres away, was a humanoid shaped being that was perfectly still. The appearance of the beings skin at least, looked like it was emitting some kind of bright luminescence, or was that intense heat, or both? Deno had been assured that the beings temperature was low enough to advance, so she made her way closer at a steady speed, circling slightly away from the beings form so that she could make her final approach towards it from the front.

She was mindful of her training and had seen how the traumatised could respond when approached from the side or from behind, she didn't wish to cause the being, if it was Major Mitchell or anyone else, any further anxiety than what she thought they must already be experiencing.

With a final touch of the boosters on the rear of her suit, Deno began to make her final approach, hoping that Steph, her friend would recognise her. Inch by inch she went, desperate to see if it was her commanding officer in need of rescue, or if Raena had been wrong all along, and it was some other kind of strange anomaly.

She continued slowly making her way towards the form, until finally it was within just one metre of her. She noticed that she couldn't feel any heat, that was good, but she wondered why this was, especially as the being looked to have some sort of fusion taking place across its skin. No, this was vastly different to anything that she had ever seen.

Deno had passed across the fifty-metre-wide hole that had quite literally been carved through the centre of the Crucians ship, effectively killing the ship and most of its crew onboard. Whatever this being was, it certainly was very impressive, and extremely powerful, she thought. Deno felt a slight tinge of envy, just for the briefest of moments, as Kevin wasn't quite as powerful as this being appeared to be.

The humanoid shape lifted its arms up slowly, as Deno approached in a gesture that appeared to be one of peaceful intentions. Deno recognised the shape as Mitchell's, and she appeared to be suggesting that she was not a threat to her. Deno looked into where Mitchells eyes were and for a brief moment could only see a type of white hot infinite fusion. Mitchell appeared to be looking directly at Deno, and from what she could tell, she did seem to recognise her.

Deno noticed that Mitchells heated appearance was beginning to subside somewhat, as small patches of bronzed skin were appearing briefly, before the skin would return to its radiant form. intermittently at first, but gradually and very slowly Mitchell transformation appeared to be returning her skin back to that of her human form.

Deno didn't know what, or if Mitchell had sustained any physical injuries and felt that it was probably a good idea to recover Mitchell back to the craft so that she could receive appropriate medical attention and be around those that she knew and trusted. She reached towards her thigh tugging at the blanket to free it from the strap. Showing it to Mitchell, and opening it out, then in a single movement she gently put it around her shoulders, almost covering Mitchel entirely, giving her the thumbs up and a wide smile when she was done. Carefully, and slowly she held her hand out towards Mitchell, Mitchell reached out towards Deno's hand, grasping it tightly.

Deno took great care to move cautiously and at a

constant speed, reaching the shuttle relatively quickly. She held Mitchell in place for a moment until the medics and Summer could pull her safely through the medical vessels outer atmospheric shield and into the craft. Deno noticed that Mitchells skin was now rapidly transforming back to its human appearance, she also noted that she could not see any kind of physical injury. She wondered to herself if Mitchell had known that she could do this. Transform into… this, whatever it was.

As soon as they were both onboard, the shuttle's engines fired up and it quickly sped off back towards the Amaranthine.

'Chief Martin, what is Major Mitchells condition?' General Eastwick enquired, there was urgency in his voice.

'General, we have her secure, she's safely onboard the medical shuttle. We are heading back to the Amaranthine right now. Hang on, just one moment Sir. I'll just put you through to the medic.' Deno held her arm out allowing the medic to speak into her chip.

'General, although she appears physically well, she is in an acute state of shock, which given what we witnessed in relation to the Crucian ship and its destruction is not at all surprising. I have given her a mild sedative, and she is currently resting.

I'm pleased to say that we have detected no visible physical injuries so far. She isn't talking to anyone yet, but that's understandable, given the circumstances. We just don't have any experience of this… situation, this transformation you experienced. It is unique, I recommend that a full medical examination be carried out on the Amaranthine. We will advise you further once she is medically fit and available for debrief.' The medic nodded to Deno, letting her know that he had finished his report.

'General Eastwick.' Deno said, her voice calm. 'We will of course update you immediately if anything changes.' Deno closed the conversation down.

'Thank you, Chief Martin, make sure she gets some rest and give her whatever she needs to help her recover. Eastwick out.'

∞

The deck was a buzz with activity when Fetch arrived. She looked about for a place to stand and saw a number of storage crates. She climbed them quickly, checking her view and steadying her feet. She then out an almighty shout.

'Listen up!' Everyone on the deck turned to face her. 'Anyone that is not linked directly to the support or care of Major Mitchell or providing direct assistance to the incoming medical team will clear this deck immediately. That's an order!' Most unnecessary staff withdrew immediately, but a few appeared to ignore the request. Fetch jumped down from the crates and made her way at pace towards a small group that were stood chatting.

'Hi there, you medical staff?'

'No.' They turned away.

'Then why are you still on this deck, I just requested that all non-essential staff leave the deck.' One of the staff then responded in a sarcastic tone.

'You're not our commanding officer, you don't give us orders. We want to see if she's still glowing.' Fetch bit down on her lip, she was seething.

'You know what… I've had an incredibly stressful day and you're right, I'm not your commanding officer. But she is mine, and furthermore asshole, she deserves to have some dignity, the way I see it, is that she just saved all of our asses. So, I suggest you make yourselves scarce and take yourselves off this deck NOW, before I lose my shit and throw you off.' Fetch stood and eyeballed the man, both of them standing off for the briefest of moments, she was wolf like, as if she were vying for the meat from a fresh kill.

'Alright, alright… jeez we only wanted to see it.'

'Her.' Fetch didn't say another word to the group, as her eyes tracked their movements off the deck. Only then did she allow herself to take a few gasps, inhaling, tasting, and noticing the mixture of metallic and fume filled air from the deck. She felt nauseated with stress, bending forwards, she immediately lost the contents of her stomach.

They had rattled her, and she was never rattled. It had been the kind of day that she longed to forget, and one that she would no doubt drink away in the bar later. She silently hoped to herself that the ships bars were fully stocked with Vodka, because tonight she intended to drink the bar dry.

In the medical shuttle six medics surrounded the bed that Mitchell lay on exhausted. It hovered just above ground level moving forwards slowly, to ensure the safe transition of Major Mitchell. The medics shouted at the air crew ground staff to clear the way their voices full of urgency, as they moved tentatively forwards. Deno, Summer and Fetch followed the medics desperate to help, but not able to do anything, other than hope, and watch as their commanding officer was transferred to the ship's medical facility.

When Joe, Cat and Tommy landed, they made their way to where Mitchell was being cared for, when they arrived, they could see Summer, Fetch and Deno. They looked to be deep in conversation.

'Hey, how is she?' Tommy said, placing a large bear like hand onto Deno's shoulder.

'Well, she's alive, but from what we could see she's in severe shock. She's not spoken at all, though she did grab my hand. I guess that's something. I'm really worried about her, and I don't know how to describe what I saw, I just can't process it.'

'Thank goodness, I'm not on my own here.' Said Cat, relieved. 'I don't know what we just saw either. I can't explain it, I–'

Fetch interjected. 'It's OK Cat, just cos she blew a hole right through that ship, well it don't mean she isn't the same person ya know. Think about what she just did for us all.'

'I know… I just… I just don't know what that was. Does anyone else?' Cat looked at her squad mates in earnest.

'Nope.' Said Deno. 'But what does it matter anyways? She saved us all, and we might want to remember that it's her in that bed right now, and not any of us. Maybe we just need to fully accept it, that she's… well that she's fucking awesomely kick ass. She's definitely more powerful than Kevin and that's saying something.' Deno smirked. 'Truthfully though, I just want her to be alright, even if we never see the whole nuclear fusion thing ever again. She's my commanding officer, my drinking buddy, and my friend and that's all that matters… I just want her to recover.

10 RECOVERY

The first thing that I was aware of was that the light was hurting my eyes. My eyes were aching with every slight movement and my eyelids felt heavy. I prepared myself and tried to open them, slowly at first and little by little a crack of even brighter light crept through, causing me a deep and throbbing pain at the back of my head.

I squinted, whilst trying to get my bearings. Where was I? I turned slowly onto my side and moved my arm over my face trying to relieve my eyes from the worst of the rooms glare. I was thirsty and the back of my throat was dry and sore from it. I tried to open my eyes once more, I was in a bed, but this wasn't my bed. I moved my arm once more and tried to heave myself up, I needed to know where I was.

My memory started to return to me, slowly at first and then after a few minutes it all started coming back to me, in small segments one piece at a time. I needed to get up, I needed to make sure that they hadn't launched those missiles at Earth. No, that wasn't right… All the countries were there in support and, we fought.

Yes, we fought, and I had the fusion missiles on my fighter, the crafts weapons system wouldn't launch… they hacked my weapons systems… yes that's right, but I think I delivered the payload, yes. I delivered the payload, all was fine. No, no, the payload it wouldn't release. But I'm alive so… No, you died. I died, no that's not right, I'm here. I don't understand. Light, the light, so much light. I don't understand. I DON'T UNDERSTAND.

'I DON'T UNDERSTAND, I DON'T UNDERSTAND ANY OF THIS!' I rocked and I sobbed, I could barely breathe, endless tears soaking the cheeks of my face and running onto and down my medical gown. I could hear fast approaching footsteps, but I couldn't make out anything more than that, as my vision was blurred, and I still struggled to focus my eyes.

'Major Mitchell. Are you ok? Please drink all of this water, you are dehydrated, and take this medication, it will help you to relax.' The medical officer handed me a small blue capsule, and I immediately swallowed it, feeling it stick to my throat on the way down, I took a large gulp of water.

'Where am I? What happened to Earth. Where are my crew?' The questions poured from my mouth like the water that I had just swallowed.

'Major, you need to rest. There are some people, I think they are your friends, wating outside to see you. They haven't moved for more or less two days solid. A real stubborn bunch I would say, would you like me to let them know you are awake?'

'Yes, please would you tell them that I told you that they need to all go and get some sleep. Tell them, that's an order, but please let them know I'm ok, that everything is going to be ok.' The medic nodded and left Mitchell's bed, walking towards the door. He opened the door efficiently, and it was of no surprise to him that they were still there.

Fetch, Tommy, Adari and Joe were pacing about, though they weren't talking. Whilst Deno, Raena, Summer and Cat were dozing on the padded benches that were situated to the left and the right of the main door.

'Hello, I have been asked to pass on some good news to you all. She's awake and has started speaking, she is still a little confused, but she's making good progress.' Joe approached the medic with a serious look of concern on his face.

'When you say she is awake, is she really alright doc? What has she said?'

'Well, she told me to tell you all to get some sleep, and followed that up by saying, that's an order. I would say that she has finally remembered who she is, and some of what has happened, for a time she was very confused and didn't seem to know if she was alive or dead.

However, considering what we know she has been through, that's understandable. She thought she was going to die and didn't. What her body and mind have been through though… Well, let's just say that it might take some time for her to heal.' He smiled at the group. 'She is lucky to have such friends, now go and get some rest.'

'That's really great Doc, any idea of when we can see her?' Deno spurted out.

'Well, I think providing she continues to improve, I may allow her back to continue her recovery in her quarters. Perhaps even as early as this afternoon, with regular check-ups, of course. I'm sure that she will be in touch.' The eight dispersed quickly, leaving the once full corridor, now completely empty.

The Chief Medical Officer walked across to where Mitchell was now sat upright in bed. He checked her stats on his computing device.

'How are you feeling, still feel like you are improving?' He peered through the pale blue visor that he wore on his head, it was running cycles of continuous data about Mitchells condition in front of his eyes.

'I'm starting to feel absolutely fine now, better every minute… other than being confused about what happened. I'm famished. Can I get some food?'

'Yes, I will have something brought in, anything in particular that you would like Major?'

'A burger and fries, oh and onion rings too, and maybe some ice cream and a shake, a strawberry shake.' The Chief Medical Officer smiled, tapping his chip, and requesting the same be brought to the medical centre as soon as possible.

'We do need to talk Major Mitchell, about the incident. We need to understand what occurred. I know it's early days, but can I ask you something?'

'Yes, of course. I'm a bit of an open book, aren't I? What with the crashing through a cruiser and coming out the other side of it and still being alive thing' I paused. Did I actually just say that? I couldn't quite remember everything, but a lot of it was beginning to come back to me now.

'Well, before you went on the mission, you said that there was something that you wanted to discuss.' The doctor said curiously. 'Was it linked to what happened to you during the battle by any chance?'

'Yes, I've had a few strange experiences, recently. The truth is that I just don't have any experience of this at all, and I don't know anyone else who has experienced this either. But what I do know is that humans, or at least all the humans I know, don't shimmer like I do sometimes, with this… this intense heat.

It was happening periodically. It was something that began initially in my late teens, but not at the level of the last few weeks and months. It's been getting really bad, really frequent, and well…It was beginning to scare me, and I'm not scared of much.

I dunno, I guess my imminent death must have, well… triggered something in me. I just don't know what, or who I am anymore. Am I human even? I know that I shouldn't have survived that blast, but I don't have an explanation for you in case you were wondering. I was hoping that you might have one for me, but I know that's a long shot.'

'Well, the initial DNA tests indicate that you are indeed human. Maybe a different type of human though, we found something that will be of interest to you, but we are in the early days of studying your results. You are right about other human types though. I certainly can't light up space like you did. Tell me, do you have any control over it at all?'

'The only thing I know, is that it seems to link to my emotions, such as states of stress or duress, but not always. Sometimes it just happens randomly.'

'Interesting, there may be two things occurring here, you may be awakening, or should I say maturing, but it may well also be something that in time can be controlled, by your emotions and, or your will.'

'Maturing, hell doc, I'm forty. That's a hell of a late puberty.' I smiled.

'Maybe, something triggered it, I will have to think on it more.' He said, clearly, he was curious about what had occurred.

'I'm worried doc, worried that I will hurt someone by accident. I couldn't bare it if–'

'Major, I didn't see you harm a single ally in that battle. With that kind of power, the kind that you demonstrated. It would suggest that you do have some control of it, even when the fusion event is taking place.'

'Fusion, is that what you think is happening to me? I had considered it but–'

'Yes, some kind of fusion was occurring in your body. I think it is quite unique, when we scanned you in space, your temperature, it was completely normal, and yet you had just burnt out and disintegrated ten internal decks of that cruiser. You also survived the vacuum of space with no suit and no helmet. It certainly is a mystery Major, but needless to say, I'm really glad that you're on our side.'

The door opened and in walked one of the ships cooks, she was carrying a large, covered tray which she put down on one of the many medical cabinets whilst she moved the medical beds table in front of me. I straightened myself up, whilst she retrieved the tray from the cabinet and placed it onto the table. She lifted the lid and the smell of freshly cooked food hit my nostrils.

'Oh wow, I'm really hungry. This looks delicious, I don't know where to start.' The cook smiled at me.

'I would start with the onion rings. They are beer battered, an old English recipe and one of my personal favourites.' She smiled, nodded, turned, and headed towards the door.

'Enjoy Major, hopefully we will see you in the mess, once you're feeling better.' I tucked into the food, I didn't think that I had ever tasted anything as good, in my entire life. Every mouthful was like the first, full of flavour, and it wasn't long before the plate was completely cleared. The Chief Medical Officer then appeared at my bedside once again.

'I think it's safe to say that you enjoyed that meal.' He smiled, whilst moving the tray from the bed, back across to the cabinet.

'I'm going to discharge you back to your quarters Major. I want you to get some rest and see how you are tomorrow. Please update me if you have any further episodes, vacancies, or any pain that causes you concern.'

∞

I opened my eyes once again, this time there was no glare, and no disorientation. I instantly noticed the fragrance of orange blossom and a soft breeze. I had awoken safely back in my quarters. I stretched out like a starfish in my large and comfortable bed, my body felt strong again, no I felt considerably stronger than before. I felt energised.

Looking at the back of my hand and palm, I moved it about in front of my face, magician like. Just underneath my skin the fusion had returned and was shimmering gently like molten, golden fish iridescent scales. I concentrated, and in my minds-eye requested consciously that it cease. *Stop*, when I looked again it was just my bronzed arm, the same arm I had seen day in and day out since my birth. I breathed in, and out came a sigh of relief. It seemed that I may be getting some control over this… well, whatever it was.

I jumped in the shower, it felt really good. The streams of hot water running down my body, cleansing me of the battle and washing the Crucian ships memories from my physique. The metallic, meaty smell of the vacuum of space was at last, irradicated from my skin and hair.

I looked down at my body, not a single bruise or cut was visible, yet I had blown clean through that ship. I had absorbed every bit of its core, everything around me had turned to nothingness, not even dust or ash remained. I had done my job, gotten the payload into the Cruiser, but really, did I need to, was it the missiles, was it me, or some combination of both? Could I do it again, and if I could, would I even be aware of it?

A multitude of questions ran through my mind, I needed answers and I also needed to know how my DNA had gotten into that room on Pluto. I needed to talk to mom, but first I needed to see my eight. I opened ship a wide communication on my chip.

'This is Major Mitchell, requesting that her eight attend the briefing room for an urgent meeting, Mitchell out.' I dressed quickly but did not put my uniform on. Instead, I chose to wear my favourite synth jeans, some training shoes, an old t-shirt, and my favourite leather jacket.

I wanted to speak with them about what had happened, and then I intended to leave for Earth immediately afterwards, to visit and talk to mom. No, it really couldn't wait any longer. I walked down the corridor from my quarters to the lift, each person I passed appeared to be studying me more closely than before. I took in a long and deep breath which filled my lungs with air, reminding me at least that some part of me was still completely human.

I was becoming more and more aware that everyone on board must have questioned what they had seen, they must be wondering what I am. Now, that would be a luxury, as even I do not know what I am, I thought.

I entered the briefing room, it felt different than before, heavier, and I felt tense. I could feel it in my shoulders and neck, and I stood at the table rotating my head in an effort to stretch the tension out. I must have only been in my own company for around thirty seconds though, as soon after my eight entered together, each one pausing momentarily, taking a quick look at me before taking their place at the table. Was this how it was going to be now?

I felt nauseous, and I wondered if I would be able to keep it together, what if their opinion of me had changed, what if they didn't see me as human anymore… what if they were frightened of me?

'Good morning.' I spoke and they all replied in unison. Good, that was a good sign.

'I'm not often lost for words, but I wanted to call you all together. I wanted to let you know what I know. I do not want there to be any secrets between us.' I paused. 'You're probably aware that something is happening to me. It's something that I can't explain, I just don't know what it is. I don't know why it is happening either.'

I walked back over to the window and looked at Earth once again, she was radiant. I stood there for a short time, just admiring the view before I spoke once again.

'I think… I think it all started when I was a teenager. I would have these… episodes of intense heat. But these passed as quickly as they began, and I wasn't all too concerned about them. I thought it was just something peculiar to me.

However, during the last six months or so, these episodes had started to intensify, and they were getting much more extreme in nature. I began to notice changes in my skin's composition, and the heat... The heat, well it was significant, and I wasn't sure how to cope with it, if I'm being completely truthful.

The last two episodes that I had, they happened not long before the battle. I thought I was going to die. I even updated my will. I was absolutely convinced that I was dying. I was going to tell the Chief Medical Officer, but then we had the Crucians and their Cruiser to deal with. I put that first, and well... we all saw how that worked out.

If any of you have any questions, I will try to answer them. I'm not sure I have answers though, but I would like your help to find out what this is. I don't want to endanger any of you and I–'

At that moment Joe intervened. 'Major, you ended the immediate threat to Earth, quicker than anything I have ever seen before in my life. You chose to crash your fighter into the Cruiser and in so doing, you saved millions, if not billions of lives, probably all of humanity for that matter. I do not believe that you are a threat at all.' Fetch followed up, jumping right in after Joe.

'What you did, well I'm damned if I know what it was, but it sure as hell worked.'

'Yep. Major it was also pretty awesome. I've never seen anything like it. I sure wish Kevin could do that, though I'm not sure I could hold onto him though if he did!' Deno smirked, whilst tapping her holster. I smiled warmly towards my friend, remembering her courage during my rescue.

Cat then joined the conversation. 'We understand that this is a mystery and that you have many questions. We all do, but we will find out what it is, and you need to trust us in that Major. We have your back, just as you have always had ours.' Cat smiled and then continued. 'In fact, you could say that we have made a good start.'

'Explain, please. Anything you can say would be helpful at this stage. I'm sure you can all understand that I'm having a hard time trying to understand this myself.' I pointed to the Holo-screen.

'Yes Major. Well, it would appear that you are connected in some way to what has been happening on Pluto. Traces of DNA matching your own were found at the Pluto site.' There were quiet gasps in the room from those who weren't already aware.

'The object that you picked up. We believe that it was encoded to your DNA. We also believe that when it released the mist like substance, that it, whatever it was, was meant for you. If you remember, the central chamber of the site lit up soon afterwards.' I nodded to Cat, acknowledging her statement in full, whilst looking at the 3D projection of the central chamber on the holo-screen.

'We have some of the pieces Major, but without any context at all.' Cat said.

'I want to make sure that we fully understand how I'm linked to that site. More importantly, I need to know why. I need to know who I am, what I am.' I could feel that my resolve was just about to cave in, when Raena finally spoke.

'Major, what you are, is maybe not as important as

who you are.' She looked about the table. 'We all saw you give up your life, for your species very survival. The fact that you survived is almost irrelevant, you risked it all, for all of them. Who you are, therefore is the most important aspect of all the many questions that you should have. We will find those answers with you, together.'

At that moment the door slid open and General Eastwick entered the room, he had an air of determination about him. Everyone instantly stood to attention.

'At ease.' He said, making his way directly to the top of the table to where I was stood.

He stopped right in front of me and then reached his hand out to me, offering to shake it. But instead, he took my hand and pulled me into him. I felt his strong arms momentarily hold me and then he released, stepping back, and looking at me directly in the eyes, he said.

'I don't usually forgo the formalities Major.' He said. 'But there are always exceptions to the rule. Major, what I saw you do. No, what we all saw you do, and then what followed. Well, I'm still trying to process it all. I just wanted to thank you, and I also wanted to say that I am sure glad you are one of us.' I felt a smile cross my lips, one of us.

'General, thank you. You don't know what that means to me, to hear those words from you. I wanted to put everyone on forty-eight hours leave. I understand that the Okai have invited us to celebrate our combined victory on their home world Nemeranth in just three days' time. I would also like to visit my mother. Deno, I would very much like to spend some time with you when I get back. I will pick up something for us to drink whilst on Earth.'

'Sounds like a plan Major.' Deno beamed. Then General Eastwick spoke once again.

'That sounds like an excellent plan Major. You jump in fifty-two hours to Nemeranth, enjoy your time on Earth.' He turned and walked towards the exit pausing just before he reached the door, turning quickly on his heel.

'Major. Thank you once again, for everything.' He then stepped through the open door and disappeared. I looked around the table, I felt better than I did, a little calmer. My head though, was still a wash with questions.

'If there isn't anything further, you are all dismissed with forty-eight hours leave. Go see those you love and have some fun.' I paused remembering that Adari and Raena couldn't do this.

'Adari, Raena you could look at taking in some of the night life, or some of the natural sights and cultures of Earth, like China Town in LA, or perhaps a museum. I'm sure you would love it.' Deno then looked towards them excitedly.

'I'll show you both around, don't have anyone down on Earth so… It would be my pleasure.' Deno looked at me in a questioning way, seeking my approval.

'Sounds like a solid plan to me, you all have fun.' I picked up my jacket from the chair and left the briefing room, heading back to my quarters. Once there I made myself a coffee and sat back in my reading chair, letting it hold all the weight and the stress that I had felt. I needed to speak to mom, I had so many questions, that only she might be able to answer.

∞

I awoke and realised that I must have dozed off, looking at my chip I realised that just over an hour had passed. I called Fetch immediately, in the hope that she hadn't already left the ship.

'Fetch, it's Mitchell. Yeah, I'm feeling much better thanks. Listen, I need to take a quick trip to Earth, and I wondered if… Oh you will, that's great. How quickly can you be ready as I want to be back on the ship by late evening. Yep, that sounds good. I'll meet you there. I'm going to see my mother, there are a few things I need to ask her. Yeah, I figured I best take someone with me to watch my ass. See you soon, oh, and no uniform.'

Fetch stood by the shuttle panther like. I noticed that she had shaved her head, just above the ears and had it closely cropped it at the sides. On top it was considerably longer, bright vivid and very purple, it stood up on end, cockatiel like. She looked a complete bad-ass, her synth-leather black jeans, the racing biker jacket, and those heavy thick soled boots that completed the look. She had her side arm neatly tucked away in a shoulder holster. I could see the butt of the pistol peeping out of the jacket, and if I could see it, so could everyone else, and that was the point.

'Hey, Major. It's really good to see you. Are you sure that you are fit enough to take a trip out?' A look of concern flashed across her face, which was quickly replaced by one of excitement.

'Yep, honestly, I'm fine. I brought you with me just in case. I thought we could take a couple of bikes instead of an A V. I quite like the feeling of being in control of my own shit right now. You ok with that?'

Fetch beamed, and nodded in acknowledgement towards me, continuing to speak about the trip as we both alighted the shuttle.

'Am I ok with that? Just a bit. I'm also looking forward to being on solid ground too. I heard you say that we are all travelling to Nemeranth in two days, at the invitation of the Okai species.

'Yes, it should be quite a thing. I've never been before, but I hear it's a beautiful planet.'

'Raena told me after the meeting that she is looking forward to showing you around. Just out of curiosity, how did you let her know you were ok… when you, ya know, blew out the front of that Cruiser?'

'What do you mean?' I was a little puzzled, we sat down in our seats and the shuttle began to move out of the hanger.

'Well, Raena was the one that told us that you were alive. She said that you relayed to her. Catch me on the other side, that's apparently what you said to her, and that's when Deno and Summer left the hanger to rescue you… Sorry Major, I thought you knew.'

'No. I don't remember that. Most of the battle, I do remember now. Are you sure she said that I communicated with her? If so, that's something new. I didn't think humans could communicate telepathically with the Okai, or any other species.'

'Well, we can't. But you did. Raena looked quite shaken by it, stunned even.'

'I will have to discuss it with her later. I'm going to have to be mindful of that for several reasons.' Fetch laughed, raising an eyebrow, and fixing her stare on me.

'Well Major, she is stunning, and Deno might have also mentioned the arm thing.'

'Oh. Well, err. I already explained to Deno that we were just talking, and she was trying to reassure me. You know Deno and her fertile imagination, it can be quite a wild and vibrant thing.'

'I do indeed.' Fetch responded. 'So, no bullshitting me Major, off the record. Do you like her?'

I could feel myself begin to blush. 'I, well I think she is extremely attractive, but–'

'But what? Come on Major spill it.' Fetch's eyes were homing in on my resolve and I needed to find a way to break her steely, and investigative gaze.

'I'm not sure this is a conversation we should be having Fetch, and I certainly won't be spilling anything, but–'

'Major, I promise you. This conversation won't go any further.'

'Fetch listen, I can't even begin to consider it. 1. I have a job to do and 2. She might not be remotely interested and 3. I'm not even sure if our species are compatible, and I can't even go there. It feels weird to even think about it.'

'Ok. So basically, it comes down to biology and duty. I get it, Major I really do. Well Major, if it will help, I can tell you that yes, they are a little different. I can also tell you that it's not really that different at all. They are in fact remarkably similar to us.' I could feel myself begin to blush.

'Fetch. Just how the hell would you even know this?' I could sense the surprise, embarrassment, and intrigue that were written right across my reddening face.

'Oh, come on Major. I've lived, if ya know what I'm saying.' She smirked and looked out of the shuttles window.

'Can we just stop this conversation now Fetch, and think about something else?'

'Yep. Of course, we can put the extremely attractive

Raena right out of our minds, there, poof… gone. But ya know where I am, should you find yourself ever needing to talk.'

'Thank you, I think.' From now on, I thought. I definitely need to be more mindful of my body language and any eye contact around my eight, and on that note, I quickly changed the subject.

'So, I thought we might take a couple of fusion bikes from the Space Port to my mom's. I need to see her in private Fetch, we have a lot to talk about. There is a good coffee shop just around the corner and I thought you could wait for me there, whilst I meet with my mother. Then, afterwards we might catch some of the night life. I've had a hankering for some authentic Chinese food and a few local beers, you up for that?' Fetch paused for a just second, as the shuttle began to move slowly out of the ship.

'Yeah. I could go for that. I miss real coffee, you know. The ships coffee is OK, but it's nothing like the bean to cup of a real Earth café. You've got yourself a deal Major.'

I sat quietly closing my eyes for the rest of the journey whilst Fetch spoke to just about everyone on board. I ran it all through my mind, again and again, trying to think of what I would say to her. What could I ask her that would give me any clue about my past?

11 HOME

The shuttle landing took place without incident, and we left the space port walking across the site to a large freight and storage unit which was on the periphery of the arrivals and departure complex and situated just outside of the central space port itself. Large metal containers that were uniform in appearance, and white in colour were stacked six high in multiple rows.

The site itself was approximately one square mile in size, but thankfully all the containers were electronically coded and numbered. We headed to the reception area, where a large balding man stood behind an older model holo-screen. He was drinking coffee out of a stained recyclable synth-plastic mug, whilst frantically tapping his chip.

'Good morning.' He said cheerily, as we entered the modest reception area. He looked up at us momentarily, whilst still continuing to use his chip.

'Hi. I'm here to open my container, I contacted you last night. The names Steph, Steph Mitchell.' The man paused, looking up towards me and smiling.

'Oh yes. Let me just retrieve that for you now. I

have it in the holding area, it won't take long to bring it across.' He touched his chip once again and paused for a brief moment.

'Forgive me, but your name. Mitchell. Are you by any chance related to the great Major Mitchell who just kicked those damnable Crucians out of our system?'

'Ha!' Fetch let out a loud laugh from her gut. 'Is she related? She IS Major Mitchell, and we are just about to take some well-earned shore leave.' Fetch was the most animated that I had seen her in a while. The man held out his meaty hand towards me and I instantly shook it.

'Major Mitchell, never in my life did I think I would meet a real hero. Forgive me for not recognising you. I only heard it on the news, I didn't know what you looked like.'

'Hey, don't worry about it. I'm just pleased that today I get to spend the whole day here, without having to worry about the Crucians and their plans.'

'Amen to that! I never did like em, something off about them if you ask me.' He spoke, nodding his head in agreement. 'Your container is just outside and to the left. I will put it back in the holding area when you have retrieved your items, just let me know when you are done.'

'Thanks, I will'. We turned and walked out of the reception area. The odour of strong coffee still lodged in our nostrils.

We headed left as instructed by the receptionist, and I caught sight of the large freight container in a cleared space on the ground. Walking up to the door I scanned in my access code from my chip. The door hissed as air from the vacuum sealed unit was released, its two large white secure doors opening, revealing the containers contents.

Fetch peeked into the container, her curiosity getting the better of her. It was full of the things I had collected during my life, things I intended to put into a home one day. There were sculptures and paintings, real ones, not the cheaper digital versions. Fetch stood in amazement, just taking it all in.

'I wouldn't have put you down as someone interested in the arts Major.'

'Why not? I love art, real hand crafted art that is. To me art should be full of texture, and colour, something you can feel with the tips of your fingers, really experience it in real time like the artist that created it. Don't get me wrong, digi-art has its place, but it's not my personal preference.'

'Well Major, you look to have a fine collection, and these here. Are these real bikes?' Fetch looked at two objects that were situated in the middle of the container, both were covered with white synth sheets.

'How did you guess?' I laughed. 'You can remove the dust sheet, that one is yours.'

Fetch pulled the cover back slowly revealing a powerful motorbike. It was sleek and its carbon black metallic tank and black chrome exhaust, seat and fairing screamed power. Fetch's face lit up, as she ran her fingers over the tank and onto the seat.

'I think I may be… I don't have words.' She uttered, whilst continuing to touch the bikes faring. 'In love, that's it. I'm in love.' I laughed, she was very rarely lost for words, and it was nice to see that there was something that could still inhibit her speech.

I pulled back the sheet nearest to me, underneath was a bike of equal power, but it had all the colours, from the darkest red, right through to the sunniest yellow, all impinging on each other. The paint was pearlescent, and the colours were merging into what could be a sunset, or a sunrise depending on where you stood to gaze at it.

'Here, place your chip onto mine.' Fetch raised her arm out towards me, and I placed my wrist directly over hers. A light beam connected the two devices, changing colour from red to green a few seconds later.

'There you go. You now have the key, turn it on.'

I straddled my bike and picked up the self-fitting helmet, which was resting on the handlebars. Placing it on my head and touching a small pad at the front, the helmet instantaneously moulded to my head, it fit snugly, and the visor then changed to my preferred colour. Fetch then turned on her bike, placing the machines helmet onto her head. She waved her arm towards me, giving me the thumbs up and we rolled out of the storage container. I stopped the bike and held my arm out, the front of the container rolled down and sealed tight, whilst I began to speak into the helmet.

'Fetch, our helmets are synced. Can you hear me?'

'Yep, crystal clear Major.' She nodded as she spoke.

'I've already put the co-ordinates into the bikes computer-nav, you should be able to see the route we are taking any second. I thought we could open these beasts up along the coast road, and then cut back into the other side of the city to my mom's. What do you think?'

'Sounds awesome, I can almost smell that sea air and taste that coffee.'

'Great, let's go'. We roared out of the storage facility and onto the open road. I could feel the breeze waft gently against my skin and I noticed the smells and tastes of everything around us. It wasn't long before we were on the coast road, to my right I could see the sea, and in front of me lay the miles and miles of the twists and turns of the old coast road.

It was beautiful here, the warm salty breeze and the smell of the ocean, instantly brought back memories of frequent happy childhood visits to the beach with mom, beach combing for shells and snorkelling, whilst searching for crabs and small fish, their silver scales glistening in the sun as it pierced the blue water with its light.

We opened the throttles up and I felt just as invigorated as I had done whilst in the fighter, but this time I had no payload and no planet to defend. It was just me, in this perfect moment, on the planet I loved, heading home.

We rode the coast road for a good hour before we turned off and headed towards the outskirts of the city. The sprawl started off small, a few buildings here and there, I noticed a derelict service station, with old charging points and remnants of the days before we achieved clean fusion technology.

It wasn't long after that, that we finally reached suburbia. We could see houses and convenience stores at first, in various states of repair. The more we rode the taller the buildings got, until we reached a smaller block of apartments that had recently undergone significant renovation.

I pulled the bike over to the sidewalk and got off. Fetch pulled up at the rear. I walked to, and opened the lockup with my chip, which just happened to be situated directly opposite the apartment block.

We quickly parked the bikes up inside the lock up, and then we parted ways. I gave one last wave to Fetch, just as I saw her disappear from my sight. I crossed the street and headed up the apartment blocks external emergency exit stairs to moms modest apartment, number seventeen.

I rang the bell on the door. For some reason when the renovations had taken place, mom had insisted on keeping the doorbell, though I never did understand why. My heart was now racing. I tried to calm its pace, with little success. Mom would be pleased to see me, as it had been several months since we had last spoken face to face. So much had happened, and I wondered if she would be aware of any of it. The door opened slowly and a woman in her mid-sixties stood there smiling.

'Hi Mom. How are you?' I smiled back towards her, her smile was contagious, and I was sure that she could have made even the Crucians smile.

'Come in, come on inside dear, I have just put some tea in the pot.' She said excitedly.

The blue door swung open wide, and I walked into the small apartment, noticing once again that familiar smell of orange blossom, both hers and my own favourite scent. I walked into the living room, nothing had changed at all, everything was still in its place.

'I'm so pleased to see you Stephanie, I have missed you, let me get you a cup of tea, and then we can have a good old catch up.'

'Yes, mom. I would love a cup.' I breathed out a contented sigh.

I sat down in my favourite chair, the same chair that I had watched TV in, the same chair that I had read for my exams in. The chair that I had eaten supper in, for so many years. This chair I had in my quarters onboard the Amaranthine, an exact replica of this very chair that

I now sat in, other than the fabric. I'd had it made for me in exactly the same style, because in a way it felt like I had something of home with me wherever I went.

I could hear the old kettle begin to boil, and then the water pour, the sound of the stainless-steel spoon clinking on the inside of the mugs, and then a splash of milk in each. She would return with two mugs, on a round tray with a small plate of biscuits and cakes. I was home.

Placing the tray onto a small wooden coffee table, just as she had done a thousand times before. She handed me my mug, being careful to turn it so that the handle was facing me. I took the tea and sipped it, it was too hot and yet I always did the same thing, every single time.

She sat down across from where I sat, I could see her toying with what she wanted to say next to me. She looked a little uneasy, but after a few seconds passed, she finally spoke.

'I saw it on the news… about the battle, with the Crucians. I heard that you played a critical role in their defeat. How are you? It must have been a hard battle. The media, they are calling you a hero. My daughter, a hero, you make me so very proud Stephanie.' I hung my head, looking down toward the floor. How could I tell her? I took a long and deep breath.

'Mom, about that.' I reached for her hand.

'Yes dear, is everything alright?' She looked concerned.

'Yes and no, there are a few things I need to tell you, and something that I very much need to ask of you.' I spent the next half hour telling her about the promotion, Jevargh's death. My new ship, our new crew members and finally I began to speak about the onset of the battle.

'Mom, about the battle. There is something I… something I have to know, and something I need you to know, but I don't even know where to begin. So, I will just come right out with it… At the battle, I was meant to die. What I mean is, there was a payload of missiles that I was meant to deliver into the stern of their ship, only the missiles, well, the damn missiles wouldn't release because the Crucians hacked the weapons system on my craft. I had no choice, no choice at all, and I… I had to try and save everyone. Mom, they were going to kill all the children on Earth. Then they were going to kill us, all of us. I had no choice.

I was meant to die mom… but I didn't, and I don't know why, and I don't know what I am. I don't know what else could possibly survive what I did. Every time I think about it, I come up with a big fat zero. Mom, I'm so sorry.

I know this must be a lot to take in, and if there were any other way, I wouldn't ask, but please mom if there is anything you know, anything at all. Right now, even the smallest detail could be relevant.' She squeezed my hand tightly, and her eyes began to fill with tears.

'I knew this day would come my dear. But before I tell you my story, I want you to know that I love you. I don't care where you are from, or what you are. You are my daughter, and I will always love you.'

She stood up and began to pace around the room a little. Stopping only, to pick up a picture of me in my uniform, holding it closely to her chest.

'They said a time would come, a time when you would ask the right questions. They asked me not to say a single word until that time came. I made a promise to keep you safe, and as your mother I found that their request came very naturally to me my dear.' She held the picture up, looking at it, studying it.

'I want you to know that what I tell you next, I didn't know, or have any thoughts or suspicions about until you became a teenager and started to mature into a woman. Until then, well, let's just say I was oblivious to the truth of the matter. I haven't told another living soul about what happened that night.' She looked saddened.

'What, mom. What night?'

'The night the stranger brought you to me.' A cold shiver ran down the length of my spine.

'Stranger? A stranger brought me to you, what do you mean?' I asked curiously.

'I was a young woman then. I'd recently been told by the doctors that I wouldn't be able to carry my own child to term. I hadn't even come to grips with it fully.'

'I didn't realise mom, I'm so sorry.'

'It's ok dear. As it happened, I was settled in for the evening. There was a hell of a storm that night, so much rain, and it was freezing cold outside. The doorbell rang, there was a stranger at the door. They asked me my name and told me that they had a package for me…'

'Go on…'

'Well dear, it really was such a cold night. So, I offered the stranger some tea. I remember thinking they must have been really cold because they had a heavy hood on their coat, well dear it covered everything but their face. And the coat, it was very thickly padded, or so I thought.'

'The package, what was it?'

'Well dear, this is where it gets very interesting indeed. I returned with the tea, and the package dear, well it was you.' My jaw dropped open. I shook my head in disbelief.

'No. Mom, you always told me that I was adopted.'

'Well, you were. It just wasn't a conventional adoption. The stranger asked me if I would care for you, told me it wasn't safe where they were going. They left me more money than I could ever spend to raise you. I've hardly spent any of it. I only ever touched it when I needed it for you. To pay for your education, or to send you on trips with the school and university.' She placed the picture back onto the bookshelf, taking one last look at it before returning to her chair. She sat down, taking my hand once more.

'I don't really know how to tell you the next bit Stephanie, as it will make no sense to you at all. It doesn't make sense to me and believe me I have often thought on it.'

'Tell me what, mom? Please mom, what happened?'

'You must understand, I didn't know. Not really. Not until you were an adult. Then, well I was scared, scared for you. I was scared of what I had come to realise.'

'What mom, what had you come to realise?'

'The stranger, she was female. I hadn't realised it at first, not until you were a teenager, and then one day, I saw it, and it scared me, Stephanie. I just couldn't rationalise it away… but there is no other way to say this to you. The stranger that visited me that night dear… well, it was you.' I looked mom in the eyes, she was telling the truth, and I could see that she knew exactly what she had just said to me.

'Me? It was me? That's impossible mom, I'm here

right now. I can't have brought myself to you. Are you sure, maybe she just looked a little like me?'

'Listen my dear, all I can say is that it was you, it was you who brought you to me. She looked just like you do right now apart from one small thing. There was something in the way she moved and carried herself. She looked weary, tired, like she was carrying a heavy burden.

You, I mean this woman, she was so very warm and caring, her eyes were full of compassion for me and my… situation. She… offered me the child, you, on the understanding that I wouldn't tell you anything, not until you asked the right questions, she said there would come a time, and then she asked me to keep you safe, and to raise you with love.

The visitor, well she knew that one day you would ask, and you did, just as she said you would. Stephanie, I told you that you were adopted because it is the truth. I wanted to protect you, and she also asked me to do so. I don't know where she was going that night, but I don't think it was going to be safe… for a child.' She glanced at the still full cup of tea that was cooling besides her.

'I may be a simple woman Stephanie, but I know what I saw, and I know I can't explain it any more than I have. I wish I could, with all my heart.' I pulled my mother close to me and we held each other for a short while. I loved her very much, she was my mother, she was all for me, regardless of who, or what I was.

'It's alright mom, there are a lot of things happening to me right now, that I can't explain. This is another piece of the puzzle. I'm trying to find out more about myself. I've had a few recent experiences that I can't rationalise. I run them around and around in my head time and time again and, well nothing makes any sense. I need to find out where I come from, who I am, and I need to know what I am becoming.'

'Becoming?'

'Yes mom, my body, well it's been doing some unusual things of late. You don't need to know the details. I'm not sure I understand any of it myself.'

'You must be very concerned dear, to visit me and ask me these questions.'

'I am mom, but rest assured, I will get to the bottom of it. I have a good crew and my own ship. They have promised that they will help me. I believe them mom, and I won't stop searching until I get some answers.'

I spent the next hour talking things through with mom, exploring the different possibilities. I very soon came to realise that I had missed her immensely, and her wise counsel. It was always so very hard leaving mom, closing the door behind me, felt like shutting off an important part of my life, and I always felt a tinge of sadness in my gut, every single time I walked away and closed the apartment door behind me.

∞

The sun was at its brightest now, as I walked swiftly towards the cafe where I would meet back up with Fetch. The cafe hadn't really changed that much in the last twenty five years or so that I had ate and drank there, it was one of the few places that still held, at least some of its original charm. Outside, there were small wooden tables and chairs placed neatly around the café's frontage. I could make out small groups of people that were sat chatting, and passing the time of day, either people watching, or being people watched.

As I drew closer, I could smell the chocolatey aroma of their signature blends freshly brewed coffee, there really was nothing quite like it. Where food and drink were concerned, only freshly baked bread and real butter gave me the same amount of sensory joy. The smell of their coffee always stirred up old memories of education, reading the news, and planning my day, before I would set off to university for a long day of study.

A small bell hung over the top of the doorway, it jingled lightly as I entered the café. It was the very same bell that had been there for at least the last thirty years or so, if not longer. I could see that Fetch had gotten herself a nice cosy corner, she looked relaxed and comfortable.

She was chatting casually to an elderly couple who had taken their small dog along with them. The small dog sat perfectly still, other than its bushy tail, which it was wagging expectantly, as it waited patiently for any crumbs or leftovers. It looked just as content as its owners, who were eating their freshly baked blueberry muffins, whilst Fetch told them some tall tale of her exploits. She was always in her element when she was holding court, and the elderly couple appeared to be utterly mesmerised by both her tales, and her charm.

I waved to Fetch as I approached the cafés counter, she pointed eagerly to her cup letting me know she wanted a refill. I ordered two large coffees and a slice of blueberry cheesecake for myself. I paid and collected the hot brews at the far end of the glossy black marble counter.

Then, whilst walking carefully over to Fetch with a large tray in my hands, my mind suddenly took me back to the battle. What if we had lost? All of these people would now be fighting for their lives, their children, grandchildren, nieces, and nephews all gone. Today would not be cups of coffee, cheesecake, and chit chat. Today would be a living hell for humanity, and most likely the beginning of the end.

I stood still for a moment, whilst trying to breathe steadily. I was struggling somewhat to take it all in and fully process the thoughts and reflections that I was having as they raced and competed with each other in my head. It would be easier and more convenient to box it all away, I thought. If only it wasn't the stark truth.

Fetch saw me approach and moved a little to the side, allowing me enough space to sit down beside her. The elderly couple promptly excused themselves and thanked Fetch for the riveting, and entertaining conversation. Fetch stood up shaking both their hands in turn, and just like that, the couple and their dog went happily on their way.

'Hey, how did it go with your mom?' Fetch said, as she turned to face me. She had a worried look upon her face, and her brow was deeply furrowed. I placed the small tray onto the table and sat down beside her, still contemplating what might have been, had we not taken direct action, had I not... I struggled to think of the right words. What was it that I had done?

'Truthfully Fetch. I can't get my head around it, any of it.' I took a sip of the coffee. It was sheer bliss and gave me the distraction that I needed. I had missed this little café so very much.

'Why? What did she say?' Fetch shuffled forwards slightly, paying attention and waiting patiently to hear my news.

'You won't believe me Fetch, it's surreal… no it's much more than that! Believe it or not, I now have even more questions than I had before. I mean, how does that even happen, considering everything we have all been through, and what happened to me during the battle.'

'Wow, that's pretty intense for you to feel that way. So, tell me, what exactly did your mom say to you?'

'Well Fetch… the main gist of it was, that I'm not adopted in the conventional sense, and that forty years ago, a complete stranger delivered a package to my mom, to her home. Well, that package… It was me, and furthermore, and this is where it gets really fucked up and weird, the stranger who brought me to my mom… was apparently, me.' I paused for a second, allowing both myself and Fetch some time to let the words I had spoken sink in.

'No way!' Fetch said almost instantly, she was clearly astonished. 'I, well… that's gonna take some processing. I… well, how? How does that even happen?'

'I don't know Fetch. I mean, I have no memory of it and mom told me that the person who looked like me, told her that they were going somewhere where it wasn't safe for a child and that it could be dangerous. But why, and how could they look exactly like me? I mean, who was it? I certainly don't remember any of it, and why would I? It can't have been me, can it?'

'Well… one thing is for sure. This has all got to be linked. I mean, think about it. You have been changing, mostly physically. I mean the shimmering, glowing skin thing. That weird shit on Pluto, that freaking pebble like object, and the activated mist thing. The central chamber lighting up straight afterwards, ya know, right after you got misted.

The star system maps, traces of your DNA at the site, even though you have never been there before.

And not forgetting of course, that you disintegrated a giant cylindrical void through the centre of the Crucians Cruiser, just like you were coring out the inside of an apple. Also, not forgetting that you survived it, and you survived the vacuum of space. I mean that's, well if I hadn't seen it with my own eyes…

It's… well it's damn right impossible. I think, and this is a wildly uneducated guess. I think that you were at that site forty years ago, and so was the stranger that your mom met. Major, the answers you seek… I don't think you will find what you are looking for within our Solar System.'

'That actually makes a lot of sense Fetch. You're right, I don't have any of the answers, but I do have a direction, or six if those charts are right. Thanks Fetch, I mean it. I smiled and drank another mouthful of the chocolatey blend, before speaking again.

'So, the next step we should take is to follow the breadcrumb trail. There's gonna be a hell of a lot of space travel and a significant number of jumps ahead. Let's be honest we don't know what we will find. I don't know if that excites me or causes me dread, but regardless we have to find out.' Fetch nodded slowly, as if she was running it all through her mind, then she spoke once again.

'Yes, we do. I think those breadcrumbs are yours to pursue Major. Of course, you wouldn't want to do that without the support of your eight, and the full support of the crew onboard the ship of course. It's gonna be an adventure, that's for sure.' She laughed heartily.

'You could say that's one thing we do know for sure Fetch. It certainly will be… an adventure. I know that I cannot do this alone. I need all of you, the crew, my eight. You're the ones that have helped keep me balanced, helped me keep it together when I really thought that I might be losing my shit. Thanks Fetch, talking with you like this, it means a lot, it means everything.' Fetch smiled and gazed out of the window, not uttering a single word more.

Finally, I tucked into the cheesecake. Each mouthful was pure heaven. We had a plan, a way forward, and I for one, would turn the entire galaxy upside down in my search, if it meant that I would find the answers to the questions that I was seeking.

∞

The rest of the afternoon passed quickly, and it wasn't long before the suns light began to fade from the clear azure blue daylight sky, into the evenings inky blue-black starlit night heavens.

Fetch and I were ready for some good food and strong alcohol as we took a leisurely walk into the city, taking in the atmosphere and watching the many shuttles and personal flight vehicles darting about in the skies high above us. It was warm, but not so hot that it was unbearable, and there was definitely an energy in the city tonight.

'What do you fancy to eat Fetch?' I said, as I ran the many different food options through my head.

'Hmm… I could go for some king prawn kung po, a basket of prawn crackers, oh and some of that sticky egg fried rice. What about you?'

'Yeah, I could fancy some chicken in oyster sauce, fried rice and maybe some banana fritters.' I said enthusiastically. 'I'm really hungry, got a real appetite tonight.'

'We always manage to order way more than we can eat, but to hell with it.' Fetch said drily.

'Well, it's probably the last time we will eat Earth

food for a while. We leave for Nemeranth in just under forty hours, so best we make the most of it tonight.'

'Can't say I'm looking forward to jumping again, lost all my breakfast the last time we did it.' Fetch said, as she put her hand over her mouth.

'Trust me Fetch, it gets easier. Just try closing your eyes before the jump, you won't get as nauseated.'

'Ok. I will definitely give that a go. Don't let me forget to have plenty of vodka sent up to the ship before we head back, got a feeling I'm gonna need it. If there's one thing I hate, it's the thought of wasting good vodka'

As we approached the entrance to the China Town area, we could see many bright red holographic Chinese lanterns that swayed gently on holographic chains, in an imaginary gentle breeze. Holographic cherry blossom wafted from the nights sky down and across the entrance, creating an atmosphere like no other.

This was the reason I had chosen China Town for our evening meal. I wanted to savour and remember the atmosphere, the food and of course the alcohol. I intended to get thoroughly shit faced tonight. I could do the regret and the recovery tomorrow, in the comfort of my quarters.

Fetch and I looked at the street menu displays of several good restaurants, until eventually we found a small but obviously popular restaurant. It was situated on a street corner, and Fetch was insistent that we try it. The aromas of the many different foods being prepared drifted down the street towards us, pulling us by our noses towards the restaurant door.

We swiftly headed inside towards a small podium, where a striking woman of Chinese ethnic origin stood, clothed in a red qipao dress, it was lavishly embroidered in silk and satin threads, it really was quite exquisite, and I felt that it enhanced the atmosphere of the restaurant beautifully.

'Welcome to The Golden Koi. Table for two?' She beckoned us to follow, and we did.

As we were walking, Fetch excused herself to the hostess, speaking to her once more.

'Any chance that we could have a larger table? I'm not sure a small table would hold everything we intend to order. This is our last night on Earth for a while.' The hostess smiled and nodded politely, as she changed direction, leading us elegantly to our new table.

At this point, our appetites were driving us forward. I think we would have both followed her back into the centre of the Crucians Cruiser, if it had smelt as good as the food being cooked in this restaurant. She eventually led us to a quieter area of the restaurant, which was softly lit, and was very pleasantly decorated in traditional Chinese artwork. Our allotted table was indeed quite large, and Fetch and I took this as an opportunity to spread ourselves out accordingly.

'I will bring the menus over to your table shortly, would either of you care for a drink, whilst you decide what you would like to order?' She said courteously.

'Yeah, that would be really great, can I get an ice cold lager please. Fetch?'

'I will have a large vodka and ginger ale.' The restaurants hostess nodded politely to us both, and I noticed that in the middle of the table there was a single large candle, that had three wicks. The hostess lit all three of the wicks in quick succession, before walking elegantly back towards the restaurants podium.

Our drinks came shortly afterwards, and we drank and chatted, whilst we waited patiently to order our food. Fetch shared with me just how awesome the 'V' wing was, yet again, and I listened to her tell me how great it had felt shooting at the Crucian ship during the battle. It then began to dawn on me that some time had passed, and our menus still hadn't arrived.

'Do we need to chase up the menus Fetch? I'm ravenous.' Fetch looked towards the podium, and for a moment I thought she was looking for the hostess, when suddenly I saw three familiar faces walk in through the door and down the aisle towards us. Without saying a word, I looked at Fetch who hurriedly shrugged her shoulders, whilst trying to look innocent. A look that she wasn't all that great at pulling off.

'Hello, fancy meeting you two here.' Deno said, a wide smirk across her face.

'Yeah. Fancy that.' I said, looking first at Deno and then at Fetch. It was clear, by the look on their faces that Adari and Raena, were a little surprised also.

'Would you like to join us? We haven't ordered yet.' I said politely.

'We sure would.' Deno said cheerfully. 'Lemme get the three of us some drinks.'

Deno then spontaneously waved to one of the waiters and everyone sat down around the large table, it was at this point that I interjected.

'Tonight's food and drink are on me, by way of a personal and heartfelt thank you for all of your support and hard work. And of course, I would like us to take the time tonight to celebrate our combined victory, friendship, and the upcoming journey to Nemeranth.' Just as I had finished, the waiter arrived and started to take a drinks order for the table. Adari and Raena both looked puzzled, as they studied the copious drinks menu.

'Tell me Major, what is a pleasant drink?' Adari said.

'Well, do you prefer, sweet, sour or strong alcohol?'

'Sweet and strong.' He smiled respectfully.

'Well, in that case perhaps you would like an Amaretto with a whisky shot and just a dash of lemon'.

'Yes. I will try one of those, thank you.' He nodded and placed the drinks menu back on the table, he looked contented.

'And Raena. What do you like? Sweet, sour or strong?'

'… Oh, I like mine strong Major.' Deno nudged me and giggled under her breath.

'Err, well. Ok. So… whisky, rum, tequila, vodka or gin?'

'I think I would like to try them all.' Raena said innocently, as Deno burst out laughing.

'Are you sure? I think we best keep an eye on you tonight.' Deno spoke, a glint of wild mischief in her eyes.

'Ok. Let's get you started on a tall drink then. I think maybe a rum and cola with lots of ice. We should order our food soon, as I think we are gonna need to eat, in order to soak up all this alcohol.' I smiled.

The drinks came and we ordered our food, Deno went for her usual vegetarian chop suey, Adari had the same as Deno, and Raena ordered a king prawn chow mien, due to her love of sea food. Four steaming hot meals soon arrived, and we all tucked in heartily. Adari and Raena had a quick lesson on the use of chopsticks from Fetch, and we laughed as Raena wrestled with a prawn that kept slipping out of her sticks. In the end she pinched it between her fingers, popping it into her mouth with a deep look of satisfaction.

Adari told us that he had found his new all-time favourite drink, he told us that he would need to share it with his people, because it really was very good. Raena and Deno had moved on from tall drinks and Deno was about to order tequila slammers, and I was still waiting for my order of banana fritters. They were a personal favourite of mine, and I couldn't wait for them to arrive.

The tequila shots were soon brought to us on a large silver tray. On it, was an entire bottle of Tequila, small heavy bottomed shot glasses, and numerous slices of lime that had been coated in salt. Deno explained to Raena and Adari the right way to down a shot. We all bit down into the salty limes, feeling the sharpness of the lime juice and the contrasting taste of the salt enter our mouths. We then quickly tapped our glasses on the table, downing our shots in one mouthful.

Raena and Adari sat frozen for a few seconds, their faces contorted, whilst Deno, Fetch and I laughed uncontrollably at the expressions upon their faces. Raena said that she wanted to try a second shot as she didn't know if she liked the sensation or not. Deno quickly obliged her request by filling up her shot glass once more.

'Banana fritters?' The waiter looked about the table, I stuck my hand up in the air waving it about.

'If you will excuse me, I must now indulge myself in an utterly orgasmic experience'. Raena looked at me puzzled, as I placed some of the crispy, syrup covered fritter into my mouth.

'Oh my… that's so damn good.' I said, I was after all feeling a little tipsy from all the alcohol. I noticed Raena glance at the fritters and then at me.

'Wanna try some?' I said, holding a piece on the end of my fork.

'Yes. I think I would like to try it, you made it sound very nice.' Deno and Fetch were now looking at each other and talking with their eyes.

I put a piece onto the fork, moving it around the bowl and covering it in the golden syrup. I held it to her mouth, and she took it off the fork in one quick and very adept movement of her jaw, mouth, and lips. Just as she did so, she raised her eyes to mine for no more than a millisecond, but it was enough for me to recognise the connection once more, it felt so intense. I had no choice but to look away briefly and compose myself, then I looked back towards her.

'Well? What do you think?' I said, raising my eyebrows.

'Major. I think your description was perfect, and even if you had not explained verbally, just how delicious you found it. I need you to know that I… felt how much you enjoyed it.' What did she mean, she felt it? I wondered.

'Raena is there something that I should know?' I said, my eyes searching hers for a clue as to what she might have meant.

'Oh, well yes there is Major. It's really not that unusual to me, or my species in normal circumstances. I mean to say that the Okai, well we do this all the time. The thing is that I have been able to sense some of your emotions since the incident during the battle. I wasn't sure at first what it was, as I know that humans cannot communicate their emotions, feelings, or thoughts to the Okai, and it felt a little different to what I am accustomed to. Much hazier, as if your emotions are tucked just beyond a fine veil, occasionally though something from you manages to drift, eventually permeating right the way through it.

I have picked up on certain emotional responses from you, and some sense of your thoughts. Though the words feel much further back than the emotions. The only time your thoughts clearly came through to me was the once, when you communicated telepathically with me following the incident, after you left the front of the Crucian Cruiser, when we all thought you were dead. I can't say that I understand it myself, but it makes our relationship… well a bit more open I suppose.' She looked around the table, reading all four faces of its occupants.

'Well Major, that's sure gonna make everything a bit more interesting.' Fetch said, looking for a response from Deno, who had a surprised look on her face, but said nothing.

'Thanks for telling me, Raena. We should discuss this more, and in private as I don't wish for you to feel any more uncomfortable, than I can see you clearly are with this right now.'

We spent the rest of the evening in bars, drinking cocktails and shots. By the time we reached the Spaceport, we were all very much the worse for wear. Adari had begun singing his favourite Nadaal songs, whilst Raena was giggling to herself, propped up by both Fetch and Deno who were walking, swaying, whilst trying to sing along to Adari's songs.

If memory serves me right, it was around 02:00 hours in the morning when we finally boarded the shuttle back to the amaranthine. it had been an eventful day, and a wonderful evening, and as my head hit the pillow, my final thought as I drifted off to sleep, was one of home.

12 NEMERANTH

My head was once again thick from heavy alcohol, and when I awoke the next morning I recalled the events of the previous day, and night. I adhered to my morning ritual, making myself a strong cup of coffee, sitting in my reading chair, checking my emails, and browsing the net.

I wanted only two things today, to relax and read, and I intended to spend the entire day in my quarters, nursing a hangover, eating delicious food, and reading a good holo-book. I made myself a second cup of coffee and settled down into the first pages of an ancient memoir, written by a legendary rock star.

I must have been reading for around thirty minutes, when the comm went on my chip. I answered it reluctantly.

'Major Mitchell?' A voice called out urgently from the comm.

'Yes, this is Mitchell.' It was a woman's voice, one that I didn't recognise.

'This is General Descheene. Major Mitchell, General Eastwick is a close personal friend of mine, and I believe we too share a common interest. We have both been investigating the Crucians for some time, that, and we would do anything to save our people, and our planet. I need to speak with you in person, today, before you leave for Nemeranth, and before you start further investigations into those star charts.' She paused. I could sense her rank, and the weight of her authority, waiting for my response.

'Yes. Of course. General, where would you like to meet?' I said respectfully.

'I will come to the Amaranthine, expect me in about one hour'. And with that the comm cut off.

'So much for having a relaxing day.' I sighed heavily, the words escaping my mouth somewhat rebelliously. I got up and out of my chair, its comfort quickly releasing me back to my hangover, and to my sense of duty. I went to the bathroom, showering quickly, efficiently. Meeting a new General was the last thing that my aching head needed today.

I dressed, again reluctantly. I had just wanted to spend today in sweatpants and an old t-shirt, but it would have to wait. I brushed my hair back tightly and tied it up. I looked in the mirror and was surprised that I looked much better than I felt, as I felt terrible.

I promptly left my quarters and headed for the mess. I desperately needed something to eat, something that would line my empty stomach. I pondered for a moment, thinking that a full cooked breakfast should do it, I hoped.

The mess was half empty, and the main flurry of staff had already eaten, they were either on duty, or were in bed asleep, as it was late morning now. I sat down on a synth-metal bench, and not long after a steward came over, taking my order and then hurrying back to the kitchen. He returned a few minutes later with my breakfast of, sausage, eggs, bacon, beans, fried mushrooms, and grilled tomatoes. He placed the hot plate down, and then placed a steaming hot mug of tea on the table next to my full plate. I tucked in wholeheartedly, the food was delicious, and I hoped that it would settle my stomach a little. I placed some mushrooms onto the crispy bacon and put it into my mouth.

'Major Mitchell.' A booming female voice caught my attention immediately. 'I'm very sorry to interrupt your breakfast. I'm a little early, please do continue.' I looked up, there in front of me was a woman, of indigenous American descent, she was dressed in full uniform, it was immaculately pressed, and she carried an air of power and intelligence about her.

'You must be General Descheene? Please accept my apologies General. I was just having some breakfast. I had hoped I would finish it before you arrived.' I said, feeling a little saddened that I might not get to finish the food.

'Breakfast… I see. It would be a shame not to indulge as I haven't eaten yet. It smells wonderful.' She eyed the contents of my plate enviously.

'Oh, yes. Well, I don't usually eat a full cooked breakfast General, but myself and a few of my squad took the opportunity to celebrate our victory against the Crucians yesterday. They needed some R n R and to be frank General. So did I.' She smiled, sitting down at the table.

'So, tell me Major. What do you recommend from the ships menu?' Her poise was composed, as she momentarily looked about my plate.

'Well General, if you are hungry the pancakes are

really good, I mean to say, I have them most of the time. Only today I needed–'

'Something more substantial, I know that feeling well, and it's written all over your face Major.' She laughed, it appeared she had me all worked out.

'Is it? I'm sorry General. It really was a good night.' I waved once again to catch the steward's attention, ordering the General a stack of pancakes, with bacon, syrup, and a fresh cup of coffee. She looked about the mess and then gestured for me to continue eating my breakfast, which I did with gusto.

Finishing quickly, I pushed the now empty plate to the side, just as the Generals pancakes and coffee arrived. General Descheene began to eat, and the fluffy pancakes had soaked up the sweet syrup. I could tell from the expression on her very contented face that she was truly enjoying them.

'Oh Major, you were right. These are really very good.' She said, whilst taking another forkful of the food into her mouth.

'General. It has crossed my mind that you must be wondering if General Eastwicks accounts are–'

'Accurate? No Major, I trust him with my life, and yours. What does intrigue me though, is what you did, and how you did it. But I'm told that our best scientists do not fully understand it yet. When such things occur, there is only one other thing you can rely on Major, and that is character.'

'Yes, General. You will appreciate that I have questioned the events myself. I have reconciled this… anxiety and the worry that I had, and I am determined to search for the answers. There are questions I have, General. Most are unanswered at this time. I need you to understand that I intend to find those answers and rid the galaxy of any threat to humanity and its allies. I will not allow the Crucians, or this Species X to control us by fear, which is exactly what they have tried to do to us, by deceit. I trust I have your full support in that General?'

'My support? Yes, of course you have that unconditionally. Major, I want you to know that I intend to give you much more than that.' She paused, I could see her studying me and weighing up her options.

'More than your full support? Meaning what exactly?' I asked directly, as I was not sure where she was going with this.

'Your own fleet Major. We have just secured a tri-planet alliance, both the Okai and the Nadaal very much want in on it… and they want you to lead it.'

'Me, really? Wow! Sorry, I mean that's good, that's really good news.'

'No, Major. You were right the first time. It is definitely a wow. It's never been done before. Both the Okai and the Nadaal wish to support us, they wish to support you. They believe that you Major, that you are the only reason that they still have their offspring to raise, and I'm inclined to say, that I agree with them.'

I took a large mouthful of tea, noticing that it was just the right temperature for drinking and gaining maximum satisfaction. My thoughts were a buzz.

'So General, this fleet. What is the offer?' I said seriously.

'You will take command of two Titan Class Cruisers, one from the Nadaalian fleet and one from the Okai fleet. Each ship will be fully crewed, and weaponised. Furthermore, each ship will have a full contingent of fighters and other tactical support, scout, and science craft, should you need them.

The Amaranthine will also be taking delivery of Earths newest stealth fighters today, and your crew will soon reach full capacity. Adari and Raena will be assigned as your commanding officers for each of their species respective Cruisers. Though they will remain stationed onboard the Amaranthine, as part of your eight. The Okai and the Nadaal have assigned experienced deputies onboard their ships. It is hoped that they will take care of the day to day business.'

'I can't quite get my head around this General, I don't know what to say.'

'We want your mission to be a success Major, we hope that it will of course be a peaceful journey of discovery and building new alliances. However, we want to give you a fighting chance, should you encounter any further hostilities or species X. Our planets have entered into a much stronger and more trusting alliance, thanks to your endeavours.

All three species are now mutually sharing technology and expertise with each other, and in all disciplines. All of our interplanetary defences will be much stronger for this. Major, I cannot thank you enough for what you did. If you need anything, anything at all, please just ask.'

'It's a lot to take in General. Thank you.' I felt a hot tingle run up the length of my entire spine, across my shoulders and deep into the back of my neck.

'Oh.' The General looked at me with a surprised expression on her face.

'What's the matter?' She pointed at my face.

'Your skin Major, it is shimmering, just around your temple at both sides. It appears to be just underneath the surface, and it looks very much like–'

'Fusion. Yes General. I'm sorry about that, it must be a little alarming. It still concerns me General, as to what it is.'

'Major. It has just ceased, almost as quickly as it began. Well now, that is very intriguing. Remember, if you need anything at all… In fact, let me see if I can assign you your own medic. I think I know just the person, a real expert in all things… unusual. But first I need to finish these pancakes, they really are delectable.' She continued eating the pancakes, until all that was left on her plate were a few smears of syrup, and a several lonely crumbs.

'Well Major, I must be off. You know how it is when duty calls. I'm heading straight back to Earth now to finalise the arrangements for your new fleet. The Okai and Nadaal Cruisers will join you at Nemeranth tomorrow evening. Safe journey, Major.'

She got up, straightening her uniform, and walking away from the table at speed. A couple of officers that had clearly been assigned to protect her, caught up with her quickly, following behind at a fair pace, attempting to attend to her personal security as she left the mess. But if my encounter with her had been anything to go by. I felt that she was more than capable of taking care of herself.

I sat at the table for a few minutes, soaking up the peace and quiet, whilst mulling over my conversation with General Descheene. I didn't know why but I liked her a lot, even though I had only just met her. She seemed like the type of woman that got things done, and any friend of General Eastwick had to be alright in my books. I wondered if, even he could have seen this coming. My own tri-alliance fleet. I felt much more reassured by the significantly stronger alliance with the

Okai and Nadaal. I knew now that we weren't in this on our own and that this alliance would make the journey ahead easier for everyone involved.

I left the mess hall's now empty table and headed swiftly back to my quarters, taking off my uniform and placing it back in my storage closet. It felt damn good to be free of it again, I really didn't want to be disturbed again today. I wanted to relax, and to process what had happened over the past few weeks. Everything just seemed to have been thrown at both myself and my six and I hadn't had a minute to think about it all, on my own. Lately, it seemed that I was always surrounded by others. I desperately needed some peace and quiet, and if I was honest, I felt like I had earned it. I called the Bridge on my chip, to reinforce my own personal wishes.

'Good afternoon First Lieutenant, can you ensure that I am not disturbed for the rest of the day. That is, unless there is an emergency. I will be resting up in my quarters, thank you. Major Mitchell out.' I smiled, allowing myself this indulgence. I quickly put on an old t-shirt, and some washed out sweatpants. I luxuriated in them, relaxing with nothing more than my own company, my own thoughts and I spent the rest of the day, reading, watching old movies, and drinking coffee.

∞

Today was jump day. The crew and my eight were up, and already at their stations well before I entered the Bridge. The ship had a buzz about it, an energy of sorts, and as I walked the long corridors, I was passed by crew that were hurriedly readying themselves for the jump.

Jumping was the term used for the manipulation of the fabric of space. That is, the space in and directly around the ship. When jumping, the ship doesn't actually jump as such, space folds in on itself, and then almost instantaneously unfolds in a chosen new location, giving the feeling of jumping from one point in space to another.

A successful jump means that in effect, the ship and its entire crew are transported to within nought point one thousandth of a single millimetre of the set navigational co-ordinates. Some describe a feeling, almost as if the ship were momentarily slipping into a wormhole, whilst others describe it as, how it would feel if the ship fell out of space. It certainly is a unique experience, and I am always grateful that the sensation only lasts a few seconds. I reached the briefing room, and I was looking forwards to visiting Nemeranth. On entering, my eight were sat waiting for me, they all looked eager to get on with the day.

'Good morning.' I spoke, enthusiastically. They all responded and stood up momentarily, as I entered the room.

'Please, be seated. Does anyone have any questions about the upcoming jump today?' I looked about them, searching their faces.

'I do Major.' Cat responded, her tone of voice, clearly curious. 'This is my first ever jump. Fetch was just telling me, that you told her that it's better to close your eyes. Is this true Major?'

'That's right Cat, I find it easier to just close my eyes for a few seconds and when I reopen them, the jump is complete.' Cat nodded in acknowledgement. I could see that she was going to try it.

'We will be jumping to Nemeranth shortly. We are likely to be away from Earth for some time, and we will be jumping again shortly afterwards, to the star system

Wolf 359. The red dwarf star is located 7.9 lights years from Earth. It's a fair distance, but not one that can't be achieved in a single jump. Once there, we will continue our search for answers. Our science team is still working at the Pluto site, and they will join us at Nemeranth shortly before we leave.

I understand that they have an important update for us about the meaning of some of the transcripts found on Pluto. They have also identified all four remaining star systems that we saw lit up in the central chamber at the Cthulhu Macula site.

I don't know what we can expect, but I do know that we all need answers, and if I'm honest with you all, none more so than myself. Earth will remain on high alert, currently there has not been a response from the Crucians, which is unusual, given that we destroyed three of their best Cruisers. Perhaps they are licking their wounds, but do not underestimate them. They will not be at all happy with what we did to them.

I expect a retaliation, but right now they are not strong enough to launch a counter. That being said, they still have considerable power, and I would advise you all to let me know if you see or suspect anything unusual, anything at all.

One last thing. We are still trying to establish a credible theory about Species X. We know that they are working with the Crucians, but at this time, we just don't know what their capabilities are, both as a species, and as a potential military adversary.

We hope to combine our research and intelligence with the Okai's and Nadaal's, in order to further our joint investigative knowledge going forwards. Do any of you have any further questions before we jump?' Tommy chipped into the conversation.

'Major. I'm told that there will be a celebration following the formal duties on Nemeranth, is this correct. I–' Raena intervened.

'Tommy, you will need to wear something comfortable, and something you can dance in.'

'Dance. Hell, I like the sound of that.' He beamed with enthusiasm.

'Number one uniform for the formalities, let the crew know. I want everyone looking their very best. Once the formalities are over, the crew can relax and enjoy the festivities. Cat, I want a skeleton crew to remain on the Amaranthine. Volunteers would be my preference, and then draw straws if needed, ok?' I nodded at Cat, and she left the briefing room.

'Ok. Everyone to their stations. It's high time I was on the Bridge.'

The room emptied and I made my way through the door, opening a secure channel on my chip. I took one last long look at Earth out of the viewing window.

'This is Major Mitchell. Prepare to jump in three minutes. Ready the jump drive. Blue alert.' The call went out across all the comms on the ship. All non-essential crew returned to their quarters, laying on their beds, and on their sides. The ships corridors fell silent and were completely empty.

'This is Major Mitchell. All crew, one minute to jump.' The lighting on the ship changed to a slowly pulsating deep blue, the rooms, corridors, and halls darkened across the entire ship.

'Preparing to jump in; ten, nine, eight, seven, six, five, four, three, two, one.'

I momentarily closed my eyes and felt the oddest sensation and feeling hold in my throat for just a second, before it settled back down once again into my stomach. Several of the crew situated around me threw up into their provided sick bags, whilst other members of the crew, seemingly unaffected rushed to check that their colleagues were alright, which of course they were, other than losing their composure, and their breakfast.

A new view greeted us now, Nemeranth. She was one third larger in mass, than the Earth. Her surface was covered with gigantic jade green oceans, fertile lands of red, green, and blue terrain, dusky pink rocky mountain ranges, that tumbled into the pale blue beaches that surrounded the immense coast lines.

'Have you ever seen anything so–' Raena said calmly, I could tell that she was pleased to be here, back at her home planet.

'Breath-taking?'

'Indeed, it is certainly that. What is the word Major? Ah yes, biased, I am indeed biased.'

'There's just so much vibrant colour, your planet reminds me of a beautiful multicoloured glass marble that I used to play with as a child, it utterly fascinated me then, just as your planet does now. The colours Raena, I can't even begin to describe them, other than to say that they are just simply amazing.' Raena looked to the planet's surface, smiling at my simplistic description of her home world.

'Let me share with you something about the history of our species Major. We Okai, evolved over millions of years, so that we could share all the colours of our planet. Who we are currently, this is the most recent stage in our evolution to date. There is a period of growth that we all go through, this is when we reach 'Arimianoran' this is our, how would you say it? A coming of age, a maturing, or passing into adulthood.

We Okai, we seek our planet's blessing and ask her to choose our adult colours at the Arimianoran.

My skin colour, this was awarded to me by our planet. It is the colour of our fields of Cabass. Cabass, is a type of lavender, this is what I believe you would call it, on Earth. We Okai retain our childhood colour in our bodies skin memory, and we can return to it just once a year at the annual celebration, known as the great joining.

At the joining, we celebrate the day that our planet shared her vibrant colours with us. It is a great blessing to receive one's adult colours, and a great blessing to be able to recall our childhood colours too. We are able to awaken our skin memory at the Arimianoran.

All Okai adults return to their childhood colours on this night, just for a few hours, to remember who we were before our planet gifted us her sacred vibrance. You are very honoured Major tonight, I will, along with my people, return to my childhood colour. When I first travelled to Earth, well it struck me how alike we are to you humans, and in so many ways how very different we are. Tonight, you will understand why I say this to you now. I believe that we can learn a lot from each other Major.'

'I hope so Raena, as Fetch assures me that we are not so very different at all.' I smiled briefly, remembering the blushing conversation that I had with Fetch. 'The thing is that we humans were once so very judgemental about all of our differences, including skin colour and ethnicity. Historically, some people also believed that they had a right to say who someone could fall in love with too. It took us a long, long time to overcome these prejudices as a species. Let's just say that it damaged an awful lot of people throughout our history and leave it at that.

I'm just glad it's not who we are now. It's hard to think that looking back, there was a time when some of us were just so very ignorant and cruel to one another. Afterall, our history tells us time and time again that our species greatest assets is our diversity, our inbuilt ability for acts of great courage and compassion, and of course, our ingenuity.

I could go on, but I'll stop there. Thank goodness that we left those times behind… I know we are a better species for it.' Raena stopped, looking thoughtful and a little saddened, and I could see that she was reflecting on the words that I had just said.

'Our species, the Okai… well, we have always encouraged connection, attraction and the love that can evolve from it. So long as it is shared mutually, between adults and that it harms no others.'

'Indeed. I couldn't agree more. I really am looking forward to seeing those blue coastal sands Raena. Is there anything I need to know about the ceremony, any formalities or traditions that I need to observe?'

'No Major, it will just simply happen. We will be attending a party, under one of our planets Sycoramth Trees. They are most like a cross between your Earths great oak and willow trees. Gigantic in size, they flower just once a year. The tree is unusual, in that instead of where its leaves would be, it has petals. These petals are every colour that you can imagine, and of course some that you can't.

When the Arimianoran concludes, the trees drop their petals upon us, covering the ground in a blanket of infinite colours. This will look very similar to your cherry and apple blossom trees during the spring season on Earth. Major, it is a site to behold, and I would like it very much if both you and the squad were with me for this moment. It will teach you all a great deal about our people and our culture.'

'I'm looking forward to it Raena. We should all need to ready ourselves for the formal ceremonies and dress accordingly. Raena you should leave the ship ahead of us and prepare for the celebrations, I imagine that you have lots to do.'

'Thank you Major. I will leave right away. Oh, and Major.'

'Yes?' I turned on my heel, looking towards her as she stood in the doorway.

'When you emerged from the Crucian ship… your colours… well, they were magnificent.' She smiled once more, it was a smile full of warmth and sincerity before she quickly turned and headed through the door. I felt humbled, and I hoped that today the day would go well for her, and all of the Okai people.

As soon as she was out of sight, I immediately returned to my duties and began running standard checks via the ships comm channels once more.

'Ship report.' I uttered calmly across the comm. At once the ships different section leaders reported back to me, no damage to the ship, and no injury to the crew. Good, I thought, then for just the briefest of moments my thoughts drifted back to Raena and her description of the Sycoramth trees. Your colours were magnificent… what a lovely thing to say to me, she had a different perspective to how I felt about the changes that I was experiencing. I held the thought for a short time, allowing myself the compliment, before returning my focus fully to my duty. It was time that I briefed the crew.

'All crew. As you are aware today will go down as a

significant day in history, with our friends and allies the Okai and the Nadaal. Today is a day marked for celebration, a day of stronger alliances and the shared common values of our combined species. We are much stronger for these friendships and alliances.

You will have been asked about your preference for today's celebrations. I wish to thank all those who have chosen to stay onboard the ship and look after her whilst we are away. To all crew not staying onboard the ship. You are to wear your number one uniform for the formal ceremonies. You will also need to take some casual clothing with you, that you can wear for tonight's celebrations. I'm told you may be asked to dance, so dress accordingly. Please be mindful, that you are all human ambassadors today, regardless of rank or role. Safe journey to you all. Mitchell out.'

I returned once again to my quarters, taking out the airtight sealed suit bag from the wardrobe, laying it carefully on the bed. I retrieved my best uniform shoes, removing the synth cloth from around them, they gleamed and reflected my quarters lights back at me, they shone like black glass. A gentle reminder of the hours spent working on them, and the reward for doing so.

I dressed, checking every detail, creases as sharp as knife edges ran down the front of my arms and trousers, the navy blue uniform cloth was beautifully accented in gold. I tied my hair up into a tight neat bun on the back of my head, ensuring it was neat, and pinning my hat to my hair, so that it would not blow off if there were a breeze. I took one long look in the mirror, before taking an electronic lint roller to my uniform, ensuring that it was pristine.

I met my seven in the shuttle bay. They were

chatting easily amongst themselves when I arrived. I noticed that they all looked incredibly smart, and they were all carrying their number one hats. Adari was wearing his best uniform which was black with fine specks of gold interwoven in the cloth. His uniform was also highlighted in gold. He looked very smart indeed and I decided that I very much liked the Nadaal military uniform that he was wearing.

'Ok everyone. Are we all feeling ready for this?' They all nodded, and we boarded the craft. The journey to Nemeranth took around thirty minutes. I spent the last five minutes of the journey looking out of the shuttles window, taking in all the colours as we flew closer to the planet's surface.

We sat for a few minutes whilst the usual docking procedures took place. Finally, and with a familiar hiss, the door to the shuttle opened. Warm, but not hot air hit my face, and I estimated the temperature to be around twenty five degrees centigrade. The sun was shining, but what met my eyes was both astonishing, surreal, and utterly captivating.

The sky was blue, and yet everything else was different. The colours were so vibrant, and instead of a mass of green there were also many shades of blue and reds. The architecture was exceptionally stunning, and reminded me somewhat of ancient Greece, but these buildings were not in ruins. There were many contrasts here, modern, tall buildings, of what looked like glass and polished marble rose up from the ground, high into the sky, looking like they might almost pierce the planet's atmosphere. There were many older buildings that were quite obviously lovingly cared for and respected by the Okai.

It was a feast for the eyes, and what complimented

this planets majesty and mystery were its people. So very different, so very at one with nature and so content in that connection, that they positively glowed with it. Everything from their beautiful appearance, to their magnificent braided, shaved, jewelled, or otherwise adorned hair, in every colour to either match or complement their skin and attire.

The squad looked about trying to take it all in, I could tell by their faces that they were as awestruck as myself, as they didn't say a single word. We walked across the landing platform to where a gleaming vehicle awaited us. Crowds had gathered in the streets and on the rooftops, they cheered throwing multi coloured petals at our feet, whilst placing garlands of unfamiliar flowers around our necks.

'I didn't expect this kind of reception.' I uttered to Joe, who was smiling and waving to the crowds.

'Me either, news must have gotten around about the battle and what we did, what you did.'

'And some. I'm just not used to this Joe, I'm a soldier, not a celebrity. I feel very humbled right now, and I'm not too sure what I should do with it. I don't have a frame of reference for any of this.'

'Well, I would just go with the flow Major. They clearly want to show you, their gratitude. Try to see it as them simply thanking you for a job well done.'

'Yes Joe. You are right.' I began to wave and smile at the crowd, they cheered loudly, it was almost deafening.

The transportation system across Nemeranth was different to that on Earth, though it was similar, in that it was clean electric. All vehicles in the city appeared to be on some kind of unique track system. The tracks reminded me of the ancient train and tram lines of

Earth, though these tracks were far more sophisticated. They were translucent blue, like the summer suns light, as if it were captured and held in a deep Mediterranean pool. The tracks flowed water like and were no more than a few feet ahead of the moving vehicles at any time. They tumbled gently and silently ahead, propelling each vehicle forward in effortless liquid motion.

The vehicles we travelled in were open topped, and the crowds that were made up mostly of the Okai people continued to roar jubilantly in their celebrations of our great victory. The squad by this time were lapping it up, revelling in it, and why not. They had earned every bit of it.

Each one had risked their life for every sentient being across the three worlds. A little kicking back was most definitely the order of the day. We had all been through so much together, I thought, as I continued waving to the crowds, as we made our way towards our destination.

The vehicle slowed, eventually pulling to a complete stop. From the vehicle I could see that there were many Okai ushers lining the route, into what was an incredible looking building. The building reminded me somewhat of an amphitheatre, but instead of it being circular, it was in fact horseshoe shaped. It had row after row of seating, seating that appeared to rise much higher than any amphitheatre I had ever seen on Earth. Its walls appeared to be pure white, almost like sculpted exotic marble, and its walls were covered in flora of many different colours and varieties.

The buildings crowning glory was a large triangular stone entrance that was carved with what looked like historic murals of the Okai people and their history.

There were also many depictions of different varieties of trees and plants and noticeably huge willow type trees. I wondered if these were the trees that Raena had spoken about to me before she left the ship, for her journey to Nemeranth.

We walked slowly through the entrance, admiring the sheer scale and beauty of the stonework that took us from the outside of the building, straight through and into its vast interior. We exited into open space once more, walking into the centre section of the amphitheatre itself. A single pure white path led us towards a rectangular stone platform that had thin strips of a gold type metal embedded into it in beautifully elaborate patterns.

The platform itself was highly polished, and there were row upon row of elegant seating that was neatly arranged in symmetrical formations. For a brief moment, I tried to count the number of seats in the rest of the amphitheatre, but as I drew closer to the platform, I estimated that there must have been tens of thousands of seats in the main seating area alone, and only around twenty seats on the central platform itself.

At the rear of the platform was an elegantly carved podium. It was adorned with gold and a scarlet heavy fabric of some kind that reminded me very much of crushed velvet. The same fabric covered all of the seating positioned on the central platform.

We were asked to be seated, which we did. My squad were usually comfortable in any situation, but I don't think I'd ever noticed them so out of their depth. I don't suppose that they had imagined this type of ceremony, and to be frank, neither had I. I shuffled in my seat, trying to get comfortable and fidgeting with my uniform, attempting to make sure that I looked my best as this was so obviously a very special occasion for the Okai.

We had just settled into our seats when music started. It was wonderful, and unusual music, it felt tribal, mystical, and futuristic all at the same time, and although I had never heard anything quite like it before, I instantly liked it. In the distance I could see large numbers of Okai, begin to fill the vast theatres seating areas. There was an electric atmosphere building in this space, and it was radiating from the Okai.

Once the seats were nearly all occupied, I realised that I had never seen so many beings together in one place. It made Earths top stadiums and parks look like tiny venues in comparison. I was struck by the incredible diversity of the Okai, they all shared similar facial traits that were indicative of their species, such as the shape of their noses and ears, and yet they were all completely unique in their appearance. I couldn't remember a time that I had ever seen so many colours, hues, and styles all in one location, my eyes and my senses were completely in awe of their individuality, and I found myself becoming utterly mesmerised by them.

All at once the chatter and conversation ceased. I could just make out a small group that were slowly walking towards us, their walking was at a steady pace, and it reminded me of a slow military march. Their outfits were intricate and spectacular in both colour and texture. Their garments were covered in smooth polished gems of many colours, that had been individually stitched into luxurious, and vibrant fabrics. The garments moved against their bodies like rich, thick fluid, and I soon realised that it was the way the gems were put together on each outfit. Each of the gems different colours impinged onto the many gems surrounding it, light catching the gems in an infinite number of places, resulting in the watery effect.

Walking easily and in the middle of the group, I noticed Raena and also another female who was clearly of Nadaalian descent. She was dressed from head to toe in a brushed gold and black gown, her honey coloured skin was one of the most beautiful skin colours that I could ever recall seeing, along with her perfect, porcelain like complexion.

At the very front of the procession was a tall and muscular Nadaalian male. He was clearly a powerful man, confident in his stature. He wore a long blue-green gem encrusted tunic, that reminded me of all the colours of the seas, in every shade of blue through to green, his attire perfectly representing the colours of all the Okai oceans. His trousers looked like the finest satin, and his skin was a deep sea blue, his hair was set in dreadlocks. These were blue, but lighter in colour and they contrasted perfectly with his skin. I noticed that his hair sat heavy and thick upon his broad muscular shoulders, not unlike that of a lions mane.

I was enjoying this unique experience, I don't think that I had thought that I would feel so moved, but I did. As the group grew closer, I could see more of Raena's dress. It was a very pale lavender outfit, pearlescent in its appearance, as the vibrant violet hues of her skin blended and contrasted with the shimmering dress, resulting in the most exquisite effect, which appeared to me to be one of every colour conceivable to the human eye. I found myself utterly transfixed, and it wasn't until Deno nudged me gently in my left arm that I was able to gather my composure, adjusting my gaze slightly, and removing the stupid look that was written across my face, refocussing both my fascination and my eyes elsewhere in the theatre.

Most of the precession parted at the podium, and all sought their seats on the centre platform. Only the Okai and Nadaal representatives remained standing. I noticed that Raena took her seat at the side of the rest of the squad, and I was pleased that she had joined us. One solitary figure remained standing in front of us. In the distance, and near the theatres entrance, I could see that this was a female, human in appearance, and she was walking slowly towards us.

I squinted slightly trying to see who it was, realising almost immediately that it was the President of the United Nations of Earth. It was Alexia Sasaki. I certainly wasn't expecting this. She arrived, greeting the Okai Sage, and then the Nadaalian Queen respectfully and warmly. All three stood in front of us, my squad. Here we were, a group of regular career soldiers, that just happened to find themselves on the front line defending the planet. Ordinary people, who had found themselves in a completely extraordinary situation.

Loud music began to play once again, and some Okai holding small trays approached the front and stood perfectly still. There were eight of them in total, but I couldn't make out exactly what it was that they were carrying. The amphitheatre fell completely silent now. Turning to face us it was the Okai Sage that spoke first.

'Welcome all to this celebration of friendship. My friends, stronger alliances have been forged, and today we are all here to enjoy, no savour, this historic moment for all of our peoples.' He paused and looked to the Nadaalian Queen who then stepped forward to speak.

'We are here today because our combined species defeated a malevolent threat. A threat that had it succeeded would have left us in turmoil, with our offspring gone and our hearts broken, beyond repair. She stood back and Alexia Sasaki stepped forward.

'It is not enough to say that we are thankful to Major Mitchell and her crew. Mere words will never be enough to thank them for what they did, and what they risked saving us all. Which is why we have created a new tri-planetary military commendation. This is the first time in our history that the recipients represent our three species, our three planets combined, and our homes. She stepped back and the Okai Sage stepped forwards once again.

'Major Mitchell. Would you step forward please.' I got up out of my seat and walked to meet him. He held out his large hand and I shook it. He turned and reached for a single medal that had the images of our three planets combined and engraved into a rich blue metal. The ribbon was blue, gold, and green. He held it for a moment, admiring it, and then pinned it to my uniform, above the neat row of medals, that were already pinned across my chest.

'Major Mitchell, friend and protector of the Okai.' He stepped back and the Nadaal Queen stepped forwards.

'Major Mitchell, friend and protector of the Nadaal.' She held out her hand and I shook it, she stepped back, and the President of the United Nations of Earth stepped forward.

'Major Mitchell, friend and protector to all the peoples of Earth. Major Mitchell, we salute you!' At that very moment, the Amphitheatre roared as the Okai cheered, music began, and the crowd threw petals into the air. I nodded respectfully and returned to my seat. My crew were then asked to step forward one by one and receive their medals. They beamed with pride, their spirits were high, and I felt immensely proud of them.

I sat and watched them showing off their unique medals to each other. I stood up to congratulate them, and the crowd roared once more. The Okai certainly knew how to celebrate. I caught up with Tommy who was beaming, he looked so proud.

'I wish the missus could be here now. She would love this, the atmosphere and the people.'

'When we have leave, why don't you invite her over. I'm sure we can arrange transport for her on one of the ships.'

'Really? Major, that would be incredible. I was thinking of asking her to renew our vows you know.' He said sincerely.

'Do it Tommy. How magical would it be to ask her here, I mean look at the place, it's truly magnificent.'

'It certainly is, I can't believe how many colours there are here, there seems to be more colour here than Earth, or it feels like I can see more colour here. It's like going from black and white to colour. It's unreal.' At that moment Raena approached me.

'Major, may we speak? I believe we will shortly be moving to our accommodations for the day, where we can relax for a bit, change, and get ready for the evening's celebrations. I would very much like to speak with you, if that is, Ok?' I looked about me and walked slightly away from the crew.

'Yes. That's fine. Are you looking forwards to tonight's celebrations?' She smiled warmly.

'I am. I am also looking forwards to all the

adventures that lay ahead for us.'

'Me too, I feel like we have a direction now... Also, and I hope this isn't inappropriate, but I wanted to say that your dress is absolutely stunning. I don't think I have ever seen anything quite like it.' She stood now with her back to me, the violet skin on her back catching in the sunlight, taking on shades of mauve, purple and pink.

'Is it truly the dress Major... please, there is no need to answer. Just remember that I said that I could sense some of your emotions.'

'Well... I er.' I felt my face heat up once more.

'Let us celebrate tonight Major. We can continue this conversation another time.' I didn't know whether to feel relieved or saddened. Once again, I pushed it to the back of my mind, where it could sit, behind all my other buried feelings.

∞

Ok, ok, how do I look? I thought, I stood in front of the long dress mirror. Carefully checking out my new outfits fit, my eyes running up and down the entire length and breadth of my body. I had chosen some dark blue silk pants and a silk sleeveless top in ivory. I had matched these with some wedged beaded sandals and wore a single string of blue pearls around my neck. Smart enough, and comfortable enough to dance, I thought. I had put a little more make up on than I usually wore, and I was happy that the dark eyeshadow I wore, would make my eyes pop.

The gentle waves in my long dark hair had been released from duty for the night, from their usual formal styling. If someone passed me by, drink in hand, the first thing they wouldn't assume was that I was a soldier, and that was what I really wanted, no I needed it tonight. I wanted just one night off to celebrate, before we continued our mission. More than this though, I wanted to enjoy the party with the eight beings that I trusted the most in the entire galaxy.

I headed out of the building and met up with Tommy, Joe, Fetch, Cat, Summer, Deno and Adari. Raena had arranged to meet up at the venue later as she was taking part in an Okai gathering beforehand. We were headed to the Vaznerah, it was the oldest and largest Sycoramth tree in the city. Raena had said that it would be surrounded by marquees and stalls selling traditional Okai foods and alcohol. Honestly, I couldn't wait.

We entered the large vehicle. It was almost entirely cream inside. It was carpeted in a deep pile cream carpet type flooring. The seating too was cream, and it was thickly padded, it was much more lavish than the average vehicles of Earth. We all sank deeply into the seats as we sat down in the vehicle, the seats hugged our bodies snugly and I couldn't think of anything that I had experienced that was as comfortable as this ride, not even my favourite reading chair.

This transport was moving much faster than the vehicle that had taken us to the ceremony, bearing a resemblance to the transport on Earth. I couldn't make out any of the streets or roads, as we were travelling that fast, the blue fluid tracks stretched out in front of the vehicle, pulling us forwards at incredible speed.

Everyone's spirits were high, Tommy looked very smart, and was wearing a casual suit, Joe was in Japanese designer jeans and a high fashion t-shirt. Deno had black synth leather pants, a cropped t-shirt, and very funky shoes, whilst summer looked elegant in a black dress with matching high heeled shoes, and stunning diamond jewellery to match. Fetch had navy blue synth leather jeans, black boots, and a white synth leather blouse. Her hair was styled upwards and had been neatly shaved on one side. Adari wore a casual two piece outfit in many different shades of red, he looked very smart. Cat had chosen to go for a dress in teal blue silk, with a velvet shawl and the jewellery to match, she looked great.

After a short period, no longer than around ten minutes the vehicle came to a complete stop. The large doors slid open, and we got out. The streets were full of revellers, making their way around the nights festivities. We were escorted by a group of Okai elders to a large domed marquee that was full of Okai who were intermingling, chatting, drinking, and eating.

On entering, we were offered drinks and what looked to be some kind of canapes. I took one and tasted it, popping it into my mouth. It was amazing, the flavours were familiar and yet new to my palate. I couldn't place what food it reminded me of, but I was sure that it wasn't something I had tried back on Earth. Fetch and Deno were trying all the canapes on offer, and I wondered if they had eaten at all today. They were trying everything going. It brought a smile to my face, seeing them so happy.

Thousands of Okai populated the area, Okai of every skin colour. I couldn't recall ever being anywhere so vibrant, so full of life, and so full of joy. Exotic music was now playing loudly, and the crowds continued to mingle, drink, eat, and dance. The joy evident in their faces, their bodies flowing like water to the music that was being pumped loudly across the venue.

I couldn't ever recall an experience like it. The Okai,

what a wonderful species, so spiritual, so very in touch with who they are, so deeply rich in their diversity. I couldn't help but be pulled in by the energy, I felt so alive.

I reached for a drink and took a large mouthful, my hand shimmered as subtle iridescent patterns and sensations ran up my arms and across the top of my shoulders in waves. This atmosphere was clearly stimulating my body, as it responded to the energy all around me. Deno and Fetch approached me, they had obviously noticed my skin changes.

'Well, that's certainly a new look.' Deno commented, Fetch handing her yet another canape, which she popped efficiently into her mouth.

'I like it, wish I could do that.' Said Fetch, as she bit into what must have been her twentieth morsel.

'You should feel it, it's… an interesting experience.' I said reaching for another drink. 'I feel like I'm absorbing all the energy here, and believe me, there is a ton of it. My body seems to be responding to its vibration. I don't know why, and tonight I don't care. I just wanna kick back and relax.' I could feel the alcohol begin to kick in. I took another large mouthful, swallowing it swiftly.

'Oh, is that… Raena?' Deno commented curiously. I looked towards where Deno's eyes were fixed into the distance.

'What the… dat outfit. Oh my… Major you just gotta see this.' I turned my head and saw Raena approach. She wore a pure white dress. It clung to her curves and was cut deep down from the centre of her cleavage and onto the top of her stomach. I took an even larger mouthful of my drink. Raena drew closer to us, effortlessly picking up a drink from one of the waiters as she passed by them. As she grew closer, I could see that her skin was still violet, and her hair was a much darker shade of the same.

'Major. Are you enjoying tonight's festivities, I hope that it is very much to your liking?'

'I am… we all are. I love everything, love the food, love the atmosphere, and the energy here, can you feel it, and have you seen what it is doing to my skin. I held my hand out towards her and my skin shimmered once more. 'The energy here, I can feel it all around me. You look amazing by the way... Are you looking forward to the Arimianoran?' Raena smiled, it must have been so obvious to her that I was full of alcohol, as I elegantly tripped over my own words.

'It will begin soon. Actually, in just a few minutes,' the ceremonial music will begin, and the tree will then be flooded with lights. Try not to be too alarmed when we change to our childhood colours, when this happens. It lasts just a few hours and then we return to our adult colours, we don't feel any discomfort Major, none at all.' She gave a reassuring nod, along with just a hint of a smile.

'Amazing Raena, that's just incredible.' I said enthusiastically, eating another canape, they really were quite delicious.

Tommy and Joe were now standing just across from us and appeared to be in a drinking contest with a small group of young Okai adult males, who looked to be giving them both a run for their money. All at once the music began to play again, the tree lit up brightly from root to leaf canopy in a deluge of countless vibrant colours and millions of multicoloured petals covered the entire tree.

The tree must have been at least around two

hundred feet high, its branches bent down thick and heavy, creating a large and natural umbrella like awning for the revellers. Its long and supple branches touching the floor in parts, it was an incredible site. The music continued to play, getting louder and louder, and it wasn't long before it reached a crescendo.

Okai, human and Nadaal alike were now dancing under the trees immense canopy, and an infinitesimal number of stars that shone brightly, like diamonds piercing the inky black vastness of space, provided a fitting and wonderful backdrop for the nights celebrations.

All of a sudden, the lighting cut out, leaving us all stood in complete darkness, other than the company of the stars, reminding us that we were not alone on this night. The crowd were mostly completely silent, with just a few quiet conversations taking place, from those who didn't know what to expect next. Then, all at once was the brightest of pure white lights, it rose into the sky at speed, it looked as bright as any comet that I had ever seen.

The light shot high into the stratosphere and then exploded into a million tiny white hot sparks that flew in every direction, lighting up the entire nights sky all around us. What happened next, I couldn't have predicted as a newcomer to this world and her people. I knew of course about the ceremony, but to actually be here and to witness it for real, was another thing altogether.

The tree, that was now lit up by the white lights in the sky began to shed its petals to the ground, music began again, building slowly at first which was then accompanied by more rhythmic drumming. Many of the Okai had started humming some kind of ancient chant. Thousands of Okai surrounding the tree began to dance, I looked across to Raena, and just as I did so I saw that her skin had changed colour. She was now the most exquisite blue-black colour, and her skin had the most lustrous sheen to it that I had ever seen. Her hair now black, matched her skin perfectly, and I found that I couldn't take my eyes off her. She stepped towards me the contrast of her curvaceous figure, the pearlescent white dress, and her blue-black skin, utterly captivating my attention, yet again.

'Major, come and dance with me.' She beamed with joy, and I could see how important this moment was to her, and all her people. I put my drink down and walked towards an area where large numbers of Okai were celebrating. I reckoned that I could afford to let my hair down, just a little, just for one night. I crossed the floor, stepping down a few steps to where she was stood. Deno and Fetch were already dancing, Summer was in deep conversation with a handsome and clearly confident Okai male. Cat looked wonderstruck, she was still watching the millions of petals that were falling from the tree, they continued to float down slowly, gently landing on her head and all the other revellers, the petals covered every surface, in every colour imaginable.

I walked a few paces more towards Raena, eventually standing just a few feet away from her. Then suddenly, my ears were pierced by an almighty deep and pulsating sound, which was followed by a loud sonic boom. The drinking glasses vibrated on their trays and in the hands of the party goers, and everyone just seemed to pause, motionless for a moment, looking up to the skies. I then looked up myself. What had they seen?

Above me was a large white-silver ship, its sleek shape and length immediately caught my attention. I'd never seen a craft like it before, it certainly wasn't one of ours, and it didn't look like a Nadaal or Okai ship either. it wasn't a crucian ship, from what I could tell, it appeared we had a new visitor. I looked towards Raena, smiling, and shrugging my shoulders, whilst briefly looking up to the sky again, before once again stepping forwards towards her.

13 HELLO, OLD FRIEND

'What the f–'

I felt my body phase out from where I had been stood and then, almost instantaneously I phased back into matter again, only now something was very different. I immediately knew that I was no longer where I had been stood just a few seconds ago, I wasn't sure where I was at all. I felt my stomach settle back into my abdominal cavity once more, it was an unsettling feeling and one that I did not enjoy.

How and what had just moved me, and more importantly, why? Everyone that I knew was now gone and I found myself high up in what I assumed was Nemeranth's atmosphere. I looked about me, this… was this the ship that we had just seen arrive? I felt concerned. Looking about me quickly gathering my wits, whilst I hurriedly tried to get my bearings again. I soon began to notice and take in more of these new and unexpected surroundings.

Pale grey glass like floors ran along the length of the room, everything else was pure white, the lighting was white, the walls around me and the entire interior of the ship was also white. It was pristine inside, like some kind of medical or science vessel. It was almost laboratory like, it looked so clean, sterile even. The one thing that I was glad of was that I didn't sense any aggression or hostility on this ship. There was no one greeting me, no gun pointed at my head, that was somewhat reassuring, for the time being, I thought.

Instead, I noticed that it felt quite soothing. I tried to rationalise why I felt like this, thinking that it was probably the effect of the alcohol I had been consuming. But still, something wasn't right, I had just been tele-phased without my permission and put aboard this ship with no warning, or request. As far as I could tell, no one was holding me hostage, or trying to restrict my movements.

It felt odd, very odd indeed. I walked around for a short time, looking in some of the rooms that were situated off each of the twin corridors that ran parallel with each other and ran down the entire length of the ship. Each of the rooms off the immaculate corridors looked strangely homely and far different from the sterile walkways.

From what I could tell, this ship was meant to be comfortable, it was meant to be lived on… and yet not a single living soul appeared to be on board. Where were its inhabitants and why had it appeared in Nemeranth's sky? I wondered what my squad would be doing right now, their commanding officer, seemingly abducted and on board an unknown ship. They would be readying to board, I thought. It's what I would do.

After a few minutes, I came to the end of one of the corridors. A large circular doorway was in front of me,

I looked at it, studying its form, it felt enticing almost like it was trying to pull me through it. I stepped forwards, touching the door and it appeared to dissolve in front of my eyes, revealing the next room. I walked into a larger room that was filled with many, mostly mystery items that I did not recognise. I did, however, see a guitar and a few other items that looked to be of human origin, but they looked to be incredibly old, even ancient. Most of the other items that I could see did not look familiar to me at all, and I concluded that they must be alien artifacts of some kind.

One thing that caught my eye, was a single glass sphere that sat upon a display plinth. I touched it, and its shape began to change, it appeared to be malleable. Picking it up in my hands, I moulded the soft pliable glass like material into different shapes. After a short time, I placed it back on the plinth, where it slowly returned to its original sphere shape. Fascinating, I thought. This room was obviously a room of curiosities, keepsakes, and memories. Someone had coveted and collected these objects, and once again I noted that they did not appear to be the collection of a malevolent being, but rather, a curious one.

I walked a little further and left the room at its far end, entering yet another, but much shorter corridor. I walked down it swiftly, trying to find my way to the ships control centre, or bridge, maybe there I would find the owner of this ship. Maybe we could talk, and they would return me to the celebrations, peacefully if I were lucky.

Another circular door lay in front of me, touching it once again, it dissolved in exactly the same way as the first circular doorway that I had passed through. This was the largest doorway that I had found on the ship, so far. I walked into a large and open room that very much resembled a bridge, but it looked very different in its design. The consoles formed a complete circle in the centre of the room. The centre floor area where the circular console was located, rotated slightly when I stepped upon it.

I realised that the bridge of this ship could move in a three hundred and sixty degree circular rotational motion, if needed. Anyone operating a console on this bridge could move their stations position by rotating the floor, putting them directly in front of the ships massive viewing window.

The viewing window appeared to be covered by a smooth and silver like sturdy metallic substance, that made the window appear to be solid, not transparent. I pondered on whether this was for privacy, as I could not see anything out of it at all. I positioned myself in the middle of the circular console area wondering what I should or could do next. There didn't appear to be anyone on board who could help me. Maybe they were in a room I hadn't visited yet, I thought.

'Hello. This is Major Mitchell, is there anyone onboard this ship? I called out loudly.

'Can we talk at least? I mean you no harm, but you must allow me to return to my squad. They will send a rescue party soon, and I…'

The consoles on the bridge began to light up, bright white lights now edged every panel and console, the metallic substance on the bridges viewing window dissolved, melting away almost instantaneously and I could once more see Nemeranth's surface, and the Amaranthine within my field of view.

'You must allow me to leave, I do not sense that you are aggressive, but it's not the done thing to abduct someone, even if you are not hostile towards me. Maybe we can talk about this?'

In front of me and on the floor to the left of the viewing window was a flat black circular plate. I hadn't noticed it before, but it appeared to have become active. I watched in silence as a pure white mesh of laser type lights began to form a shape. Gradually the shape grew taller and taller, and I realised that at around two feet in height, that I could make out what looked to be… feet and legs, its shape appearing to be humanoid in nature. I stood still, waiting to meet my abductor.

I watched as an abdomen, a chest, male in shape, shoulders and then finally a head shape formed. I gazed at it, and I was utterly astonished at what I saw. But more importantly, I was wondering what it was going to do. I could have run at that moment, but where would I go. I couldn't see anything that I could defend myself with… the guitar maybe? The mouldable sphere? Or perhaps one of the many other collectables? No, I would have to wait this one out. All of a sudden, there appeared to be some comm chatter within the ship.

'This is Joe Tanaka, please release Major Mitchell immediately or we will have no choice but to fire upon your ship.' His voice sounded stern, tense even.

I walked slowly towards the humanoid shaped figure that was stood perfectly still, having now fully formed. I reached out slowly towards it, pushing my hand gently against its lighted mesh, three dimensional shape. As soon as I did so, it moved, its face appeared to be studying the look of astonishment upon my face, it looked calmly and inquisitively at me.

It then stepped off of the plate and walked slowly

towards the Comm, it didn't appear phased by me being there at all. Turning towards me, as it operated the console directly in front of the ships viewing screen. It began to turn slowly to face me. Then, it finally spoke.

'Hello, old friend. It's good to see you.' It's voice was upbeat and if I didn't know any better, I would say it appeared to be happy to see me.

'Old friend? I'm afraid I don't know you at all. We've not met before... Who are you and why am I onboard your ship?' I tried to look into and connect with the digital constructs eyes but found only pure white light.

'My assigned name is Yahga, a name that you gave me, quite some time ago.'

'Well... Yahga, that's impossible because I've never met you before. Perhaps you are mistaken? Please listen to me, if you wish to help me, is there any way that you would allow me to communicate with my ship?'

'Oh, I see... the situation has developed since we last spoke. These people in the large ship docked off to port. They are your new crew? Of course, they are, please let me open a channel for you. But before you leave this ship, it is imperative that we must speak.'

'Ok Yahga. Just let me tell them that I'm alright, it will save them damaging this ship, they will assume that I have been abducted if I am not able to speak with them.' I tried my best to reason with the AI.

'Oh, please be reassured that they cannot damage this ship, but as requested, I will open a channel for you so that you may communicate with your squad and tell them that you are indeed safe.' Yahga said cheerfully.

'Yahga, what do you mean they can't damage this ship?' I was interested in the AI's assumption that it couldn't be damaged.

'Put simply, their weapons systems would be ineffective against this ships defences.'

'They are extremely powerful ships Yahga, the best that we have.'

'No. I can confirm that this ship is the best that you have.'

'Wait, this ship is the best that we have? Yahga this ship isn't mine.'

'That is incorrect… Mitchell. There is much to discuss, please request that they stand down.' I stood in front of the console, shaking my head slowly in disbelief at what had just transpired. I had the opportunity to call for aid, but my intuition was telling me to hold off. If the AI had wished to harm me, it could have done so long before now.

'Joe, it's Mitchell. I am alright, the AI being aboard this ship appears to just want to talk with me.'

'You sure Major? Ok, let me know if you need anything. We will sit tight in orbit and await further orders. Tanaka out.' I walked back across the bridge to where the being stood. It appeared to be running checks on the ships systems.

'Can I ask you something Yahga?' I said, whilst walking up to where the AI was stood.

'Of course. Please ask me anything.'

'Why have you come here, and why have you beamed me onboard this ship?'

'Simply put, I came here for you. I beamed you aboard this ship as you requested… Stephanie.'

'Wait, I didn't ask you to beam me aboard. I was at a party, about to dance with… well about to celebrate with my crew and… how in hells name do you know my birth name?'

'Forty years ago, your final encoded orders to me were, that I was to locate you and beam you onboard the ship, your ship once I had located you.' The AI said reassuringly.

'Forty years ago, I was… just born… wait. Tell me, what was my last mission?'

'You left the ship, your ship, for the planet named Earth. You needed to leave yourself in a safe place, I have come to pick you up, as you requested Stephanie.'

'How could I… leave myself in a safe place. Oh... shit! Oh fuck… Mom!'

'I can tell by the expression on your face that we do indeed have much to discuss. You don't remember any of it do you?' It asked me sympathetically.

'No, Yahga I don't, but I do know that some unusual things have been happening to me, and my mom told me of a stranger visiting her forty years ago. A stranger with my face Yahga.'

'No. Not your face. You.' Again, its tone was sympathetic towards me.

'Yahga… Listen, this is really bending my brain. You tell me that you know me, you tell me that this is my ship… and yet I don't remember any of it. You tell me that I took myself to Earth and left myself there. What happened to the other me, the me that took me to Earth? I feel like I'm tying my head in knots here.'

'Ha! You would say the exact same thing to me when we would play chess together.'

'…We would play chess?'

'Yes. You are quite good at it… for an organic brain.'

'A what brain?'

'Oh. It is a term of endearment. I meant no offence, the other you would call herself it… quite regularly.'

'Non taken, Yahga. She seemed to have quite the sense of humour, the other me.' I sat down and put my head in my hands.

'Is everything alright?' Yahga asked.

'Yeah… No. It's just a lot to take in Yahga. So, back to my other self. Where are they now?'

'Sadly, they are no longer with us. You see, in order to protect you, them, they had no option but to stop your pursuers. They pulled their adversaries into your Sun, along with themselves. They did this whilst ordering me to relocate and wait in a safe location.

I was ordered to wait for your return. The Pulsars systems, and my own systems came back online when you activated the room on Pluto, and your final encrypted message to me was then released. You really did have no other option Stephanie, you had to stop them from discovering you, so that you would continue.'

'So, they… me, stopped me from being discovered on Earth, is that right?'

'Yes. It was very important that you survived, and in order to do that, you needed to die.'

'I see... I think.'

'There is much more that you should know, but there are somethings, that even I do not know.'

'Please go on Yahga.'

'The last you, believed that it was vital that you survived. We had been trying to understand the reason that the cycle kept repeating.'

'What cycle?'

'Your rebirth, the endless cycle.'

'Endless cycle?'

'Yes. An endless cycle of your rebirth'

'Endless, just how many times have I done this?'

'You visited the site on Pluto. This site is the site of your very many rebirths, I don't know how, or why it is there. All I know is that the site is very ancient indeed. Someone or something created that site, for you, and someone or something created this ship, for you. Did you discover anything of interest on Pluto?'

'Yes, we found six star charts and a lot of other weird shit happened. Lots of weird shit has been happening to be honest of late, look.' I held out my arm and it shimmered, the fusion clearly visible, just under my translucent skin.

'Now that, that is something new Stephanie. It must have started. I know you won't realise the significance of this, but if you have waited as long as I have…'

'I'm changing, aren't I?'

'Yes, but more than that, you are evolving. I do know that you are meant to change. But I do not know in what way, or why you are changing. Perhaps now would be a good time to tell you who you are to me, and your one true name?

'My one true name, what do you mean?'

'Many years ago, when we deciphered the texts on Pluto for the first time, we discovered some reference to an ancient being, a being that is reborn, time and time again. A being that will awaken in a great time of need. In the texts they refer to the being as The Luminary, and written in those same texts, it states that their true name is Sol. Your true name Stephanie, I believe is Sol, named after the Earths sun, though we do not know why.'

I gazed out of the window. My head felt numb with all of it, but I still needed to know more.

'Is that as far as I got, what about who originally built the site on Pluto, do we know who or what that is?

'The only thing we know for sure, is a single reference within the texts that recalls *the first ones*. You and I have both spent many thousands of years looking for information and any scrap of evidence that relates to these, first ones. We were unsuccessful, though we did enjoy our travels together. Your creators Sol, I'm afraid at the moment are a mystery, but maybe you will have more luck, than your last incarnation did.'

'So, this ship really is mine then… literally?' I slumped down in one of the ships chairs, I suddenly felt exhausted.

'Yes. This ship is yours to command. She can comfortably accommodate a crew of fifty.'

'And her capabilities?'

'The Pulsar out guns all three Cruisers docked around us.'

'Wait, how can that be?'

'The Pulsar is an ancient ship. It may well have been created by the first ones, the technology onboard this ship is many times more advanced than that of the Okai, the Nadaal and the Humans.'

'Could I move some crew onboard this ship and utilise it for our missions?'

'Yes, it is your ship.'

I took a deep breath, I felt safe here. I couldn't recall Yahga, I couldn't recall our travels together. I couldn't recall any of it, and maybe that was a good thing. I stood and walked, pacing a few steps forwards.

'Which of these is the communications console?'

'Just say open channel and I will take care of it.'

'Ok… Yahga. Would you open me a channel to the

Amaranthine.'

'Channel opened.'

'Joe, Mitchell here. Everything is alright, and it appears that we have a new ship, please allow the crew to continue celebrating tonight. We leave for Wolf three-five-nine in thirty six hours, I will brief you in the morning. Mitchell out.'

I sat back down, the effects of the alcohol had begun to wear off now, and I realised that I had just given the order that would lead us out of familiar territory, and far into the unknown. Wolf three-five-nine was a red dwarf star located in the constellation of Leo, approximately seven point nine light years from Earth.

But it was much more than that, after Pluto, Wolf three-five-nine was the second destination in my search for answers. In the endeavours that I had so far undertaken with my crew, I hoped that I might succeed where the other versions of myself had previously failed, time and time again. A star lit path was mapped out in front of me, leading me deeper into our Galaxy, and far away from my home world.

It was a challenge that I could not turn away from. I had been here before, and yet I couldn't remember any of it. Was that for the best? I had gained so very much in those initial moments that I had spoken with Yahga… and yet, now I found that I was thinking more and more about what I had lost. The memory of who I am, who I was. I couldn't let it go, I need to know who, no… I need to know what I am.

∞

I slept onboard the Pulsar that night and I felt something that I hadn't felt for a while, I felt safe. The morning came and I awoke to a full breakfast which had been situated neatly at the side of my bed. I didn't know how it got there, but then I didn't really care. It looked delicious and I didn't waste a single moment, consuming it enthusiastically, until not a morsel was left on the plate.

Afterwards, I dressed and made my way once again towards the Pulsars bridge. I needed to brief my squad and the crew today on our new ally. I needed to talk through this incredible discovery, though in reality, Yahga had found me. I thought of the irony of it all, they were new to me… unknown to me before yesterday, and yet so familiar, like a distant memory that I couldn't quite put my finger upon. I contemplated the conversation with Yahga once more, an AI that calls themself an old friend, I felt a smile draw across my face.

I still had no recall of any of the past incarnations and thought that maybe a fresh start with no preconceived ideas about the coming missions, or anything else that lay ahead of us for that matter was probably for the best. I felt energised, excited, like another piece of the mystery had been resolved. Though it occurred to me that there was probably more that lay ahead of us, than lay behind us.

I reached the Pulsars bridge door, I could see that Yahga was stood by one of the consoles, they turned towards me as the door melted away once again, allowing me safe passage onto the bridge.

'Ah Stephanie. Good morning, did you sleep well?' Yahga sounded cheerful, like they were genuinely pleased to see me.

'I slept very well thanks, and thanks for breakfast it was… just perfect.'

'Good. I am pleased that you enjoyed it. What are

your plans for today?' They asked curiously.

'Well, firstly there is a new house rule on this ship. So, when I'm in my quarters alone, please call me Stephanie, but if I'm in any other part of this ship or anywhere off this ship, please address me as Major Mitchell, or just Mitchell is fine too. It kind of comes with the territory of my role and responsibilities. Is that, ok?'

'Yes, Mitchell. I understand. Please let me know if there is anything else I should be aware of. Will you be residing onboard this ship or the Amaranthine?'

'Yes, I think that I will reside here, unless I'm needed on the Amaranthine for any reason.' I looked out of the viewing window and could see the Amaranthine in the distance, her hull reflecting the sun's rays. Almost everything and everyone I cared about was onboard that ship. I would need to think about who would join me onboard the Pulsar. I definitely wanted my eight with me, I didn't know what this ship was capable of, but I was pretty sure from what Yahga had said that it was far more advanced than anything our tri-planetary alliance had.

'Yahga, can you request docking permission from the Amaranthine. I need to brief the crew.'

'Mitchell, we could tele-phase you onboard. It would be much more efficient.'

'I think I'll stick with something less advanced, at least for now. I need everyone to be aware of the Pulsars capabilities, wouldn't want anyone to freak out about it. We've had a few Major surprises lately Yahga, and everyone's nerves are a little bit fraught right now.' Yahga acknowledged my concerns with a single nod, pausing for a second before hurriedly rechecking the communications console.

'Docking permission has been granted Mitchell, shall I take us in?'

'Yes. Let's get this done, I'm sure they are all very… curious to meet you.'

'As am I, these eight you speak of, they are your squad?'

'Oh, they are much more than that, but yes. In essence they are my squad, they are also my dearest friends. I try to lead them in the best way I can, it's not always easy and I'm sure that I get on their nerves from time to time. But that too comes with the territory of my rank.

You could say that we have been through a lot together, things that no one else would understand, unless they had actually been there.' I paused, as did Yahga before they spoke again.

'I believe I understand. I suppose that I could say the same of you and I Mitchell. In time I hope to share with you some small part of your past, so that you may understand our relationship and some small semblance of… its importance to me.' Yahga turned to me and smiled, it was a warm smile, the smile of a friend.

'Then take us in, Yahga and don't spare the horses!' Yahga looked a little confused their head tilting slightly to one side. 'It means take us in to the Amaranthine, at speed.'

'Acknowledging your request, Mitchell.' Yahga touched the console and the ship heaved to one side. I felt my stomach rise into my throat slightly, whilst all of time and space appeared to flash past the ships viewing windows in the blink of an eye. A millisecond later, the same feeling arose in my throat as the ship came to almost a complete stop.

'Docking at the Amaranthine Mitchell, further

orders?' My mouth must have been wide open, as Yahga seemed to question the look on my face. 'Is anything wrong Mitchell?'

'Well, er no. That was just very fast. How fast was that exactly?' I noticed that the Amaranthine's docking clamps had just secured to the outer hull of the Pulsar.

'Mitchell, we can talk about the Pulsars speed and capabilities later. You also have some upgrades available from your extensive travels that the Amaranthine and your allies might benefit from, but all in good time. For now, may I suggest that you board the other ship?'

I nodded to Yahga and was about to leave the bridge when a thought crossed my mind. Here I was with an AI that calls themself my oldest friend, and I am about to brief the crew without them by my side. I didn't know why, but it just felt wrong. If Yahga really was my oldest friend, whether I could remember them or not, then they needed to be part of my crew.

'Yahga, is there any way to get you onboard the Amaranthine. I think you should meet the crew, and you definitely need to get to know my eight.' Yahga stepped forwards.

'Yes Mitchell, I can partially relocate myself at any location up to three parsecs away from the Pulsar. Would you like me to join you?'

'I would like that very much.' Yahga approached me and placed a single small silver nodule that looked like liquid mercury onto the smooth skin of my lower left arm. It sank a little into my skin, appearing to solidify into a small domed shape before setting solid. The process was completely painless and took only a few seconds. I touched it, and it appeared to have completely and seamlessly melded into my skin. It didn't move at all, and I knew for whatever reason, that I couldn't simply remove it with my fingers.

'What is this?' I asked curiously.

'If you touch this nodule and I am anywhere within three parsecs. I can relocate to your position instantaneously. However, your former self had a password, as initially I kept appearing in the strangest of places. She felt that it was probably safer… and more dignified for us both, if I didn't do this.'

'It sounds like she had some sense. Yes, a password, how about just simply using your name and my date of birth? That would make the most sense to me. Hang on…' I paused, trying to gather my thoughts. 'Isn't three parsecs just short of ten light years? You mean to tell me that you can relocate almost ten light years from this ship?'

'Yes, I can. My name and your birthdate as a password does indeed sound like a good choice Mitchell. We can test it out when you are ready to brief the crew, and as I said we can talk about mine and the Pulsars capabilities later.'

'That sounds like a plan. I will call you over when I'm ready to introduce you to the crew.'

I gathered my thoughts as I walked towards the docking area of the Pulsar. I had quite the update for my crew, and I was sure that my eight would want to know everything I had just discovered and more.

The interior of the Pulsar felt so advanced and yet there was something quite ancient about it, I wondered how old this ship was. It looked immaculate, brand new even, but I knew it wasn't. Yahga appeared to have… wisdom and I had never met an AI with this quality. I wondered if they had been programmed with it, or if it was the same as it was with many older beings, in that it mostly came with age and life experience.

The doorway that linked the Pulsar to the short docking corridor was the same style as the interior doors on the ship. I stood and waited for the corridor to repressurise before I made my way across to the Amaranthine. As before the circular door melted away to allow me safe passage, I looked back at the door, I still wasn't used to it.

Deno and Fetch greeted me at the door, whilst Joe stood observing my entrance. I could see that he was checking for any sign of a hidden party trying to board the ship covertly, but there was none. It was just me and my thoughts alone, that would accompany them to the bridge.

Deno was the first to speak. 'So, this is very unusual Major. Wouldn't you say?'

'Yep. Unusual is one way to put it, but I think that you will like this unusual development Deno. It's quite something.' I could see Deno's semi perplexed expression. She was desperate to know more, but why spoil the fun of my latest great reveal to the crew? I felt a slight grin cross my face.

'So, when we gonna find out who took you away from us? It kinda put a dampener on the afterparty to be honest with you.' Deno looked like she was a reporter after the latest scoop.

'All in good time, I promise that I won't keep you waiting. Oh… and it didn't take me anywhere Deno. They came back for me.'

'Came… back… for you?' She was definitely intrigued by my reply, and by the time she had finished her drawn out response we had reached the bridge. I strode in energetically towards the briefing floor.

'Open me a channel to all ships in the fleet.' The

console operator nodded towards me, and I knew that I had the attention of the entire crew.

'Good morning. Yesterday at the celebrations I was tele-phased on to an unknown ship, a ship of unknown origin, bearing no markers or flags of any known adversary, or ally.

The ship that is currently docked off the Amaranthine is named the Pulsar. It has capabilities that far outmatch ours. Whilst onboard I also met its sole occupier, Yahga0210.' I touched the silver nodule on my arm. Immediately and to my right Yahga appeared.

'Meet Yahga, the Pulsars AI, but more than this Yahga is now a fully-fledged member of the crew and will be given all rights and privileges befitting of their rank, which will be assigned to them by me in the morning. The other news is that the Pulsar will be joining the fleet... it can host a crew of fifty and for this reason I will be relocating my eight and thirty crew to the Pulsar to learn its capabilities and to ensure that it is mission ready in one week's time when we depart for the next phase of our mission.

I would like a diverse multiplanetary crew onboard the ship, so I will be hand picking ten human, ten Okai and ten Nadaal crew members. Those chosen will report directly to me and will also act as liaison officers and ambassadors to the rest of the fleet.

I'm sure you will appreciate that Yahga would like to get to know you all much better. We now have our next mission and it's going to be unlike anything that any of us have ever been tested on.'

An intergalactic trail of six cosmic breadcrumbs, and a myriad of undiscovered truths lay ahead of us. Somewhere deep within me, I knew that it had always been fated in the stars. The journey was ours, but its destination, this was mine alone to discover. I turned to the crew, facing my eight.

'You know what? I, for one am sick of letting these intergalactic bullies think that they can have their way, cos that's the way it's always been for them. I'm sick of being dictated to by their actions. These attacks on home worlds, they have to stop. We don't know how many other species are at risk, or how many planets are under the direct rule of species X and their allies. The brutality… the cruelty… and the control, do we just let it continue unchallenged?

If we do allow it, at what cost will this be to our own species soul? No, enough is enough. It's time we stood up to them. There will be a reckoning in this galaxy, I can feel it. Their way… it cannot continue. I won't allow it. Will you stand with me?' I looked out towards my eight, knowing full well what I was asking of them, yet again. They approached me slowly, all putting a hand upon my shoulders.

'We stand with you Major, as always.' Joe said, with a determined look upon his face. I nodded silently, whilst lowering my gaze. I was feeling resolute, this was the right thing to do, Yahga lifted their light filled face towards mine and smiled. Lifting my head humbly, I looked at them all once again, my eyes narrowing as a single sentence escaped my lips.

'Then let's go after them.'

ABOUT THE AUTHOR

TL Marston is a self-proclaimed Sci-fi fan who believes that a good story cannot be contained. She has been an avid lover of the science fiction genre all her life, and she wanted to bring new stories to the reader.

She believes that science fiction is like no other genre, in the way that it can open our minds, removing all limitations of what we, the human species can achieve, if we work together.

She hopes that the reader will enjoy the story, just as equally as getting to know the characters. She would love to hear from anyone who has enjoyed this, her first book in the series. She can be contacted by requesting to join her authors page on Facebook.

Printed in Great Britain
by Amazon

71627339R00246